Praise for Kristopher Jansr
The Unchangeable Spot.

"Kristopher Jansma accurately nails the yc
unnamed young male writer narrator also h.
fact that makes for a playfully weird narrative experience. I'd call this book
'postmodern,' but that makes it sound like it's not as pleasurable to read as it
is."   —Meg Wolitzer, author of *The Interestings*, on NPR.org

"[A] tricky picaresque thick with literary allusion from Fitzgerald to Amis . . .
[A] clever, tightly paced novel of ever-upping stakes."   —Vogue.com

"Though one might recognize bits of Dickens, Fitzgerald, or Hemingway,
this is simply a good case of stealing from geniuses. It's a breathless work that
celebrates literary tradition, while making a strong case that its author
belongs on the shelf beside his forebears."   —*Time Out New York* (five stars)

"Couched in Jansma's wildly recursive funhouse of a novel is a coming-of-age
story . . . filled with clever literary allusions and insider jokes. . . . There's
plenty to relish in this noteworthy debut."   —Heller McAlpin, NPR.org

"F. Scott Fitzgerald meets Wes Anderson. . . . The novel strikes a chord on
questions of authenticity, love, and ambition, and it reminds us that life is
often out of our control, even if we're writing it down."   —*The Village Voice*

"One of the best books of the year."   —Jeff Glor, CBS's *Author Talk*

"[Jansma is] a writer of extreme promise, who seems to belong to an older
generation."   —*Electric Literature*

"[A] slippery and energetic debut novel . . . rapid in pace, the language and
details tightly controlled . . . It's tremendous fun, this book."
                                        —*San Francisco Journal of Books*

"This mind-blowing spiral of a book will also appeal to anyone who enjoys
their fiction as playful as it is intriguing."   —*BookReporter*

"The layers of the pastiche at work here are so intricately laid down that the
disparate tones don't jangle. They sing. . . . The truth of the matter is, it's
damn fun."   —Joanna Robinson, *Pajiba*

"An enchanting, transfixing, and intricate codex of mirrors—an unabashedly pure, witty case study of literary fiction." —*Tottenville Review*

"[A] masterful web of literary lies and metafiction." —*Full Stop*

"*The Unchangeable Spots of Leopards*'s intricate narrative game and its carbon-burning escapades add up to a novel that is wise about identity and aspiration, competitive storytelling, romantic obsession, and the assertion that 'all these stories are true, only somewhere else.'" —*Shelf Awareness*

"Layered, nuanced, and compulsively readable; a feat of linguistic legerdemain that treads perilously close to being just too clever for its own good—without ever actually crossing that line. A delight." —*Chatelaine*

"While an imaginative plot is often all it takes to please a reader, debut author Kristopher Jansma supports his plot with remarkable writing. . . . The novel is probably best described by these lines pulled directly from the book: 'It is a rare sort of book that resembles nothing else and yet somehow seems intensely familiar. From the first line you feel your own heart begin to beat differently. Once it's over you want to begin it again. It is a love letter; it is an atom bomb; it is literature we'd forgotten could be written.'"
—KMUW, Wichita Public Radio

"Captivating . . . [A] smart, searching debut about art and identity." —*Library Journal*

"[A] canny, seductive, and utterly transfixing tale about the magic of storytelling and the misery of writing . . . Like a magician pulling a seemingly endless string of colorful scarves from a hat, Jansma streams stories-within-stories-within-stories, each a diabolically clever homage. . . . Readers will detect riffs on Fitzgerald, Hemingway, Truman Capote, Bob Dylan, Tolstoy, Salinger, Borges, Kipling, and many more. . . . A first novel with the strength and agility of a great cat leaping through rings of fire."
—*Booklist* (starred review)

"[An] arresting debut . . . Jansma's characters deftly explore the blurred lines between fact and fiction, discovering the shades of truth that lie in between."
—*Publishers Weekly*

"A terrifically fun book that's a little bit Calvino, a little bit Jennifer Egan, and a little bit the inside of every young artist that ever was. Concerned with the nature of storytelling, art, fallacy, and f**king up, and told as only a witty wordsmith can, we're pretty sure it'll be one of your favorites in the new year."
— *Flavorwire*

"*The Unchangeable Spots of Leopards* is my new exhibit A for the defense of literary fiction. A great read—a must-read. Kristopher Jasma is more than the real deal. He's made himself, with this book, essential."
—Darin Strauss, author of *More Than It Hurts You*

"Light and airy, *The Unchangeable Spots of Leopards* is a funhouse of a novel about the outsized ambitions of authors and the sneaky power of storytelling. Kristopher Jansma's debut is a whimsical round-the-world tour that recalls Calvino, Millhauser, and *The Confidence-Man*."
—Stewart O'Nan, author of *Last Night at the Lobster*

"Emblematic of its many delightful complexities, the writer-as-narrator of this exciting debut novel brings to mind both Holden Caufield and Tom Ripley. This is a coming-of-age novel, albeit not an especially tender one; rather it is infused with wicked satire on the pursuits of wealth, fame, and love. As if he were running the literary equivalent of a game of three-card monte, Jansma's protagonist artfully charms and deceives his friends and readers as a means to revealing what is true. *The Unchangeable Spots of Leopards* is a remarkably smart novel and it's great fun, too."
—Binnie Kirshenbaum, author of *The Scenic Route*

"Kristopher Jansma is a brilliant writer of energetic, original, intelligent, skillful, and highly imaginative and hysterically funny fiction. Few writers of any age succeed in the chances he took with *The Unchangeable Spots of Leopards*. That he does so with such finesse, ease, and maturity is astounding."
—Stephen Dixon, author of *What Is All This?*

"Lies are as essential to our lives as truth, time, and love. With *The Unchangeable Spots of Leopards*, Kristopher Jansma escorts us through a carnival funhouse of literary mirrors where truth and lies are so delightfully melded that we, like the characters themselves, don't care to distinguish between them. The result is a dynamic, imaginative adventure featuring a trio of characters that are constantly shifting, yet instantly recognizable, as endearing as they are flawed. But the true leopards of Jansma's novel may be the deep questions crouching deftly within its pages. I, for one, may never regard my own reflection with quite the same certainty again."

       —Kenneth Slawenski, author of *J. D. Salinger: A Life*

"The brilliance of this novel slays me! With an extravagance of wit and grace, Kristopher Jansma has masterfully composed a chimerical, *matroshka* doll of a story as gripping as it is inventive, as moving as it is hilarious, populated with fascinating, singular characters about whom you long to know more and more and more. (Even the extras are drawn in pitch-perfect detail.) It reminded me of so many favorite novels, from David Mitchell's *Ghostwritten* to Gary Shteyngart's *The Russian Debutante's Handbook*, and yet it's so deeply original that all comparisons fall out the window. This is the most fresh and exciting novel I've read in ages."

       —Joanna Smith Rakoff, author of *A Fortunate Age*

"Behold *The Unchangeable Spots of Leopards*: an eloquent, witty, and inventive debut novel about a promising young writer's persistent quest to reinvent himself. Kristopher Jansma masterfully explores the ways in which we lie in order to grasp the most inexplicable truths in art, life, and love. The protagonist is a trickster-artist and con artist alike; he is Houdini, Tom Ripley, and Hemingway rolled into one. But despite his web of lies, we can't help but root for him all the way to the end. *The Unchangeable Spots of Leopards* is a tour de force—a nest of Russian dolls, with stories within stories, each tale bringing us a little closer to some glimmer of the truth."

    —Mira Bartok, author of *The Memory Palace* and winner of the
    National Book Critics Circle Award

"Clever, smart, and beautifully written, *The Unchangeable Spots of Leopards* is not only a story about storytelling but also a true celebration of the art. At times hilarious and heart-wrenching, Jansma has managed to produce a mind-bending and utterly unforgettable book."

    —Andrew Porter, author of *The Theory of Light and Matter*

PENGUIN BOOKS

THE UNCHANGEABLE SPOTS OF LEOPARDS

Kristopher Jansma lectures in creative writing and writes the Literary Artifacts column for Electric Literature's blog *The Outlet*. His work has also been published in *The New York Times*, *The Believer*, *Slice* magazine, the *Blue Mesa Review*, and *The Millions*. He lives in Brooklyn with his wife and son. This is his first novel.

To access Penguin Readers Guides online,
visit our Web site at www.penguin.com.

The Unchangeable Spots

of Leopards

KRISTOPHER JANSMA

PENGUIN BOOKS

PENGUIN BOOKS
Published by the Penguin Group
Penguin Group (USA) LLC
375 Hudson Street
New York, New York 10014

USA | Canada | UK | Ireland | Australia | New Zealand | India | South Africa | China
penguin.com
A Penguin Random House Company

First published in the United States of America by Viking Penguin,
a member of Penguin Group (USA) Inc., 2013
Published in Penguin Books 2014

THE LIBRARY OF CONGRESS HAS CATALOGED THE HARDCOVER EDITION AS FOLLOWS:
Jansma, Kristopher.
  The unchangeable spots of leopards / Kristopher Jansma.
p. cm.
ISBN 978-0-670-02600-5 (hc.)
ISBN 978-0-14-312502-0 (pbk.)
1. Authors—Fiction.   2. Friendship—Fiction.   I. Title.
PS3610.A5873U53 2013
813'.6—dc23
2012027179

Printed in the United States of America
10 9 8 7 6 5 4 3 2

Set in Dante MT Std
Designed by Alissa Amell

For Leah

All good books are alike in that
they are truer than if they had really happened . . .

—ERNEST HEMINGWAY

Truth, like gold, is to be obtained not by its growth,
but by washing away from it all that is not gold.

—LEO TOLSTOY

Contents

If you believe that you are the author of this book,
please contact Haslett & Grouse Publishers
(New York, New York) at your first convenience.

The Unchangeable Spots

of Leopards

Author's Note

The truth is beautiful. Without doubt; and so are lies.

—RALPH WALDO EMERSON

I've lost every book I've ever written. I lost the first one here in Terminal B, where I became a writer, twenty-eight years ago, in the after-school hours and on vacations while I waited for my mother to return from doling out honey-roasted peanuts at eighteen thousand feet.

I used to sit very quietly, at this very table, at Phil's Coffee Hub, under the watchful eye of Ms. Barlow, or bellied-up to the Formica countertop of W. W. Gould's Good Eats with Mrs. De Santos, or on a small stool inside the cramped Jewels, Jewels, Jewels! kiosk with Mrs. Nederhoffer. Now these people are all gone and I'm as old as they were then.

It was a wonderful time in my life—before I became a writer. I had an endless supply of books from Mr. Humnor, the great-girthed man who ran Emerson Books, and I spent many happy hours spying on Mr. Bjorn, who ran Ten-Minute Timepiece Repair.

Mr. Bjorn was the only person in Terminal B who wore a full suit, every day, with a real bow tie. His ancient eyes permanently fixed in a squint—the result, I imagined, of studying the tiny gears of wristwatches all day. When he was not seated in his high chair, fixing watches, he stood upright to read the big New York City newspaper. I wanted to be just like him some day.

We first spoke on the day after my eighth birthday. So that I would always know when she would be arriving home again, my mother gave me a gold wristwatch that had been left behind on one of her flights. Its band was twice the diameter of my little wrist, so our first matter of business was to have some links removed by Mr. Bjorn.

When I handed the watch to him, he let loose a fluttery whistle and polished it respectfully to remove the little oily fingerprints I'd already gotten all over it.

"This is quite a watch for a boy your size," he told me. "What's your name, son?"

I did not even dare to speak. My mother smiled her wide smile at Mr. Bjorn and, checking her own watch to see how long she had until her next flight, said, "There are no clocks in this place. Have you ever noticed that?"

Mr. Bjorn's low voice rose sweetly as he spoke to my mother. She had a way of flushing men's cheeks and causing them to stare at the toes of their shoes.

"Yes, ma'am. They don't want passengers getting upset that their flights aren't on time. There is a row of ten clocks over in Terminal A. But not one of them is set to Eastern Standard Time."

I listened intently, for I had never set foot in Terminal A. My mother never flew internationally and did not know anyone willing to look after me over there. I had dreamed about Terminal A many times. I imagined it to be just the same as Terminal B, but in reverse—a looking-glass terminal, where everyone did everything backward. Or, if it was A, and we were B, perhaps it was the original and we were the copy. Perhaps I was only a reverse version of some other boy whose life was the other way around.

My mother chided Mr. Bjorn for calling her "ma'am" as he slipped the newly shortened watchband around my wrist. Then he handed me the removed links in a little plastic bag. "You save these, son. Take care of a watch like this and it'll last longer than me or even you."

My reflection was small in its gleaming curves. "OK," I said.

After that, once every week or so, I would return to Mr. Bjorn's shop, and if he was not too busy, he would open the watch for me and inspect the tiny gears inside.

"This is the tourbillion, and that's the hairspring back there. And this over here is called the escapement." He gestured to a little anchor-shaped arm that swung like a pendulum, clicking as a tiny-toothed wheel turned beneath it. "That's what makes that ticking sound you hear." The little gear struggled against the anchor. After a second it built up enough force to turn one click, swinging the pendulum, and then it stopped again. Struggled, turned, and stopped.

"Each time it goes around a little bit, a second goes away."

"Where?" I asked, as the pendulum swung again. And again.

He winked at me. "It escapes. That's why they call it that. Escapement."

I barely blinked as it swung and swung again. I think I believed that if I watched closely enough, I could figure out where the seconds were headed.

Sometimes I just sat and listened to the watch ticking. Each tick was another second less before my mother returned. Each tick was another second older that I grew. Each tick was another word that I scribbled into the many notebooks that Mr. Humnor gave me.

I wasn't a writer—not yet, of course—but I wrote. From the days before my feet could touch the linoleum floor beneath my seat, I had been jotting little things down about the odd parade that flowed through Terminal B: pilots, passengers, and the people waiting to greet them. I began doing this so that I could tell my mother about all the things she'd missed while she'd been gone. Every day I saw so many new people, rushing through the terminal to one place or another while I remained still. For all my hours spent in Terminal B, I'd never flown on an airplane—not once. I wondered where all the people kept escaping to, like those little seconds inside my watch. But in between arrivals and departures, I got bored, and sometimes I made people up, to see if my mother could detect the false woman in a pink blazer, with the hamster in her carry-on luggage, among the actual transient citizens of Terminal B.

Not long after receiving the gold watch, I wrote my very first book, a mystery I called *The Pink Packet Thieves*, twenty-two pages in length, including illustrations. It concerned an unnamed boy detective who is summoned by the Chief of the Airport Police to discover who has been stealing all the pink packets of artificial sweetener from the various restaurants in the terminal. The boy detective cleverly conceals himself in a trash can and lies patiently in wait for the criminal mastermind to appear. All day long, the boy endures the garbage that the travelers are heaping unknowingly onto his head. He is resolute and, indeed, the long wait pays off. By the light of the full moon, the boy detective spots two suspicious figures sneaking around. The boy detective confronts the shadows and discovers they are Xavier and Yvette D'Argent, a wealthy brother and sister who are new in town and who confess that they have been stealing the artificial sweeteners to feed a horrible addiction that they developed during their idle youths in Paris. (I had learned a few things from eavesdropping on Mrs. De Santos, talking about her sons.) In the end, the boy detective is moved by their tale and agrees to keep their secret, in exchange for the return of the sweetener, a promise that the thievery will cease, and assurances that both siblings would consult their parents about treatment options. Just as the story appears to come to a wholesome conclusion, however, the boy detective recalls his earlier sufferings in the trash can. Then, on the next page, he is seen telling the Chief of the Airport Police that he has been unable to find the culprits, and he walks away with the stolen sweetener in a black suitcase. A brief epilogue reveals that the boy detective then sells the pink packets on the black market, retires for good, and that the newly cured Xavier and Yvette become his best friends, now that he is as wealthy as them.

The Pink Packet Thieves was universally adored by the women in the terminal, and for a few days I had my first taste of a writer's celebrity. But I was not really a writer—not yet. Not even then. Mr. Humnor said that if we made copies and put them up for sale in his shop we could split the profits. For a night or two I dreamed of the hundreds of dollars I would surely make—perhaps even enough so that my mother could retire and we could fly around the country together.

One person hadn't seen the book yet. That was Mr. Bjorn and there was no one in the concourse whom I wanted to like the book as badly. For days I watched him, waiting for my moment, and finally I walked over, on a slow Tuesday afternoon that summer, to offer him my story. I don't remember finding it strange that, on this day, he was reading the newspaper in his high chair and not standing.

"You get any bigger yet? You ready to put one of those links back in?"

"I wrote a book," I said meekly, as I held it out.

"So you have," he said, squinting down at it for a moment. His hands were shaking and he kept sort of clearing his throat.

"You could read it," I explained, as I pushed it toward him.

He lifted it up, made a little show of admiring the title and the cover art, and released a familiar fluttery whistle. "I'll take a look at it as soon as I'm done with my paper. One hour, son. All right?"

I agreed, happy to see him smiling. "A book," he laughed as he set it down. "Sounds like someone wants to live forever."

I didn't know what he meant by this but I didn't care. I rushed off again through the concourse, giddy with pleasure, and I did not stop running until I reached Emerson Books and snatched three candy bars while Mr. Humnor pretended not to look. I camped out there, beneath the rotating rack of romance novels, watching the little hands on my wristwatch twisting slowly around, the little ticking of the escapement seeming to grow louder and louder.

When an hour had finally passed, I rushed out of the store and followed a crowd of passengers to the other end of the concourse. When I got there I was surprised to see a crowd massed around Mr. Bjorn's shop. Ms. Barlow and Mrs. De Santos and Mrs. Nederhoffer were all there, but Mr. Bjorn was not. His high chair was on the ground, on its side. His newspaper lay in a heap beside it.

"Old guy's ticker just stopped," I heard a rough voice say. It was a policeman—a blue pudgy ball with a buzz cut—and he was holding *my* book in his hand. And he was laughing. Not like Mr. Humnor laughed.

Laughing as though he thought something was awful. And all of my daytime minders were just standing there, letting him laugh.

"Was this the old guy's?" the officer asked, that horrible smile still on his face.

"No," said Mrs. Nederhoffer. "It's just this little boy's. His mother's one of the flight attendants, and she leaves him here all day like it's some sort of day-care center."

"We all sort of look after him," Mrs. De Santos chimed in. "Honestly, I live in fear every day that some nut will run off with him."

Ms. Barlow agreed, loudly, that if one ever did, it wouldn't be on her chest.

The officer laughed—a hacking, barking sort of laugh. "No father?"

This time the ladies laughed—their cackles were high and excited—as if there were nothing they liked to laugh about more. They all began talking at once, and I heard them say bad words before I could hold my watch up to my ears. Soon I couldn't hear anything but the ticking. I stood there in a dark forest of strangers' knees, listening to second after second, escaping. Then with one careless motion, the policeman chucked my book into the nearest trash can. None of the ladies even noticed.

I started running away, back down the concourse. At first I meant to hide back at Mr. Humnor's, but when I got there it still wasn't far enough. Leaping down the escalators, the concourse rose up around me, and below were the great snakelike conveyor belts that slowly ferried luggage to waiting crowds. I kept on running, out past the big orange car rental sign and through the revolving glass doors. I ran down the sidewalk past the taxicabs and the luggage collectors in their red caps. I didn't know where I was going or where I wanted to go. I wanted to go wherever my mother was, or wherever Mr. Bjorn had gone. I wanted to go where all the seconds went.

I stopped when I saw a sign pointing inside again. TERMINAL A it said. Timidly, I went inside and up some more escalators to the concourse level. Finally, I would see it. Terminal A. And maybe I would find Mr. Bjorn, winding all the timepieces backward, with the same serious smile. The little round tables were the same. The linoleum floor was the same. The skylights high above me were the same. But there was no Emerson Books. There was no Phil's Coffee. There was no W. W. Gould's, and there was no Ten-Minute Timepiece Repair. There was no Mr. Bjorn.

Finally, I sat down on the ground under a long row of clocks. There were ten of them—each exactly the same except for a little sign that said the name of a place. Some of these places I'd read about, like Paris, where Xavier and Yvette had come from. And some I'd heard of, like Mexico City, where Mrs. De Santos was born. These were places that were very far away, I knew. And they all had different times from the time on my watch. In Mexico City, it was still an hour earlier. If I were there, I figured, and it was an hour earlier, then Mr. Bjorn would still be around.

I sat there listening to the clocks' little ticking noises. Inside each were little gears like the ones inside my watch, struggling and turning. I listened to the seconds escaping. And I knew then that each second was just escaping to a different clock, somewhere even farther away, and that the seconds just went on and on escaping like that, forever.

So. That is the story of how I lost my very first book. I've lost three others since—a novel, a novella, and a biography. The first is disintegrating steadily at the bottom of a black lake. The second is in the hands of a woman whom I love and will never see again. The third is in a dusty African landfill, wrapped in the bloody tatters of my tweed coat, my gold watch still in the pocket.

Only fragments remain, which I've carried with me around the world and back again. Sitting here in Terminal B, setting them beside one another, I've been trying to get them to add up to something true. I'm staring at the margins between them—just an inch on each side—but the distance may as well be the Grand Canyon. Yet I feel certain that somewhere in this empty space, between my lies and fictions, is the truth.

It occurs to me, as I finish writing this, that perhaps these surviving pieces aren't so different from those clocks in Terminal A. In each of them you can see what the time would be, but only somewhere else. Between them all, you can, if you wish, determine what time it is here.

These stories are all true, but only somewhere else.

What Was Lost

1

The Debutante

What can be said at all can be said clearly,
and what we cannot talk about we must pass over in silence.

—LUDWIG WITTGENSTEIN, *TRACTATUS LOGICO-PHILOSOPHICUS*

The autumn of my sixteenth birthday, I worked after school and on Sundays, serving *apfelstrudel* and *einspänners* at Ludwig's Café in the Raleigh Museum of Art. Sundays were the best days for tips, because all the patrons getting out of church were feeling simultaneously undercaffeinated and overcharitable. Before the bells were done ringing, all the most affluent ladies in North Raleigh were rushing over from Methodist Saints United, wearing hats that my buddy Rodrigo said ought to be in the abstract art exhibits. But the real reason I looked forward to Sundays was that the Terpsichorean Society held its debutante classes in the event space across the hall, and while the well-heeled mothers lost track of time gossiping at Ludwig's beneath the golden *Portrait of Colette Marsh*, Rodrigo and I would go back to the storeroom window and stare at the debutantes.

After their class ended, the debutantes would line up in the narrow space between the café's dumpsters, where their mothers couldn't see them, and pass Camels carefully, so as not to fleck ash on their white rehearsal dresses. When they saw us looking they tossed cigarette butts at the window, but they couldn't do anything too loudly or they'd risk blowing their cover. It was the end of 1993, and we knew we'd become adults inside of a new century—and there these girls were, being trained for the last one. Mostly they ignored us until Rodrigo tapped on the window to warn them that the mothers were calling for their checks and that they had better hurry back inside.

Some Sundays Rodrigo just looked and some Sundays he called out to Suzanne White, the tall girl from our school whom he swore he would marry. Together, he claimed, they would breed a superior race of half–Puerto Rican/half–Southern Belle babies. For my part, I slunk down, hoping that none of them would see me in my feathered cap and olive lederhosen, and pretending that I just happened to be passing my break reading *The Woman in White* near the window.

"We were supposed to read that for school or something?" Rodrigo would ask.

"Extra credit," I'd lie.

The truth was that I liked to read—especially old books about eccentric heiresses and menacing counts and guys with names like Sir Percival Glyde, but I'd learned long ago that this was a preference best kept to myself.

"What is *wrong* with you?" Rodrigo would ask. "Don't you want to look at these fine ladies?" He gave his cap a stylish slant and let one suspender fall off his shoulder, as if he wore this sort of thing especially for them.

"Sure," I'd say, "I just don't want them to look at *me*."

"Well, how are they ever going to talk to you unless they know you're looking?"

"I *don't* want them to talk to me. *They* don't want to talk to me. They don't even want to talk to *you*."

Rodrigo's eyes would bug as if I'd just tried to convince him that the sun would burn out tomorrow. "Hell *yes* they want to talk to me."

"We clean tables at an Austrian coffeehouse, in a city whose residents generally think *Austria* is where kangaroos come from. Come on. Your mother is a housekeeper and your father mows lawns."

"My mom runs a cleaning service. My dad owns a landscaping company. We're entrepreneurs, jerk."

"But they're *debutantes*," I'd remind him. "They're going to go to Princeton and Duke and marry inbred trust-funders with yachts who play polo and shoot skeet."

"That's pretty funny, coming from Mr. Ten-Under-Par."

Rodrigo liked to tease me for playing golf on the high school team. In truth, being on the team did my reputation more harm than good. I loved to play, but the other boys on the team all hated me, because I was better than them and because my mother was a flight attendant and didn't belong to the Briar Creek Country Club like their mothers did. My father was a man she'd met seventeen years ago, during a layover in Newark. Together they'd gotten swept up in the heady, romantic winter of 1976.

"So, they marry Mr. Trust Fund," Rodrigo would say, cracking open the window so the girls could hear. "But they'll be home all day making sweet, sweet love to me!"

Suzanne would glare, and as the other girls pretended to be shocked, she'd flip her perfectly manicured middle finger straight up in the air, and smile.

Meanwhile, I'd angle one of the silver baking trays toward the window so that I could catch the reflection of Betsy Littleford, the only other girl there from our school. A silent blonde with ice blue eyes, Betsy Littleford never smiled. Not as far as I could remember. Not even all the way back to the fifth grade when I'd first seen her.

"That's funny," she'd say flatly whenever some teacher tried to coax even the slightest giggle from her with a joke in class. "That's really very funny."

Rodrigo called her "Stepford Betsy" and liked to theorize that inside she was just all Disney animatronics. He loudly speculated about someday finding out for himself, but I dreamed of simply someday making her smile. Just once.

And I'd never have done it if her brother hadn't gotten his skull caved in during our match against Asheville late that fall.

It started on the seventh hole, when Mark White had sliced a shot deep into the woods, and both teams wound up shivering for ten minutes in the chilly November air, watching the golden leaves spiraling down from the trees, until the judges went in after him and caught him sipping a little airport bottle of vodka. Our team took a double penalty and Coach Holland angrily sent White to clean everyone's clubs. When I, then, had the audacity to hit a beautiful two-hundred-and-ten-yard drive on the eighth hole, Mark dumped my golf clubs into a water hazard "by accident." I didn't really care. The other boys had Titleists and Mizunos; mine were just an odd mix of yard-sale finds, half rusted already at purchase. But while I quietly fished them out, the real trouble began.

Billy Littleford, our captain, enjoyed putting his friends in their places, especially Mark. Everyone in our school adored Billy—even me. In movies, the king of the school was always a tyrant, taking lunch money and breaking hearts with reckless abandon. But our king, Billy, was as kind as he was suave. He didn't stand for anyone picking on either the quiet kids, like me, or the loudmouths like Rodrigo. Once, when I was short a dollar at the front of an impatient lunch line, and in front of everyone was about to put my burrito back under the warming lamps, Billy Littleford strolled up suddenly to spot me a five. "Thanks for getting me those cigarettes before the game on Saturday," he said earnestly, though I'd done no such thing and he did not smoke. "I'll pay you the rest by tomorrow, I promise."

If Billy ruled our school, he did so benevolently, and for this he was beloved by teachers and classmates alike. Hence, Billy was forever able to charm his way out of whatever trouble he got himself into. That afternoon on the golf course, he'd seen Mark dump my clubs in the water. He waited until Mark was hovering near a sand trap, and then Billy tackled Mark headfirst into the sand, kissing him, deeply on the mouth.

"Oh, Mark, you're such a stud!" he shouted. Both teams erupted in laughter.

When Mark began pushing him away, Billy clutched at his broken heart. "But *Mark!*" he cried. "You said we could finally *tell* people!" As Billy minced around in fake tears, even some of the judges were laughing.

Mark spat sand out and wiped at his eyes. Half blind, he grabbed a rake from the edge of the trap. We were supposed to use these rakes to smooth out the sand, like they were little Zen gardens; Mark tried to use his to smooth out Billy's face. Billy dodged the swinging rake and began to bob and weave around the course like a cartoon boxer. Grinning boy-ishly at the laughing Asheville players, Billy did not realize he was weav-ing directly into the backswing of their teammate, who was warming up for the ninth hole. The boy from Asheville brought his 3-iron out of the swing, clean through an imaginary ball, and straight back down into the side of Billy's head.

The following day, every newspaper left behind on the tables at Lud-wig's had run a photo of a grinning Billy at last year's Homecoming Parade. The reports said he was at Wakefield North Hospital, in and out of consciousness, and the doctors' prognosis was that he could lose half his IQ and that his motor skills would be greatly reduced, forever.

Even Rodrigo was upset about it. "They ought to throw that *pendejo* in jail," he snapped at a photo of Mark White that had made the inside page, after the jump. Mark was Suzanne's older brother, so Rodrigo didn't like him much to begin with.

The café was closing, and the museum outside was teeming with glitzy people who had come for the Terpsichorean Society's Annual Debutante Ball. I doubted that Betsy would still be going, but I hurried through my table wiping just in case.

When I next looked up, I noticed that a woman had come into the closed café and was peering at the *Portrait of Colette Marsh*, a small golden nude that hung above the bricked-up fireplace. Most people didn't notice the painting because it was about the size of a page in a paperback book, but when the light came through, late in the day, it gleamed. I'd passed many wayward hours staring up at this golden woman, filled with as close to a religious feeling as I had ever had. I wondered who Colette Marsh had been, and who had painted the portrait. The tiny plaque said merely that it was from 1863. ARTIST UNKNOWN.

"We're closed for the day, ma'am," I said to the woman, who wore a long black fur. Her hair was swirled up in a severe blond vortex on the back of her head.

"It's simply *sickening*," she muttered as I came closer.

My cheeks flushed as I glanced up at the painting's golden nipples. "The managers got some complaints. That's why they moved it so high up." She did not look away. So I added, "Plus, that's real gold on there, I guess."

The woman finally looked at me for the first time since I'd approached. She did not seem all that impressed, and she did not in any way hide this evaluation.

"Clearly. I meant that it is sickening that Genevieve Von Porter would donate it and then allow it to be hung in the coffee shop instead of the museum proper."

"Oh," I said, looking back up at the painting again. I'd never thought of it as something anybody owned. "Well. We're closed anyway, ma'am."

I gestured at my wristwatch and she seemed to admire it, momentarily. A gift from my mother, and gold as well, it was the nicest thing I owned.

The woman attempted to smile, though her taut face did not allow for much movement. "My name is Cecily Littleford. Are you available this evening to help me with a minor jam?"

Littleford. Betsy's mother. I stuttered as I pledged I'd do absolutely anything she needed. She handed me a small plastic keycard.

"Take the staff elevator upstairs to Conference Room B. You have twenty minutes to clean up and put on the tuxedo that's hanging on the door."

"Excuse me?"

She pinched one of the newspapers between two disdainful fingertips.

"My daughter is coming out to polite society this evening and needs an escort. My son Billy is otherwise engaged and my husband is away on business. Betsy mentioned that she knew someone working here at the museum who could wear Billy's size." She looked at me again, disparagingly. "Or close enough."

I could barely speak. Fortunately, Rodrigo rushed over. "He'd be honored, Mrs. Littleford. Could I offer you some tonic water, while he goes to change?"

After Rodrigo ushered her to a clean table below the golden portrait, he pulled me back toward the door. "Don't screw this up now, Cinderella. Have some goddamn balls. She *asked* for you, you *suertudo* motherfucker."

Twenty minutes later, when I saw my reflection in the inside of the elevator doors, I did not even recognize myself. Billy's tuxedo was a little long in the sleeve, but I looked all right. I thought that surely I could impersonate a proper member of the leisure class for two hours. But when the doors parted, and I saw Betsy Littleford standing there, my confidence withered like grass in winter.

The voluminous lower folds of her white dress flowed from the waist like collapsing waves, descending from where the defined V of its northern border intercepted an orbit of tiny pearls. Her hair was down, covering her bare shoulders. A second V was formed by the neat crossing of her gloved hands. A third and final V came in the shape of her sharply plunging eyebrows: already I'd done something wrong.

"Come on," she said, grabbing my hand and jerking me toward the ballroom's arched doorway. "They started going in four minutes ago."

Red velvet curtains covered the high windows that normally illuminated the rotunda. Tall Roman columns supported a great glass dome, through which the moon could be seen, full and yellow and high above us. Briefly I felt as though I were being led into the Coliseum to be fed to the lions. The room swarmed with older women in scarves and slinky evening gowns, and distinguished men in finely tailored tuxedos. The debutantes were there—perhaps twenty girls—all the ones we'd seen out by the dumpsters in their rehearsal garb. Now they wore the full regalia—white gloves, floor-length dresses, and pearls that had belonged to their mothers' mothers. They stood in a line, arm in arm with fathers or brothers; the only guy I recognized was Mark, who was escorting Suzanne and looking more than a little pale.

A man at a podium called the girls' names aloud, one at a time, and with each presentation, he announced the name of her escort. Each girl then stepped out into a spotlight, curtsied politely, and smiled. Next she took her escort by the hand and moved on, to allow the next young pair to take its place. Betsy's face remained in total lockdown, but I wondered if I would finally see her smile tonight.

"Sorry about your brother," I whispered weakly.

Betsy's face did not change even slightly. Her eyes stared off at nothing at all. Soon a harried little man rushed over to us with Mrs. Littleford in tow.

"He's right here. I told you," Mrs. Littleford said. "Just have Mr. Isherwood say, 'Presenting Elizabeth Littleford, escorted by . . . '"

Mrs. Littleford looked blankly at me. She did not know my name. "He's an old friend of Billy's, this is . . . " And again she trailed off.

Betsy's crescent lips began to form my name, but before she could speak it, I blurted out another name instead.

"Walter," I lied, thinking of the detective in my Wilkie Collins book. "Walter Hartright."

Instantly I regretted not saying "Sir Percival Glyde," but the harried man was already scribbling down "Walter Hartright." The name seemed more plausible for a resident of suburban Raleigh, and the twentieth century, anyway.

Betsy's eyes bulged, ever so slightly, and her lips eased gently back into place. There was no smile, and no laugh. Just an odd blankness. She wasn't angry—that much I could see. She was amused, I was sure. Only, rather than smile, she somehow *un*-smiled. Then I saw it at last: Betsy's smile was the absence of smiling.

As the man ran off to give the speaker my fake name, Betsy pushed her mother's hand aside and said, "Walter. When did you and Billy become such good friends again?"

"Acting class in fifth grade," I lied. "Billy was Vladimir in our production of *Waiting for Godot* and I was Estragon." It worked. Betsy un-smiled again. Her mother seemed puzzled but Betsy stepped in suddenly.

"You were in Switzerland with Grandma."

And before Mrs. Littleford could question this, the couple ahead of us stepped away, and Betsy dragged me into the light. The audience assumed a solemn silence.

"May I present Miss Elizabeth Littleford," Mr. Isherwood said, "escorted by a close friend of her brother's, Mr. Walter Hartright."

The applause was sudden and electrifying. Betsy curtsied elegantly but did not smile. Not even a little. She took my hand in her gloved one and led me out of the light.

After a hundred hands had been shaken and a hundred platitudes exchanged, Betsy drew me to a table, where we sat side by side in front of gold-inlaid plates and silently consumed Niçoise salads and wagyu steaks while the adults talked of Morningstar ratings, Croatian catamaran chartering, and hunting tundra swans. I watched Betsy closely out of the corner of my eye, making sure I lifted the same utensils when she did. To my fascination, I found this new role was an easier fit than I'd expected. I was like one of the people I'd made up in Terminal B— blending naturally right in with all those around me. Plus, it seemed that no one really expected much from the escorts, anyway. While the girls got a year of debutante training, the boys seemed to be winging it. I did a damn sight better than Mark White, for instance, who sat across from me, using only one fork and dribbling sauce conspicuously down his shirt front.

He acknowledged my existence but once, when Mrs. Littleford asked me to tell everyone about Billy's early acting career and addressed me as Walter. Suzanne firmly squeezed Mark's hand as he began to correct her, and he winced in confusion. Before dessert was even served, Mark had vanished to the men's room three times, returning slightly clumsier after each visit. I didn't blame him—the conversation kept spiraling back to Billy, no matter how much Mrs. Littleford and the others tried to avoid the subject.

"Early decision notices will come in soon," Suzanne's mother said. "Walter, where have you applied?"

"Princeton," I answered quickly. Everyone smiled, except Betsy, who un-smiled.

Walter's bright future at Princeton grew to involve a position on the golf team and an old friend who'd promised to take me sailing on the Delaware. And then, of course, there'd be writing classes with prizewinning authors. The mothers all approved. I was so engrossed in it all that it wasn't until my water glass was being refilled for the third time that I recognized Rodrigo holding the Waterford pitcher, wearing a staff uniform.

"Mr. Hartright?" he asked, smirking somewhat. "May I refresh your glass?"

I shifted down in my seat as he poured. Suddenly I felt sure that everyone knew I was full of it—that clearly, none of these rich people believed that I was really some well-to-do son of a paper manufacturer. Just as they didn't believe that Mark was in any way sober, or that Betsy Littleford's father was really away on business, or that her brother was sure to recover in a few weeks.

"Time for the waltz," Betsy said, suddenly removing her napkin from her lap.

"Waltz? Like, *the waltz* waltz?" I mumbled, struggling to stand on my suddenly shaky legs. Rodrigo was trying to help Suzanne get Mark to his feet, and no one was looking at us. I leaned in as close as I dared. "I don't know *how*."

"The boys are *all* disasters. Just try to look like you're leading."

So we stepped out onto the dance floor with the others, and the girls prodded their partners so as to form a wide circle. The stiff-looking Mr. Isherwood made some sort of announcement regarding the sponsored charity, and then there was a crash of music and Betsy beckoned with her right hand for me to extend my left. I did so, shifting all my weight onto my right foot as she took it. She then drew herself in against me, slightly to my right, so that just half of her pressed up against just half of me. I half passed out.

Betsy guided my right hand to the smooth skin below her shoulder blade, and placed her right hand into my left and held it out high, opposite my neck. Then, through what I can only assume was girl sorcery, she began to move her feet in such a way that my feet knew just where to go.

"One, two, three," she whispered into my ear. "Forward, side, together." And we began to revolve around the floor, like a clock's hands in reverse, spinning around our own axis like two sides of one moon.

"I had no idea you were an actor," she said. "How unexpected."

"Oh, no. I just made all that up," I said quickly. "About me and Billy."

"Exactly," she said. "Very funny."

But her amusement was silent. Just between us.

"It's very hard to tell with you," I said.

I smiled. She didn't. We waltzed.

"Did *you* know," she said drily, "that the waltz was originally a peasant dance? And that Viennese nobles initially were *shocked* by the indecency of dancing so closely?"

"I did *not* know that."

"You should try taking debutante classes. For a *year*. And I'll peek out of a kitchen window and watch *you* every Sunday."

Before I could decide if she was joking or upset, the song came to its end and she began to pull away from me. "Thanks for filling in. *Walter*."

The mothers were all on their feet as we came back to the table. Mark White, somewhat dizzier from all the waltzing, was vomiting semi-raw tuna and well-massaged cow meat all over the table, along with about a quart of Jack Daniel's.

"He's hardly slept since Billy's accident," Mrs. White apologized before the flow had even ceased. "It wasn't your *fault*, dear . . ."

Suzanne was anxiously trying to get Mark to the bathroom, but the large boy had gone limp, and she could barely lift him. Before I knew it, Rodrigo was on the scene.

"Please," he said sweetly, "allow me to assist you, ma'am." Suzanne looked at him—possibly for the first time realizing that he was the same boy whom she'd seen leering at her out of the kitchen window—and then without a word slid aside so that Rodrigo could get Mark to his feet and then to the bathroom.

Understandably, the whole incident had put everybody off, and Mrs. Littleford, sensing that the evening would go only downhill from here, tapped Betsy on the hand and said, "Come, dear. Visiting hours will be over at ten. We're expected back."

"Walter and I need to say good-bye to the Von Porters," Betsy said, her face showing nothing—no resignation, no urgency.

"So," I said, thinking, *So that was it then*, as we walked away, in the direction of the Von Porters. But as soon as she had escaped her mother's sight, Betsy began to move quickly toward a set of double doors that led to the sculpture garden. Before I knew it, we were outside. Thick clouds had moved in from the south, covering the full moon like a wash of ink.

"We spent the whole *morning* at the hospital," she complained.

"How's he doing?"

"Not too good," she said. "He's got this big hole in the side of his head."

"Oh," I said, a little surprised by her even tone. Was she mad at me? Did she know that I had been, at least indirectly, responsible for Billy's current state?

"That was a joke," she explained, her blue eyes dancing like fireflies in the dark.

"Sure," I said. Mystified, I continued to follow her down the gravel paths of the sculpture garden.

"Want to hear something else funny?" We stepped gingerly over little artificial streams, jumping from rock to rock with our shoes in our hands like children. "Well, something that *I* think is *very* funny?"

"All right."

"He woke up while I was there this morning. He had this breathing tube in, so he couldn't speak until they pulled it out. And then his mouth was real dry, but he kept trying to *say* something. He pulled me in real close, because he can hardly even whisper, and, you'll never guess what he said."

"What?" I asked.

"He goes, 'Who *are* you?' He didn't know who I *was*. So I say, 'I'm Betsy. Your sister.' And he goes, 'Betsy, I'm *gay*. I'm gay, Betsy. I'm gay.'"

I nearly slipped off the rocks and into the water.

"What did you say?" I asked.

"I said, 'Yeah, I know, Billy. I know.' Like I didn't see him making out with our neighbor Roger when we were in the eighth grade? But he couldn't remember."

"Jesus," I mumbled. I couldn't quite believe it. And yet, while I couldn't quite tell how Betsy felt about it, I sort of admired Billy all the more.

Betsy went on. "He didn't remember who *I* was. But he remembered that. And my mother is standing there bawling—pretending she didn't hear what he said—and I'm standing there thinking, *Huh. He finally comes out on the day of my coming out.*"

And there it was—another distinct un-laugh—and then, still barefoot, Betsy began to run across a long green field, empty except for us. I was surprised at how fast she was able to run in her gown. I could not see the museum at all anymore, just neat curves of trees along the sloping grass. Betsy kept on running. Not until we came to the top of the hill and I saw a little oasis of sand in the distance did I realize we'd come onto the Briar Creek Golf Course. She slowed down at last, as we crossed onto the eighth hole and sat down on the edge of the bunker.

"So this is where it happened?" she asked.

"I guess so," I said. The spot where Billy had fallen had been smoothed out into a neat spiral. Not a single bloody grain of sand remained evident in the trap.

Nervous, I took my hand and pressed it on top of hers. I didn't know what I was doing. I didn't know what I was saying. It didn't seem as if there could be anything worth saying.

"You don't seem that upset," I said finally.

"It's all just so . . . " she began, and then stopped. "Unexpected."

"Of course."

"No, I mean . . . my family, we—well, *they*—see to it that nothing unexpected ever happens. No grade lower than an A-minus. No winter we don't spend in Colorado. No summer we don't go to the Outer Banks. My mother will host the Spring Leukemia Fund-raiser, and my father will say he'll be home for our birthdays, only something will come up and he'll send a savings bond instead."

Though I'd have preferred a father who sent excuses and treasuries to not having one at all, I said, "That's awful."

"It's not. It's just expected. How can it be awful if it's expected?"

"I guess."

"Two days ago, Billy was going to go to Chapel Hill, like my father, and then Wharton, Stern, or Harvard, and then take over my father's company someday. Everyone sitting in that ballroom knows that was the plan. Just like they all know that I was going to go to a liberal arts college and read some Emily Dickinson and talk about slants of light, join Alpha Gamma Pi, and then get a degree I'd never use because I'd be married to an econ major I met in my first semester. Then while he'd be at business school—Wharton, Stern, or Harvard—I'd start popping out babies and choosing window treatments. The expected treatments. The expected babies."

She looked up at the wide black sky.

"But now?" I asked.

"Now Billy's not going to be the next Littleford to go to Chapel Hill. He'll be lucky if he can go to the bathroom. He's not going to go to Wharton, or run the company. He can't count to ten."

"It's terrible," I said.

"It *is* terrible," she agreed.

"So? Now you'll go to Chapel Hill and Wharton and run the company? Is that what you mean?"

"I don't know," she said. "I'm going to do . . . "—she turned her head to look at me—". . . *What. Ever. I. Want.*" She relished each syllable. The corners of her lips were just barely curling. Then she lay her head down on my shoulder.

"Billy told me once you snuck out here at night to practice."

Face turning a deep red, I asked, "How did he know that?"

She shrugged. "You're the best player on the team, and the only one whose dad doesn't drag him out here every Saturday. Billy's not an idiot. Well. He *wasn't* an idiot."

"Was that another joke?"

"Walter. What kind of monster do you take me for?" she said, batting her eyelashes.

I had to do it: "How come you never smile?" I asked.

" 'Smile.' " She repeated my word flatly. "That's what they told me in every debutante class. For a *year* of Sundays. 'Smile, Betsy! Smile! It's *your* job to put everyone else at ease. Make them feel welcome.' " She shrugged, her bare shoulder nudging into mine. "My dad's been on 'a business trip in Dubai' since I was ten; my mom's miserable; my brother's gay, and now brain damaged to boot. Put *yourself* at ease. Make *yourself* feel welcome. I'll smile when there's something worth smiling about."

"Fair enough," I said, trying hard not to laugh.

"Billy liked you," she said after a minute. "I mean *likes* you. I mean, if he remembers who you are anymore, he probably still likes you. I think of all the guys he knew, Billy would have wanted me to go with you. When I told him you and that Spanish kid had been spying on us, he said that sounded just like you."

"Spying . . . "—I paused—". . . with the utmost respect."

She studied me a moment, and it seemed as though she were about to kiss me. Or, possibly, devour me. It turns out I was right on both counts.

First she kissed me, and then came the devouring—the devouring of any hope I ever had of forgetting her, or that night, or Billy, or any of it.

Later we lay on the fairway watching the airplanes line up for landing. It was still cloudy and there were no stars, only airplanes. They were efficient machines—tons of perfectly sculpted steel and wire, each containing three hundred people, or more, a thousand feet up in the air, moving hundreds of miles an hour. But from where we lay it was impossible to believe: they seemed to just hover there, blinking lazily, like fireflies.

"Do you like me?" she asked.

"I sort of thought that was obvious," I said.

"No, I mean, *me*," she said. "*This* me."

And she did seem like somebody else, suddenly. Her tough, sweet front was gone. Her teeth were chattering, faintly.

"I do," I said. I thought about Rodrigo's theory that she was a robot, through and through. "I'd always hoped, I guess, that this was what you were like. On the inside."

She said nothing, but the faint chatter of her teeth began to get louder. "Let's go back," I said finally.

"I don't want to go back. If I go back, they'll drag me out to the hospital."

"I'll hide you in the café. I can make you a Viennese hot chocolate."

"Vell, can ve keep talkink about mein pater, Herr Freud?"

"Vhat better place?" I replied, scratching my imaginary goatee. "Ve've even got a little couch you can lie on."

Her eyebrows lifted and her cheeks quaked, but she covered the erupting laugh by kissing me again.

We gathered up our things and walked down off the bunker. We crossed to the stream and stepped over the rocks that led into the sculpture garden. I climbed up on the dumpsters behind Ludwig's and squeezed through the back window, so that I could unlock the side door for Betsy. And I was so deliriously happy that I did not even notice the two bodies entangled on the couch in the front, until I'd invited Betsy to sit on it.

"Well hello, Suzanne," Betsy said flatly.

The half-naked girl scrambled to her feet and, glaring furtively at Betsy, yanked her dress up and extracted herself from the still-amorous Rodrigo.

"Get *off* me!" Suzanne shouted, as if he had been the one holding *her* down. Then, avoiding Betsy's eye, Suzanne rushed away to the lobby doors, as Rodrigo went after her, calling out in Spanish.

When the door shut, Betsy and I just stood there, unsure of how to proceed.

"He's a really nice guy," I said lamely.

"Oh," Betsy said. "Yes, I'm sure they're going to have quite a future together."

This stung, and she could tell—though I wasn't entirely sure that she minded. Immediately, I wondered what *our* future would look like. Would we go on dates? Would I have to explain, eventually, to her mother that my name was not really Walter Hartright? That I had not even applied to Princeton?

"You said something about hot chocolate? Earlier?"

Eager to dismiss this line of thought, I went to the back and with the greatest possible care, made her a perfect hot chocolate. When I came out again I found her standing on top of one of the tables, looking at the golden portrait.

"Careful!" I whispered.

She did not seem even slightly concerned, and with her perfect posture I imagined that she could have done jumping jacks up there without falling.

"Come up," she said, reaching down a hand for me.

"That table's going to break."

"In case you were wondering," she said, "the time to lose your nerve would have been before you jumped me out on the golf course."

"*I* jumped *you?*" I began to protest, but saw that this wouldn't help my case. I set the hot chocolate down and, slowly, carefully, got onto the table with her. She seemed distant again. Back to being the way she was before.

"You seem different now," I said.

"I am."

"Why?"

She shrugged and looked at the painting impassively. "Because I don't like me, that way."

"I do," I said.

"I know," she answered.

From where we stood, the golden woman was just out of arm's reach.

"That's real gold," I informed her.

"No kidding." She didn't appear so impressed, but she couldn't take her eyes off it either. "Touch it."

"You're crazy," I said. "That'll leave my fingerprints."

"On something beautiful. Something that will stay beautiful forever."

Slowly I reached out and pressed a finger to the painting. It crunched, just slightly, under the pressure of my fingertip. When I pulled away I saw a soft circular shadow where I'd touched it, just to the left of the woman's face. My finger faintly glittered with flecks of gold. It had come off so easily.

We stared at it for another moment. Then she said, "Write me something."

"I'm not *really* a writer," I explained. The last thing I'd written that wasn't for school had been illustrated, badly, and I'd been about eight years old.

"Yes, you are," she said simply. "You've been making stuff up since you first opened your mouth. And you've been loving it. So just write it all down. Write about tonight. Quick. Before you forget anything."

"Why?"

"Because," she said, turning away from the painting at last. "You could get hit in the head with a golf club tomorrow, and then it would all be gone forever."

"That's ridiculous," I said.

"Not *that* ridiculous. Apparently."

Standing there in the silent café, I wanted to tell her that if I got hit in the head and lost every brain cell but one, that brain cell would be the one that remembered that night. But, of course, I couldn't think of words that good, just then. So I said nothing. And silence said what my words couldn't.

"All right. I'll do it. If you want," I finally managed.

The corners of her mouth began to shake. She bit her lower lip. Her nostrils swelled slightly as she breathed in, sharply. And then, at last, a strange and slow smile spread across her face.

"Why are you smiling?"

"Because," she said. And for a moment I thought that'd be it. But then she finished: *"You'll* never forget me."

Then she kissed me one more time and stepped down off the table. Before I could say anything, she walked out of the café, toward her mother and her ball and her world, and I remained there in mine, sitting on the table looking up at the tiny smudge we'd made.

2

Pinkerton and McGann

Writing, at its best, is a lonely life . . . For he does his work alone
and if he is a good enough writer he must face eternity, or the lack
of it, each day.

—ERNEST HEMINGWAY

Julian McGann was the only other boy in my freshman Fiction & Poetry
class, which met at 8:30 in the morning in a forgotten sub-basement of
Abernathy Hall. While the balding Professor Morrissey squawked about
Hawthorne and Longfellow over the clanking of Berkshire College's
infamous steam radiators, Julian sat at the far end of the conference table
and, twice a week, passed the ungodly early hour watching the leaves
pile up against the raised windows. The girls spent the class mostly staring at the brown freckles that bridged Julian's nose. He always sat up
perfectly straight. His reddish hair was a perfectly kept mess. I assumed
Julian was a slacker, since he rarely spoke or wrote anything down, and
I was certain that he would never be a real writer, like me.

The first story of Julian's that I ever read was in this class. His slim
piece, "The Thirty-Third Winter," had fluttered weightlessly when
passed across our long table, unlike my story, "The Gravity in Durham,"
which had thudded meaningfully in front of each student, clocking in at
a far more impressive twenty pages. "The Gravity in Durham" was

about a rich girl who invites a poor boy, at the eleventh hour, to substitute for the Homecoming king in the town parade, after the real king is hit by a truck. I'd based it on taking Betsy Littleford to her debutante ball, but I'd changed around the names and basic details. Even though I knew no one else at Berkshire College and none of them knew me, I still imagined someone might have read the newspaper stories about Billy's accident, and they'd then despise me for mining his traumatic brain injuries for literary gold. It seemed wrong, especially when I remembered I was at Berkshire College only due to a generous scholarship from the Briar Creek Country Club, arranged by Mrs. Littleford. She'd never said anything explicitly, but still I had the feeling that it was my silence she was really buying.

Moreover, I didn't want anyone to know where I was from, exactly. Not that I was embarrassed *per se* . . . I simply had never been anywhere before where nobody knew me, knew my mother, knew of my father's absence—knew my life story. The only other time had been when I'd masqueraded as Betsy's blue-blood date, the Princeton-bound Walter Hartright—that same too-short night when my fictions first earned me a ticket into the inner circle. There, at college, I once again felt as though I'd touched down on another planet, and with each successive day I grew more convinced that I'd suddenly be identified as an alien and sent back from whence I came.

"'Tell all the Truth but tell it slant—'" Professor Morrissey proclaimed, as I returned my attention to the Emily Dickinson poem we were meant to be scanning. "'Success in Circuit lies / Too bright for our infirm Delight / The Truth's superb surprise. / As Lightning to the Children eased / With explanation kind / The Truth must dazzle gradually / Or every man be blind—.'"

As the rest of the class picked out tetrameters and iambs and other smart-sounding things, I thought about the *Portrait of Colette Marsh* back home, dazzling in its slant of light. I thought about the little smudge I'd left behind. *Tell the truth*, I wrote in large letters at the top of my notebook. *But tell it slant*. It sounded profound . . . I just didn't quite know what it actually meant. I raised my hand a nervous fraction, but Morrissey was busy outlining rhyme schemes on the board: A-B-C-B . . . D-E-F-E . . . I looked over at Julian, staring up at the leaves outside with a vaguely amused smile. Did *he* know what it meant? I was sure that he must. My hand went down again.

After Professor Morrissey ended our class that morning, I walked out across the dew-drenched quad with Shelly, a frail girl whose veil of dark hair seemed to pull her head earthward. She'd read my whole story during class, and as I bought her a cup of burned cafeteria coffee, she let loose a surprising deluge of jumbled compliments. I'd never had anyone read—let alone *love*—the things I'd written, and perhaps it was the coffee, but I found myself warmed by a gentle, acidic sensation. By evening I had returned the favor and read her workshop piece, plus another of her stories. Both were about death and both involved highly disturbing sex scenes. Shelly invited me to stay over, as her roommate was visiting an out-of-town boyfriend. I passed a nervous hour trying not to crush her in her dark-sheeted bed, under the watchful eyes of a larger-than-life-size poster of Edgar Allan Poe.

In the morning I accidentally woke Shelly as I was reaching my free arm into my backpack on the floor, trying to fish out Julian's story.

"Sorry," I said, "I just can't wait to tear this thing apart. What kind of a title is this? He must have written this an hour before class. It's not even three pages long."

But as Shelly settled back to sleep on a dark waterfall of her own hair, I began to read Julian's story and was soon astounded to find it utterly untearable. Though "The Thirty-Third Winter" was only two and a half pages, it felt epic. It was about a man skinning a hare out on the moors of Ireland while drinking from a bottle of Epiphany whiskey. I'd never read anything better. It made me so deeply ashamed of my own story that I wanted a stiff glass of Epiphany myself. Impossibly, Julian appeared to know more about being thirty-three and skinning hares in Ireland than I did about cleaning restaurant tables and growing up in the American South, which I had actually done.

I left Shelly's room that morning in a solemn autumn funk, which lingered all through the weekend. It persisted even when, in our next class, Professor Morrissey praised my monstrous story for its fine detail. It wasn't until Julian spoke up that I felt any better.

"It feels *classic* but at the same time *strangely* modern. Like Bach played on an electric violin."

I had no idea what to make of this, but it was the most he'd ever said at once in our class, so I took it as a double-underlined compliment. He said nothing at all about Shelly's piece, "If We Were Birds," a gruesome melodrama about a married couple who accidentally kill their newborn baby when a bout of their depraved sex breaks the crib to splinters. I said I liked that there were yellow squids on the nursery wallpaper and that this might be symbolic of something, though what I couldn't decide. She still didn't seem very happy.

When we finally got to Julian's story, Professor Morrissey praised it effusively, as did I, as did all the girls except Shelly. Morrissey talked for ten minutes alone about *one* description of a rock covered in lichen, and by the end I'd have believed that the secrets of the entire universe were contained in that rock. But Julian didn't say a thing. He didn't write down our comments. He didn't even smile.

My first real conversation with Julian didn't occur until a month later, in mid-November, when Professor Morrissey invited "a dear friend and old classmate" of his, a writer named Jan Sokol, to come in as a guest lecturer. For homework, we had all read his story "The Minimum Wage." I'd thought it was pretty awful until I realized that it had been published in the *New Yorker*. I decided I must be missing something, probably because I didn't know anything about Czech revolutionaries, which it seemed to be about. Sort of.

Sokol, like Morrissey, was in his nebulous forties. Plump and baby faced, with wiry sprays of dark hair, the writer slumped over the edge of the table as he spoke. From my seat near the front, I breathed in the stench of cheap vodka. I checked the time on my wristwatch, even though I knew that our class met at 8:30 in the morning. Sokol leered at several of the girls along the left side of the table as Morrissey introduced him. They seemed utterly repulsed, but I couldn't help but notice that Shelly was staring at him with curiously wide eyes.

"The university has invited Jan to do a reading here during alumni weekend. And the dean has asked me to hold a contest. The student who submits the best story will read it in front of a gathering of alumni and students in December."

"That's the first thing to know about being a writer," Sokol interrupted in a squeaky, nasal voice. "Nobody actually wants to read anything themselves. They all just want you to read it to them." This sounded like a joke, though he sounded utterly miserable as he said it. His eyes flitted to my photocopy of his story, which I had out in front of me. Slowly he reached over and grabbed it in a pudgy hand.

"Pinkerton," he said absently, "may I borrow this?"

I was about to say that my name wasn't Pinkerton when Sokol rose up out of his seat and studied my photocopy for a moment at arm's length. His face took on a look of abject desperation.

"For the love of whatever gods you believe in," he pleaded, "don't be writers."

We all looked to Morrissey while this plea echoed through the classroom. Our professor appeared only mildly alarmed. It wasn't clear if Sokol had anything else to add, but then suddenly he continued.

"You might as well walk across the desert planting apple seeds. Be doctors. Or, if you're not smart enough to be a doctor, be a security guard. That's what I do. We make pretty good money. And don't worry about getting hurt. The chances are ten billion to one that anyone is going to blow up the building *you're* in. I guard the Las Olindas Mormon Tabernacle, five nights a week. The worst that happens is that kids come and try to piss on it, and then I get to zap them with a taser. But most nights it's quiet. Sometimes I just dance down the hall like it's the darkest nightclub in Warsaw. I get drunk. Later I zap myself, just to see if I can feel it. Or I'll call a girl over. That's the real ticket. Happiness!

Happiness is making love for as long as you can stand it to the most luminous thing you can find on this rotten corpse of a planet!"

He punctuated this last point by slamming his fist on the table, spilling coffees and scattering pens all along its length. None of us breathed. Even Julian was absolutely alert. I was so sure that it was all simply preamble to some sort of inspirational speech, about how, really, writing was the only thing worth doing at all. But instead he lifted up the copy of his story that he'd taken from me and tore it in two.

"There are *enough* books in the world," he concluded mournfully. Then he sat down again, placed his head on the edge of the table, and began to weep. For a few long moments, we all just listened to this gigantic man, sobbing over the chaotic clanking of the radiators.

"Class dismissed," Professor Morrissey said finally, when it became clear these were not tactical tears. "Boys, would you help me get him to my office?"

The girls erupted into frantic whispers as they grabbed their notebooks and fled, nervously looking over their shoulders to confirm that the man was still there, crying. Only Shelly lingered for a few moments, watching Sokol's tears soak into a pile of our papers before she skittered away.

Morrissey got the door, while Julian and I got underneath each of the man's arms, yokelike and heavy, and eased him out of the room and into the hallway.

"Is he going to be all right?" I asked.

"Random House turned down his novel this morning," Morrissey explained. "He's been writing it since we met eighteen years ago. I told him to just come in some other time, but he was insistent."

Eighteen years was longer than I'd been alive. For the first time I began to wonder if this writing thing wasn't maybe a bad idea. True, Betsy had told me to write her something. The nights I'd spent writing that story, getting lost in my imaginary Durham, were the closest I'd come to reliving that night. Pretending in her presence. Making myself up. But now that the story was finished, it didn't seem like hardly enough. I felt sure that I could do better, that I could say more. As I helped to carry the weeping Sokol through the hallowed halls of Berkshire College, I could not help but wonder if this was where it all led.

Julian and I got Sokol at last into Morrissey's tiny office, where he knocked into piles of dusty books and student papers before finally collapsing into an armchair.

"Thank you, Pinkerton," Sokol sighed, shutting his eyes like an enormous baby getting ready for a nap.

"Thank you both," Morrissey said with a soft expression that pleaded for us to keep this among ourselves. Julian and I nodded then left, shutting the door behind us.

We made it about ten yards before Julian turned to me and said, "Flip you for it."

"Flip you for what?"

"The story. Flip you for the story. *One* of us has to write it. Nobody else in that class is going to, I can tell you that."

I thought he was kidding, but his hand was rooting through his pockets looking for a coin.

"Heads," I called.

Julian found a quarter and flipped it off his thumb. He snatched it expertly out of the air and checked it against the back of his hand. Tails.

"Cheers!" he shouted. "Now promise you won't write about it."

"I promise," I said.

At the time I didn't even know that I was lying.

Following this incident, Julian and I stopped for a coffee, and I soon discovered, to my delight, that Julian was not the monastic daydreamer he seemed to be in class. He explained that he simply preferred to write late at night, and on good nights he would get so lost in his writing that he'd suddenly find the sun rising and realize his classes were imminent. After a nap, or some high-test espresso, Julian became a boundless mass of chatty energy.

"That Shelly girl weirds me *out*," he told me as we walked out of class one afternoon. Another girl had written a story about watching her mother give birth, called "The Miracle of Life." Admittedly it had been atrocious, but Shelly had run out of the room, shaking.

"You ought to keep her away from open windows," Julian advised.

"And babies. Apparently."

Julian sighed. "The crazy ones are always better in bed, though."

I reddened at this. "You have no idea," I lied. Truth be told, we had not managed to get much of anything done in bed, I was so concerned about crushing her.

Fortunately, Julian appeared to be having a brainstorm. "*You* need to meet my friend Ev, from Choate."

"No offense, but 'Ev, from Choate' is a girl, I hope?"

Julian waved his hand dismissively in the air. "Evelyn Lynn Madison Demont. Our families have known each other forever. She's our age and she's already practically been nominated for a Tony. She was just in that revival of *My Fair Lady* with Richard Chamberlain. I'm not even shitting you. The character in your 'Gravity in Durham' story reminded me of her. The 'arctic-souled' Homecoming Queen, as you put it."

He explained that Evelyn was *strictly* a stage actress—film and television being nothing other than opiates for philistinic masses. Then he fumbled with his wallet until he pulled out a crinkled newspaper review for a musical called *Samson!,* and at the top was a picture of her on stage as Delilah, in sheer crimson silk. Even on smudgy newsprint, she was stunning. Slender and high cheeked, with hair tied up in a perfect knot. I could not look away. Her eyes seemed to bore right into me, and somehow she looked bored herself, by what she found there. Her lips parted, a delicate smile for the camera, but I could see it there beneath—an un-smile that matched the look in her eyes.

"Is she in something now? A show, I mean?" I'd never been to New York City before, and I desperately wanted to change that.

"She just finished *something*," Julian said distractedly. "She comes up here sometimes to do things at summer stock."

"Where does she go to school?"

"She doesn't!" Julian laughed, as if it were the most brilliant idea ever. "Although between you and me, she turned down full rides at Ivy League schools."

"Her parents must have been furious," I said.

Julian laughed again. "Don't be silly. What does she need to go to Harvard for? She's already smarter than you or I will ever be, for all the good it'll do her. I can't even imagine her there, with all those neo-con banker babies and sons of sports franchise managers." He shuddered. "On Broadway she's being taken out by ambassadors and actual *Swiss* people, for God's sake. Makes me wonder what the hell I did wrong to wind up *here*. Speaking of . . . what are you writing for the contest?"

A half hour earlier I'd been considering a change of majors. Now suddenly I wanted nothing more than to win the contest and read my story in front of the deans and all the alumni. More than anything, though, I wanted to read it in front of Julian.

I shrugged and asked, "What are *you* going to write? The Jan Sokol story? You could call it 'The Guest Lecturer.'"

He grinned and shook his head. "That's classified, I'm afraid."

Promising to show me better pictures of the lovely Evelyn, Julian invited me back to his room. He had a double all to himself, after his roommate had withdrawn in the third week, and it was truly the Shangri-La of dormitories. He'd lofted the two beds, wedged the mattresses on the top, and pushed both desks together to create a massive work space, which was covered in library books and unorganized papers. On the wall, in a frame, was a red-and-black chessboard.

"You play chess?" I asked, hardly surprised.

"Yes, but I much prefer checkers," he said. "We could play, if I had any damn pieces. I keep meaning to buy some, but the pieces always come with a board, and I've already got a board. It's the oldest game in the world. Did you know that? There are hieroglyphics in Egypt with the scores of checkers games, and in one of the tombs they found a whole set! They think it came over from India. Anyways, I keep the board around because I figure someday I'll find some pieces. You can't hang a checkerboard on the wall in act one if no one's going to play it in act two. Chekhov. Or something like that. Can I get you anything?"

He set some coffee on a Bunsen burner and found some bagels in the back of a minifridge. "Six years at boarding schools and you learn how to maximize your space." He sprinkled the bagels with a strange spice. "Za'atar. I put it on everything."

Though I'd never heard of it in my life, I nodded and smiled. "Ah . . . za'atar," I replied. "My grandmother used to put this on her shredded wheat."

Julian seemed delighted at the idea, and I was thrilled to have gotten one over on him. He continued eagerly, "Maimonides said it cures parasites and flatulence. With that sort of range, I figure it must be good for everything else in between."

This seemed to be Julian's philosophy on life: that no one could ever hope to get the breadth of the whole thing, so he would stick to the extremes and assume the middle was thus covered. He knew everything there was to know about Schopenhauer and Napoléon Bonaparte. He read every gossip rag with a headline about the marriage of Lisa Marie Presley and Michael Jackson. But he didn't seem to know normal things, like the difference between Newt Gingrich and Roger Ebert. Each night after we'd hung out for one hour, I'd spend three more at the library, reading up on everything he'd mentioned, even in passing. And in each word and place I sensed an unfolding universe of stories, just waiting for me to make them real.

Shelly hated him, naturally. As often as he invited her to join us over in Shangri-La, she refused to accept. If I even brought him up in her presence, she rolled her eyes until I stopped.

"He's totally in love with you," she snapped.

"That's absurd," I said, trying hard not to flush at the suggestion— and it was absurd. About Julian's preferences in the bedroom I didn't dare speculate, but I felt certain that his interests in me were as a kindred spirit who shared his deepest obsession. Back home, there'd been no one. Girls could dabble in poetry and keep diaries. But guys were expected to be memorizing sports statistics, not the opening sentence of *A Tale of Two Cities*. Even my English teachers seemed to hold books several feet from their bodies, as if some contagion might be multiplying within the pages. Julian held books right up close to his face—a habit formed, he explained, in his nearsighted youth—and now, even with contact lenses in, he liked to have the page within a few inches of his eyes. So close that the pages scraped the tip of his nose as he turned them. So close that, when he inhaled sharply at a particularly good turn of phrase, the paper seemed to lift up slightly and tremble before settling back again.

In class, once Julian knew he had an ally, he talked more often, and together we eviscerated the bland tales of moonlit marriage proposals and drunken deflowerings that our classmates brought in. Morrissey began to call on Julian and me as one person, and often he'd jokingly call us by the names of famous writing duos.

"Hawthorne? Longfellow? What do you think about all this?" or sometimes, "Emerson? Thoreau? Which of you wants to start?" Once we even scored a "Fitz? Hem?" but most of the time we were "Pinkerton and McGann"—which always got a chuckle as the class thought back on the day of the guest lecturer. I still wondered often what had become of the weeping writer.

As the weeks went on, Julian and I worked furiously on our contest entries. Julian would invite me over in the afternoons to work, and for hours we would sit there, me scribbling on a yellow legal pad and him hammering on the typewriter, with the humming aerator of his fish tank behind us.

We had only two rules: one, we would never write anything about each other—that was *off-limits*—and two, we would not peek at the other's work until it was finished. The first condition I succeeded in following only because I felt certain that if Julian could be captured in words, I was not yet good enough to do it. But the second condition I violated every chance I got.

When he got up to go have a cigarette outside, Julian would take his pages with him. But one day I found some old drafts, buried in a drawer, under a collection of playbills from shows that Ev had been in. Julian's story was called "Polonia," and the little I got to read involved a Polish family who, due to absurd circumstances involving a sick cow, are forced to move to Wales and take up shoe making. That night I lay awake for hours, just imagining how good the rest of it had to be. Where did he come up with these ideas? As hard as I tried to make up something amazing, I found myself returning to the dry inkpots of estranged redneck families and tedious suburban sprawl. As I lay in bed I repeated to myself, *"Tell all the truth. Slant slant slant slant slant."*

It seemed clear that I'd never get anywhere with something as cliché as a story about a kid whose mother misses his birthday party. I scrapped "The Flight Attendant's Son," knowing that if I was going to beat Julian's imagination, I was going to have to dig deeper, be edgier, and expose even more of myself. *"Truth truth truth,"* I muttered to myself as the keyboard clicked and clacked. By sundown I was half done with a passable draft of "Just Another Bastard Out of Carolina."

Only three days later, when Julian ran downstairs to pick up a new supply of *za'atar* that had just arrived at the mailroom, I found his old story was missing from the drawer—replaced by something new, titled "A Friend of Bill W.," about a twelve-year-old boy in an Eastern Orthodox church choir who steals vodka from the deacon's desk each night and then begins hiding in a confessional so he can attend the AA meetings they hold at the church every Tuesday. A frantic flip to the final pages revealed that the boy is caught guzzling holy wine in the shadow of the icon of Saint Basil and soon thereafter is expelled in disgrace.

"Son of a bitch," I groaned as I hid it back away. How did he come up with this stuff? How could I possibly top a story about being excommunicated at age twelve?

I lamented this injustice to Shelly that night as we watched television in her room.

"He's too fucking *interesting*. He lived in, like, a dozen countries before he turned ten. His parents own an import/export company that spans the freaking globe. This is the farthest from North Carolina that I've ever been. I've never been to New York City. I've never even been on a *plane* before."

"I thought your mother was a flight attendant? Don't you, like, fly for free?"

"There's just a discount," I muttered. Neither of us said anything for a moment. By now she was sick of hearing about Julian and the writing contest, although I knew she was quietly working on her own submission. She left it lying out but I never once thought to steal a look.

"Just make something *up*," she sighed. "It's *fiction*, for chrissakes."

But I could not make anything up. In Raleigh I'd hardly been able to keep from drifting off into my imagination—anything to escape the doldrums of school, the tediousness of work, and the quiet of an empty house. But now, suddenly, my imagination seemed to have frozen up, like a used car in the depths of winter. As the deadline for the contest approached, I was so miserable that I began avoiding Julian entirely. It was hard not to notice that he wasn't banging down my door, either.

The night before the submissions were due, Julian called.

"Did you finish?" he asked. It was the first time we'd spoken in a week.

"Yes," I said. Both of my stories were as done as they'd ever be. All that remained was to decide which of them was worse than the other.

"Good. Because mine is a *disaster* and I was hoping you would do me a favor?"

Was he going to ask me to read it? Was this his way of rubbing it in my face? Still, I had been dying to read the finished product, if only to remind myself how it was all really done.

"This will *just* take an hour, I swear. I'm *so* close to being done."

Something in his shaky sound reminded me of Sokol, during his visit to our class. Was Julian hammered? Or just on the brink of exhaustion?

"My friend Ev is here and I *absolutely* cannot work with her around. Could you, I don't know, take her around campus or something for an hour?"

My heart stopped beating. And I don't think it beat again until fifteen minutes later, when I arrived at the door to Julian's room.

He came to the door wearing only a hotel dressing robe, a week's growth of beard on his face, and three days' rings of red under his eyes. The room was a disaster, with old coffee on the Bunsen burner and the checkerboard hanging crookedly. Julian barely acknowledged my arrival, aside from turning back to fold down the page that had been jutting halfway up from his typewriter, as if my superhuman eyes might be able to catch a word or two from the door. What I *could* read were the golden-inlaid titles of a few enormous library books, stacked beside the machine: *The Demise of the British World Order, Convicts of Kimberley*, and one bizarrely titled *Windradyne of the Wiradjuri*. Just as I noticed a large map of Australia folded open on the desk, my line of sight was cut off by a high-cheeked girl, her face framed by a cascade of golden hair, on top of which sat a small pillbox hat made of leopard skin.

"He's *un*-believable," she announced, rolling her eyes back at Julian. Her eyes were bored; they bore right through me.

"You're, *uhm*, Evelyn?" I stammered, trying to sound cool as she shut the door behind her.

"Call me Ev," she said, with the same smile as in the picture. There, but masking something. "Julian told me your name is Pinkerton? I thought you'd be British."

I got the clear sense that she was disappointed I wasn't. According to Julian, she spent all her time hobnobbing with ambassadors and Swiss people. How could I hope to impress her?

"He's just joking. It's sort of funny, actually," I said, and quickly began telling her the story of the guest lecturer.

It was snowing outside, but she wanted to smoke, so we ventured off into the cold night together. Originally I thought we might stop at the library for some coffee, but instead we just walked in circles for an hour, and then two—trading more stories. Occasionally I'd stop to point out one of the older, impressive brick-and-marble buildings, but I got the sense she'd seen plenty of far older and more impressive ones before.

Her tone of voice seemed to say: *Oh, is this what you call a fountain? Is this what you'd call a college? Is Julian what you'd call a writer?* Of the gently falling snow she said, with heavy sarcasm, "When I was eight years old it snowed once in Atlanta over Christmas, and my grandmother called it a *miracle*." She looked at everything like it was a sad, small version of something better she'd seen somewhere else. It was how she looked at me.

The *only* thing she seemed to admire was my gold wristwatch. At first I thought she was worried about the time, but soon I saw that it was, in fact, because it was clearly nicer than anything else I was wearing. And yet she remained politely attentive as I spun out story after story— the neurons in my brain firing double time, trying to think of something that might astound her. I told her all about my drab little town, and my drab little mother, and my drab little after-school job. After a while I couldn't stand to hear her pretend to be interested anymore, so finally I asked her how she and Julian had become friends.

She composed herself before speaking, as if she were auditioning for a part.

"Julian cried for three days straight after his parents dropped him off. Hand to God—three days. This is when we were thirteen. It was the middle of the semester, and rumor had it that he'd been thrown out of two schools already, all for crying and refusing to eat, and eventually his parents would come and take him away and try another school."

"Seriously? Julian?" I said, as we came to rest finally at the edge of a fountain that had been shut off for the winter.

Evelyn sat down softly on the dry edge and straightened her hat. I was close enough that I could see it was made of real leopard skin. "He'd stay in bed until someone kicked him out, sit there at breakfast just crying, not eating, and then go to class and sniffle the whole way through. The other boys were all picking on him and making it worse. The teachers didn't even try to stop them, really. They all figured that if the boys made life hard enough for Julian, he'd stop crying. But he was stubborn. That's why I decided I liked him."

She took out another cigarette without offering one to me. I watched closely as she pursed her lips to it, leaving a rippled ring of crimson behind on the paper.

"Well, the only *decent* thing to do was to adopt him myself. We girls weren't allowed to sit with the boys at lunch and dinner, but I snuck over to him afterward and I said, 'You think if you keep on crying, your parents will come back?' and he told me to . . . well . . . I shouldn't repeat it."

"Of course," I said.

"So I told him I'd be his *new* mother, if he'd only just shut up and stop crying. And he did. And we've been close ever since." Evelyn paused, as if to take her customary bow, and then added, "A few nights like tonight as no exception."

We sat a little longer while she finished her cigarette, and I wondered what else exactly guys like me were supposed to say to glamorous actresses who had gone to prep schools and wore leopard-skin hats.

"I shouldn't smoke," she sighed. "I have a table reading tomorrow."

"For a play?"

She nodded. "A production of *Hedda Gabler*. It's got a great director, but he wants to do this modern interpretation with all young people. My agent tells me I should be glad about that, because otherwise I couldn't be in it, but still. *Ugh*. And it's Ibsen. Just *once* I wish he'd have written a play where the woman isn't miserable or dead at the end."

I nodded and said, "That's the trouble with Ibsen," as if I'd known it all along. She stared at me for a moment and I felt my mind erase itself.

"But I do love Hedda," she sighed. "Do you know Hedda?" she asked, as if Hedda were a friend of hers and Julian's.

"We've never been formally introduced or anything," I replied with a grin.

She smiled slyly and smoked some more.

"She marries this writer, because she thinks he'll be successful, but then this other writer, whom she really loved all along, seduces this other woman, and she inspires him to write this *masterful* book and, well, Hedda gets jealous and destroys him, his book, and herself, eventually."

"She sounds charming," I joked, but Evelyn was not laughing. She pushed away from me, and I felt the whole world grow colder. Flakes of snow fell from the golden streams of her hair and sank, lost, into the shadows of the dry fountain.

"She's a genius! Married to an idiot. In love with another idiot who isn't half good enough for her. All her life she's done everything expected of her, and yet she's got nothing. No power, no future, no hope." She adjusted her pillbox hat a little with one hand. "People just think she's this vicious gold digger. I mean, she's vicious all right. That's why she's *so* much fun to play. But it wasn't money she married for."

"It wasn't?"

She snorted and somehow even this seemed poised. "She was the daughter of a great general, and as a girl, when they rode up the street together, everyone in the town would come out to see them pass by. That's all she actually wanted, *I* think. Just to be seen for all that she really was."

She looked defiantly at me and took a long, triumphant pull on her cigarette.

"That's the last thing *I'd* want," I muttered. It was the truth, and the only thing I could think of to say.

She coughed a little, and there was a glimmer of surprise in her eyes, though the boredom had not left them.

"At least I'll never be married for my money," I joked.

She did not laugh. "What's wrong with money?"

"Nothing's wrong with it. I just don't have any."

She was still not laughing. "*My* mother married for money. So did her mother. So did Julian's mother, for that matter. You think any woman who considers money is a gold digger? Because let me tell you. It's *always* at least a consideration."

I thought about my own mother, and the many men she'd hoped, in my lifetime, would carry us up and out of Raleigh. Two or three pilots. The man who'd owned a racetrack, Dan. Or had Dan been the guy with the beautiful boat we never saw? Had she loved either of them? Any of them? I had to admit to myself, I'd always hoped she hadn't. I liked to believe she loved only my father, the man she'd met in Newark, and that she looked down for him whenever she flew over the Garden State.

"Maybe money could be a *part* of it," I conceded. "So long as there's love, too."

"'Love,'" she said, softly, in someone else's voice. "'What an idea!' Now you say, 'You don't love him, then?' and I'll say, 'But I won't hear of any sort of unfaithfulness! Remember that.' And then *you* say . . ."

"What's happening?" I laughed.

"We're running lines," she said, finally smiling. "You're Eilert Løvberg."

"Which one is he?" I asked. "The first idiot or the other idiot?"

She tipped her head back and let loose a hard laugh, though I still could not decide if it was really genuine. Then she bent her head down against my shoulder suddenly and snuffed her cigarette out on the cement lip of the fountain. Her hat rubbed against my cheek and I was so startled that I almost missed what she said next.

"You know, Julian asked me to *spy* on you. Find out what you were writing for this contest tomorrow."

Julian was nervous about what *I* had written?

"He said he read your story, while you were in the bathroom or something. The one about the flight attendant's kid? And that it was so good he started his over. And then he saw you'd started *yours* over, and so *he* started *his* over again. I swear, I love him, but he's completely in*sane* sometimes."

"Well, you can tell him I've got nothing," I said moodily. "Tell him to get a good night's sleep because both of my stories suck and I can't write another word."

Evelyn clicked her tongue twice and suddenly lifted her head up. "Don't make me adopt you, too, now. In my line of work we call that *melodrama*," she whispered. "All you need is a little inspiration."

And then she kissed me, and I could feel the wet pulp of tobacco and the crimson of her lips coming off on mine.

"What's the matter?" she asked.

"Nothing," I said. "I'm sorry."

She smiled and kissed me again.

And I thought about what Sokol had said: that happiness was making love for as long as you could stand it to the most luminous thing you could find on this rotten corpse of a planet. And, afterward, I thought he might be right. And so she did not go back to Julian's room that night to report back on my writer's block. And so, all morning as she slept in my bed, I furiously tapped away at the keys of my computer. Just two pages at first. *Truth.* And then five. *Forget this slant business.* And then twelve. *Tell all the truth.* And then a title. "The Trouble with Ibsen." And then it was done.

Later that morning, Julian and I turned in our stories at the end of Morrissey's class without a single word to each other. He looked as though he'd gone ten rounds with a gorilla and decided to wear part of its pelt on his chin as a trophy. There were rings around the rings around his eyes. He grunted at me, as if to acknowledge that it was over, and staggered off to sleep for as long as humanly possible. He never even asked me where Evelyn had gone, which was probably for the best, because Shelly was, at that very moment, turning in her own story, which she'd titled "Just Like Starting Over."

"I printed one for you, too," she said, offering me the copy and giving my hand a squeeze—surprising both in its affection and strength. "I knew you could do it. I can't wait to read yours."

My palms began to sweat, and for the first time the hours of sleeplessness felt caked onto my face. I hadn't showered. My fingers flew to my lips, sure that some lipstick must still be smudged there. The scent of Evelyn was deep underneath my nails.

"I'll just have to go back to my room and print out another," I lied, hiding the spare copy of "The Trouble with Ibsen" that I'd printed to give to Julian.

"I was kind of hoping you'd say that," she said, making a move to follow me there.

I'd never cheated on anyone before. I felt like slime, but weirdly grown-up slime. Shelly stood there, chewing on the ends of her black hair, dark eyes expectant. Whatever damages had been done to her already—and there must have been some—I knew I did not want to add to them. Nervously, I stared down at my watch.

"Let's meet for coffee in an hour? I really need to shower," I said as means of an apology. And I kissed the straight-cut bangs that hung in her big eyes and rushed off.

As guilty as I felt, I couldn't help hoping that Evelyn would still be in my room. But she was already gone, vanished, off reading Ibsen around a table somewhere. Was she thinking about me? Why had I told her I didn't have any money? But was there something else? The bed was empty except for her lingering smell, powdery and rich like the confections we'd kept behind the counter at Ludwig's. It was all I could bear not to dive down into it and drift off to sleep. If I never resurfaced, I don't know that I'd have minded. But I showered, printed out a copy of "Just Another Bastard Out of Carolina" instead of my actual submission, and skimmed Shelly's story. It was about a single mother, trolling around a bookstore and planning to leave her screaming baby in the True Crime section before driving her car over an embankment. But right at the end, she hears a young poet giving a reading in the café. And his poem sends her wailing baby into a deep, undisturbable sleep, and the mother feels hopeful for the first time in months.

Silently I reminded myself that Evelyn was not my girlfriend. And that after her audition she'd go back to New York. And Shelly would never have to know.

A few frigid weeks passed and I wondered, each day, when we'd hear about the contest. Julian and I did not speak—I did not know if he was upset about Evelyn, or anxious about the contest, or simply out of his mind. In class he sat, entranced by the snow falling on the windows, and said nothing at all to me or anyone else.

"Pinkerton? McGann?" Professor Morrissey called to us hopefully, when no one at all reacted to his story about how Hemingway's wife lost the only copy of his first novel on a Parisian train. We each faked a smile.

Then suddenly, overnight, Abernathy Hall was covered in flyers with Julian's picture on them. Shelly and I stumbled across one on our way to class.

> **Come see writing contest winner Julian McGann read from his story "Just Before the Gold Rush." Jan Sokol will also read from his forthcoming novel, *Luminous Things*. Tonight! Osgood Auditorium!**

Neither of us was surprised to find that Julian had won, though we were a little annoyed that nobody had even bothered to let us losers know that we had lost. Down at the bottom of the flyer were the opening lines of the story, meant to entice us into attending the reading.

In 1851, on the continent of convicts known then as Australasia, before the gold mines of Kimberley were famous and the population of that island tripled with men searching for New South Wales's very own El Dorado, young Shamus McGarry, a poor Irishman indentured to the Clarke Mining Corporation, had already spent six dark years sifting infinitesimal specks of gold from the earth. But then came the day that he and his partner stumbled upon a pure nugget the size of a man's heart. Shamus and this other man instantly turned their pickaxes on one another. By luck or by fate, Shamus's ax crushed the nameless man's skull first—or else Shamus would have been the one without a name. He emptied the man's skull, hid the golden lump inside, and then tore down the surrounding rock. He convinced the foreman that the wall had collapsed. It was easy enough to dig the man up from the grave pit that night. It was easier still to hide the heart-sized nugget inside his mouth and flee West, toward freedom, and fortune.

Australasia? New South Wales? Gold nuggets hidden in the drained skull of a murdered miner? It seemed patently unfair—just *blatant* showing off. I was keenly aware of being both outraged and jealous at the same time. Why hadn't I been able to come up with anything like this? Was this *slant*? This fantastic impossible dream? Made real with just the *right* words, with just the *right* sentences. Was I even capable of it? Or was Julian, as I'd feared, simply imbued with powers I would never possess?

That night at the reading, I arrived with Shelly, who joined me in laughing at the parade of casual pretension that was settling into the auditorium around us: a white-bearded professor in an off-kilter black beret, a girl with two peacock feathers woven into her hair, a boy in a twenties-era gangster hat toying with a cigarette tucked behind one ear.

"I don't look like a writer at all," I lamented, looking at my lightly stained button-down shirt.

"You look more like a waiter," Shelly teased. I had not even told her that I had worn this same shirt for three long summers, as I served pastries and espressos at Ludwig's Café to people dressed just like the alumni who were steadily streaming into the reading. Shelly was wearing a simple, slim black dress that almost made me forget about my fear of breaking her.

"Get a load of *this* one," Shelly said, rolling her eyes at the doorway.

I turned and to my great surprise saw Evelyn enter the room. Evelyn Lynn Madison Demont. In the same leopard-skin hat, with the same high cheeks and bored eyes. The noisy chatter of the room seemed to fall away to whispers. My heart pounded thousand-degree blood out through every capillary I possessed. I had begun to forget her, the smell of sunlight in her hair and the taste of sweet tobacco on her lips, but the moment she walked in I could smell and taste nothing else. I shrank down in my seat suddenly, trying not to let Shelly see how red I'd gotten. Evelyn was followed in by a sour-faced woman with long, glamorous dark hair and a stern-looking gentleman in a tuxedo who looked just like Julian, but with less hair. They both looked as though they might buy the auditorium just to burn it to the ground. Even in this crowd they seemed most assuredly a cut above the rest.

"Are those Julian's parents?" Shelly asked. The resemblance was undeniable. "And who is that? His sister or something?"

"I don't know," I lied. "I've never met her."

She frowned a little, so I clarified, "I mean, I don't think Julian has a sister."

Evelyn was schmoozing with some alumni on the other side of the room. I wrapped my elbows around the chair arms and lodged my hands deep into my pockets, fearing my legs might propel myself over to her without warning.

"What's wrong with you?" Shelly asked.

"Just trying to get comfortable," I replied with a shrug, keeping my arms where they were.

But just then, Professor Morrissey crossed directly over to us. His owlish face was as darkly lined as it had been on the day of Sokol's little speech in our class, and he looked me in the eye.

"Do you have a moment? Julian's asking if he can speak with you privately. We're having a bit of a dilemma."

Happy to get away from Shelly and from Evelyn's line of sight, I followed Morrissey down the hallway to our old classroom. Sokol was standing inside the door of the payphone booth, yelling excitedly in Czech into the receiver.

"Random House bought his novel," Morrissey explained tersely, as we skirted the exuberant man.

"I thought you'd said they turned it down?"

He expelled a long, wavering sigh. "They had. Until Haslett & Grouse said they wanted it. Then S&S got in. Finally Random wound up paying almost twice as much for it as they would have before."

Morrissey seemed crankier than I'd ever seen him, so I let it go. From the looks of Sokol staggering down the hall, the man's success hadn't stemmed his drunkenness, but he did look much less miserable.

In our old classroom, Julian was sitting at his usual place at the table, staring up at the raised windows again, now half covered with snow.

"I can't do it," he said with no trace of hysteria. He said it plain, like a fact. Like the truth.

"What? Read? What's the big deal? I think your parents are here . . . "

Julian groaned. "The dean's probably trying to weasel some sort of *donation* out of them. Christ!"

"Evelyn's here, too."

"Fantastic. You can sleep with her *again*, then," Julian snapped. Professor Morrissey made an awkward noise of surprise, then rapidly apologized and stepped outside.

"I didn't realize you'd mind," I said. Though we'd never discussed it explicitly, my understanding had been that Julian was not exactly interested in the opposite sex, much to the disappointment of the girls in our class.

He waved his hand dismissively, as if this were all well beside the point.

"I can't do it. I can't read the story," he said.

"Why?" I asked, taking a seat across from him. Julian's breath reeked of whiskey, and I wondered if it was Epiphany whiskey, or if there even was such a thing.

"Because," Julian mumbled, "it's all true. My great-great-grandfather really *did* steal a lump of gold from this mine in Australia. When I was little, my grandfather told me the story. He showed me the half of the nugget that never got sold. I've *seen* it."

So Julian hadn't simply pulled this story out of pure imagination. It wasn't slanted—not even one half of a degree. Somehow this comforted me.

He went on: "It's like our biggest, darkest family secret. Everything we have today is on account of a low-life thief and murderer."

This muttered confession caused me an unreasonable amount of joy, for which I immediately felt the blackest kind of guilt. Maybe he wasn't really better than me; maybe he just had a more sordid history to draw from.

"So why the hell did you write about it?"

He gave me a look, as if to say, *You know.*

He'd written it for the same reason that I'd written mine. Out of sheer desperation. Out of competition. Each in an effort to top the other, we'd driven ourselves to this. Julian had created an atomic bomb of a story, which, if detonated, would mushroom cloud his parents' lives and probably his own inheritance. It was the same thing I had done, I'd realized. Made a little bomb all my own.

"Read something else then. Read one of the other ones. They were all good."

Julian shook his head, starting to pull himself together. "I burned those all weeks ago. You're going to have to do it. Morrissey said he'll let you read yours."

My heart began pounding.

"I can't," I said quickly, looking at my toes.

"Why not?" Julian snapped.

Of course I wanted to read it—I wanted to badly. But not with Shelly there. Not with Evelyn there. I'd been in such a rush to finish my story that night that I hadn't bothered to change anything. There was no thin veil of fiction to save me. Even if I changed the names on the fly, there was the description of my dorm room. And of a girl in a leopard-skin hat. And the title, "The Trouble with Ibsen." I couldn't change that. If I read the story, Evelyn would know all the secret things I'd thought about that night. How I was sure that I loved her even though I barely knew her. Plus, I'd shatter Shelly's glued-together heart in front of her classmates, some alumni, and every professor in our department. It would be the worst thing I'd ever done.

"Why don't you want to read it? Christ, you didn't write about *me,* did you?"

"No!" I assured him. "I wrote about Evelyn."

Julian's drawn face suddenly cracked into a smile. "Well," he said. "Very nice."

Morrissey peeked in. "Boys? I need someone. Now."

Julian looked at me—waiting, to see if I was willing to do what he could not. Without his parents, Julian would have practically nothing. I had practically nothing already, yet I'd never done anything truly cruel before. Sleeping with Evelyn had been wrong, of course, but it had seemed like a victimless crime. It wouldn't be so victimless if I stood up there now and detailed that crime to the well-dressed and waiting crowd. And to Shelly. I studied Julian's face—annoyed but resigned. He could afford to wait for the next contest, or the next—but I knew that I might never again get this chance.

So I nodded. Julian's smile widened, and I took a few deep breaths while Morrissey retrieved a copy of my story from his office and got Sokol off the phone.

From the side doorway I looked out into the crowd as Morrissey urged the attendees to take their seats. Shelly sat there quietly chewing on her hair, wondering when I'd be back. She had no idea what was about to happen. As if that wasn't enough to make me sick, Evelyn was now sitting just three rows ahead of her, looking quite bored. As Sokol came to the podium, to wild applause, I studied the man's face carefully. The hugeness of his self-satisfaction was all but blinding. The sacrifice of eighteen years of his life had just been validated. The crowd adored him and all he'd done.

"I'm sorry to say that our contest winner, Julian McGann, has unfortunately become ill and will not be able to read his story, 'Just Before the Gold Rush,' tonight. Instead, we have another story called . . . *uhm* . . . 'The Trouble with Ibsen.'"

I looked out at the darkened audience and caught Evelyn's gaze. She looked back at me, and her eyes, for the first time since we'd met, suddenly widened. She was not bored now. Then, with one smooth movement, she slipped the hat off her head and tucked it into her purse. Then she looked up, almost eagerly. We weren't running lines anymore. Something vicious and fun was about to take place. Something unexpected was about to happen, for a change.

"Yes, sorry, that's 'The Trouble with Ibsen,' written by the runner-up in our contest! Ladies and gentlemen, if I may introduce . . . "

And as he extended his arm and looked warmly toward the door, I saw him falter. The smug, serene confidence on his face crumbled, and, for a moment, I could see the same man who had wept in front of our entire classroom. A deadening silence followed. He glanced at me and then back out at the audience, sure they could see what a fool he really was.

He did not know my name.

Clearing his throat, he spoke slowly. "The one. The only. Pinkerton!"

Taking a deep breath, I stepped through the door. There was more applause as I walked straight to the podium. My heart was pounding in terror. *Tell all the Truth?* I looked out at the waiting crowd, at Evelyn, and Shelly, at everyone. Julian watched me from the shadow in the wings. A spotlight shone down on me from somewhere way up in the blackness above. In my hand I held my little rolled-up paper bomb, the words still hidden safely inside.

I took another slow breath, carefully unfurled the paper, and pressed it firmly against the lectern. I prepared to lay waste to everything in my path.

3

The Unchangeable Spots of Leopards

Can the Ethiopian change his skin, or the leopard his spots?
Neither can you do good, who are accustomed to doing evil.

—JER. 13:23

This morning his name is Simon. He's sitting on our couch beside the picture windows, through which comes a golden view of Soho and Tribeca. Simon's lower half is wrapped in one of *my* towels, and he is sucking the milk out of a bowl of *my* Frosted Wheats and watching men's swimming on *my* television. They all have the same look each time, the Simons, give or take—the ribbed chests, the high cheekbones, the tidy haircuts. This one has kind of a busted nose—not one of Julian's finest. Better than last Thursday's Philip. Or had he also been a Simon? It's always something *like* Simon—Trevor, maybe; or Spencer; or Colin. One time we had a Geoff—with a G.

"Name's Simon," says Simon. "Have you seen this guy? *Phenomenal.*"

He gestures to ESPN with my spoon, sending a fine spray of milk off across our suede-upholstered cocktail ottoman. Technically, it is *Julian's* suede-upholstered cocktail ottoman, but without me around to sponge up the residue left behind by the many Simons, the ottoman would have gone out with last year's trash. In which case, he'd have replaced it with a George Bullock octagonal table with inlaid lotus leaves, or something equally absurd.

"What guy?" I ask. Julian likes me to be polite to his overnight guests, although he certainly never is.

"Mitchell King!" Simon shouts through a mouthful of frosted wheat. *"PHENOMENAL!"*

As he shouts, little flecks of cereal land on Julian's checkerboard, which he still keeps framed on the wall. I brush them off quickly.

New York Magazine has Mitchell King on its cover this month, all seven feet of him, crossing an Olympic-sized pool in a single stroke. Simon watches as the all-American *phenomenon* does an underwater turnaround in digitized slow motion. His body curls up like a beige fish and shoots away again.

Suddenly there's the sound of water from the bathroom; Julian is awake. Simon grins and sets the bowl down on the table, leaving a ring of milk. When he stands up to greet his onetime lover, I can only grin as I lift the bowl and wipe the milk with the edge of my sleeve.

"BONJOUR à toi! Et aussi un matin doré!" Julian strides into the room, arms extended to the sunny Sunday skyline. He wears a stolen hotel bathrobe and his curly hair is matted from sleep; soon he will carefully tousle it with a Venetian cream and claim it looks somehow different. *"Ouvrez le fenêtre dont je peux voir mon saint!"*

When he spots Simon, however, Julian's nicotine-scarred lungs deflate.

"Jazz Brunch," I remind him cheerily, as I make myself scarce. Julian will now eject Simon from the apartment with the cold proficiency of an East Berlin customs agent. Visa expired, this Simon won't be back in our country again.

Jazz Brunch has been a weekly ritual since Julian and I moved to this Great City in the East, three years ago. Fresh out of college, we were two writers ready for the world to anoint us as its newest young geniuses. Our heads were filled with Fitzgeraldian dreams of rooms in the Biltmore Hotel and of writing our Great American Novels at the cafés along

Sixth Avenue, then on to have steaks at Delmonico's with girls named Honora and Marjorie. In my defense, I'd only ever *read* about New York. Julian had actually been here before. Still, he acted as if the modern city, with her graffitied subways and omnipresent bodegas, was just some sort of temporary wrinkle in the fabric of civilization. Julian's parents were currently off in Switzerland somewhere, running McGann International Trading, but part of their diversified portfolio included various rental properties around the island, one of which Julian and I had taken up residence in just off Washington Square Park.

Even this morning, as we stroll toward the arch in two-tone shoes and biscuit tweed, Julian seems startled to find the square crawling with bearded NYU students, propelling themselves about on skateboards, and not a horse-drawn carriage or a top hat in sight, as Henry James had promised.

As she does every Sunday, Evelyn meets us on the corner. This morning she clutches a script in her left hand, which bears the familiar, cragged face of Samuel Beckett. Her right hand holds a lit cigarette and a clump of wildflowers, roots attached.

Evelyn Lynn Madison Demont. Even four Anglo-Saxon names cannot contain her. She should be a "the Third" or a "Countess di" something-or-other. My heart has been lost in the frozen tundras of hers ever since Julian first introduced us in our college days, seven years ago. Now the accidental thought of her sends sparks through me like I am one of Henry Adams's dynamos.

Everything I write is for her; none of it is ever good enough.

"If it isn't Jeeves and Wooster. You two are later every week." She grabs my wrist and checks the time on my gold watch. Then, pretending to scowl, she plants a kiss on each of our cheeks. Her blond hair smells of buttercream and her white skin of lemonade. Her lips brush against my cheek and they feel like the chitinous wings of a dragonfly.

"We were unavoidably detained," Julian says.

"By a Simon," I add, with a roll of my eyes. Julian is too busy stealing her cigarette to hear me. He inhales desperately, though he has only just finished one on our way over. Somewhere back inside the park comes the loud clatter of a skateboarder who has just screwed up a trick. Julian mumbles some vague threats about moving to Prague. In truth, he's been threatening to leave the city for all sorts of reasons, ever since we arrived. But we know he won't. Not without us.

He jabs the lit end toward the flowers. "Where are those from?"

"I mugged this little orphan boy for them," she says, inserting two bluebells in my lapel and a prairie aster in Julian's. She tucks a midsize daisy into her hair and drops the remainder on the sidewalk without a second's thought.

"Shall we?" she asks, tucking the Beckett away into some heretofore-unseen purse. She extends an unblemished forearm and I hook my elbow around it.

"'I can't go on,'" I say, with the dramatic air of quoting things. "'I'll go on.'"

Jazz Brunch at the Washington, once held weekly in a lush ballroom to hundreds of Manhattan's elite, has in recent decades been moved into a small cove on the basement level and done up like a high-class speak-easy. Maybe in Fitzgerald's time, jazz music was a call to revolution—chaotic, arousing, and ever changeable. It disturbed the natural order; it tore up the old millennium, with its absurd wars and its drudgerous Puritanism; it declared reckless independence once and for all. But in our era of anthemic dance beats, power chords, and casually rhymed profanities, jazz music has become quaint and old-fashioned, appreciated only by those who were born too late—namely, the three of us.

A heavyset black woman croons Etta into a microphone; a guitar player with a beer gut sweats and strums; a little Latino gentleman squeaks along on the trumpet. The tiny crowd, aside from us, all appear to be over fifty; their accents are thick with Long Island and New Jersey. Once upon a time I'd have been counted as one of their numbers, but now they look admiringly at me in the close company of Julian and Evelyn.

"Four, please," Evelyn instructs the hostess, who is also the only waitress for the room—a brunette ball of curls with a small, golden stud in her left nostril.

"Can't you count?" Julian says. "We're three. Every week, we're three."

"I've asked someone to come and meet us."

As the waitress leads us to our table, Julian, ever change-averse, begins to complain. "Haven't we spoken about inviting strangers to brunch? Haven't we agreed that foreigners must be approved by a majority, not more than two days prior to brunch, so as to allow for proper background checks?"

By "background checks," he means asking me to perform a Yahoo! search; Julian still types everything on his Remington, not even an electric.

Evelyn presses a slim, sturdy finger into my breastbone. "Well, every time I invite someone, you make *him* vote against it."

She slides onto the deep purple, crushed-velvet banquette. High above her is a small opening on the sidewalk level, where light comes down over us, in between the steady passing of disembodied shoes.

I defend myself. "You don't have to live with him when he doesn't get his way. And I said that your friend Charity could come. And Rosalyn. And Gwyneth." I sit across from her, and Julian next to me, as usual.

"Yes and, funny how, afterward you wind up taking them to the *zoo* or something and then I never hear from them again," she says with an indecipherable smile.

"I feed them to the leopards," I say, flashing an arched eyebrow.

She sighs and studies the menu, though we all know it by heart. There is very little about Jazz Brunch that we don't know by heart. By heart, she knows that I will try to make her jealous by going off with her friends. By heart, I know that she brings only the ones she's bored of, half hoping that I'll fall for one of them, do myself some good, and put her behind me. By heart, she knows that she'll call me within an hour of departing brunch and sulk for days if I don't pick up. Charity, Rosalyn, and Gwyneth each hardly made it to the monkey house before figuring out that my heart was still nestled far away, by her heart. Gwyneth had left me by the exotic birds. Rosalyn hadn't minded. She'd told me she thought we were "like *so* completely tragic for each other." Or had that been Charity, actually? It's always something like Charity.

"Coffee. Immediately," Julian instructs our waitress urgently. Frightened, she does a sort of unconscious curtsy and is back with coffee in moments. Julian has his idiosyncrasies, to be sure, but he knows how to get good service.

The singer wraps up "Tell Mama" and we all pause to give brief applause. I feel Evelyn's foot touching mine beneath the table, and I try to catch her eye, but it is always off somewhere else, by the door.

"Thank you, thank you. My name is Jo, just Jo, and I'm here with the talented—"

But as she moves to introduce her two band members, one of the older women in the room lets loose a guttural noise and a commotion brews. We turn to see what is going on and spot the swimmer Mitchell King, all *phenomenal* seven feet of him, descending the steps into the room. He passes several blushing senior citizens, then greets Evelyn with an eager kiss. He sits down across from an utterly bewildered Julian, rendered silent for perhaps the first time since we'd moved to New York.

"Mitchell King," says Mitchell King. "Mighty pleased to meet you both."

His buttery Southern voice sounds just as it does on ESPN. He extends a hand, larger than a dinner plate, and I have no choice but to shake it. I think I can feel my metacarpals shattering. Julian jumps to summon our waitress again, mostly to avoid shaking hands with this Goliath. "And a *pitcher* of mimosas, as soon as humanly possible."

The room begins to settle, like the surface of a lake after a boulder has unexpectedly fallen into it. The jazz singer, Just Jo, takes her boys into "Something's Got a Hold on Me," and we are left to face the gigantic swimmer.

Fortunately, Julian is highly trained in the art of dismissive small talk. "So nice of you to join us, Mitchell. We were watching you on television just a half hour ago! How *did* you get here from the pool so quickly?"

"Actually, that was taped last night," Mitchell explains rather earnestly. "At the World Aquatics Championships in Japan! I just flew back into town this morning. With all those time zones, I get confused myself sometimes! We crossed the International Date Line. Yesterday, for me, it was already today. How insane is *that*?"

Julian stares, open mouthed, just a moment longer than he should.

"How did you and Evelyn meet?" I ask, figuring that I may as well take my turn.

"I went to see her play. My agent likes to take me out when I'm in town."

"An *agent*," Julian mumbles venomously, but only I can hear him.

"Mitchell went out during intermission and bought me a bouquet of daisies, and then met me by the stage door with them," Evelyn says, running her hands up and down his hairless forearm, so slowly that each of my own arm hairs feels a pang of jealousy. Evelyn was playing Irina in the hit Off Broadway revival of *Three Sisters*. I had attended fifteen of the performances, each time leaving a crimson florilegium of roses in her dressing room afterward.

Evelyn always says that when she thinks about me sitting there in the front row she becomes afraid of losing her character. She says it would simply be the end of her. So I never tell her which shows I am coming to, and I sit back beneath the dark underhang of the mezzanine with a set of Julian's opera glasses and my heirloom roses, and I watch, and I wait.

She'd been impressed by *daisies*? Seriously?

I fidget with the bluebells she lodged in my lapel. The daisy in her own hair still hangs there, perfectly. Even the laws of gravity must obey Evelyn.

Evelyn has, no doubt, given Mitchell the impression that Julian and I must be impressed, if their relations are to go any further—which is probably why he goes on ad nauseam about his book. It is to be about how athletics showcase the triumph of the human spirit, and the meaning of human perseverance, and sportsmanship and teamwork, and just as Julian and I are getting ready to hang ourselves by our skinny neckties, the waitress finally scurries back with a bucket of Champagne on ice and a pitcher of blood orange juice.

Julian is set to launch into his complex brunch order—which always involves wheat toast without crusts and the salmon eggs Benedict but without the Benedict—only Mitchell holds out a gargantuan hand before Julian can begin.

"Ladies first," he says, gesturing to Evelyn.

Julian looks as if he might chew Mitchell's chiseled face off. This is not the usual order of things. There is a pause. He downs his mimosa in a single gulp and sulks.

Evelyn orders "the Caesar salad with smoked trout. Fish *cold*, please," and then Julian jumps right back in with his elaborate demands. Feeling shaky, I opt for the steak and eggs, "but bloody," thinking I might up my iron intake. Mitchell orders a granola and yogurt to start, and then pecan pancakes, with a ham omelet, making sure this comes with greens and home fries, and then sides of chicken-apple sausage and cheddar biscuits.

"Got this Parkinson's charity meet tomorrow. Carbs and protein. Carbs and protein. 'The Mitchell King Diet.' That's going to be my next book." He winks, like he's letting us in on some sort of insider-trading deal.

Sensing that Julian is gearing up for some epic rant, Evelyn quickly turns to me. "So, Mitchell is from the Raleigh area."

"Go Green Jackets," I say weakly. As much as it pains me to engage Evelyn's new boyfriend in conversation, it is nothing compared with the pain I'd feel chatting about my blue-collar childhood in front of Julian, who smirks continually.

"No!" Mitchell cries. "Go *Crusaders*! Don't tell me you were a Cracker?"

Just Jo is belting out a nice rendition of "Little Boy Blue," which allows me to mumble surreptitiously to Julian while Mitchell regales Evelyn with Southern high school football lore.

"He's about as cultured as a mole creature. He'll probably be on about NASCAR next. Evelyn's smarter than this. It just doesn't make any sense."

Julian sighs knowingly. *"Avez vous vu la grandeur de ses mains . . .* have you *seen* the size of his hands?" He and Evelyn have always had disturbingly similar taste in men.

We clap politely and drink. Mitchell's granola and yogurt arrive, the mixing of which occupies him long enough for Evelyn to pay attention to us again.

"You two are the worst kinds of snobs," she whispers, under cover of the trumpet singing a double-high C. "Don't think that I can't read your awful little lips. Even in French."

At the same time I can tell that she is not surprised. Not even really upset. She knew that it would remind us that she has a full life outside our little vicious circle. At the same time she also knew that if she brought this Aquaman to Jazz Brunch, we'd put him through the ringer.

"Evelyn tells me you guys are writers," says Mitchell cheerfully. "What all do you write?"

Julian jumps on the chance to tinker with Mitchell's head. "I'm working on a novel right now. It's essentially an homage to the deconstructed romans à clef of the late 1700s. Intertextually, I think it will be a smashing success, so long as the readers can be trusted to accept the basic premise that the entire thing takes place in a remote outpost in the Andromeda Galaxy, thirty thousand years ago."

Mitchell cannot think of a single thing to say to this. Of course, Julian is not writing about the Andromeda Galaxy—although he won't say what his novel is actually about, not even to me.

"Julian has had a story in the *Paris Review*," Evelyn explains to Mitchell patiently.

"I have to say . . . I don't really like Paris! I spent a week there once for an invitational," he says, as if anyone cared. "Sure, it's nicer than New York, no offense, but it's no Savannah." He looks at me as though he expects me to agree, which I most certainly will not.

Before Julian can inform him that since 1973 the *Paris Review* has been published right here in—yes, offense—New York City, I intercede.

"Mitch, how come we didn't see you in Sydney last summer?"

Mitchell's mouth stops chewing, and I half wonder if one of his ham-sized hands is about to grab me around the neck. But he forces a thin smile.

If he hadn't seen it before, he does now. He's at brunch with a pair of wild animals. And we are out for blood.

I know the story already. Everybody does. Two weeks before the Olympics, Mitchell King was caught in a hotel room with half an ounce of blow. By the time the charges had been dropped, he'd been left behind in the Northern Hemisphere.

"I've made a couple of mistakes," he says tersely. "Spent some time getting to know myself a little better. Consulted with my priest—"

"Now tell us a little bit about that," Julian urges. "What do they tell you to do? Kneel down and say Hail Marys? Self-flagellation with rosary beads? Details, please. I'm doing research for my book."

"What would *Catholics* be doing in the Andromeda Galaxy, twenty-eight thousand years before the birth of Christ?" I wonder loudly, but Julian kicks me under the table with a bruising saddle shoe.

"Wormhole," he says snappily. I don't know if he is referring to his book or to me. We are drinking the Champagne straight up now.

The rest of Mitchell's food arrives, our waitress wilting under the weight of it.

After the food has been laid out, she says, "You're Mitchell King," dabbing sweat from the nape of her neck. Her tiny golden nose stud catches the light.

"Please," Julian sighs. "We're just trying to enjoy our meal."

"No," Mitchell says firmly, giving Julian a stern look. "I'm happy to meet a fan."

Evelyn is looking on with cool detachment as the brunette twirls a finger in a curl by her left ear while Mitchell signs her order pad. "Amy?" he asks. "With an *A*?"

As I ponder any other ways one might spell the name Amy, I take a bite of my bloody steak and eye Amy's twirling finger. "Quite fetching," I mumble to Julian, loud enough for Evelyn to hear. Little flickers of lightning flash behind the grays of her eyes.

"So what's with the Beckett?" I ask lightly. My positive charge catches her burgeoning negative one, and there is a spark of electricity that recalls many mistakes of nighttimes past, which we never speak of during the day.

"I have an audition tomorrow for a new adaptation of *The Unnameable.*"

Just Jo erupts into a sweet and sultry "I Found a Love," and for a moment, Mitchell and Julian temporarily exiled from my periphery, I feel as if Evelyn and I were sitting alone. She gushes something about "the Theatre of the Absurd" and I'm arguing against "this idea of the *destitution* of modern man, as if we were ever *better* than this," even as she's trying to agree with me because it is "absolutely just so *brave*, ultimately, and all the while just deva*stat*ingly tragic and—" And then there's this prolonged instant in which I *know* that she is mine—that her mind loves my mind—and all my masks and all her costumes are off, and the great green curtains are drawn back, and it's the *real* Evelyn and me, just as plain as the noon sun coming in above us.

"So," Mitchell interrupts, staring at me as if he cannot even remember my name. "Did you and Julian ever write anything together?"

I laugh but not half as loud as Julian does. "Oh, yes," he says drolly, spinning the little purple prairie aster around in his buttonhole like a clown. "We've got a four-picture deal with Paramount. I do all the action sequences and he handles the jokes."

Mitchell lights up. "A movie? Bad *ass*! I'm a bit of a film buff myself. Have you guys seen the new *Jurassic Park* film? This third one was absolutely the best."

"Honey," Evelyn condescends, "they're joking."

Mitchell is beginning to look upset and I feel a twinge of benevolence.

"Julian's very private," I explain. "We don't really work well together."

Julian's creative process involves drinking three bottles of wine over the course of an afternoon, stalking about the apartment in his old robe from the Baur au Lac hotel in Zurich, and smoking while leaning precariously out of our windows, until inspiration, or the urge to nap, strikes. I do all my own writing at the New York Public Library.

"What do *you* actually write, then?" Mitchell asks me, pointedly waving a speared chicken-apple sausage in my direction.

"Short fiction now," I explain, "though I *was* working on this novel last year about an apprentice to a gilder in New York in the 1860s who steals—"

"Wait. *Was?* What happened?" Mitchell asks. Julian flashes an angry look at Evelyn, who tries to pat her beau on the hand to indicate it's time to shut up, but he goes right on ahead. "Don't tell me you gave up! Let me tell you something. *Winners never quit.* That's the *first* piece of advice I talk about in my book."

"It's not that I gave up exactly," I say coolly. "I lost it."

"You *lost* it?"

"Yes."

"What, like under a couch cushion or something?" Mitchell laughs, miming a look underneath his own gargantuan seat. Evelyn kicks him now and looks apologetically at me, but I ignore her. Mitchell—no idea what he's done wrong—struggles to think of something else to ask.

"So I'm working primarily on short fiction again," I say flatly. "Trying to get back to basics."

Mitchell smiles as if he understands. "Cool. So are you in the, *uhm,* 'Paris magazine,' then, too?" he interrupts.

Julian laughs—a hard, cold laugh—and it is just enough to admit something I hadn't intended to.

"Actually, I have something coming out next month. In the *Vicksburg Review.*"

Julian stops chewing. Evelyn—God, my heart might stop—is beaming.

"*Vicksburg?*" Julian asks, as if unfamiliar with the concept.

"They're *preeminent!* You should have told us earlier!" Evelyn says, her hand reaching across the table now, daintily crushing mine. "What's it about?"

Julian's face has darkened, approaching blackened. "Yes, which is it? That little thing from college about subbing in for the Homecoming King or whatever? Or is it that Ibsen story you wrote about—"

Evelyn gives him a look that could cut diamonds, and even Julian knows to change tacks.

"—that you did at my reading?"

He leans on *my* in a way that makes me itch, but there isn't time to dwell on it. I think about lying, maybe saying it's something older, but there's no way they won't read it, once it's out. It's not like Julian to forget these things.

"It's based, you know, quite loosely, with all the names changed and everything, on this road trip that Julian and I took to the lake, upstate, last winter. You remember? When you got really sick?"

Julian drops his fork on the plate. He actually drops it. The noise reverberates as the guitar player comes off the end of a long solo.

"You can't," he says slowly. "You ab-so-lute-ly can NOT!"

He yells this final word so loudly that Just Jo skips a beat in "All I Could Do Was Cry," and some of the old Long Island ladies turn and stare at him with Death's own eyes.

Mitchell, all alpha male, slides a meaty paw in between us. "Whoa, fellas," he says, but Julian slaps his hand away. Well, not so much *away*, but he does slap it.

"Mitchell!" Evelyn snaps. "Don't get in the middle of this. It has nothing to do with you." He shrinks back—losing two feet in height to the tone of her voice.

"Didn't we *agree?* Didn't we *agree* that we, ourselves . . . that is . . . that, that *one another* . . . well, that it's off-limits? That it is *absolutely* OFF-FUCKING-LIMITS?"

He's so upset that he's grabbing for his pack of cigarettes, and when he realizes that he's still inside he gets even more furious and downs another flute of Champagne. I say nothing. Not that he has never kept a single promise to me in his entire life. Not that I keep *trying* not to write about him. Not that I always wind up doing it, anyway.

Finally I say, weakly, "I changed your *name* and all that. I gave it a kind of Russian theme. After seeing Ev in *Three Sisters* fifteen times, I think it got under my—"

"You're moving out," he declares smugly, as he sets the empty flute down. "And that's that. I want *nothing* to do with you. No more." He looks down at his plate and flicks a great blob of his eggs at me. The golden yolk runs down my shirt and leaves a forbidding stain.

"You're nothing but a petty thief!" he shouts. "LIAR! THIEF!"

The old ladies are getting very upset now. "Young man, would you—"

"Oh, go back to hell!" he cries. "Or Staten Island. Wherever it is you're from!"

Just Jo has stopped, midsong. Amy, the waitress, is coming over, sliding between tables faster than Mitchell could leap off the starting block. "Please!" she squeaks. "Please! Keep your voices down!"

But Julian is past the point of no return. He overturns his plate. He launches himself out of the chair, shouts that he "will see the *manager* about this!" and propels himself past the other patrons and out of the room.

"Dude . . ." Mitchell says, scooting back from the table. A camera flashes, somewhere. "This is . . . I'm sorry. Those ladies are taking photos. I can't . . . I mean, my agent says I can't afford to be in *Us Weekly* again."

"Go, go," Evelyn says, waving her hand in the air dismissively. He promises to call, and she gives him a look that says he'd be a fool to bother. He seems confused, as if he's still not entirely sure where he's gone wrong, and then, because there's still a camera flashing, he strides off, hands hiding his face as though he were some sort of criminal.

"Terribly sorry, everyone," I say to the room. "Just a small misunderstanding."

"You know you've really done it this time," Evelyn says softly, as Just Jo begins her song over again.

"He'll get over it," I say.

Evelyn looks skeptical. True, I've never gotten a story about him *published* before, but I have been down this road with Julian many times. The truth is that without me he has no one—just Evelyn, who gets tired of him without me around, and a long string of wine bottles and a longer string of Simons, each emptier than the last. Without me around he'll lose what little sanity he has left.

I go on. "He'll break into my room now. Read it. Spend half an hour figuring out how to delete the file. But that's fine, the *Vicksburg* people already have it."

"How many times have I told you to make backups? Don't you ever learn?"

This I ignore, because what is there to say? No, I don't. None of us ever learns.

"He'll drink half our Grey Goose and pass out on the bathroom floor. I'll bring home some Campari tonight and we'll do our whole Hemingway-and-Fitzgerald routine. Secretly, he's flattered already. He *might* even tell me he liked the story."

"You'd better hope you're right. Where else would you go?"

I shrug. "Will we be seeing Mitchell King again?"

"No, I don't think we will."

It is always this way with her: she brings them here to us once they begin to bore her, and we devour them. It is all routine.

Now that it's actually just us—just Evelyn and I—strangely, I feel that there is nothing left to say. Or, really, that we've said all there is to say, too many times before. What is the point of running through these lines one more time?

She says, "You should start seeing somebody else."

And I say, "Is this about money?"

She: "Don't be absurd."

And I: "You're the one who's being absurd."

"We can't keep going on like this."

"Then go."

We do not move.

She says, "You know you only think you want me."

And I say, "You know you only think you don't."

She sighs. "You're such a liar."

"Quit acting." I grin.

Long silence. Thinking that maybe we can get philosophical about Beckett again, I ask, "What time is your audition tomorrow? I'm sure it will go well. Why don't I come along and then take you out after to celebrate?"

She sits back. "No. I have to stay focused."

And that is that. Alone together, we are worse than worthless.

Amy comes by with our bill, still terrified I think, that Julian is going to sic the managers on her, though she's done nothing wrong. The little faux-leather booklet lies between Evelyn and me for a long, cold moment. Ordinarily Julian pays. I reach for my wallet, which we both know is empty. She reaches for her purse.

"My treat," she says. "To celebrate. For the story." She drops two hundreds on the table as if it were nothing. For her, it is.

It is, in fact, more than I'll be paid for the story.

"I'll get it next time," I lie. I'll never get it. We both know it.

"See you next Sunday," she says and kisses me gently on the forehead. Then she taps my bluebells with her finger and I'm left to listen to the end of "At Last," alone.

I can't go on, I think to myself, scraping Julian's eggs off my shirt. *I'll go on.*

Curly-haired Amy comes back with the change. I siphon off an over-apologetic tip and slide it back to her. Her nose stud glints as her round face breaks into a smile. "Thanks so much."

She thinks the money is mine and I don't correct her. In fact, I tuck the ample remainder into my pocket and pour myself the last of the Champagne. As I do, I notice Evelyn hovering by the mirror at the exit, fixing her makeup. Or pretending to.

"So," Amy says, beginning to clean up the eggs *sans* Benedict that Julian has splattered, "how do you know Mitchell *King*?"

"Who, Mitch?" I say, fumbling a Savannah accent—I can only fake it now. "Oh, why . . . we went to school together down in North Carolina. Benedictine Academy. *Go Cadets.*"

Amy giggles and eyes the bluebells. "I like your little flowers."

"Why, thank you kindly, miss. My name's Simon," I lie, extending a hand to hers. She grips it, ladylike, and I glance at the mirror before I ask her, "Would you like to come with me to the zoo this afternoon? Have you ever seen the leopards?"

Note: The following is reprinted with permission from the *Vicksburg Review*.

—C.E.E-B.

4

Anton and I

"What truth? You see where truth is, and where
untruth is, but I seem to have lost my sight and see nothing."

—ANTON CHEKHOV, *THE CHERRY ORCHARD*

Winter winds howled through Union Square and snow piled up in the night; there were no pathways, only the backs of benches and the tops of trash cans. Street-lights bent up like periscopes from beneath the tundra. The tree branches were limned with white, as were the fire escapes and all the little terra-cotta pots out on them. Each pot sheltered a lump of dead earth and the dry husk of plant life within it. From the window of Anton's apartment, I sipped some of his golden Żubrówka vodka and watched three figures crossing the park from different angles, heads bent and trudging slowly, carving lines that would not intersect.

Rose lay on an Oriental-blue divan by the fireplace, her hair still pinned up from her rehearsal of *The Cherry Orchard* earlier that day. The only finished copy of my manuscript lay beside her in a heavy yellow hatbox, which I'd borrowed from Anton as a means of transporting my pages to and from the public library each day. Every few moments, Rose pinched the corner of a new page with two fingers, as if it were a beloved photograph, and lifted it from the box. As she read she rubbed her thumb softly against her latest engagement ring. This one was either from His Royal Highness, Umberto, Prince of Greece and Denmark, or from Phillipos the Fifth, of the former Royal Italian House of Savoy. It got so hard to keep track, and I found it easiest to live with myself when I did not know who her suitors were.

Through the thin paper, an orange glow outlined the shadow of her fingers as they scanned beneath my lines. Her deep brown eyes flitted from side to side; her lips occasionally cracked into a smile that sent my heart thumping, or they crept down into a puzzled frown that twisted my guts until I forced myself to gaze out the window again, hoping she would hurry and deliver me from my misery.

Then the peaceful crackle of the electric fireplace was interrupted by deathly hacking from the neighboring bedroom. Anton hadn't been well in weeks. He'd wake up at odd hours and bang around the apartment while Rose and I were entangled in my room across the hall. In the morning we'd find burned-down candles, handkerchiefs stained with phlegm and typewriter ink, and discarded containers of wonton soup like artifacts for us to puzzle over.

As Rose got to the last page, I looked out into the snowy darkness again. I could still see the immortal statue of General George Washington on his horse. Before its erection, the square had been a potter's field and, according to the research I'd done for my novel, only the penniless had been buried there, and they'd hung criminals from the elms. Beneath all that snow and concrete and dead grass and damp earth lay the bodies of some twenty thousand nameless men and women—forgotten before they'd even died.

"Finished," Rose said, laying the last page on the divan beside her and stretching out like a lioness, satisfied with the day's kill.

"And?" I asked, reaching for the bottle of Żubrówka to refill my glass. Each bottle was adorned with a little brown bison and contained a single yellow blade of bison grass from the primeval Białowieża Forest. Technically illegal in the States, the spirit was Anton's favorite reminder of his homeland.

"And you're brilliant," she purred. "It's absolutely masterful."

I came over next to her and set my glass down. "You're not just saying that?"

"Would I lie?" she teased. Behind her dark eyes, folded up inside Rose's imagination, my characters were still alive, just as I'd described them. She scraped her ring gently against the back of my arm; liquor pulsed in my veins. Her head slowly moved into the orbit of my own. I kept my eyes open so I could see the gentle shake that comes when she's fighting herself and losing. And then an inhuman rasping sound burst forth from Anton's room, shattering the moment and all subsequent moments.

The sound grew louder, and soon the door pushed open and Anton half collapsed into the room, his bathrobe opened and his eyes red as beets.

"I'm dying," he announced.

"Anton, dear, you have the flu," Rose said for the hundredth time that week. She got up to look after him. She'd been mothering him since long before I knew either of them, since they were thirteen and both sent to live a continent away from their families at St. Alban's Preparatory School. Quickly I shuffled the remaining pages together and slipped them back into the hatbox before Anton could see them. "Do you want us to order you more wonton soup?"

"Damn the soup!" Anton bellowed, tossing a checkerboard sans pieces over the divan and against the window. "Damn all the soup!"

"He's delirious," Rose said, chasing after him to try to tie his robe together.

"Melodramatic, you mean," I said, and we both knew it was more likely that he was drunk.

Anton seemed to be offended by this. "There isn't a melodramatic bone in my body," he coughed. "And *you* ought to know the difference." He seemed eager to go on, but he erupted into another coughing fit that he covered only barely with his sleeve. When he pulled the sleeve away, we could both see that it was specked with blood.

"How long have you been coughing up blood?" Rose asked.

Anton lifted one cupped hand high in the air. "It will have blood! They say, blood will have blood!"

"What the hell is he saying?"

"He's doing Macbeth," Rose said calmly, finding her phone in a voluminous handbag. "Anton, dear, sit down. I'm going to call your parents."

"But they're out on the Crimean Peninsula somewhere," I said. "We've got to call an ambulance. We should have called one a week ago."

I'd let it slide this long because Anton's nocturnal schedule wasn't all that unusual. We had always gone through long stretches when we were each so engrossed in our writing that we barely spoke. I worked best during the harsh light of the morning, when my dreams from the night before still danced in my mind. Anton preferred to wake in blackness from nightmares and push them away slowly with sips of Żubrówka and taps of his Remington hammers on ink-soaked ribbons.

Now, I felt that it was little wonder he'd gotten so sick; every day he waged new campaigns in the war against his own body.

Rose ignored me and dialed twelve digits from memory. A moment later she was connected to a palatial mansion on the Sea of Azov that I'd heard about many times but had never seen.

"Dobroye ootro, Gospodin Prishibeyev. Eto Rose. Vash syn, Anton, bolyen . . . " she spoke in flawless Russian. As the one-sided conversation continued, Anton led me in a waltz around the room, pausing only briefly to mist his other sleeve with airborne blood. I wondered how contagious tuberculosis was, or if he might have gotten some kind of STD from one of his gentlemen callers.

Rose looked up, holding her hand over the receiver. "Mr. Prishibeyev says we should take him to see a Dr. Ivanych. He's a friend of the family's."

Anton shouted, "Pasha! Pasha Pasha Pasha!"

I didn't know what "Pasha" meant, but Dr. Ivan Ivanych's name I knew from the many bottles of Lotosil, the antidepressant Anton took daily, as well as the various barbiturates and painkillers that hid farther back in Anton's medicine cabinet.

"Great. Yeah. 'Pasha,'" I said, coaxing Anton onto the divan to lie down. "I'll buzz downstairs for a taxi."

"The doctor is ice fishing at his lake house," Rose informed me after a bit more Russian dialogue with Mr. Prishibeyev. "Somewhere upstate?"

"Waccabuc!" Anton shouted suddenly.

"He's delirious," I said, laying the back of my hand on Anton's forehead. "Just tell his father we're taking him to St. Vincent's."

"Kak naschyet yesli mi voz'myem yevo v blizhayshooyoo bol'nitsoo?" Rose checked the time and then said to me, "I have rehearsal for *The Cherry Orchard* in six hours. I can't go upstate tonight."

"*Nobody* can go upstate tonight. None of us has a car, for one thing. For another, there's two feet of snow on the ground!"

"Waccabuc!"

"What does that mean? Is he saying something in Russian?"

"It's not Russian," she said to me. Then to the phone, *"Zdyes' mnogo snyega."*

"His son is coughing up blood," I continued. "The man is twelve time zones away. Let's just go to the hospital."

Rose shot me a tired look and whispered, "He says to take the Jaguar in the garage down the street. It's for emergencies. He says his son has numerous rare conditions, and if you don't take Anton to see Dr. Ivan Ivanych at Lake Waccabuc, then he'll die, and then Mr. Prishibeyev will fly over here and kill you with his bare hands."

And so it was settled. I got Anton into a too big overcoat and grabbed a mismatched wool cap and scarf for myself. Rose pushed the yellow hatbox full of manuscript pages under my arm. More than anything, what I wanted to do now was read it all again, to relive each and every detail that was now dancing around in her head.

"*Masterful,*" she said again, as she gave me a quick kiss good-bye.

Then, with Anton leaning heavily on my other arm, he and I trudged out into the worst storm in several years, in search of the parking garage where Anton's father kept the for-emergencies-only Jaguar. It was times like these, which cropped up more often than they ought to, when I wondered why exactly Anton and I were friends at all.

A sleepy Pakistani attendant unearthed a camel-colored X300 from the bowels of the garage. The man seemed skeptical, double-checking Anton's crimson Russian passport—his only form of photo ID—and jabbering in Urdu while motioning at the snow at the mouth of the garage. But I tipped him a hundred dollars out of Anton's wallet, and the attendant reluctantly handed over the keys.

Soon Anton was dozing in the passenger's seat and I was guiding the Jaguar through a maze of plowed streets, going the wrong way on Sixth Avenue only briefly before finding my way onto West Street. There I found four empty, freshly plowed lanes and the great frozen Hudson to the left. It was a challenge keeping the sports car under thirty miles an hour, and I could only barely see the red lights I was running. A few snowplows passed in the other lane, but otherwise I had the roads almost entirely to myself—a good thing, because I hadn't driven since high school and was feeling the effects of the Żubrówka.

Fumbling with the radio controls in the dark, I managed to get the tape deck on, but the only music available seemed to be a scratchy recording of Zero Mostel in *Fiddler on the Roof.* I hadn't suspected Mr. Prishibeyev to be a fan of Broadway musicals.

As we passed the George Washington Bridge, I listened to Tevye sing about tradition—accompanied by Anton's faint dream humming—and drifted back to thoughts of my novel. Titled *Just Before the Gilded Age,* it was about a young

Southern gilder in the late 1800s in Manhattan who falls in love with the daughter of a railroad tycoon. I was going to dedicate it to Rose, as a wedding present if she gave me no other option.

We were past Fort Tryon Park and rising up out of the city. Soon I found I could not keep my eyes open another second, so I pulled off the highway, under the shelter of an overpass. I checked the time on my watch and decided to skim through the final pages of my novel until I woke up a little.

Monday the 13th. July 1863. Heartsick and thinking only of Colette Marsh, I went uptown to report for the Union draft. Colette would be married in a few days and my own life would be forfeit anyway. Why not go back down South to shoot my own cousins on some muddy battlefield? The Union had claimed victory at Gettysburg after three of the bloodiest days since the Revolution, and President Lincoln had declared every able-bodied man in New York must sign up to step onto the front lines. Fearing the wait would be epic, I clutched a well-worn Wilkie Collins novel as I rounded the corner of Third Avenue. I stepped onto Forty-seventh Street and found the 9th District Offices in flames.

Smoke poured out so thickly that it plunged the block into grayness. Men swarmed all through it, heading in every direction at once. To my left, an Irishman in faded overalls clawed a paving stone out of the street, shouting, "Aileen! I'll see you again, Aileen!" He reeked of whiskey. It was barely past ten. He pitched the stone up and it arced right into the window of the draft office. The crash was drowned by the roar of the fire, but shattered glass still rained down on our heads as fresh plumes of blackness burst from inside.

A rock flew past my ear with a hollow whistle and then I heard it thwack into something behind me. Terrified, I spun, just in time to catch the falling body of a policeman whose club had been raised to split my head open mere seconds before. The front of his uniform was the color of cherry juice and his face nothing but a pulpy hollow. I let him fall, and I screamed, and I ran for my life—thirty-three blocks without stopping—until I arrived at Tammany Hall.

I charged through the main doors, anxious to warn the others about the riot. But before I could, Colette Marsh appeared around the corner. Breathless, I stopped, almost forgetting why I'd come, and what I'd seen.

Colette was of "the Railroad Marshes" of Georgia, and heiress to a fortune larger than I could begin to imagine. Her impending wedding to Bertram Vanderbilt was the talk of the Hall, where I, and my fellow apprentices,
scrambled daily, making preparations for the big event.

Many times, I had tried capturing her with my crude charcoals and my
penny paints. All this failed. Only when I layered thin leaves of gold onto the
columns of the hall had I ever felt near to capturing the deep hue of her
Southern sun-kissed hair. Only when I delicately painted golden highlights
onto the murals of the Revolution in the Great Room—glinting medals on
uniforms and in the sunlight behind a musket blast—had I ever come close
to the electric spark behind her eyes. But Chausser only kept a single day's
supply of gold paint on the premises at a time, locked in a back cabinet, and
he weighed our jars at the end of the day to be sure none had been wasted. A
single drop was worth more than I'd be paid in a week, but I had become so
meticulous with my brush that I could conceal a few drips of gold each week,
and with these precious drops I had painted a single portrait of Colette on the
blank back page of my book.

"D'you happen to have a match?" she asked, approaching me lazily, and
withdrew a cigarette holder made of purest bone.

Of course I did. I bought seven matches each week, at the tobacconist's
down the block from my boardinghouse, even though I had no money to buy
tobacco. A Hungarian man there dipped a bundle of pine sticks into a great
vat while I watched. He brought the sticks out with beads of lead and gum
arabic and white phosphorus on the tips, exotic and potent substances that
were befitting only of Colette Marsh.

And so I took out a match then, as I did each time she asked me, and
struck it against the buckle of my belt. The little stick sizzled into white
flames while I lifted it to the slim line of bone and paper and tobacco that led
directly to her perfect lips. She inhaled with ladylike deliberation.

Then her eyes widened, and—bliss! Her hand reached to my face. "Is that
blood on your cheek?" The policeman's blood stained the white lace of her
gloves. Her eyes flicked down to my Wilkie Collins novel. "The other men
are always reading the newspaper. Not you."

"No, ma'am," I said, pulling the novel out to show her. "This one's called 'No Name.' It's not quite as good as 'The Woman in White.'"

"That's my favorite," she said, plucking the book from my hands and turning it over in her own. I was so surprised to still be speaking to her that I completely forgot about what I'd painted on the blank page in the back—at least until she paused there, the blood-stained tip of her glove resting on a golden portrait of herself.

"Oh. That's just . . . "—I grabbed for the book—". . . a sketch. Of a woman. I knew back home."

But the verisimilitude was too great. Either my imaginary Southern woman was her identical twin, or that was a portrait of her. With no further word at all, Colette closed the book, tucked it into the folds of her flowing yellow dress, and left me standing there in the echoing hall. Far away, a clerk was rushing in the other entrance, shouting that the Colored Orphanage on Forty-fourth Street had just been set on fire.

Later I listened to the booming voice of Boss Tweed, discussing with the others how to best protect Tammany. Still I couldn't think of anything but Colette as I gilded the arrows of fat-faced cherubs, drawn and ready to pierce the hearts of men like me. The riots continued on and off for days. I was reassigned to touch up the ceiling in the room where Colette's wedding reception was to be held. Below, the little tables were laid out with gold-rimmed china teacups. Once or twice I dared to peek down from my perch and I caught sight of Colette, bobbing below, like a star fallen from my ceiling and submerged in the sea.

The Vanderbilts saw no need to cancel the wedding just because of the riots. The fires didn't dare spread their way downtown; even the smoke seemed to always blow in the other direction. When, the day before the wedding, a servant clumsily slammed a vat of tomato soup into one of the Grecian frescoes in an adjacent portico, the Vanderbilts demanded even that tiny crack be repaired. Chausser sent me in to be sure it was done right. In the cracked fresco, Leander, the young Greek, swam across a turbulent river toward his forbidden love, Hero, a priestess of Aphrodite, who kept a light on in her tower so that he could find her. It was as I limned the rays of this light that I first heard Colette's whispering.

"You're in there, aren't you?"

Jerking back from the wall, I looked all around me, but Colette was nowhere. And then I saw the shadow that had come over the crack in the wall. I bent down to peer through it. On the other side, out in the main hall, was a luminous blue eye. From where I stood, it seemed almost a part of the deep sea that Leander swam through.

"It's masterful," she whispered, holding her sweet lips to the thin fissure. "In your book. The painting, I mean."

"It's just a silly sketch," I said. "I'm so sorry. Please—"

"I'd love to see what you can do with more time," she whispered.

Before I could respond, one of the Vanderbilt daughters shouted Colette's name, and she rushed away. I watched through the gap in the wall as Colette looked back over her pure white shoulder, just once, at me.

The next thing I knew, I was shivering in the pale light of early morning and Anton was awake.

"What happened?" I asked, snapping forward sharply into the leather-wrapped steering wheel. My eyes were so glazed over that I could barely see.

"Apparently," Anton said drily, "you tried to kidnap me and steal my father's car but fell asleep in the middle of the getaway."

"You were dying. Coughing up blood and—"

Anton protested, even as he let out another long hacking cough. "I'm from Russia. This is my natural state of being. What? You think I have tuberculosis? Consumption? Like some character in *this* terrible thing?"

Suddenly my eyes focused on the pile of papers on his lap, and I twisted around to find the yellow hatbox, violated on the backseat.

"Who said you could read that?" I grabbed the pilfered pages away from him. I felt my heart pounding harder: back in our college days, Anton had written a story not *entirely* unlike this one, about his great-great-grandfather, and for months now I'd feared his reaction when he realized I was, somewhat, stealing his story. He seemed, if anything, amused—hardly what I'd been expecting.

"I wake up next to your snoring body, in a car with a dead battery, in the middle of nowhere. What *else* am I supposed to do to pass the time?"

"Dead battery?"

"Yes. I know *Fiddler* is enchanting, but perhaps you could have turned it off before you tucked in for the night?"

Anxious to escape him, I shoved my door open and stepped out onto the side of the road. We were on the side of the Saw Mill Parkway. The snow had stopped, at least, and I waved at some approaching cars, hoping to find someone with jumper cables.

Anton got out of the car. "Aren't there perfectly good hospitals in Manhattan?"

"That's what *I* said, but Rose called your dad and he said you had some rare—"

"Preposterous!" he shouted.

"—condition and that we had to go see Dr. Ivanych at his lake house. And I thought you were, you know, *dying,* so it seemed like we'd better get on it."

Six cars sped past before a rusted blue Suburban slowed to stop, blocking half the neighboring lane. A large gentleman with a raccoon's beard leaned through his passenger's-side window.

"You got cables?" he asked.

I looked hopefully at Anton, who shrugged—possibly not even sure what jumper cables were. "We don't know," I admitted.

The raccoon man seemed to consider leaving us there, but it was clear that he thought a fine piece of British engineering didn't deserve to be stuck in Yonkers with two idiots like us.

"She's a beaut," the man said. "Pop the hood and check your trunk for cables."

Anton fumbled about in the front, looking for a latch for the hood. I popped the trunk, where I found two huge crates marked heavily in Cyrillic. The only English I could find was on the Customs declaration, which read PRISHIBEYEV CAVIAR—SEA OF AZOV. Beside these was a complete roadside-safety kit, thankfully including jumper cables.

I delivered these to the raccoon man. Anton was searching for his cell phone, which was ringing—the aria that ends the first act of *Eugene Onegin.* Suddenly I realized the phone was in the pocket of his coat, which I was wearing.

"I'll get it," I said. "You start your car."

I answered the phone as Westchesterians honked and flipped me the bird as I nervously flailed at the traffic to go around us.

"Where *are* you?" Rose asked, her voice warming me deep down to my toes.

"We're coming back. Anton is back to his usual, charming self again."

Had he really called my novel *terrible*?

"Anton's father keeps calling me for updates. You'd better take him the rest of the way up there." Through the phone I could hear Rose instruct a taxi driver to head up Madison Avenue to avoid construction.

"Where are you going?" I asked.

"The Tea Room," she said after a pause. "I'm meeting someone."

"I thought you had a rehearsal?"

Rose mumbled something to someone else in the cab with her, and somehow I just knew that she was with her prince.

"It's been canceled, because of all the snow," she lied. If the cabs were running then the show, as it were, would be going on. And she would never miss a rehearsal, which could only mean there never had been one scheduled at all. She'd lied to get me out of town. I felt sick.

There was a shout, either of pain or panic, and the roar of the Jaguar's engine, followed by the booming bass of Tevye at the end of "Sunrise, Sunset."

"Got to go," I said quickly. I heard her hesitate, as if there were something else that she'd just been about to say, but then she said, simply, "Good-bye," and hung up.

Anton was trying to tip the raccoon man when I came running back up to the car.

"Let's go," I barked at him. "Before somebody takes a shot at us."

And so we eased out into the honking river of cars and headed up the highway again. As we drove in silence, I imagined pulling a U-turn through a break in the divider and heading back down to the Russian Tea Room to duel with whichever prince it was. Maybe it would move Rose to stay with me. Maybe I'd get shot and my novel would be published posthumously to great acclaim. Either way, it didn't sound like a bad plan, compared with sitting next to Anton another minute.

"It's *nice* to get out into the country for a change," Anton said, reclining a little in his seat. I ignored him. Anton pretended he didn't care what was bothering me for about five minutes, at which point he simply couldn't resist anymore.

"Troubles with *Rose*?" he mocked. "Is the Prince of Dullsylvania back in town?"

Though I was sorely tempted to sink into a long, disparaging discussion of Rose's latest fiancé, a subject which Anton never tired of, I ignored the jab.

"Rose is fine. *She* loved my book, by the way."

"Oh, is *that* your problem? Of course she loved it. It's practically *about* her."

Another long and stony silence, as I sped through the thin traffic, angrier and angrier, toward the nearest exit.

"I never meant you couldn't fix it," he said finally. "You've got a perfectly serviceable first draft."

"You said it was *terrible*. And it's my *sixth* draft."

Anton reached back for the hatbox. "Well, I only got through part of it. Let me take another look."

"Leave it!" I shouted. As we came into some small town, I suddenly wondered why I was even still driving. For weeks I'd barely heard from Anton, only finding little messes around the apartment in the morning and hearing death rattles through the walls, and here I was, motoring him up to the Siberian wastelands of Westchester to see some quack, right after he had insulted a year's worth of my work.

"Screw this," I said, seeing a sign for the train station up ahead. "I'm going to go back into the city." I checked the time on my watch and figured that if I caught a train in the next half hour, I'd be back in time to make it to the Russian Tea Room. I wondered if it was still considered regicide if the prince in question had already been deposed. All I knew was that I didn't want to be stuck in a car with Anton a minute longer, listening to Tevye asking Golde "Do You Love Me?"

"I suppose I do," she sang.

"And I suppose I love you, too," he replied.

"You can't *leave* me here," Anton said, looking around at the quaint little nearby shops—the sunny exterior of Paddy's Funeral Home, the shuttered Yarn Ball, and a busy little diner named Silly Nick's. To him, these might as well have been the gates to the gulags.

"I don't have a license!" Anton added. "I don't even know how to drive."

We slowed to a stop at a red light and watched a family of brightly colored fleece jackets crossing to get breakfast at Silly Nick's.

"You keep a *Jaguar* in a garage and you don't know how to drive?"

Anton didn't seem to understand why this wasn't logical. "It's my father's car."

"Which he left here, for you, to use in case of emergencies? With two crates of caviar in the trunk for safekeeping?"

At the mention of the caviar, Anton's face lit up, and he suddenly opened his car door and scrambled around to the back.

"Get back in the damn car!" I shouted.

The light turned green and I had to set the car in park so I could run out after him. For the second time in an hour, I found myself standing in front of a line of furious drivers, thanks to Anton.

But Anton was exuberant in front of the open trunk. "I thought I'd lost these! My father was practically going to disinherit me over them."

"Where did you think you had *lost* them?"

Anton, again, didn't seem to understand the question. Crates of caviar, in his world, were perfectly capable of falling in and out of existence.

Before I could stop him, he had grabbed the tire iron and pried a crate open. The cars' horns behind us were composing a collective atonal symphony. Though I was still stinging from what he'd said about my novel, I couldn't help but begin laughing at the sight of the stringy Anton, dangling in midair as he tried to use his full weight to open the crate. At least he was earnest about things, even his abject helplessness. He had everything in the world and could do almost nothing for himself.

Gesturing rudely for the cars to drive around us, I rushed over to lend my weight to Anton's lever arm. With a great splintering sound, the lid burst off. Inside were stacks and stacks of golden caviar tins, painted with pale blue maps of the Sea of Azov. Anton grabbed two of the pressurized tins with a loud cheer, and we rushed back into the car and got safely over onto the side of the road, across from the train station.

Scooping out the large, brownish pearls of caviar with our fingers, we sat on the hood of the Jaguar and watched the traffic roll by. For a while I waited for an apology, until I remembered that the word *sorry* was not in Anton Prishibeyev's vocabulary.

"Do you think Silly Nick's has blinis?" Anton asked, mouth full of fish eggs.

"No. I do not."

"And you people call this the Land of the Free!" he shouted at the commuters.

"They call this Westchester."

Three children leaned out the window of a yellow school bus to point at us. Anton's hair had bushed out in all directions, and his overcoat, which I had given back to him, was two sizes too big. My wool cap had slid back, and I was wrapped in a large red scarf and my threadbare old blazer. We must have looked like two hobos, perched on the hood of a hundred-thousand-dollar car, sucking fish eggs from our fingertips.

The chorus of Fiddler rang out, *"We know that when good fortune favors two such men, it stands to reason, we deserve it, too!"*

"How much does this stuff cost?" I asked, wishing I had some more Żubrówka to wash it down with.

"And if our good fortune never comes . . . here's to whatever comes."

"These big tins are about two thousand. Depending on how the ruble is doing."

I choked and sputtered, inadvertently spraying fifty dollars' worth of caviar onto the icy pavement.

"Ours is *osetra* caviar," Anton explained, beginning the inevitable lecture. "*Malossal*—which means a lightly salty flavor—large, and relatively dark. Darkness is typically a mark of inferiority, but ours contains a particular nuttiness that is unique to this *terroir*. The Sea of Azov is actually the shallowest sea in the world, and this makes our sturgeons particularly nutty for some reason."

"Not just your sturgeons," I joked. For that I received a flicking of eggs in the face, but I couldn't resist another: "You know, it's not at *all* surprising that you come from the *shallowest* sea on Earth."

Anton leaped from the hood and started to come after me. After a few moments' chase around the car, soon also speckled with fish eggs, we began shouting along with the tape deck in the car. *"Drink, l'chaim, to life!"*

Soon full, Anton curled up in his seat and closed his eyes. He was out like a light. Cursing myself a little for letting him off the hook so easily, I reached back into the hatbox, eager to finish rereading my novel's "terrible" ending.

Though I had hardly slept in a week, that night I could not stop dreaming up ways to somehow steal Colette away. She loved me, I was sure of it, but I had no money, no status. I could never offer her the life that she expected.

But without her, what was the point? Why go on gilding until the riots ended? I'd be shipped off to the front lines and made to shoot my fellow men, lest they shoot me. There didn't seem to be any choice. I dressed and stowed my few favorite camel-hair brushes away, along with my bundle of matches. From a hiding place behind my headboard, I took out a gold watch that had been handed down to me by my mother—one of the only things of hers that I owned. Then, like Leander, I crept out of the boardinghouse and traversed the dark night, steering occasionally away from the light of arsonists' torches. Soon I came to Tammany Hall, slipped past a dozing night watchman, and silently snuck to the back room, where Chausser kept the next day's supply of gold paint in the locked cabinet.

I plied the soft pine matchsticks into the keyhole, pressing gingerly against the tumblers, until the thing, at last, popped open. Inside, I found a jar still sealed with heavy beeswax. Holding it up to the moonlight, I studied its liquid glimmering and wondered how much I might be able to get for it out West. We could flee into the unexplored territories. Out where there was no draft, where I was not poor and she was not rich. Out where our love could begin. Suddenly drowsy with these dreams, I crept back into the portico. There, staring at the moonlight glinting off Hero's light, I slipped into deep blue sleep.

I woke to the sound of resounding cheers from the Hall. Immediately, my heart seized, as I wiped dreams from my eyes. Surely I had not slept through the wedding! I checked the time on my watch and, cursing my sleepless week, pressed one eye to the crack in the wall. There, on a dais, was a gray-haired minister, and in front of him, Bertram Vanderbilt, in a high top hat and woolen tails, his leather boots gleaming with fresh polish. I did not see Colette anywhere, but then the music swelled and people began turning toward the entrance. Without a second thought, I grabbed the golden paint from the floor of the portico and rushed out through the doorway.

No one noticed me. Every rich, joyful eye was fixed on the rear doors where Colette was entering, gowned in the most beautiful white lace and silk—her golden hair cascading in curls across those sun-kissed shoulders. The crème de la crème of Manhattan was there—every Vanderbilt from the commodore on down, Boss Tweed, and even the mayor himself. Every eye was on her. But her eyes were on mine. She froze, there, in the petal-strewn aisle, quickly grabbing the arm of her father—the handlebar-mustachioed railroad tycoon Nathaniel Marsh. The old millionaire turned slowly to follow his daughter's gaze to the painter's apprentice coming out of the portico. Others began to turn in their seats. I shouted something—Colette's name, I think—but with all the blood in my ears it sounded like gibberish. Half sure that someone, some Vanderbilt son, would rise up and fire a bullet through my breast then and there, I waited to die.

Then Colette let go of her father's arm and rushed back down the aisle. My heart leaping, I flew to meet her there. There was no time to clutch at each other, nor even to kiss. In her brilliant eyes, I could see only delirious happiness.

Bursting from Tammany Hall, we shouted like small children. Colette kicked off her stiff shoes and she ran barefoot with me into the sooty streets. Ash floated everywhere. Somewhere behind us, we could hear the noise of wedding guests rising to their feet in the echoing chamber, and shouting out in confusion. But we did not care. We did not look back. Faster and faster we ran. In another moment, as we approached the square, I began to hear gunshots, and I was sure that we would be killed by the Vanderbilts at any moment. Valiantly, I would perish in the arms of my true love. And she would leap in front of the bullets that followed and take her own life, and we would walk arm in arm through the meadows of the afterlife, together eternally.

But the bullets were not coming from behind us. Up ahead, Union Square was thick with the smoke of musket fire. Colette and I stopped short as we saw hell's own horror in front of us. The rioters were making their last stand. Soldiers and citizens alike were rampaging through the lines. The sun was blotted out completely. A black-coated fireman with no legs cried on the cobblestones, ten feet away. Flames consumed the square from the inside out. Charred black corpses hung from nooses in the trees—now blacker still. And there were no golden rays of light glinting in the musket fire. And there were no golden medals on the uniforms of the valiantly slaughtered. And there were no golden wings of angels hovering above.

I looked into Colette's eyes. In the face of this carnage she seemed like someone else entirely, for whom my love was unfamiliar. The golden paint still rested in the crook of my arm. Colette looked back at the hall and then, scared, almost reluctant, she tugged at my elbow. The look on her face was clear. We'd come too far to go back.

When Anton woke up we left the little town in our dust and traveled east on Cross River Road, through thickets of trees, past snow-covered barns and frozen lakes. Maybe it was just the caviar, but there really was something restorative about the countryside. And though our teeth were chattering, we powered the windows down and hummed along to "Matchmaker" as we zigzagged across the iced-over back roads. As we passed through a sleepy, nameless town that had not yet dug itself out of the snow, I looked over my shoulder at the hatbox.

"So. Did it remind you of anything?" I ventured, thinking of a story he'd written ages ago, back in college.

"It's *clearly* about you and Rose," he said, "I told you."

"No," I said, "I meant—did it remind you of anything of *yours*?"

Anton's face betrayed a small but earnest smile. "Maybe," he said. "Something terrible, which I scrapped *completely*, as I recall."

Was it my imagination, or did he seem—strangely—proud of me for having had the nerve to steal it?

"So do you think it's fixable?"

"It's *fixable*," Anton said gingerly. "I just don't know if you want to fix it."

"*Of course* I want to fix it—" I began to shout. I'd worked on the damn thing for more than a year. I'd spent months thumbing through metric tons of library books about the Draft Riots and biographies of the great gilders and genealogies of Southern railroad families. I'd lost hours of sleep over each of its three hundred pages. But as I tried to muster my outrage, I felt these arguments simply evaporating in my windpipe. Before I could explain the strange, sinking feeling to myself, Anton suddenly began shouting.

"This is it right here!"

He was pointing wildly at a snow-covered sign for South Shore Drive. Just in time, I swung the wheel and we skidded around the icy corner, onto a little winding dirt road that led us over the crest of a hill. At the bottom sat a small boxy log cabin, its only frill a stovepipe chimney and, behind it, the frozen lake.

An apple-cheeked boy, about our age, was shoveling snow off the walkway.

"Dr. Ivanych, I presume?" I wondered aloud.

"Don't be silly. That's Pasha, Ivan's son," Anton said, waving with the goofiest grin I'd ever seen. "We were kids together."

Then I remembered Anton's ramblings the night before, when he had shouted "Pasha." I'd assumed it was simply his delirium, but maybe this guy, not the pain-killers, was why Anton had been so eager to see the good doctor. Pasha was sandy-haired and strapping. Anton had the door half open before we slid to a stop, and a moment later I found myself watching them in the warmest of embraces.

"*Shto sloocheelos s' tvoyeemee volosami?*" Anton cried.

"*Ty tochno takzhe vyglyadeesh!*" Pasha replied with a laugh.

I lingered getting the parking brake on. They seemed as though they wanted a moment—and as I rewrapped my scarf, my eyes fell on the yellow hatbox. Anton's comment was still swirling around in my head, and I wanted to dig inside the box and pull out pages at random, scanning them for glints of literary gold so I could prove to him that it was certainly worth fixing. Angrily I grabbed the hatbox on my way out of the car and kept it tucked under my arm.

"This is my oldest friend!" Anton cried, smiling at Pasha. "The best cormorant catcher in Belosaraiskaya Kosa!"

I shook Pasha's hand and introduced myself. I could just picture them as pale boys, chasing each other up the pebbly shores of a frozen Cyrillic Sea.

"How . . . is your trip?" he asked, fumbling with the words. "You . . . slip-slide?"

He mimed twisting an out-of-control steering wheel and I laughed—it certainly had been a slip-slide of a trip.

"Pasha lives in Russia with his mother most of the time," Anton explained. "His father's English is a *little* better."

"Papa is on the ice," Pasha interrupted, stabbing at the air, which was heavy with our misted breath. He motioned for us to follow him. Trudging through knee-high snow, I kept the hatbox under my arm as Anton and Pasha bantered in rapid-fire Russian, their guttural laughs echoing through the woods as we came down to the lake. About fifty yards out was a small hut, made from the lashed-together limbs of trees and covered in what appeared to be bearskins.

Pasha and Anton trudged onto the ice without so much as a pause to check its thickness. "Don't be a pansy, now," Anton teased. Cursing at him and clutching the hatbox like a life preserver, I held my breath and stepped onto the ice. It held.

"You stay?" Pasha asked eagerly as we treaded out to the bearskin hut. "If Papa catch a fish, we have some dinner?"

Anton looked back at me eagerly. I bit my lip and smiled, hoping we might be able to discuss an exit strategy later. My mind wandered to Rose and the Tea Room, but it was too late to interfere with that now. How could I get her to see the truth? She wasn't in love with Prince Philippos, or Umberto, or whomever. I'd seen her losing her usual composure on the divan in the warmth of the fire—she loved *me*.

At last we arrived at the fishing hut. Pasha held back one great flank of bearskin and revealed the inside, lit with a dangling brass lantern and lined with great barbed hooks and augers of all sizes. And seated in the center was the wooly Russian himself. At long last, Dr. Ivanych.

"Zdravstvooytye, doktor!" Anton cried, racing around a wide hole in the ice to embrace the elderly man. Pasha stood behind his father's folding chair, and Anton crouched beside them. Immediately the three of them launched into an intense debate in Russian. The good doctor listened to Anton's descriptions of his illness while tending to a line that dropped straight down into an icy hole, nearly two feet in diameter. Pasha bent down occasionally to chop at the constantly refreezing ice with a little chisel.

As they jabbered on, the doctor suddenly reached into his things and produced a bottle of Żubrówka, with the familiar golden bison label. He waved it in the air like a murder weapon.

"Kak ti syebya choostvooyesh? How much have you been drinking?"

Anton blushed and squirmed as he mumbled his reply. I have no idea how much he *confessed* to drinking, but if our recycling bin was any indication, Anton was burning through several liters of Żubrówka each week—and he only drank more of it when he got sick, as he claimed that it fortified him against disease and had anti-bacterial properties.

"The buffalo grass in this contains a natural toxin called coumarin," the doctor barked, "which is *why* it is *banned* by the FDA! Of course, it's not enough to make you sick unless you're drinking ten liters a week!"

Mute with astonishment, Anton stared at the tiny bison design on the bottle like Caesar examining Brutus's knife.

I set the hatbox down on the ice and reached for Anton's phone again. "Guess I should go tell Rose to set the apartment up for detox again."

Anton scowled and Pasha began teasing him in Russian. Soon they began to jab at each like little children.

I ducked out of the fishing hut and stepped back onto the glacial lake. A few birds were rustling on the far end, and some smoke drifted from a distant chimney. The winter was dead silent. The cell phone barely got any reception, but after a few tries I managed to get a static-filled call through to Rose.

"Anton . . . darling . . . there?" she sounded very far away. Static burst on the line.

"It's me," I said. "Anton's going to be fine. Dr. Ivanych cracked the case. He's been poisoning himself with all that Polish vodka."

More static. I could not tell if Rose had heard me, so I went on. "Too bad. He was almost the first person to ever die of homesickness." Was she laughing on the other end?

"How's the prince?" I asked stiffly, after a moment. More static.

More static. ". . . he's well . . . look let's not . . . right now" and more static.

Suddenly it seemed that my whole life was static. Years of garbled nothingness, sitting at a library carrel, letting my imagination do the living. Static. She and I looking after Anton together, but whenever things got hard she went off on auditions. She went off with her princes. And Anton and I would drink and drown our weary ears with fizzing gin and tonics and crackling cubes of ice. Her fiancés were called on and called off like extras in a crowd scene. She and I would drink until our minds snowed over; TV sets tuned to channels that never came in. Static. I'd thought that maybe once she read the novel I'd written for her . . . But no, it was all wrong. Anton was right. *Masterful*, she'd said, just like Colette in my story. But then, what had I expected? That was the line I'd written, and she always stuck to the script.

Static. We were always. Stuck.

"I love you," I said, and, as if the phone knew that these words were not on the approved list, it hissed and burped. "Rose, don't you know I love you?"

Another burp. And then the call ended. I was alone again on ten acres of frozen water, listening to birds crying in the empty white sky. Had she heard me?

It didn't matter. If she had, she would pretend that she hadn't. We'd been there before.

For a minute I thought I might cry, and I wanted the tears to freeze to my eyes and ice them shut. But then I heard a chorus of shouts from the fishing hut.

"*Ya spoymal bol'shooyoo riboo! Ogromnaya riba!*" The whole framework seemed to be shaking, the bearskin coming to life as the three Russians danced around inside of it.

Spinning on the ice, I tried to slide back toward the tent. It seemed to get only further away from me. Careening on shoes never meant for such surfaces, I collapsed inside the tent just in time to see Dr. Ivanych thrusting the enormous spear down into the hole in the ice, which had doubled in size and seemed to have come alive. Water sprayed up in every direction. Pasha had the line tight in both hands; Anton ducked for cover. With a mighty effort, Dr. Ivanych raised the spear from the water, bringing up with it the biggest fish I'd ever seen. Its scales were black and iridescent, and its eyes opaque. The primeval thing thrashed around in the tiny space. Watery, red blood pumped from its side as it struggled to somehow escape its fate. I was in awe of it. I pitied it. In one moment, it had been the elusive monarch of its frigid kingdom, and in the next, it had been yanked upward into the bright and unbreatheable heavens.

"We'll feast tonight!" the doctor roared, getting the great, flipping tail above the lip of the hole. With a mighty heave, he launched the fish into an empty corner— only it wasn't empty. Sitting there on the ice was my yellow hatbox, just inches from the writhing beast, its great gills flapping futilely.

"Get that! Hatbox! Get it!" Anton snapped. Pasha was closest, but he didn't seem to understand. "Hatbox, hatbox, hatbox!"

I ordered my limbs to move but they were frozen. It happened in a split second. The fish's powerful tail curled away and then snapped backward, slamming into the box. It shot sideways, into the icy hole and down into the depths of Lake Waccabuc.

And it was gone.

For a moment, no one spoke. Pasha and the doctor were only mildly confused, but Anton was ashen faced. He knew what was inside. He was one of three people who ever would know.

"It's OK," I stammered, finding my legs again. "It's OK. Really."

Numb, I helped the others lug the dead fish back up to the log cabin. There were other, older drafts. Reworked endings, but none complete. I looked down at the firm, oily tail of the great fish in my hand and felt something strangely like gratitude.

Anton and I watched as Pasha and the doctor laid the fish out on a long workbench. Working in silence, father and son took turns running the blunt edge of a knife all along its silvery length, scraping away the scales to reveal raw pink flesh beneath.

"You were hiding," Anton said finally. "All that research about how paint was mixed in 1860, and where all the horses were bred, and the history of Manhattan contract law, and . . . " He rolled his eyes like he might be sick.

"So . . . ?"

"So you were avoiding the truth," Anton said. "It was a love story. Hiding in a textbook."

I knew he was right. I'd built a three-hundred-page house of cards, a carefully balanced illusion, without an ounce of the truth that would cement it in place.

Anton seemed apologetic, but I knew he was being honest. *This* was why we were friends. *This* was why I cleaned up the wonton soup bowls and recycled the vodka bottles. It wasn't about having a trunk full of two-thousand-dollar cans of caviar and an apartment with a view of Union Square. It was about having someone who gave it to you straight when you wanted to be lied to. Staring down into the great yellow globe of the fish's eye, I said a soft, silent thanks. He had freed me from something I'd been unable to escape for more than a year. Maybe it was about time I picked up an honest trade, became a doctor, or a fisherman, or a dishwasher at Silly Nick's. Anything but a writer.

We watched as the doctor set down his blunt knife and picked up a longer, much sharper one. As Pasha held the fish steady, the doctor slit open the great beast's belly from head to tailfin. Anton and I gasped as its mysterious purple innards spilled out onto the bench. Without even thinking of it, I reached over to hold Anton up, getting there before his knees even began to buckle.

"Come on," I suggested. "Let's go inside and clean off."

But though Anton's face was white as the snow outside, he stayed put. His eyes followed every motion, each slice. As he inhaled the oily stink of the fish, I saw his lips moving slightly, choosing words, testing phrases, timing cadences. He was writing the scene, already. Immediately, I felt my own pulse quickening. I wanted it, too. Here it was—right in front of me, the end of a much better story than the one I had lost. The story of how I'd lost the story.

That night, we ate more caviar—with blinis this time—and we roasted the fish in Dr. Ivanych's roaring fireplace. The food and fire and vodka soon warmed me. Anton and Pasha spoke of Mother Russia. The doctor told stories about noble fools he and Mr. Prishibeyev had known in the war. Stories about men of God and beautiful peasant women. Stories about fathers and sons and brothers-in-arms. Deep below the ice, my great, terrible novel was still disintegrating in the darkness. Paintbrushes and lovers and gold, coming apart into words and letters and dots.

5

Malice and Desperation in the Grand Canyon

"By God, if I ever cracked, I'd try to make the world crack with me. Listen!
The world only exists through your apprehension of it, and so it's much
better to say that it's not you that's cracked—it's the Grand Canyon."

—F. SCOTT FITZGERALD, *THE CRACK-UP*

As soon as I finally decided to break up the wedding, I felt much better.
Julian was absolutely right—I'd been down and out the whole trip, and
what for? I'd known I was going to do it—all along—and I was feeling
lousy only because I thought feeling lousy was the right thing to do. I'd
groused through the interminable cab ride to JFK and I'd sulked during
the five-hour flight to Vegas—the first flight I'd ever been on in my life,
and I had complained all through it, even after Julian so kindly ordered
up the second bottle of Clicquot. I was still bitching as I—for the first
time in my life—twisted the knob on the side of my gold watch and
observed the hours breeze backward. I whined while I rented the car—
even after Julian paid to upgrade us to the AC Shelby Cobra—and when
we finally checked in to our suite at the Bellagio, I'd been so sullen that
Julian had hardly any choice but to leave me behind for the night. He
had much to celebrate, what with the sale of his first novel in what all

the publishing-industry magazines had called "a major deal." I was proud of him, and at the same time so jealous I could have killed him—so it was for the best that Julian popped a few sky-blue pills and traipsed off to watch the fountains firing off in their mechanized ballet and the roulette wheels clicking and spinning and the contortionists at Cirque du Soleil twisting inside one another. If the past could be counted on to repeat, I expected to hear Julian returning to his room in under four hours, with some wan, waxed bartender in tow. I'd hear the shaking of more pills out of more bottles, followed by animalistic engagements, which I'd drown out with something on Turner Classic Movies. But until then, I stood out on our balcony, staring down thirty stories into a neon abyss. I wanted very badly to do something I knew was terrible, and only once I'd settled upon simply, really *doing* it did I feel a great weight lifting off me at last.

Just one thing still bothered me. I'd been asked to write this article about the wedding for *Esquire*, seeing as Evelyn had starred in yet another Broadway hit this season and . . . well, all right, truth: technically, *Julian* had been asked to write this article and he said he couldn't *possibly*, what with the final edits for his novel due just after the wedding, so he'd handed the assignment off to me.

Regardless, now that I'd decided to ruin everything, I wondered if they'd actually want that money back. Unless, I decided, why not write about the ruining of it? Why not become part of the story? Why not go full gonzo? "Malice and Desperation in the Grand Canyon." What a title! They'd love it—surely. Celebrating in advance, I ordered a room service filet mignon and raided the minibar.

Surely my new story would be more interesting than one about how the Aphrodite-esque Evelyn Lynn Madison Demont, beloved star of *Mourning Becomes Electra*, wedded the utterly uninteresting Dr. Avinash Singh. The good Dr. Singh was a geologist at UC San Diego, whose life's single act of spinal fortitude had been to insist to his parents—Indian royalty of one of the former princely states—that his wedding be held at the Grand Canyon, here in America, and not in India as they demanded.

Not for its immense grandeur or romantic color upon sunset—but so that he would not have to pause long from his study of the mile-deep chasm and its forty-million-year-old rocks.

Avinash and Evelyn planned all the usual trappings of an Indian wedding: the groom would ride an elephant along the rim of the canyon and they would exchange vows before the *Agni*, the Sacred Fire. I'd packed three of the New York Public Library's finest books on the subject of the traditional Hindu wedding, or *Vivaah*, and two more on the mighty Grand Canyon itself—all for research purposes. Whether or not I ruined the wedding, I had always fully intended to write the hell out of the event.

Giving Evelyn away would be Mr. Demont (accompanied by his fourth and third wives) and Evelyn's mother, the first former Mrs. Demont. Also in attendance: the bride's childhood friend, Julian McGann, presumed heir to McGann International Trading, whose as yet untitled but already acclaimed novel would be out next summer; joined by his roommate, Some Nobody, the writer of this article, who slept with the bride-to-be on six of the seven nights prior to the wedding. (It would have been seven of seven, too, if Julian hadn't dragged me out to Vegas early, in a clumsy attempt to put some distance between me and Evelyn.) The bride, incidentally, couldn't have given two shits about rocks, however old they might well be, and suffered from bouts of intense vertigo that once kept her from climbing the stairs at Lincoln Center, and, so, naturally she had privately expressed some reservations about being married on the edge of the deepest chasm in the country. I considered all this as I ate my steak—every bloody bit of it—and concluded that it seemed barely avoidable that I should stop the wedding. Satisfied, I settled in to sleep.

Julian had not yet returned, to my great relief. That night I dreamed about Evelyn's hands. Like the last time we slept together they were covered in henna for the *haath pila karna* ritual, a deep sienna except for a single empty circle on her right hand. I kissed this spot in my dream, as I had done in waking. Then I saw a magnificent elephant towering over us. On his back rode a man in a turban whose face was covered in flowers. He shrieked and lowered a wickedly curved sword toward us. Evelyn's *mehndi-tattooed* hands flew up to cover my eyes and then suddenly I was awake and the phone was ringing: the front desk, extending an invitation to please join Julian McGann and his wife, Bethany, for breakfast.

I laughed and took this to mean that Julian, and his sense of humor, had forgiven me for my grumpy trespasses of the previous twenty-four hours and that, over caviar-freckled blinis, we would soon be back on track again. However, when I stepped into the dining room to find Julian sharing still more Clicquot with a lithe young woman in a white satin dress, I suddenly wondered if it wasn't a joke after all.

"*Buongiorno, amico mio!* Meet my wife, Bethany Szabó . . . *erh* . . . McGann!"

The gorgeous dark-haired woman hugged me with two smooth arms, allowing her jawbreaker-sized diamond ring to linger in my sight line as we parted.

"Have a glass," she purred, pouring out the last of the Champagne and beckoning for another bottle. I downed my glass without hesitation and looked at Julian for some indication that he was playing some kind of elaborate prank. But he was absorbed in a Blue Period canvas on the wall—a drab, flattened beggar who seemed not quite in keeping with the flash and glamour of the rest of the restaurant.

"This *is* a surprise," I said, smiling sweetly at Bethany. "Do you and Julian know each other from school or something?"

She cackled. "No, he *won* me. Last night in a game of craps."

"Who had you before?" I asked, but Julian interrupted.

"I was up by nearly four, then down six. Now I'm back up—only down two—but I think, if I hurry, I can get in another hour. Maybe two more." If he was speaking in increments of hundreds or thousands or hundreds of thousands I did not want to know.

He was twitchy—grabbing at the elbow fabric of his rumpled suit jacket and lifting his glass as if to drink and then setting it down again without taking it to his lips.

"We've got to hit the road if we're getting to the wedding. The Grand Canyon's five hours away, at least," I said.

"That's why we got the Shelby Cobra. We'll be there in four."

"I'll go and find myself something to wear," Bethany announced suddenly, pushing back from the table as the waiter arrived with the new bottle of Champagne.

"You're— She's coming?" I asked Julian.

"That's the idea," Julian said. Bethany smiled, as if this were a great compliment. He kissed her awkwardly and said, "Buy yourself something lovely, my love. Charge it to our room."

As she slipped away to the shopping area, I repeated, "Well, this *is* a surprise," because I couldn't think of anything else to say. Julian had brought boys back to our apartment of every size, shape, color, and creed, but I'd never once seen a girl tiptoeing out of his room in the morning.

Julian said nothing else and drank no more of the Champagne. Was he pleased with himself? Was he waiting for me to ask him why he would do such a thing—or if he was at all serious?

Somewhere, once, I read that the only mind a writer can't see into is the mind of a better writer. When I watched Julian watching the world, I was always reminded of this.

After breakfast, Julian returned to the casino floor and put his money down on the first table he found—something involving Chinese tiles and ten-sided dice—and before the hour was up he had won back his two (thousand) and made two more—which I had hoped was enough to cover the chiffon monstrosity that Bethany emerged in, twenty minutes later. We cashed the chips and checked out of our room.

Being far soberer than Mrs. McGann, I at least got to drive the Shelby Cobra again. The car was built for two, so Bethany squeezed herself onto Julian's lap, a position he seemed extremely uncomfortable with until he took three red pills from his bag. Then he loosened up instantly.

As Bethany scanned the radio stations for atrocious pop music, I drove us first along the unlit-neon corridors that led out of Las Vegas, and then past the billboards along the highway heading south. I kept checking my watch as we went along, but in the Shelby Cobra time seemed to stand still. Soon the billboards were replaced by scraggly pines, and then these were gone, leaving nothing but flat red earth—dry as far as the eye could see. With less fear of running into passing troopers, Julian dipped into his medicine chest more liberally and soon was wrestling the radio tuner away from Bethany.

"Synth and drivel!" he shouted. "I demand *Bach*! I demand the *Magnificat*! Look at all this fucking *flatness*! Barren as the Martian plains. Driver! Take me to Olympus Mons!"

"*Tutto pronto, signor!*" I barked as Julian located something from *Tosca* that must have been classical enough for his current mood.

"So how did they *meet*?" Bethany asked me. It took me a moment to realize that she was referring to Evelyn and Avinash.

"He came to see her doing *Cat on a Hot Tin Roof*," I shouted over a soaring tenor. "He was in town for the American Geological Society's annual conference. Presenting a paper on some fancy rocks he found."

Julian interjected in a robotic monotone, "Dr. Avinash Singh's research centers on the so-called two-billion-year-old Vishnu Schist at the bottom of the canyon and its relationship to the Brahma and Rama Schists. His paper concludes with a suggestion of how the younger Zoroaster Granite came to be stratigraphically lower than the older Vishnu Schist."

Bethany blinked and said, "Well, that all sounds very interesting."

"Believe me, even if you understood it, it wouldn't be," Julian said.

Glad to have Julian's support, in a sense, I continued: "Supposedly, Avinash was so moved by her performance that he insisted on coming backstage afterward and asking her out to dinner."

"Unfortunately he was so nervous about it all that he threw up halfway through the soup course," Julian added.

"That is so romantic," Bethany giggled. I begged to differ, but considering that her engagement had involved a pair of dice and a high-stakes wager, perhaps it was all relative.

"Pull over!" Julian shouted. "I must make number one!"

I pulled over the Shelby Cobra and while Julian ducked behind some boulders to relieve himself, Bethany stretched out on the leather seat and helped herself to some of the contents of Julian's pill bottles. Dedicated as I was to Evelyn, it was still hard not to notice Bethany's ample décolletage as she fumbled with his overnight bag.

"What's this?" she asked, pulling out a sheaf of typewritten pages, covered in editorial pencil marks.

"Julian's novel," I replied.

"He's a *writer*?" she said, clutching her throat as if the pills she'd swallowed might come back up. "I thought he was *rich*."

"Well," I said. "He's a very good writer. But that's not why he's rich."

She skimmed the first few lines, and the look on her face did not improve. I reached over and pushed the papers down below the edge of the door so Julian couldn't see them as he returned.

"He'll go berserk if he thinks anyone's been reading it," I said.

"Well, isn't that the whole *point*?" Bethany asked.

"It isn't done yet. He's a perfectionist."

The truth was that he'd never let me read a page of it, and he'd been working on it for as long as we'd known each other. Even now that it had a publisher and the advance check had been cashed, he wouldn't let me see it. I strongly suspected that his increasing mania over the past few weeks was a result of realizing that, now that it was slated to be published—now that he no longer even technically *owned* it—that soon people would actually be *reading* it.

"Well, *you've* read it," Bethany said.

"I haven't," I lied.

I had. I had read every draft. I had read it while Julian was occupied by alcoholic stupors and off on pharmaceutical benders. I had read it again just the night before, while I'd been moping about whether to break up Evelyn's wedding. The book was good. In fact, it was extremely good.

"But I'm sure it's good," I added hastily.

"You're lying," she smiled. "The only person you can't lie to is a better liar."

"I've heard that," I admitted with a grin, as she shoved the book back into the bag while we waited for Julian.

"Can I ask you something?" she said finally. From the look on her face I could tell what she wanted to know. She kept glancing at Julian behind the rocks, then down at the radio, still quietly playing its opera. "Is he . . . uhm . . . ?"

"Indeed," I said. "I'm assuming he didn't exactly consummate the marriage?"

She giggled and leaned in secretively. "It's all a joke. We're not really married. He just wants everyone to think he is. We're going to have a *terrific* fight at the wedding reception and call the whole thing off."

I began laughing as I grabbed her hand and held her ring up to the light.

"Cubic zirconia," she giggled.

"So, what? Is he *paying* you?"

She nodded mischievously. "I've had stranger requests."

"So you're a . . . uhm . . . ?" I asked. Now it was my turn to be too embarrassed to finish my question.

"Escort," she said cheerfully. We both turned, silently, to see what had become of Julian. He was still behind the rocks—either making quite a number one or having moved on to orders of greater magnitude.

It wasn't unlike Julian to try to upstage the most grandiose wedding I'd ever heard of. Not that I wasn't hoping to upstage it myself. Still, I wondered. Was this Julian's lunacy, ever-increasing? First there'd been the incident with the hummingbird feeder, which he'd hung out of our twelfth-story window and watched for days, though no bird ever came, humming or otherwise. Then there'd been the episode at Petrossian with the high-heeled shoes and all the oyster shells. And last week, there'd been the disappearance of Mrs. Menick's always-barking shih tzu puppy. There'd been the scratch marks on Julian's left arm. And then a cabbie had found "Shihtzy" a day or two later, outside Hempstead, Long Island. The dog was doing just fine now, except that she had yet to emit even a single bark or whimper since her disappearance.

"*Why?*" I asked Bethany, finally. "Why would he hire you to be his fake *wife?*"

Bethany shrugged, the desert sunlight glancing off her bare shoulders as she eased back against the headrest falling under the grips of whatever medicine she'd found in the bag. "I just do what I'm paid for. You'd have to ask Julian."

I considered this, but then I noticed my roommate, having removed all his clothing, running through the bramble and dust. Golden-hued in the noon sun, he flew with arms wide and fingers stretched wider, like Icarus.

The best thing to do—usually—was to let him play these things out. Who was I to tell a genius it was time to put his clothes back on?

"You tell *me* a secret now," Bethany giggled, sliding over toward me and laying her head down on my shoulder as I looked at my watch. We had time.

"I'm going to ruin the wedding," I said. "I'm in love with the bride and I'm going to tell her not to go through with it."

Bethany cackled madly, as if this were the funniest thing she'd ever heard. Then she kissed me, deeply, and I felt her climbing on top of me, blocking out the warmth of the desert sun. Julian was still off howling in the distance. "That's so romantic," she breathed in my ear, as her hands searched downward. I could have stopped her but I didn't. A hundred miles away, Dr. Avinash Singh would be promising Mr. Demont to secure eternal *dharma*, *artha*, and *kama* for his daughter. And Mr. Demont would be pouring sacred water as a symbol of his acceptance of the arrangements. Then he and his first former wife would place a conch shell in Evelyn's hands, filled with gold and fruit and flowers, completing the ritual of *Kanyadaan* and granting their permission for the wedding to proceed.

We arrived three hours later—not exactly on time, but by no means too late.

I'd heard that the Grand Canyon is the only thing in the world that lives up to the hype when you finally see it. While I can't speak to the hype of everything else in this world, I can confirm that the Grand Canyon does, indeed, live up to its own. Sheer walls fell down and down for miles, changing from blood-dusty reds to golden sandstone and back again. At the very bottom was an acid snake of green and black, river water running lazily in places, as still as glass, and in others it roared and rampaged in frothy rapids. For the first time I half understood Avinash's hesitation to stray very far from it. No one inch of it was like the inch above it, or below, and there were more inches of it than any of us could ever see in ten lifetimes.

The wedding ceremony was to take place on Grandview Point, on the traditional *mandap*, a prominent raised stage covered in flowers, which contains the *Agni*—the Sacred Fire. Around this dais, to allow guests some shelter from the heat, were two rows of white tents, the dry wind blowing them all a little westerly. Here the aristocracies of both Manhattan and Mumbai were gathered, the women in gowns that could walk a red carpet and saris and veils woven of gold and the threads of Bombay's finest silkworms; the men wore Armani tuxedos and *sherwanis* and ornate, flower-covered turbans. The air surrounding the bar was thick with jasmine and Chanel No. 5. Our landing party quickly appropriated glasses of Scotch and moved over to dutifully admire the chasm. Far off from the proceedings was an incongruous elephant, finished with its journey and resting happily under a shade. And even the elephant looked pathetically small, with the canyon behind it.

"Oh, I do not like this one bit," said Julian loudly, of the canyon. He had been successfully cleaned up and re-dressed at eighty-five miles per hour by the industrious Bethany.

"Makes one feel rather small, eh?" chuckled a bald-headed guest with the distinctive look of a doctor.

"Yes, it does make one," Julian agreed. "And when one doesn't prefer to feel as small as one does, it is certainly time one does something about it."

He raised a pill bottle directly to his lips and tossed back an unknown quantity of its contents into his mouth. The balding doctor looked somewhat alarmed as Julian passed the orange plastic cylinder to Bethany, who daintily tapped two out into her palm.

"Vertigo," I explained to the bald man. "Crippling cases. The both of them."

The man rejoined the crowd, mumbling something about being off duty. Soon people were giving the three of us a bit of a wider berth. I knew Julian well enough to know that he did this, at least somewhat, by design. He seemed at peace, however, there beside the empty chasm.

Not only was the canyon more beautiful than anything I could ever hope to produce—and so big that it defied comprehension—but it was also literally as old as the very life on Earth. The rocks at the top were an unimaginable 230 million years old, and the ones at the bottom were more than 2 billion years old. And it had endured. It had endured because it was nothing. Because it was only an abscess. An absence. A void that patiently expanded and that nothing could ever fill.

I watched Julian watching the canyon. I wondered what he was thinking about it. What else did he see that I could not see? What more did it mean to him that I would never understand?

"Julian McGann!" called someone from the crowd. "Didn't think I'd see *you* here!" A trim boy with owlish glasses emerged, and I was sure he was a classmate from the prep school where Julian and Evelyn had done their time together.

"Charles!" Julian said in the high pitch I knew he used when he was, in fact, cursing the very gods for this surprise. "May I introduce my wife, Bethany?"

Charles nearly fell over at this announcement, which I imagined was just the sort of reaction that Julian had been hoping for, especially with so many old schoolmates bound to be there—and with so many, like Charles, I imagined, who had been with Julian in many a darkened broom closet. Was this why he'd planned the whole Bethany deception?

In that moment, I felt a rare kind of pity: the sort that comes only when you feel it for the person of whom you are the most envious.

While Julian was distracted, I tailed a bridesmaid in an ornate mulberry sari back to a wide white tent, where I'd hoped to find Evelyn. I didn't know just what I'd say to her, but I had decided not to overthink it. For years now we'd danced in circles. She'd let me lead for a while and then I'd let her. But now we were at the end of it. She didn't love this *geologist*. I'd seen it in her eyes on six of the seven preceding nights. Probably she was expecting me to stand up during the ceremony and object in some dramatic fashion—and I *would*—if she wanted that particular drama to unfold. But wouldn't it be kinder, and ultimately less tiring for each of us, just to slip away before things got going? If we did it now, the assembled Singhs could all be back in Vegas in time for dinner and a Tom Jones show.

There were far too many mothers and bridesmaids and junior wedding planners circling the main entrance to the tent, so I worked my way around to the back, where I gently untied a flap in the tent fabric and peered inside.

Evelyn sat alone on a white-padded stool, staring into a mirror, putting makeup on with a gentle touch. She was more stunning than I'd ever seen her before—more radiant than the desert sunlight, more magnificent than the canyon beneath it. Every few seconds, she looked down at a photograph in her left hand—a picture of an Indian woman in traditional bridal makeup. I'd been to many of her shows but I'd never gone backstage to her tiny dressing rooms. I'd never seen her do this before.

She touched a brush to a rouge in a small plum-colored container and painted it onto her lips with careful strokes. I'd seen her wear the same color on stage. It made her lips catch the light, she always said, so every seat in the house could make out each quiver and curl. Some acted with their hands; others, their eyes; but as I watched her, for the first time I realized that Evelyn acted with her lips. She studied them in the mirror, trying out the various possibilities. She pursed; she pouted. She bit the lower one, then the upper. She let them twitch a little. I caught a rare glimpse of tongue, running across them. Then an even rarer smile—the corners drawing back like the panels on a pair of velvet curtains.

She looked away, once, toward the door to the tent. Was she looking for me? Was she wondering if I would come? If I would stop her? Was she wondering if she would stop, if I did come? She lifted another brush to her eyelids and shadowed them over. There was no spark behind them now. And if I did nothing? Would she and Avinash settle down here, in the desert, while he chipped away at pebbles? Would his parents buy them a Frank Lloyd Wright manse in Los Angeles, where she and I would pass the time as always, no change but for a ring she'd remove beforehand? What if he finished his work and they returned to India? How far would I follow?

She set down the eye shadow and lifted another brush to her lashes. They were long and dark, and her hands were now sienna with the dye. Only that single circle was still exposed. I wanted to press my thumbs to it and push, down and outward. Wipe away the *mehndi* in all directions. Perhaps tonight—if we took the Shelby Cobra we would be at the coast in five hours—we could wade into the salted waters of the Pacific and let the colors wash away. We could head south into Mexico, where no one would ever find us. We could return east, and hope the scandal blew over with the seasons. In the vineyards in the north we could drink until we forgot who we'd ever been. West seemed the only proper way to go, and yet there was only a little more west left. On the other side of the ocean was just the world again, and eventually we'd come back to where we'd begun, and still nothing would have changed.

Evelyn turned away from the mirror and bent down to lift something from her bag, a small painting in a golden frame. I wanted to see it more closely, but suddenly a car horn honked, somewhere off on the side of the canyon. I lifted my head from the flap and looked out at the chasm. There was a faint echo as the blaring sound kissed the edge and bounced back. And then nothing. The noise was swallowed up and gone. The source of the noise was a silver Bentley that had nearly rear-ended a Rolls-Royce. The Rolls honked back, and this time the sound was like a whisper, as it journeyed the other way, into miles of desert. The two cars stayed, squared off there, in the middle of the small sea of limousines and Town Cars. Each refused to let the other by, and the Beamers and Benzes began to pile up behind them, all honking their horns in time, like seconds ticking in a snarled clock, and vanishing into the empty canyon. Red-vested valets started scrambling over, their hands clamped to their ears protectively. There, in the heart of the lot, the sound of all those pricey cars making their urgent demands must have been deafening, but it was barely audible from where I stood, just a hundred yards away.

All around me, the wedding preparations spun on, last-minute affairs being quickly settled. Florists hung heart-shaped slipper orchids from the tent poles; caterers sailed about with silver trays of curried prawns. A harpist and three accompanying sitar players argued over some detail in the sheet music. Two of the bridesmaids rushed by, carrying an industrial sewing machine. Looks of desperation were written on their faces. Something had to be hemmed, or mended. Everything had to be perfect.

How many millions had it all cost? The white silk tents? The single-malt Scotch and the imported flowers and the jet fuel and the fucking *elephant*?

It was at this moment that Julian's fist suddenly connected with my jaw. The entire Grand Canyon at once swerved upward into a right angle as my body crumpled to the ground.

Julian's other fist connected with my neck, and the first again with my shoulder blade. What he lacked in aim he more than made up for in enthusiasm.

"What the *fuck* are you doing?" he seethed.

"What the fuck are *you* doing?" I managed to gasp. Julian's eyes were as dark and impenetrable as ever. Was he seriously trying to stop me?

"You slept with my *wife!*" He began dragging me away from the tent so that Evelyn would not hear.

"Your—. She's a fucking *escort*, Julian!"

But he didn't seem to hear me. Was this it? Had his nominal ties to reality finally been severed? Had the pharmaceuticals chewed through? Or was it whatever else was wrong—whatever had always been wrong— in the wormy folds of his brain? I managed to shove him off me. I tasted blood in my mouth.

"No, I'm saying you *just* slept with her. An *hour* ago. And now you're going to go in there and ask Evelyn to run off with you?"

Suddenly I felt deeply ashamed. I had hardly thought about the escort. She'd barely seemed real. Regardless, I charged at Julian and threw a punch that connected up around his eye and sent him staggering backward.

"You're out of your mind!" I spat, releasing a thin stream of blood that disappeared into the dry earth. "You're *completely* insane! You know that, right?"

He flinched but agreed. "Definitely," he said, brushing himself off. "Definitely I am. But at least I *try* to make a point of only ruining my *own* life."

His eye was swelling, and I imagined that by morning it would be a lovely shade of eggplant. I didn't even want to think about what my own face would look like.

"You really think you love her," he said, surprised.

"Of course I *love* her, you idiot. I've loved her since the moment we met. Since the moment you sent her off to roam the college with me because *you* were too caught up in your damn story to spend any time with her."

"God," he said, rolling his eyes in desperation.

"What, you think she doesn't love me?" I challenged, ready to remind him about six of the past seven nights.

"I don't know if she loves you or not, you solipsistic son of a bitch, but I hope to hell she doesn't! Because what I do know is that you don't love *her* at all." Julian shook his head. "You've gotten *just* good enough to fool yourself, haven't you?"

"You don't know what you're talking about," I snapped.

"It's *fiction!*" he shouted. "She's just this character to you. Both of us are! And we always have been. You don't know what goes on in our heads. You don't know where we come from or who we *are* . . . Can you even tell the difference anymore between what you've written about her and who she really, truly is?"

I didn't understand *what* he was talking about. Clearly he was losing it.

"But how could you?" he continued. "You've made *everything* up— even yourself, for God's sake. Well, here's the truth. Let me remind you—*The Biography of You*: Son of a man who had a layover in Newark and the flight attendant who brought him peanuts with a smile that afternoon. Recipient of a Vacheron Constantin watch that your mother found wedged between two first-class seats and *stole* for you, so you'd be able to count the hours she'd abandoned you. One-time escort—*paid* escort—to a debutante ball and introduced to high society as a character from a *Wilkie Collins* novel. You project these *fantasies* onto us. It's fun playing the people you think we are, but this is where it stops. This isn't some story anymore; this is her *life*. And you don't get to do this. *You* don't get to."

And for once I thought I knew exactly what was running through Julian's mind. He was out of his mind, of course. But underneath that was something else. Something I'd never seen before, but that had always been there, whenever he'd looked at me, from the very first day: he pitied me. Not in the same snobby way that he pitied everyone and everything, but because I had no idea who I really was. He'd seen me all along, like a moth fluttering repeatedly against a windowpane. He'd grown attached to me, gotten to know the pattern of my wings against the glass. I'd always been on the other side of it, though. I'd been circling out there for so long that I'd forgotten.

I thought he would hit me again, or drag me away, but instead he let me go. He just began walking off the other way, toward the blazing, open sands and the red distant hills. Perhaps he wanted some space, or just to lick his wounds. Perhaps something had finally snapped inside him that would not be mended. I didn't understand exactly. And I didn't know then that I wouldn't see or speak to Julian again for ten long years.

I hurried back to Evelyn's wedding tent.

When I slipped my head back through the rear flap, I saw that she was not alone anymore. Avinash stood a few feet from her, dressed in magenta silks that leant him no aura of impressiveness at all. A shirtless man, whom I took to be the priest, was chanting and pressing a golden coin onto the untattooed void on Evelyn's hand. There were no other people in the tent—no relatives or bridesmaids or elephants of any kind. This was the real wedding ceremony; everything that would happen out on the *mandap* in front of the others was technically just for show.

Evelyn could not see me. The little picture frame that she had taken from her bag earlier lay beside her makeup tray. I watched as the priest clasped her hand to Avinash's and began to bind them together, with the gold coin pressed between them. I opened my mouth to speak, but only dry desert air came out.

There she stood, only a few feet away from me, but she looked like she looked on stage—completely real and yet entirely someone else. I'd never been so close to her while she was in character. When Julian or Avinash or any of the other men—and there had been many—came to see her, they sat in the front row, center. Only my eyes had the capacity to unravel her.

She gazed into Avinash's heavily lashed eyes with a serene confidence. It was a gaze of expectations being firmly met. Of plans having at last come to fruition.

The priest's voice reached a higher pitch as he knotted their hands together and reached for the fringe of her sari. I watched as he wove these tiny threads to Avinash's *dhoti*. She breathed a little deeper, but she wasn't really nervous. She was only playing the part.

I said nothing. I did nothing.

When the priest's fingers parted from the knot, he concluded his prayer and it was done. Evelyn and Avinash were wed.

She never saw me. And when she moved away from Avinash, her face did not change at all. This character was permanent now. Evelyn had become someone new. In a few minutes they would go out to the *mandap* and revolve around the *Agni*, and they would make their traditional promises to each other in full view of their families and assembled international guests, but it was already done, so I took off to find the car. I couldn't stand to stay and watch the rest. I knew how it all would go down.

Up on the *mandap*, Evelyn and Avinash would place strings of flowers around each other's necks. They would circle the holy fire seven times and make their seven vows to each other. And as they stared into each other's eyes, they would come to what was really my favorite part of the whole ceremony, when it came right down to it.

We are word and meaning, united.
You are thought and I am sound.
May the night be honey-sweet for us.
May the morning be honey-sweet for us.
May the earth be honey-sweet for us.
May the heavens be honey-sweet for us.
May the plants be honey-sweet for us.
May the sun be all honey for us.
May the cows yield us honey-sweet milk.
As the heavens are stable,
as the earth is stable,
as the mountains are stable,

as the whole universe is stable,
so may our union be permanently settled.

Whenever I made it back to the hotel, I would throw these details together and finish this article and get very drunk and catch the first flight out in the morning. Most of these holes could be patched together. Everything else was just the Grand Canyon.

As I drove off along the rim in the Shelby Cobra, I found it easier and easier to remind myself of how incredibly small I was, and how incredibly small everything about me, and my life, and my love, and my world, was, too.

What Was Found

6

A Plagiarist in Dubai

It is good to know the truth, but it is better to speak of palm trees.

—ARAB PROVERB

Even with the full moon, it's terribly dark out there tonight, isn't it? That's the desert for you. You should try the 51 cocktail here. It's quite good. Are you in Dubai on business? Honeymooning? Oh, wonderful! I should leave you two alone then. You're sure? Well, if you insist, then, of course, I'll join you. Just for one drink—on me. Three 51's, min fadlik. There we go. So, you two just arrived from—? Oh, lovely. I'm from New York, myself. Pleasure meeting you both. Call me Timothy Wallace. Professor Timothy Wallace, actually.

    How did I wind up in Dubai? Well, it's certainly an interesting story—one of my better ones. Unless, of course, you want the truth. The truth is only slightly less interesting than the story. But, then again, it's the truth—so it has that unique quality. Of all the possible stories out there, from the fantastic to the mundane, only one of them qualifies as the truth. It's OK! You can laugh. I won't take any offense. Perhaps I've had one too many. It's just, you see, I don't usually tell the truth, as a rule. But every rule has exceptions. Maybe mine is that I can tell the truth only in strange bars to lovely couples, when the moon is full behind the Burj Al Arab and the night is especially dark. Fortunately for you both, tonight is just such a night. Ah! Here come our drinks.

Now, see, I've gone and made you a little nervous. That's good. Will he tell us the truth? Or will it be a lie? How will we be able to tell, one way or the other? If I told you, for instance, that I lived for many years with the international bestselling author Jeffrey Oakes? If I told you that the woman I love is, today, Her Royal Highness, Princess of Luxembourg? No, no. Don't apologize for laughing. Of course, you wouldn't believe that. Tricky thing about the truth . . . that it is often stranger than fiction is only the beginning. But, I'm sorry—I'm lecturing already. It's something of an occupational hazard. You fall a little bit in love with the sound of your own voice. You start chasing little threads and before long you've lost the point entirely.

Now, how did I come to Dubai? Well. I'll begin at the middle, which is where all good truths begin.

One year ago, in May, I stood in front of a poorly ventilated room in Manhattan, packed with thirty-five jittery students, all just moments away from completing my course on New Journalism. Pacing back and forth in front of the blackboard, I swirled my hands through the dead air, bringing the final, trembling chords of my class to its crescendo. It went a little something like this:

"A few final thoughts, then, on this, our last day. What is *New* Journalism? Not quite fiction and not quite reality. We began the semester by looking at Gay Talese's piece 'Frank Sinatra Has a Cold.' Talese followed Sinatra around for three months, trying to get an interview and ended up talking to every person around Sinatra instead. *Esquire* shelled out five grand to cover his costs, making it one of the most expensive articles ever written at the time. And in the end, he never spoke to Sinatra, not once. But Talese constructed an interview, anyway: *he wrote what he knew Sinatra would have said.* Now, compare this with what we've just read: the work of Stephen Glass, rogue fraud reporter of the *New Republic*, who fabricated not just interviews but facts, and entire people, and the corporation of Jukt Micronics—even inventing the subject of his piece: a young hacker who violated Jukt's servers, and *then* conned Jukt into paying him a fortune to protect them against future attacks. Is there a difference? Where is the line? James Frey. Jayson Blair. Kaavya Viswanathan. Blair Hornstine. The countless others out there who have surely gone undiscovered. Ours is a new generation of plagiarists. Armed with Wikipedia and Google, we can manufacture our own truths. What else should we expect in an age when even the real reporters, off in the Middle East, sent back only government-approved messages? Move over Jennings and Murrow. No need for the cold, uninterpreted facts. Make way for Stewart and Colbert! In our era, *truthiness* is in the dictionary, and Dan Rather got fired for not authenticating the Killian documents. And in his wake we've found, twisting and shouting, the Bill O'Reillys and the Chris Matthewses, spinning us sugar-sweet falsehoods. Plagiarism, class, is the new American art form."

Just a brief pause for poignancy, and then—"Have a great summer. Leave your final papers by the door."

They just eat this shit up. With their little silver spoons, they do. Every year a couple of kids even applaud before rushing out the door. A little irreverence, a little old-fashioned fire and brimstone, and you've got them. Back in the sixties, I might have been one of those professors who got everyone to join a cult or march on Washington in protest, but as fun as that may be, it's not my MO. After I charge their brains with my own brand of skeptical electricity, I unleash them—the New Cynics—upon a world that is slowly and happily critiquing itself to death.

The truth is that I actually have the greatest respect for those fantastic liars. Someday I'd like to teach a class entirely about them. Late Great American Fakes. My humble thesis will be that America no longer desires the truth, only the reasonable facsimile thereof. Like battered lovers, we're willing to settle. Our sense of values still holds us to dismiss that which we know, outright, to be blatant lies, but we avoid the truth with equal intensity. We wish to remain in the gray interregnum of half belief, when at all possible.

But. How I came to Dubai. Yes. Well, that final day of class, after the students had all wandered away, I erased the board and brushed off the chalk dust. Then I threw away the stack of term papers waiting for me by the door, hit the lights, and headed out.

There, just in the doorway, I collided with Saiyid Ghazali, a particularly bright-eyed student of mine, who always sat in the first row, paying rapt attention to my lectures. Probably as a result of his upbringing, Saiyid was impossibly respectful and polite. Without fail he raised his hand before speaking, and he never spoke without making full eye contact. He never slouched in his chair. His notes were written in neat shorthand, and from what I could tell, as accurate as a court stenographer's. He'd gotten a perfect score on every quiz, had never missed a single class, and his final paper, had I read it, would surely have been flawless and insightful.

"*Uhm* . . . Saiyid. Good to see you." I wondered if there was any way that through the door he'd seen me dumping the term papers.

"Professor Wallace," he said, "I just wanted to tell you how much I enjoyed your class this semester."

"I appreciate that," I said. "I'm teaching Methods and Practices of Modern Journalism in the fall. It's past registration, but if you come on the first day, I'd be happy to sign you in."

He looked crestfallen. "I am afraid that I will not be able to accept your kind offer. My parents are transferring me to another university next semester."

"Your parents are quite smart," I said. "Truth is, this is not a very good university."

This remark received a few stares from passing students and one elderly professor, who knew I was right. The older ones have been around long enough to remember when our city-funded university was still a pioneer of urban schooling, instead of a cesspool that hands out degrees like lollipops at a barber's.

"Every year," I explained, "our standards decline, our attrition rate rises, faculty retire and are replaced by adjuncts, and all the while our class sizes swell with ill-prepared students with no idea why they're here. It's no surprise. It's America. Even our little public institution is a business. We soak the FAFSA money out of the freshmen, knowing they'll drop out after a semester and return to their dead-end jobs. Then we funnel everything to the graduate school, where the students actually accomplish things that make the university look good—because most of them were properly educated elsewhere, and the cycle continues."

"You are very wise," Saiyid said, nodding. "I shall miss you greatly next semester."

Saiyid was certainly smart enough to join the ranks at NYU or Columbia—more advanced practitioners of these same shell games—but I didn't get to ask where he was bound, because just then, the chair of our department came marching down the hallway.

"Professor Wallace?" he called down the corridor as soon as he'd spotted me. I pretended not to have heard him—the chair and I had never officially met. To be honest, I wasn't entirely sure how he knew my name. Then I realized that I was still lingering in the doorway of my assigned classroom, still wearing my checked-tweed blazer.

"Professor Wallace?" he called again. "May I have a word?"

My first impulse was to pretend to be another professor, or a student—just overdressed for the final day of school—but Saiyid, at that moment, pressed his hands together in gratitude and said loudly, "Excuse me. You must be busy. Have a wonderful summer, Professor Wallace."

There was no way out. The chair continued his advance—staring directly at me. I looked at my watch. "Sorry, I've got to run to a meeting with another student," I said.

"Oh, this should just take a second," he said with a nasty little smile.

I was trapped in a badly tiled hallway with buzzing fluorescent lighting, about to face up to my crimes.

For the problem, you see, is that I am not really Professor Timothy Wallace.

You see? I told you. It's much better told from the middle. That's

Storytelling 101—not that I've ever taught such a class, though I think you'll agree I'd be quite good at it—no, but I've certainly taken my fair share of such classes. Before I became Professor Timothy Wallace, you see, I was something of a writer myself. Now, for the beginning part.

The real Timothy Wallace was a Scotsman I met at a writing course at the Gotham Workshop—Narrative for Fiction and Non was that professor's clever little title. I'd have called it something more like, Stories: Straight and Slanted, but I digress. Tim was, then, an eager young journalism student who sat beside me at the great round workshop table where our works were weekly eviscerated. He wrote with great passion about the city's crumbling public school system—about boys named Deshawn and girls named Jessina who kept their feet up to avoid the roaches in their classrooms and who sheltered their heads daily from falling chunks of plaster as they filed up and down institutional stairwells into hallways funneling five times the number of students anticipated by the architects of days past.

I admired Tim's sense of civic responsibility. At first I suspected his outrage for the underprivileged was just a way of getting bleeding-heart publishers to print his work, but soon I saw that he genuinely cared for these children. He was certainly very different from any writer I'd been friends with previously.

The children wrote him letters, and he spent Saturdays with them at the park. He was a *good* person, in other words, and being around him made *me* feel like a good person too, even as I was furiously rewriting old stories about all the *not good* people I'd known and loved, before. Egotistical and insane writers. Self-absorbed socialites with emotional distance issues. The very people who had chewed me up and spit me out. I dreamed of tying it all together into a novella that could encapsulate an article I'd written for *Esquire* (though they'd refused to print it), as well as my only published story—"Anton and I"—a chilly little work of fiction that had received little fanfare and vanished with even less. The larger novella that I envisioned followed a young man from Raleigh who sells his soul to become a writer; moves to Manhattan with his college roommate,

Julian; and proceeds to lose everything—his epic first novel is lost in a lake; Evelyn, his one true love, marries an Indian prince; and he and Julian get in a fistfight on the rim of the Grand Canyon; etcetera, etcetera.

One evening, after a particularly brutal disembowelment of Tim's piece, "No Number-Two Pencil Left Behind," about the suspicious relationship between the standardized-testing industry and the Bush administration, he and I went out to the Lion's Head Tavern on Amsterdam. There we often acerbically discussed the latest flashes in the pan while we pretended to be great writers ourselves—like Norman Mailer or Lanford Wilson—even though their Lion's Head had been in the Village and closed for years.

"I thought it was very well written," I told him. "I liked Deshawn's line about how the tests were like evolution, like survival of the fittest, except the people who survived were just the ones who cheated the best."

"It doesn't matter," Tim moaned into his beer. "I can write it as well as I want, but without hard evidence from former Department of Education people, it all may as well be fiction." He paused a moment and then added, "No offense."

"None taken," I said, getting up to order a fourth round. From the bar I could see that poor Tim was truly crushed. When he thought I wasn't looking he took out a small photograph of Jessina that he kept in his wallet—taken on the steps of the New York Public Library, while she chased pigeons at the bases of the great stone lions. He'd taken her there on a Sunday, after her family had finished church. He told me she'd read for four and a half hours without stopping. At home she had no books. The ones that Tim gave her, Jessina's mother kept throwing away; I'd never understood why.

As I returned with our beers, I watched Tim slip the photo back into his wallet. Then he folded up the pages of his essay in resignation.

"I'm going to have to go back to Scotland," he sighed. "Do you know how goddamn *cold* it is in Scotland?"

His student visa was past expired, and his application for dual citizenship had gotten him nowhere fast. He'd been writing freelance, for blogs and other nonpaying entities, and barely getting by. All in the earnest hopes of someday landing a job as a real reporter. Honest work wasn't easy to come by and Tim had been down every available avenue, twice, and still always wound up right back where he'd begun. There was only one thing I could think of to do to help him. Something I was terribly good at. Something I had not done in far too long.

I lied.

"You know, I have a brother-in-law who works for a company that scans all those SATs and GREs and everything," I said. I didn't have a brother-in-law. I didn't even have any siblings.

"Scantron!" Tim said excitedly.

"That's it, Scantron!" I said. "I can't believe I didn't think of it before. Anyway, I'd be happy to get in touch with him to see if he knows anything."

The rest was easy. With a little help from Google and Photoshop, the twin engines of modern-day con artistry, I produced a perfectly passable letter from an anonymous colleague of my fictitious brother-in-law's, which suggested that Tim was, indeed, onto something. Nothing damning or concrete. Just enough to give the ring of truth to Tim's article. Armed with my letter, Tim went on to finish his piece, publish it in *Educator's Monthly*, and win the Dunnigan-Pyle Award for Investigative Journalism. Jessina and Deshawn got to shake hands with the mayor, and some philanthropist donated two hundred thousand dollars to their school. Tim moved to a bigger apartment and asked me to take the spare room, free of charge.

Talk about your win-win situations.

"It's all thanks to you," he'd say whenever I protested—which I made a point to do each month when the bills came. "Your big break is coming any day now, I can feel it."

In the mornings we woke and toiled away in the apartment, dreaming of becoming the next Mencken and Dreiser. Tim sent out résumés to newspapers, television studios, and magazine publishers—anyone who might have been looking for a young, eager reporter. Though he kept on calling about his application for dual citizenship, the wheels of government ground slowly. Still worried about deportation, Timothy applied for a job teaching courses in journalism at City University. Just something to fall back on.

As June came to a close, I heard from the first round of literary agents, who collectively declared my novella "forced," "unrealistic," and filled with "less-than-charming characters." As I drank my way through the dog days of July, Tim began to get offer upon offer for his brilliant journalistic mind. And while everyone loved his work on the standardized-testing piece, citing his "bloodhound's nose for the truth," the insults continued to come flying toward me through each mail delivery—my hardly fictional writing was, apparently, also "fantastical," "emotionally dishonest," and "frankly, simply not believable."

Aside from my appreciation for a little irony, you can imagine my frustration. When Timothy Wallace left in August on a year-long assignment in West Africa for the BBC, I stayed behind in his apartment, still hoping that my luck would soon change.

Drunk and depressed, I neglected to transfer the lease, or the utilities, to my own name. A few bank statements arrived from a Chase account that Tim had not had time to close, so I just found a refill checkbook and began paying the bills. When the account ran out, I deposited my own money into it. Gradually, I became a little more Tim, and a little less me. My novella, and everything that had inspired it, began to feel like a distant memory—part of someone else's life. Someone else's beginnings, not mine.

Then one day, sifting through the stacks of mail, I found a letter from City University, offering Timothy Wallace four sections of Introduction to Journalism. The semester was slated to begin the following week. Desperate and a little inebriated, I wondered if that maybe I could substitute for Timothy, seeing as how the school probably wouldn't have time to find another replacement. Tim had left behind his books and syllabi, so I spent the week studying Harrower, and Zinsser, and the AP style-book, and putting together my own thoughts on these subjects. I stayed up late at night, reinventing myself as an expert on truth telling, and when I woke from bleary half sleep, I was one fraction less of the man I'd been when I'd fallen into bed.

On the first day of class, I threw on an old corduroy blazer and a button-down shirt and went uptown to the university. Thirty-five eager freshman faces sized me up as I walked into the room. "He seems young," I heard someone whisper. "Is this a joke?" someone else asked. I began to sweat and flush red as they snickered. Standing there before their doubting eyes, something in me finally snapped. With all the rage only an unappreciated genius could muster, I slammed a stack of syllabi on the table.

"Who knows how much tuition costs at this school?" I thundered.

No one raised a hand. Everyone sat up straight, even the jocks in the back.

"Why am I not surprised?" I muttered. Truth be told: I didn't know myself. Then I let out a companionable laugh—only two students in the room dared to smile back.

"If you want to learn about journalism, you're not going to do it sitting in a classroom," I barked. "Everybody stand up. You have twenty-five minutes to go out onto the city streets, find someone to interview, and get their life story. In exactly twenty-five minutes, come back here and be prepared to tell me everything there is to know about your subject. I'll be quizzing you on the details."

No one moved. One of the students who had smiled raised her hand. She, at least, was zipping up her bag. "What if you ask us about something that we don't find out?"

"Then you make it up," I said. "But if I don't believe you, you fail."

A few more people began sliding their notebooks into their bags. A boy with a Mets cap on backward raised his hand. "Isn't that . . . whatchacall . . . inethical? Isn't that, like, plagiarism?"

"No," I said flatly. "*Plagiarism* is when you steal someone else's words and pass them off as your own. When you just make them up from nothing, it's called *fiction*. We'll discuss the difference more thoroughly when you all get back. Now you have twenty-four minutes."

Five or six people jumped up and bolted for the door.

"Professor?" one girl called out. "Professor . . . *uhm* . . . I forget your name."

"*Tim . . . o-thy . . . Wal . . . lace . . .* " I said as I wrote it on the board in big chalk letters.

"Yeah. Ain't you even gonna take attendance?"

"I'll take attendance when you come back," I said coolly, taking off my jacket and slinging it over my chair. Checking my gleaming gold wristwatch, I said, "*If* you come back. Twenty-three minutes now."

With that I sat down and watched the students filing out, looking at me as if I'd lost my mind. Maybe I had. All I knew was that I was someone I did not recognize, but it felt right. I liked me, this way. And twenty-three minutes later, every one of the thirty-five students was back, with pages of scribbled notes, all fighting to read first.

The rest is the rest. Timothy's backup plan became mine—and with a little practicing of the scribble he called a signature, I started cashing his paychecks and paying his bills. At one time I suppose I planned to just get a teaching job of my own, with my own name. But a strange thought came back to me, which had first surfaced back in those dark, drunk days in July.

I'd been pondering my chosen vocation—to write fiction and to slant the truth—to tell lies, for a living. But I wasn't good enough at it. At least not in writing yet. No one believed me. And then my mind wandered back to little Deshawn, sitting at his desk avoiding the roaches, filling in those little Scantron bubbles with his yellow number-two pencil. He'd said that taking the tests was like evolution in action—only instead of the brightest and most capable students surviving, it seemed that victory fell to those who could scam the test, learn the rhythms of the answers, the tenor of trick questions, take educated guesses, and budget their time. The teachers had stopped teaching science and English and started teaching *how to pass the test*. Was it gaming the system? Or was it an evolutionary necessity?

The best novelists make you believe, as you read, that their stories are *real*. You hold your breath as Raskolnikov approaches his neighbor with a raised ax. You weep when no one comes to Gatsby's funeral. And when you realize you are being so well fooled, you love the author all the more for it. Up in front of my students each day as Professor Timothy Wallace, I discovered the thrill of getting away with the manufacturing of reality. I had a way not only to pay the bills, but to become a better purveyor of make-believe. I had put myself into an evolutionary situation wherein my failure to deceive would result in disaster. Wherein I'd be forced to risk everything. Where I'd be rewarded for my successes at dishonesty. And the greatest reward was that I barely thought of my old life anymore. Only when I saw a certain novel by Jeffrey Oakes in the bookstore windows, or caught a headline about Luxembourg as I passed by a newsstand.

Oh, yes, that's right. You didn't believe me when I said that part, before. Now you're not so sure, are you? It's perfectly fine. I understand. After all, you're talking to someone who, really, for a time, believed he *was* Professor Timothy Wallace. So much so that, one day, when I opened the mailbox to discover that the United States of America was proud to accept Timothy Wallace's credentials for dual citizenship, I felt genuine relief, as if *I* were the one avoiding deportation. I signed Timothy's name on the dotted lines as if it were my very own. I tell you, at that time, I'd all but forgotten it wasn't. A few weeks later, when I went down to Hudson Street and collected a crisp blue passport, it hardly occurred to me that I was committing a federal crime. I bought myself a hot dog, afterward, to celebrate.

I'd made something of myself. Or someone's self, anyway. I was actually a wonderful teacher—if I only channeled equal parts Mr. Kotter, *Full Metal Jacket*, and Professor Keating from *Dead Poets Society*. At the end of the first semester, my students filled out their Scantron evaluations of my performance, deigning me "Excellent" with unanimity of graphite. Over the holiday break, I dug out the old novella I'd written and, for the first time, it felt more like fiction than fact. When I returned to my post for the spring, I took on four new sections. This time the students were expecting the theatrics—they had heard about me, it seemed. They had heard about the professor who tells it "like it is."

The brilliance of teaching for a large university department is that it involves surprisingly little oversight. If I'd tried to be a middle school teacher for little Deshawn and Jessina, I'd have been fired in a heartbeat. Little children still tell their parents what they do at school all day. The Department of Education hands down a curriculum, and textbooks, and any deviation from the prescribed course is noted. But at the university, oversight only ever came once a semester, when a member of the tenured faculty materialized to sit in on my class. And this faculty member was required to give advance notice, so it was simple to merrily plan more mundane and traditional activities for that day. The students played along—happy to help me in damning "the man."

In the end, my flaw was that I was really *too* good. My name came to the chair's attention when I was overwhelmingly voted Teacher of the Year by the freshman class. This lifted my name out of the crowd of nearly a hundred adjunct professors and, that same night, when the chair saw the real Timothy Wallace on the BBC, reporting on corruption in the UN foreign aid program, he finally put two and two together.

My little conversation with the chair in the hallway was uninteresting—he called me a sociopath, which, I'll admit, *did* sting— but otherwise, he seemed simply flabbergasted that I had so thoroughly charmed the hundreds of university students in my charge. An uninspired dinosaur himself, he asked me, more than a few times, none to my surprise, how I'd done it. I'm sure you'd like to know the same. So here's the truth:

Students *want* you to tell them that everything they've learned thus far has been bullshit, served up steaming by people far stupider than themselves. They've all made it through high school, where they're guaranteed to have encountered worthless instructors of all kinds, peddling information that has not even the slightest relevance to their lives at all. So, first things first, you tell them that their suspicions have been correct all along—most of what they avoided learning wasn't all that important, anyway. But then comes the right hook, now that their guards have been dropped. What is the *one* thing that is valuable in this world? The ability to lie. That's right. And they know it well by then, only no one has acknowledged it to their faces before. *Language*, you go on to explain, is not a boring and worthless system of grammar and spelling, but a *tool* that can be used to manipulate the weak and the stupid. Students sit up straight in their chairs when they hear this.

A master of the English language, you go on, can convince and manipulate anyone into doing anything the master pleases. You show them Socrates—they know him as just some ancient dead guy. No. You show them a man who uses his superior wit to convince ordinary people to think exactly the way he wanted them to think. You show them speeches by Stalin and Marx, JFK and FDR. You look at the Gettysburg Address. Don't quiz them on the year and the date—they know that's what Wikipedia is for. They can get that on their cell phones.

My favorite lesson plan involved simply walking over to the TV and turning on CNN for the hour. Any time of day, even in commercial breaks, the students could identify an endless stream of manipulation. The truth is bent constantly into lies—right before our very eyes and ears, every day of our lives, and they are hip to this fact. Change the channel to MTV and they can see their idols doing the same thing: pop singers who reinvent themselves to seem like the girl next door in one interview and little better than porn stars in the video that follows. Or rappers who back their words with claims of rough streets, so we'll forget their bank account balances are in the triple millions. And the students idolize these frauds. They dress like them and speak like them *because* they're frauds. They're heroes because they're *good* frauds. And the students then reinvent themselves as ever-better miniatures of their fraudulent role models.

Of course, you will occasionally find a young, idealistic kid who believes that art contains *truth*. This may seem initially to be anathema to your entire being. But these rare souls are even easier to win over. For you will deliver your speeches with amusement, but also with *grave* concern. Your passion bursts from the heart, which you wear on your corduroy jacket sleeve, and it runs, bloodred, down your jeans and onto your Italian leather shoes. Never take your eyes off these genuine students, for they have not yet been crushed, and you will not crush them. You will nurture this idea that there *is* truth and beauty behind that veil of lies. Indeed, whenever you draw back that curtain, you will show them that there is Good and there is Right and there is Better Than and there is Best. And if you tell this lie well enough, you may even begin to believe it again yourself. You may even regain a sliver of the innocence and ignorance you treasured once, too. And this is your reward at the end of the day.

But there I go again. Sometimes I forget I'm not in my classroom anymore. We're having a nice night in a quiet bar, on the fifty-first floor of one of the finest hotels in Dubai. There's something about this place. It's the air, I think. Makes you want to fold stories inside of stories inside of stories. But I'll get to the end, finally, and explain how I got from there to here.

The department chair fired off some empty threats about getting the police involved—but I knew he would never do this because it would require him to admit the truth about the university's lack of oversight to hundreds of parents, perhaps even to real reporters. So I told him to do what he liked and I walked downstairs. Stepping out onto the rainy streets of New York, I wondered where to go next. A long summer stretched ahead. The downside was, of course, that they wouldn't let me teach at any of the other city universities now—and I couldn't exactly put my experience of the past year on a CV. The economy was in the toilet. I was about to turn thirty years old. I was unemployed, friendless, and loveless. My sole possessions were the disaster of my "forced," "unbelievable," and "less-than-charming" novella, and the knowledge that I'd spent the better part of a year being someone I actually enjoyed being instead of myself. And I would be damned if I was going to go back.

Just then, I noticed Saiyid, my favorite student, hovering under the awning, smoking a hand-rolled cigarette. The golden tobacco smelled sweet, like dark secrets, and when he saw me looking over, Saiyid happily offered me one.

"Where did you say you were going next year? Hunter? NYU? Columbia?"

"The University of Dubai," Saiyid declared proudly.

"Ah, good old U-Doob," I said, though I had never heard a thing about it before.

"My father knows some people who teach there," Saiyid explained. "You would like it there. The people in the Middle East, they all want to know . . . what is America, really? You know, Professor. You tell it like it is. You do not pretend this country is perfect and pure and wonderful. You can tell them."

"America might not be perfect," I said, not really thinking, "but I've always thought it must be a hell of a lot better than anywhere else." Truth was I'd never left the country in my life.

"My father told me that I had to come to America to see for myself just what the rest of the world wants so badly to be," he said with a smile. "With all due respect, Professor, how do you know you won't like Dubai better?"

"I read a lot," I said, giving him a warm, authoritative pat on the shoulder. "Enough to know I don't want to be in the Middle East at this particular historical moment."

"But you said yourself in class, Professor. These things are not all the truth. United Arab Emirates is a friendly, peaceful, democratic country, just like America."

"Our partners in peace," I said with a wry smile. He looked back at me—for the first time as a fellow human being and not just my student. And he laughed.

"My father, perhaps he can talk to a friend? They pay a lot of money for American professors in my country."

And that is how I found myself boarding Emirates flight 24, with Timothy Wallace's American passport in one hand. As I checked the time on my gold wristwatch, I looked up to see a row of polished clocks, each set to different hours around the world. I'd gotten a little drunk—insurance against the long flight ahead—and so I saluted as I passed the men in army fatigues, with guns the size of me. The sight of them was quickly replaced by the vision of my flight attendant, all almond eyes and smooth, coffee-colored skin. Her name tag said SHAHRAZAD, and she graciously ushered me into the first-class cabin. Saiyid's father had been generous enough to supply the ticket.

"Professor, please, make yourself comfortable."

She pulled open a small divider, and I peered into what was set up as a miniature luxury hotel room. I ran my hands over the swirling walnut burl of the countertop, opening a small compartment to find, to my great relief, a fully stocked minibar. My seat was folded down into what resembled a snug twin-sized bed with 450-thread-count sheets and a silk comforter. A wide flat-panel television invited me to surf hundreds of channels, browse the Internet, or plug an iPod into a smartly concealed receptacle. I set my bags in the spacious storage area and lifted the remote control. Scanning through the guide, I felt like the commander of a futuristic battleship, the world at my fingertips. More a part of the next century than the current one.

I scrolled through The Buddha Channel, MTV Brazil, Fashion International, Szechuan BabyNet—I froze when I saw the listing for Radio Télévision Luxembourg.

"Is your suite prepared to your liking?" the attendant asked.

"Am I still on a plane?" I gasped.

"Yes, sir," she answered with a smile.

"How much does this cost?" I asked.

"I have no idea, sir," she replied.

"About twelve, round trip" came a voice from behind Shahrazad. An adjacent panel slid open and I found myself eye to eye with a harried-looking businessman, already half into a miniature bottle of Scotch.

"All this for twelve hundred?" I said, looking back at my bedchamber.

"Twelve *thousand*," the man said casually.

Taking my cue from him, I coolly suppressed my own shock at the statement. "Right. Twelve thousand. That's what I meant."

The man smiled at me as Shahrazad excused herself to board the rest of the passengers.

"Gene Packard," the man said, extending a hand. "Nice to meet you, son."

I was suddenly wishing I had gotten dressed up for the flight. Mr. Packard was wearing a golden-silk-backed wool vest and a gleaming tie to match. I was wearing my usual teaching gear—a pair of Italian shoes, some dark blue jeans, and my thrift-store blazer, with a shirt I had meant to iron. Packard seemed to note this, for he said, "You know, they'll press that for you."

"Of course," I said. "That's why I didn't press it before. Might as well have it done fresh."

"What's your line?" Packard asked, pouring me a Scotch without asking.

"I'm in journalism."

"Well, you're headed to the right place," Packard said with a wink. "The future is in Dubai, sure as I'm standing here before you."

After takeoff, over several Scotches, Packard told me the whole story of Dubai. One of seven emirates that banded together when the British left the gulf in the late seventies, Dubai had made its place in the world in the expected way—by peddling shitloads of oil and petroleum to freedom-loving countries such as our own, keeping profits high by relying primarily on underpaid and often-violated South Asian workers. But in recent years the forward-thinking emirate realized the inevitable end-game of the oil business, something that America, despite Al Gore's admonishments and the recent rash of celebrities espousing greenness, has collectively failed to realize. There's simply not enough oil to go around forever. So Dubai decided that while the rest of the world continued slaughtering one another over who would get the finite amount of oil that remained, they would begin diversifying their portfolios. Dubai turned into a playground for the wealthy, particularly those in Europe, featuring seven-star hotels, man-made islands, and even indoor ski slopes. If there was one thing that a lifetime in the oil business taught an emirate, said Packard, it was that people are addicted to opulence. A growing number of American businesses came to set up shop in the new Silicon Valley, where Microsoft, IBM, Oracle, and the EMC Corporation were merrily cashing in on expansive tax-free zones. Packard assumed I was headed just down the block to where CNN, Reuters, and the Associated Press had all set up their offices of late.

"All these people here," Packard said, motioning to one of his three cabin windows. I could see the New York skyline clearly against the horizon still, and I silently bid it adieu. "They think they're living in the center of the universe. But we're headed to the real McCoy."

And it's funny, but, looking down at all those hard lines of Manhattan, the grids of streets and office windows—all getting smaller and smaller—I felt as if I *had* evolved, after all. Not just into Timothy Wallace, but into someone cleverer, more confident.

Up and down Park Avenue and along Canal Street scurried millions who felt they had the grit of the Real World beneath their fingernails. Because they were making it there, they assumed they could be making it anywhere. And in the blare of taxi horns and the roar of subway tunnels, they bought and sold, networked and dialogued, listened to NPR on podcasts and read the headlines off the *New York Times* website. It was the city where I'd written my first novel and where my first real friendships had flourished, grown ripe, and eventually rotted. I'd come to it as a stranger, only to learn its every avenue and alleyway. But from a few thousand feet up, I could see that it was all just a little island in a vast and unfamiliar landscape. On the plasma screen in my suite, I could see the city I was bound for, Dubai—self-proclaimed land of make-believe—a city with ski slopes in the desert and sheiks in limousines, a city where the hotels kept leopards in cages in their lobbies and gave themselves seven stars out of five. A city where no one expected anything to be true.

But all of that is another story, and I can see you are getting tired. Get your new wife to bed. There is a lot to see and do around here. Maybe we'll meet again tomorrow night. Maybe I'll continue with the truth. Maybe I won't. Would you know either way? Would you care, truly? Or perhaps I'll be long gone by then; who can say? We're all just travelers, after all, telling stories, passing time. Get some rest, then. Tomorrow could bring anything. Al Wada'—good-night.

7

Outis

> "The far east. Lovely spot it must be: the garden of the world, big lazy
> leaves to float about on, cactuses, flowery meads, snaky lianas they call
> them. Wonder is it like that. Those Cinghalese lobbing around in the sun,
> *in dolce far niente*. Not doing a hand's turn all day. Sleep six months out
> of twelve. Too hot to quarrel. Influence of the climate. Lethargy.
> Flowers of idleness."
>
> —JAMES JOYCE, *ULYSSES*

With only ten minutes left before my train leaves toward Sigiriya, I jam down on the Necto-soda-sticky keys of the Internet café computer. As quickly as possible, I pound out the final lines of a truly ponderous conclusive paragraph:

> The essay's closing image of a young George Orwell laughing with British soldiers and Burmese natives while the man they've just executed hangs "a hundred yards away" is surely a haunting vision of the colonial world order: oppressor and oppressed amicably sharing a Lethean drink, while the unnamed voice of dissent swings ominously in the winds.

I hit Save, double-check my PayMeNow account, and then click Send. In a millionth of an instant, my impenetrable thirty-five-page wall of rhetoric is dissembled into hexadecimal electrons and fired off into the stratosphere—bounced down thirty-five hundred miles clockwise around the globe and into the high-tech library of the Shanghai International Students' School, where an obese and princely little Chinese boy who goes by "simon/西蒙" has been waiting eagerly for his midterm assignment. I've never met this particular Simon personally, of course, but after teaching for several years at a school in Dubai, attended primarily by the hashish-addled children of the House of Saud, I've come to know his type quite well. During my teaching days I had often wondered how my students managed to turn in shining theses that included words like *hegemonic* and *pedagogical*, or even *agitprop* and *autarky*. It didn't take long to figure out that most of them had anonymous Internet ghostwriters cranking out every paper they turned in. So when being a teacher finally lost its charm, I decided that taking up professional plagiarism could grant me decent pay, freedom to travel, and unlimited opportunity to lob my own thought-grenades into the halls of academia. In just a year at it, I'd traveled the Mediterranean, been through Singapore and Hong Kong. I'd visited every single European nation (except for Luxembourg)—all while writing somewhere on the order of two thousand pages of literary criticism, disseminated happily into the thesis collections of universities worldwide.

I feel a fleeting sense of pride over the Orwell paper. I'd managed to take his tidy essay "A Hanging," which clocks in at about five pages, and spin out seven times that length in tedious, diligent analysis. Thinking it may be a personal best for me, I take a long sip at my cold tea in self-congratulation. With what Simon was paying me, I'd have enough money to roam north into the central region of Sri Lanka for at least a week. I could drop into Buddhist temples, get lost in Ceylon tea farms, and enjoy the unique charms of this land: *Serendib*, the Arabs called it, and from there the British colonialists invented the word *serendipity*, to explain the magical ways in which the invisible cogs of fate itself seemed to turn against one another in this verdant paradise.

I stretch back. I peer through the glass walls of the café and out into the station. I have always done my best work in crowded transportation hubs. Airports, train stations—a bus stop, one time—these have been like my personal little cafés dotted along the Seine. I'd given up on being a writer, aside from the essays that I sold to my shadowy students around the globe. I'd become accustomed to a certain lifestyle—particularly when it came to traveling through these third-world countries. I'm trying to see the world and as many of its plenty-splendored wonders as I can. I'm trying to stay on the move. I'm not one of these typical Americans, mind you, trying to *find myself*. No, if anything, it's just the opposite. I'm trying to get as far away from myself as at all possible.

Typically, my students are the children of the well-to-do; the heirs apparent of the world, who are too busy spending their parents' money on the beaches of Ibiza and in the shops of Rodeo Drive to learn how to compose a thesis. And why should they? What possible use will it be to them to be able to deconstruct a Dickens novel when they're merrily employed by some white-collar firm, overseeing the outsourcing of its customer service department to the east side of Bangladesh?

Actually, a lot, probably.

But I digress. Eight minutes left until my train leaves.

The Colombo Fort Railway Station has truly come alive while I've been working my way through the wee hours. I can smell cardamom coffee and *moong kavun* oil cakes being fried up in the shape of diamonds. Somewhere someone is mixing up some fragrant mutton rolls and I wonder if I'll have time to grab one on my way over to the train. I still have seven minutes. Anxiously, I tap on the keys as if to summon Simon, so he can confirm receipt of his paper and I can enjoy a week off exploring the Buddhist temples of the Matale region.

As I wait, I watch the Sri Lankans lining up along the benches in the lobby. I try to make sense of what appears at first to be a single mass of dark hair and skin and eyes. I try to drown myself in the distilled noise of their chirping chitchat. What I realize quickly is that nearly all of them are *reading*. Reading *books*. An old man with a paisley necktie dangling beneath his trimmed white beard is absorbed in what looks like a detective thriller. A gaggle of boys in little purple school blazers and shorts are studying cloth-bound readers, their little heads hunched over and the odd golden epaulets on their uniformed shoulders jutting out. They look like a tiny, scholarly fighting force. An older boy with mini-dreadlocks and a tattered black BAD TO THE BONE T-shirt is flipping through an old Penguin paperback while he tries not to stare at a flock of peacock-patterned flight attendants who are picking out magazines at the newsstand nearby. While nearby India continues to slump behind the world literacy averages, the island-dwelling Sri Lankans read more than most anyone in Asia, though perhaps this is because their seventeen measly television channels are so thoroughly unentertaining. Or perhaps it is because now that—thanks to a tidy mass-slaughtering two years ago—the Sinhalese have finally ended their bloody twenty-six-year civil war with the LTTE, the Liberation Tigers of Tamil Eelam, Sri Lanka has been rated one of the world's most promising emerging markets by the Dow Jones and has just been named a 3G country by Citigroup, whatever that means. Looking out at the crowds, I can *feel* their excitement. They don't know what it all means, either, just that venture capitalism is coming soon to a theater near them. Perhaps it is because of the promise of all this growth that they are reading—boning up for the return of the imperialists. It reminds me of a T-shirt I saw on a kid a year ago when I was weekending in Turkey. GOD IS COMING the front said in bold letters, while the back warned LOOK BUSY! This is what comes to mind: the Sri Lankans *look busy*. Soon, perhaps, they'll all be rich as kings, with important-looking cell phones and Louis Vuitton purses clutching custom-sized chihuahuas. I wonder how much they'll be reading by then.

Finally, the computer blips at me.

simon/西蒙: this loks grt!!! Ooooooo shit! U gunna get me an A for sur

Wincing, I crack my fingers, check the time—only six minutes to go—and nimbly tap back a reply.

Outis/ΟΥΤΙΣ: My pleasure, Simon. Do take care now.

simon/西蒙: wait wait man i gt anuther papr. is do on nxt Saturday, what yu say, huh?

Outis/ΟΥΤΙΣ: Like I told you earlier, Simon, I will be gone all week.

Outis/ΟΥΤΙΣ: Good-bye, Simon.

simon/西蒙: WAIT dammmti! Im going to pay u doble!

Outis/ΟΥΤΙΣ: Double?

simon/西蒙: what i said

Outis/ΟΥΤΙΣ: You said "doble" which is neither an amount of money nor an adjective indicating twice the former quantity of something.

simon/西蒙: whaaaaaaaaaaaaaaaat????????

Outis/ΟΥΤΙΣ: Good-bye, Simon.

simon/西蒙: WAIT

I'm about to click off the computer screen, satisfied that poor "simon/西蒙" more than deserves to fail his next assignment, when suddenly the sweet, high pitch of American English reaches my ear. I glance up and see two female backpackers arguing just outside the door to the Internet café. The first girl is beautiful and tall, with skin that has been methodically browned at the sides of a dozen crystal-clear swimming pools between here and—I'm going to guess—Philadelphia. There's something self-assured and forlorn about her that reminds me of a Phillies fan. Her long, dark hair has clearly been carefully blow-dried and straightened that morning in one of Colombo's finer hotels. The way she teeters a little on her cork-platform sandals makes me think that she also kicked back a few minibar items while she was preening.

Her friend is shorter and fairer-skinned—actually, she's quite pale, white as blank paper—with hair as red as sweet vermouth and eyes so green that I suspect she is only a generation removed from the shores of Galway. While her friend's clothing is so sheer and sleeveless as to verge on nonexistence, this girl is wearing a high-collared linen dress that looks like it walked off the set of *Citizen Kane*, and which falls down well past her knees. She must be about a thousand degrees, and she looks miserable and lost, in a hat so ridiculously broad-brimmed that all the flies in the train station seem to think it is a runway strip. They circle around her like landing planes, to her adorable annoyance.

> simon/西蒙: where r u anywayy? Hello??
> Outis/ΟΥΤΙΣ: I'm in Sri Lanka.
> simon/西蒙: whats that
> Outis/ΟΥΤΙΣ: Look it up.
> simon/西蒙: ur funny. U going to helpme or not, what?

"Come on, Tina. Let up! I just want to get this DVD so I have something to *do* on the train!" barks the dark-haired girl, as her friend with the hat tries to wrench her out toward the main doors.

"Carsten, we have *four* minutes to get on the train!"

I check my watch quickly and verify that I, too, have only four minutes to get on my train, which means that their train is probably also my train. I wonder if they, too, are on their way north toward the ancient city of Sigiriya, the Buddhist mountain monastery known as the Fortress in the Sky.

"Just let me grab the DVD!" Carsten begs, snatching one of the cardboard-wrapped packages off the rack, which nearly tips over before the newsstand keeper manages to catch it. A barrel-bellied man with little hair left does not even dare to shout at the girls, though he does look around in astonishment toward the other natives.

Curious, I watch as Tina, the girl in the hat, apologetically hands the man a few hundred rupees more than necessary for the DVD—which I can see from the cover is *Surangani, Surangani,* currently the country's most popular Bollywood love story. It's about a Tamil boy who falls in love with a forbidden Sinhalese girl. There've been posters up for it nearly everywhere I've been for the past month.

"Jesus, fine. You've got the goddamn DVD. So let's *go.*"

Tina stalks away as Carsten follows, clutching her prize to her fairly overexposed chest. With about three minutes left to go, I decide to give "simon/西蒙" the second-best news of his morning.

Outis/ΟΥΤΙΣ: Send the money to the PayMeNow account. DOUBLE.

simon/西蒙: yaaaaaaaaaaaaaaaaayyyyyy thank you thank you

Outis/ΟΥΤΙΣ: Now, Simon, I'm in a hurry.

simon/西蒙: ok ok

Outis/ΟΥΤΙΣ: What's the assignment anyway?

simon/西蒙: Papr for Modrn America Lit.

Outis/ΟΥΤΙΣ: On anything in particular, Simon? Hurry hurry.

simon/西蒙: hold on, just chking the books name now I hve in my email smwhere

Outis/ΟΥΤΙΣ: You have one minute, Simon, and then I have to go.

These Simons are all alike. A few months ago, before heading to Sri Lanka from Chennai, I'd been doing some Internet research for one of them about the Tamil Tigers and came across a funny story that stuck with me. Allegedly, back in the late 1980s, some government wildlife official had given a televised interview explaining that, despite the name of the rebel group, the tiger was actually not indigenous to Sri Lanka—in fact there were no tigers there at all. Accidentally, the man misspoke and said that the "*kotiyā*," which was actually the Sinhala word for "leopard," was not native to the island.

But, of course there *are* leopards in Sri Lanka—the Sri Lankan leopard, or *Panthera pardus kotiyā*, has been a recognized subspecies since the 1950s. And so, the confused English media translated the word as "tiger" anyway. Somehow, some way, this misnomer had actually stuck. Slowly, the Sri Lankan people just began to use "*kotiyā*" to mean "tiger." Nobody wanted to be wrong. They'd seen it on television; it had to be true. Eventually locals began to refer colloquially to the Tamil Tigers as "*koti*," the plural of "*kotiyā*," and, another word, "*diviyā*," had to be reassigned to mean "leopard" in order to end the confusion.

Spots changed into stripes. All it took was just one serendipitous mistake.

When I look back at the screen I see that thirty seconds have gone by. Finally, *blip*, I see Simon's money arrive in my PayMeNow account. Enough to keep me quite comfortable on my journey northward— maybe even enough to make it two or three weeks before I need to be on a computer again.

I count off five, ten, then twenty more seconds, but he still hasn't sent the assignment over.

Outis/ΟΥΤΙΣ: You're out of time, Simon. Find someone else.
simon/西蒙: wait wait! its some book. Nothing Sacred. Jeffrey Oakes?
U know it?

The flash of that name on the screen stings me more sharply than Simon's offensively bad grammar. I don't know why I'm so surprised— the book's been everywhere for eight years now: an international best-seller, translated into thirty-seven languages. No matter where I have gone, and I've gone far, I find remaindered hardcovers and tattered paperbacks in every used-book bin I've peered into. From Eastern Europe to Cambodia. But now, somehow knowing that they're teaching it in schools is an especially great blow. Isn't that how it happens? Just one tidy step closer to immortality? I continue staring at the little pixilated letters, and I can hear the ticking of my wristwatch. Suddenly my eyes refocus and I catch my reflection in the screen. Hollow, tired eyes. A beard that hasn't been trimmed in two weeks, maybe three. It hardly looks like me.

Then, before I quite know what has happened, my fingers have flown to the disconnect button and I am running, running to catch my train.

Our train prowls slowly up out of Colombo, through the slums and then the suburbs, and eventually into the monsoon-swept rain forests to the north. I've paid the extra 1,600 rupees, about 14 dollars, to get a seat in the small first-class observation compartment in the rear, where I also find the lovely Carsten and her friend, Tina. The fourth seat in the compartment is empty for a few minutes, until we are joined by, of all people, an old Italian nun in a crisp black habit.

The girls seem just as tickled as I am to be in the nun's tiny wizened presence. She is reading a little blue-covered Bible, written in Italian from what I can see. I wonder if she ever reads anything else? Does she just read those same best-stories-ever-told over and over? Does she ever take a quick break and dip into, I don't know, some Calvino or something? I ponder this singular commitment as I flip lazily through a collection of Hemingway stories that I found in my hotel back in Chennai. I haven't read most of them since my freshman year of college, and it's nice, if not a little nostalgia inducing, to look over them again.

Aside from the advantages of comfort, with individual armchairs and air-conditioning, we've all more or less wasted our money on the observation car. It has been raining for four weeks, as long as I've been off the mainland of India, and there's not much to observe. Great, god-enraged gusts of wind carry down opaque curtains of gray rain. Beyond it, the dense, dark verdigris of rubber trees has grown back with a vengeance over the old British plantations. Occasionally we pass low stretches of tea trees, which curve and wriggle over the hills like hedge mazes in a Victorian garden or the wormy gyri of a brain. But most of the time the rain hides all but the nearest-reaching branches.

Carsten happily passes the first hour of our journey with her headphones clamped on, watching her movie on a little portable DVD player. Tina, meanwhile, flips through the *New York Times* International Edition. My heart leaps suddenly, when I see LUXEMBOURG in a headline as she turns the page, but it is only an article about a soccer game. I manage to catch that they lost 0–5, and that there is no photograph with the story of, perhaps, some members of the royal family in attendance— then Tina looks up and catches me looking, and I glance away at the nun as a diversion. To my surprise, the nun has set down her Bible and taken out a cellular telephone—an ancient model roughly the size of a brick—and she is punching buttons on it, trying to get a signal. When I look up at Tina again, I can see she is smirking but trying to pretend not to look at me. Still, I know how this game goes. She'll crack first; she's too curious not to.

It happens ten minutes later when, as we roll into a clearing, a far-off mountain range comes into view, and we both look up suddenly to take in the sight.

"They look like white elephants," Tina says to me smartly.

"I'm sorry?"

"The hills." She nods at my Hemingway. "'Hills Like White Elephants'?"

I look down at the book and then skeptically back out the window. "I think those are more like mountains than hills."

"Semantics," she scoffs. "You're from the States?"

"Maybe," I say with a smile. "And you?"

"I'm from Boston," she says. Then, thumbing at her friend, she says, "She's a Philly girl."

I smile at Carsten, who blinks up at me through heavy lashes and then back down at her DVD player. She hits Pause with a manicured nail and then pulls the headphones delicately away from her carefully straightened hair. She smiles with teeth so perfect that they're utterly unnatural. There's not a chance they haven't been braced and bleached.

"Carsten Chanel," she says, extending a hand to shake mine lazily. It's the fakest fake name I've ever heard in my life, and the look on Tina's face confirms my suspicions.

With a much more aggressive shake, Tina introduces herself, "Christina Elizabeth Edgars-Boyleston."

"My name is Outis," I say.

"Otis?" Carsten laughs.

"*Ow*-tis," I enunciate. I'm about to explain that it's Greek when Tina says, surprisingly, "That's an old Greek name. Right?"

Caught off guard, I stare into her great green eyes. Like cat's eyes, I think. I wonder what she thinks of mine.

"That's right," I say.

"We've both been living in Manhattan for *years* now," Carsten explains with a dramatically bored flip of her hand. Since they are in their late twenties at most, I'm guessing that they were Barnard students who stuck around after graduation.

"Manhattan! I've never been," I lie.

"You'd *love* it, Outis," Carsten says.

"If it's so great then why aren't you there now?" I ask.

Carsten smiles and attempts to look mysterious. "We thought we'd take some time off from our careers and, you know, *find* ourselves."

"Any leads so far?" I ask.

Carsten looks confused; Tina snorts and hides a smirk behind a pale hand.

"Is that supposed to be funny?" Carsten asks.

I back down graciously. "My apologies. It's been a long time since I've had a real conversation with anybody but myself."

Carsten seems to consider this, but fortunately we are interrupted by a knock at the door and a tall Sri Lankan boy enters pushing a cart. He is maybe sixteen and wears a golden traditional-looking uniform. "Excuse me, please. Stuffed fig? *Bibikkan?* Pastry?"

"Drinks?" Carsten asks immediately. The boy nods his head.

"Portello soda and vodka?" Carsten orders.

I like the lovely little lilt of her *"vah-kah?"* though I immediately gag at the mention of the purple, hypersugary berry-and-cream-flavored soda brought over long ago by the Brits and gleefully sold now by the Coca-Cola corporation. I think I can see the guy gag, too, as he bends down to prepare the drinks. There's something about the way he moves, actually. Cocky, smooth motions that belie the somewhat nervous look in his eyes. He reminds me of a boy I used to know, when I was his age, when I strung rackets at a Carolina country club.

"Arrack and ginger beer," Tina orders. The boy nods approvingly, and I must concur. It is an excellent combination.

I see that the boy is drinking a thick, milky syrup from a small glass on the edge of the cart.

"Toddy for me," I say, pointing to his glass.

The boy balks. "No, no, man. You don't want toddy."

"I do," I say. "I'm sure. Don't worry."

"Outis, do you mind if I ask . . . what's a toddy?" Tina is eager eyed.

"It's kind of like the arrack but not as refined. Basically it's a wine made fresh from palm sap. Sort of local swill. Usually they don't have it on the trains, but our friend here has some stashed down there, I can see it."

"Two of those then," Tina says.

"No no no no," the boy laughs. "Not for ladies!"

Tina takes direct affront to this. "*Yes*, for ladies. Come on! You think I can't handle it? Let's go. You and me, kid!"

The boy, delighted, reaches down for a repurposed soda bottle and pours out three glasses. The nun has stopped playing with her cellular phone and is now watching us with very curious amusement from behind her round-rimmed glasses.

"That looks *foul*," Carsten weighs in as the boy passes the cups. The liquid inside vaguely resembles detergent.

"The Tamil people have this book of little parables in couplets," I say to Tina, "called the *Thirukkural* . . . "

"*Thirukkural*," the boy whispers happily. "You have read?"

"Parts," I say, pinching my fingers together to indicate a small amount. Then, back to Tina, I explain, "There's a whole chapter called 'The Abhorrence of Toddy.'"

Tina's great green eyes are fixed wide, with curiosity befitting a jungle cat. I certainly do like a girl who appreciates a forbidden drink. Meanwhile, Carsten has begun holding her nose against the smell.

Our glasses in hand, the boy whispers, "Cheers!" We toss back the toddy. It is coconut sour and yeasty sweet, and it chills and burns like liquid nitrogen going down our throats. The kid is pouring out three more before Tina has stopped coughing. There is a wide smile on the little nun's face, and it just about makes me want to ask her to join us.

"Grrr-*oss*," Carsten pronounces as she sips her drink. The purple seems to stick to her teeth just slightly.

"So you two have been, what? Eating, praying, loving?"

"Something like that," Tina answers with a smirk, and is about to say more but, predictably, Carsten has become tired of not being the center of attention.

"Have you ever been in a threesome, Outis?" she asks daringly.

Tina squeaks unhappily and looks awkwardly at the nun, who does not seem to understand anything we're saying.

"Once," I say, "but it was the wrong kind."

Carsten doesn't know quite what to do with this, and as she puzzles over it, I ask, "And so what do you guys do back in New York?"

"She edits books and stuff. *I* work in public relations," Carsten says, leaning forcefully past her friend and—in what I suspect is a well-practiced accident—allows the sleeves of her blouse to fall down so that her bra straps show. A bright, pleasant mango color.

"Really?" I say. "Is that like advertising?"

"*No!*" Carsten asserts suddenly. She unrolls a speech she has doubtless given before. "Advertising is just, like, when you're promoting a product, or a company directly, in the media."

I nod as if I'm interested. Tina flips back to her newspaper. Carsten finishes her sugary drink in an instant and orders a second *and* a third before the boy can escape our car.

"Public *relations* is when you're actually shaping the company's entire image. Like, you might spend a lot of time online posting, like, positive *reviews* of the company on different forums, and making sure their Google searches aren't, like, *negative*."

"Wow," I say, and I guess I don't sound impressed enough because Carsten redoubles her efforts.

"Or we might *lobby* for them so that local government stuff works out the way they want it to. Back before I started working for this company, we had this pharmaceutical client that makes—you know Lotosil?"

I know the name quite well. It was one of the many prescriptions that had populated Jeffrey's medicine cabinet.

"So, like, it's like *awesome* at helping people with depression. But—big problem—everyone already knows that if you're depressed you take Prozac, right? I mean, that's just branding. So what they did was they lobbied the AMA to create this *new* diagnosis for 'societal apprehensiveness disorder' so, like, Lotosil could be the drug for *that*."

I blink two, three times, waiting for her to continue, but she's reached the punch line. I try not to look aghast, and Tina is now smirking at *me*.

"That's . . . so *interesting*," I manage.

But what I am thinking is that this airhead has just told me that she, or at least her international corporation of airheads, has invented a disease. A disease with the repulsively clever acronym of SAD, all so as to increase sales of a drug, one that Jeffrey took for years. Years during which he, yes, wrote an international bestselling novel, but also years during which his depression, or his "societal apprehensiveness," was pretty damn high, considering that I was one of two human beings on the planet whom he could halfway stand. It seems unconscionable that Carsten and her PR cronies have perpetrated this falsehood, and that's coming from a guy who plagiarizes people's papers for them.

"Plus, like, you call other businesses and try to, like, *promote* whatever your client is doing and, like, build some *buzz* around it. One of *my* first projects was this book—"

And then, before I can quite catch up to what's happened, she reaches into Tina's bag and pulls out a paperback copy of *Nothing Sacred*.

"That's *mine*," Tina snaps, though she does not stop Carsten from handing it to me. I run my hands over the familiar title; note the immense number of dog-eared pages. Many pages are also half blue with underlining, with notes in the margins.

"It's actually how Carsten and I met," Tina explains. "I worked on the book right when I started at Haslett and Grouse."

I stare awkwardly at the author photo on the back. There is Jeffrey, frozen in black-and-white, looking somehow warmer and friendlier and happier than I've ever seen him look in his entire life. He looks like he'd just love to be your best friend, with invitingly big eyes and a half smile, as if he's just now thought of something amusing and wants to share it with you and only you.

Right after the book had come out, he'd stopped giving interviews, quit his teaching job at Iowa after three days, and effectively disappeared. Christ, the thought of Jeffrey in Iowa! A story about him would sometimes catch my eye as I hopped around the Internet researching students' papers. Someone would snap a photograph of Jeffrey exiting a Bavarian coffee shop, or walking a strange dog in a park in Portugal. Someone would have snuck onto the property his parents owned in Surrey, where he was alleged to be staying—writing his *Ulysses*, they all hoped—and the mystery would suddenly be reignited. It hadn't taken long before websites emerged, dedicated to his whereabouts, great Wiki-landscapes of facts and fictions and, worst of all, *fantasies*—tales told by lovers of both genders, of their torrid evenings in Jeffrey's embrace. The one I'd glanced at was so rife with un-Jeffrey-like details that there was no doubt in my mind it was utter nonsense. But always I had the creeping worry of how horrified Jeffrey would be if he ever read a word of it. I was grateful that he'd never been very good with computers.

"You edited this?" I ask.

"Sort of," Tina says, almost a little embarrassed. "Officially it was my boss's book, you know? Russell Haslett? He's like the main big-shot editor in chief. But I did a lot of the actual work."

Carsten doesn't care. "Right, yeah, and I used to work for this super-small company that, like, took on the publicity once it started getting kind of big. Of course this was before he went totally fucking *bonkers*."

"He didn't go *bonkers*," Tina says defensively. "I used to talk to him on the phone—"

She breaks off again and looks down at the book. I wonder if she's gotten her hands on anything as good in all the years since she began. I wonder if this is why she's here, now, on an extended leave from Mr. Haslett's offices, only to "find herself" stuck in Sri Lanka in a monsoon with Carsten "Chanel."

Carsten is happy to have someone new to gossip with. "I heard he turned into like a Buddhist-Scientologist. And that he, like, saves his used pen nibs in jars. And that this one time he actually got in a *fistfight* with this Olympic runner, what was his name . . . Mitchell-something . . ."

Just as I am about to slip up and snap that they had never actually come to *blows*, Tina turns to Carsten and says, "Would you please please please please please please please stop talking?"

Not aware that her friend is once again plagiarizing "Hills Like White Elephants," Carsten snaps, *"Fine!"* and puts her headphones back on.

"You did a hell of a job," I say quietly to Tina. I turn Jeffrey's book over in my hands. "Editing it, I mean."

"How would you know?" she says, sipping on her second toddy.

Because, I want to say, *I'm probably the only other person in the whole world who read every tattered, tangled draft—more drafts than even you read, probably. Talk about serendipity. Jeffrey wrote it in* our *kitchen, drinking the booze that* I'd *picked up when he couldn't bear to go outside, wearing the slippers he* thought *were his except that* I *bought them the weekend we drove down to Delaware*—only I don't get to say any of this, because before I can decide if I should admit to being who I am, the train suddenly and sharply stops moving.

Carsten screams as she tumbles out of her seat, tangled in her headphone wires, her third drink spilling all over her blouse.

Tina doesn't even scream as she flies from her seat, but she clutches *Nothing Sacred* to her chest as if she might shield it from harm.

And I? I grab the nun. I don't know why, but I throw my arms in front of her little old holy bones and keep her from hitting the seat in front of us. She screams, *"Gesù Cristo! Madre di Dio! Maria! Maria!"*

When the world has gone still again, I let her go. She looks completely frightened, and so completely relieved that she has not died. And though my own head missed the pole of the luggage rack by only an inch, maybe two, I never felt scared and I don't, now, feel any relief. I can't remember the last time I felt truly scared for my life—or relieved to be alive, for that matter. Here I am, a man with no faith in any afterlife, who makes his living by helping others cheat, and who last saw his soul on the other side of the Atlantic. And here she is, frantic tears wetting the insides of her glasses, a woman who has dedicated her life to God and who has lived accordingly. But she loves this life and does not want to see it go. And I?

"Holy *shit!*" Carsten coughs; the headphone cord has half strangled her.

"Is everyone OK?" I ask.

"I'm OK," Tina says softly, and checks the book to ensure that it is, too.

"Bless you, bless you, bless you," the nun praises between breaths, rubbing my face with her wrinkled, soft hands.

"No problem," I say, pulling away from her. I don't know why.

She immediately begins crossing herself vigorously and clasping her hands together, praying in Latin, if I'm not mistaken. *"Credo in Deum Patrem omnipotentem, Creatorem caeli et terrae, et in Iesum Christum, Filium Eius unicum, Dominum nostrum . . . "*

Carsten suddenly looks down at the purple that covers her blouse and wails, "Look at my *shirt!*" She grabs her bag and runs away to change in a huff.

As I help Tina to her feet, she tries to uncrush her hat. I take it from her and fold it back into shape with my hands, and she seems grateful.

Then, suddenly, she says, "Your name's not really Outis, is it?"

I think about denying it, but the look in her eyes tells me that she's already guessed where I stole it from. Then she explains my own reference to me.

"Odysseus, after he rescues his men from the Land of the Lotus Eaters, is captured by Polyphemus the Cyclops. And Polyphemus says that if Odysseus tells him his name then he'll eat him last. So Odysseus says—"

"Outis," I interject. "That's my name—Outis. So my mother and father call me, and all my friends."

"Outis," she says with a grin. "Which means, 'Nobody.' And so later when Odysseus blinds him, Polyphemus wails out to the other Cyclopses—"

"'Outis! Outis is killing me!'" I interrupt with a chuckle. "And so they think that he must be being killed by the gods, and so they don't even attempt to help him."

Tina claps her hands happily.

"And you must know all about Poe, then, right?"

I shrug. Her green eyes, again, grow wide with delight. I find myself thinking that I would never grow tired of watching them. "So Poe had this big problem with Longfellow," she said. "He thought he was a terrible poet, even though he sold, like, one hundred times the number of books of poetry that Poe was selling at the time. Poe didn't like that Longfellow had basically married into money and gotten a cushy Harvard professorship—"

"While Poe was broke and . . . trying to marry his fourteen-year-old cousin?"

"This is before that, I think. But yes, very broke. So, Poe wrote this article claiming that Longfellow had ripped off Tennyson in this poem about the end of the year being like a dying old man. He called it 'barefaced and barbarous plagiarism.' And Longfellow doesn't really care. He's, like, 'I'm Longfellow. Nobody's ever heard of you, Poe.'"

Despite everything, I'm laughing. Her Poe imitation winds up sounding like Groucho Marx, while her Longfellow sounds vaguely like Charlton Heston.

"So Poe keeps going on and on about this. And pretty much nobody cares. And then he publishes *The Raven* and still nobody really cares, until this mysterious guy named 'Outis' starts to publish these articles defending Longfellow against Poe's plagiarism charges . . . by analyzing

The Raven and showing how Poe does the same thing . . . takes ideas and images from other poets. And suddenly, because there's this controversy, people start to read *The Raven* and Poe starts to get famous, finally."

"So who was Outis?" I ask.

"I don't know," she teases. "Who *are* you?"

Suddenly I'm somewhere between telling her everything and kissing her. Troubled by this rush of confessional impulses, I clear my throat and glance awkwardly over at the nun, who is now done praying and back on her cellular brick, speaking in anxious Italian to whoever is on the other end. I look down at the DVD screen. There is a riotous dance number going on around an elephant, and a Sinhalese woman is dramatically being tossed to-and-fro between a prince and her Tamil suitor. Looking back into Tina's green eyes, I feel my heart begin to pound in a rhythm it hasn't known for some time now.

Tina acquiesces. "They think it may have been Poe himself, drumming up a little good PR for *The Raven*."

Just as I am about to kiss Tina, she turns away from me and looks toward the window. I follow her emerald gaze and see that just a little ways away, to the left of the train, a camouflage-painted Jeep has parked on a little dirt road that leads back into the rain forest. Several official-looking men wearing dark rain ponchos, with what appear to be military uniforms underneath, have hopped out of the Jeep. Some have bushy black mustaches and others are barely grown boys, but they all have guns that glisten wickedly in the rain.

Before Tina or I know quite what to say, the door to our car opens. We turn, thinking that maybe it is Carsten coming back from changing her blouse. But instead we see the young man who served us our drinks. I assume he's come to ensure that we are all right, but once he comes in, he yanks off his golden uniform and looks anxiously at me.

"Please please. Can you give me your jacket?"

"My jacket?" I say, looking down at the brown tweed Brooks Brothers coat that I've been wearing for so long that I fear it's begun to grow fur.

"Please. Please. My friend. Please."

With the nun looking at me, and not entirely sure what else to do, I take off my jacket and hand it to the boy. He throws it on and then looks desperately at Tina. "Your book, please. Can I hold your book?"

Tina looks unhappy about this but hands the boy the book and then, her hat. He accepts it with a flood of Tamil that we cannot quite translate but which feels like thank-yous—and then he quickly sits down in the right-hand corner of the observation car and tries to take up as little room as possible. He hides his head behind the open book so that he seems like an innocuous student, trying to study. It's not much of a disguise, I think.

"What's he doing?" Tina hisses.

"Hiding," I say quietly. "I'm not really sure why. Except that I think our friend is Tamil."

"But I thought the civil war ended."

"They never end," I say, thinking back on my relatively civilized area of Charlotte, in North Carolina, where my neighbors had Confederate-flag bumper stickers and our landlord had DON'T TREAD ON ME tattooed between his shoulder blades. We learned about "The War of Northern Aggression" in school, and instead of Martin Luther King Jr. Day, we had off from school in honor of Robert E. Lee. I'm about to tell Tina all this, but it's been so long since I told anyone anything resembling the truth. The last time I can remember is a story I told a couple in a Dubai bar, and then it was only because I'd had three more cocktails than I ought to have had.

Slowly Tina and I take our seats and pretend to be watching Carsten's DVD—which seems like the most unassumingly American thing to be doing.

"She loves this stupid movie," Tina mutters.

"She's seen it before?" I say in surprise.

"It was on television in the hotel the other night when she was too hungover to go out. The main guy is Tamil. He's very poor but he's been sent to the big city full of Sinhalese, so he can learn to be a painter. Have you seen this thing they do here where they highlight the frescoes in their temples with gold leaf?"

I cough in surprise and then study the little screen closely, watching as the Tamil boy paints gold onto the horns of a strange minor deity on the wall of a Buddhist temple. There is a crack in the wall, and he suddenly notices a great brown eye staring through it at him. The music swells so loudly that we can hear it through the headphones on the floor.

"And there's the girl he's in love with. She's Sinhalese, from a very rich family. And she's supposed to marry this member of the former royal family in Anuradhapura, of course, but she's in love with painter boy."

I watch closely as they sing to each other through the hole in the wall. Once, long ago, I wrote a novel with this exact moment in it. The only copy I had had been destroyed, though this moment and some surrounding fragments survived as part of the only story I'd ever published, in a tiny literary review. Was it possible that somehow my story had made its way into the hands of some Bollywood writer, halfway around the world? Had someone plagiarized *me*? Or had my original idea been so hackneyed and cliché that it had simply resurfaced? Could I have plagiarized it myself, from some book of myths I'd read or some film I'd seen when I was growing up? Was it still plagiarism if I'd done it unknowingly? Does it sting like this because I've been robbed or because it was never mine to steal? I watch their eyes trying to catch each other's through the tiny crack in the wall. Maybe an idea, like love, cannot ever be stolen away, just as it cannot ever have belonged to me and only me.

Just then the door opens loudly. The observation car fills quickly with mustachioed Sri Lankan soldiers. Two of them begin barking at Tina and me, "Passport, ma'am! Passport, sir! We need to see identification."

Another soldier storms over to the nun and demands she hang up her phone, which results in more frantic screeching in Italian, this time it sounds more like curses than blessings.

Still more soldiers are bringing the Tamil boy to his feet. Can he be even eighteen? He looks at me suddenly, with those same cocksure eyes, and as the men are pulling at him to remove my jacket, the boy does an astonishing thing. He looks away from me and back at the book in his left hand and he reads. His hazel eyes move left to right across the page. I watch his dark lips part as he sounds out the words in front of him. Given how rough his English had been earlier, I have to guess that he can understand only a fraction of what he is reading. It seems a completely insane thing to do, and the men grab him roughly for not coming easily. Why would he do it? I barely have a second to process it before the book and my coat are being thrown roughly to the floor. The soldiers rush the boy back through the open doors and then they're gone.

"What. The hell. Was *that*?" Tina says in complete disbelief.

"I'm . . . I'm sure it's nothing serious. These guys, they just act really blustery probably to scare everyone into respecting them."

"Where's Carsten?" Tina says suddenly.

"Carsten's fine," I say. "These people. Even if these are bad people, they're not going to hurt—"

Americans is about to be the next word out of my mouth, but it dies on the way up my throat.

"He looked very young," Tina says.

"I'm sure he'll be fine," I lie.

Just before the end of the civil war, when skirmishes were breaking out everywhere, the Sinhalese government rounded up native Tamil civilians into "no-fire" zones, where they were promised protection from the fighting. The concerned government then proceeded to shell the no-fire zones until they looked like the surface of the moon. Soldiers chased the survivors to the beaches and slaughtered them in the rocky surf until the water had gone red. The leaders of the Tigers turned themselves in, hoping to save the few Tamil civilians who had been captured. The Sinhalese executed every last one of these leaders and then they killed every single captured civilian.

I want to tell Tina this. Then I think maybe it's better if she doesn't know it. I wish that I could *un*-know it. I'd give all the money in my Pay-MeNow account to un-know it. The nun is praying again, crying more than she had when she thought she had nearly died. I wonder again why she felt something and I didn't. I wonder if, even believing in a better world after this one, she loves this place more than I have ever loved anything in my life. I don't know.

All I really know is that I feel something now. I feel a sinking horror as I watch the soldiers, out in the rain, shove the boy roughly into the back of the Jeep and begin to drive away. Happy music plays out of the headphones on the floor as, I presume, the Tamil boy in the movie has at last run off into the sunset with his one true love. Tina clenches at my hand and I grip her like a life raft. I tell myself that it's going to be fine, but I can't shake this horrible feeling. There was something about the way that the boy's lips were moving as he read the book. Something that made me think that he knew he was about to die. And that he wanted one of Jeffrey's lines to be the very last to pass his lips.

There is a long, long nothing, and then the train begins to move again.

8

The Doppelgänger

[He] met his own image walking in the garden. / That apparition,
sole of men, he saw. / For know there are two worlds of life and death: /
One that which thou beholdest; but the other / Is underneath the grave,
where do inhabit / The shadows of all forms that think and live, / Till
death unite them and they part no more . . .

—PERCY BYSSHE SHELLEY, *PROMETHEUS UNBOUND*

Down one lane of the bustling Kumasi Central Market I see him. Or,
rather, I see me. In the swirl of surly northern grocers and Ashanti
women with baskets on their heads and a boy who juggles for ten pesewa
pieces—there I am. Or there he is. An *obruni*. A white man. My age, in
Brooks herringbone tweed, despite the fact that in August, it is 82
degrees in Ghana. We have the same haircut. His mouth twists in the
same puzzled amusement that mine does as he inspects a smooth teak
carving of a jungle cat. I've been in Africa five weeks, which is five weeks
too long. It's the heat, surely. Or something in the food. Or whatever it is
that Tina has been rolling in her cigarettes. And last week I drank gin
with ice in it—why? Just frozen cubes of salmonella, no doubt! It is not
just that this other man is white—though there are rarely white men in
the marketplace. The tubby British tourists, the unwashed backpackers,
the dreadlocked college dropouts—they all generally avoid this place.

This is the real Kumasi. The man takes a notebook out of his left breast pocket. It is the *same* leather-bound notebook that I keep in my left breast pocket. He scribbles onto it with the same nib-point pen. *This is it,* I think, *the parasites have wormed their way into your brain, you phenomenal fool.* Christ, even our shoes are identical—weathered buck-leather tennis shoes. I haven't replaced mine in fifteen years. I've tried; they don't sell them anymore. The only difference I can seem to find is that his wristwatch is silver and mine is gold. As I'm standing there, holding a melon or something in my left hand, he turns and catches my eye. He sees me. Then he quietly turns down a side alley and disappears.

For an hour I search the endless maze of stalls, hoping to catch another glance of him. There are thousands of men and women in all directions, buying raw chicken, salted fish, shoe polish, kente fabrics, bubble gum, Oxo soap, Highlife and Gospel CDs, eggs, gasoline, and sandals printed with American flags. They're calling out in Twi and Fante. They're selling ivory crosses and Muslim headscarves and soccer balls and bags of loose tea. The marketplace is grotesque; it is enormous. Soon all I see are blurs of ebony and teak and sunbursts of textiles and I need to escape it. Somewhere there is a fair-skinned woman with a cold drink waiting for me.

Tina waits at O'Bryan's, an Irish pub not far from the market. There is something patently ridiculous about an Irish pub in the middle of Africa, and so we have made it our main base of operations. Trading in our cedis for mincemeat pies and warm Guinness, we stretch out in a dark, cool corner beneath a rotating fan and a framed blurry photograph of James Joyce, taken during his rocking-the-eye-patch period. He still wore glasses, though. There's something about that clean little lens over his blind, covered eye.

"Did you get the old man his yams?" she asks me as I stumble in and order two beers from the bar. Both are for me; Tina's on her second already.

"I didn't," I confess.

"What is the *matter* with you?" she sighs, planting a kiss on my cheek before I can wipe it clean. "We've been here five weeks and I'm about ready to die."

Tina and I are technically here on business. She, on behalf of Haslett & Grouse, international booksellers extraordinaire, wants me to write a definitive insider's biography of my former best friend, the perpetually enigmatic and bestselling novelist Jeffrey Oakes. After she and I met in Sri Lanka and spent some time touring its holy places, the lovely Ms. Tina had persuaded me—by *all* means at her disposal—that as the former roommate, confidant, and classmate of the brilliant and secretive Oakes, I had a perspective that was sorely needed. Jeffrey, sadly, had finally, completely, tragically, cracked up, and it was up to me now to tell his story.

"I'm sorry. I went to the market for them and then . . . this'll sound crazy, but I *saw* myself," I say, pausing to drink half of the first beer before continuing. "I saw a man who looked exactly like me. I mean *exactly* like me." Over the remainder of the first beer I go into detail—the haircut, the pen, the tennis shoes.

"Why do you wear those torn-up things, anyway?" she asks.

"I bought these shoes with the money I made at my first job," I say. "Restringing rackets at the West Charlotte Country Club. Growing up, I thought I'd be a tennis pro."

"I *knew* you hadn't *always* wanted to be a writer. How's your backhand these days?"

She burrows constantly—what were my parents like? what are my earliest childhood memories?—I suppose it's this inquisitive side that makes her such a good editor, but it has made her an increasingly tiresome travel companion.

"Can't malaria give you delusions? We had the last of those pills days ago. Either that or it's worms," I speculate.

"You haven't got worms," she sighs, fanning herself with the newspaper, the *New York Times* "Theater" section, in particular. I grab it from her and she grins. The American papers come only once every week or so. She watches me coyly as she rolls a fresh cigarette. She waits a minute for me to offer to light it; when I don't look up from the paper, she lights it herself.

"Well, has she got any new reviews or not?" she asks.

"She hasn't performed since—. She hasn't performed in nine years," I remind her.

"Well, she's busy with her billionaire," Tina sighs. "What is he, the prince of Yugoslavia or something?"

"Or something."

I could tell her that it's Luxembourg, actually—what would the harm be? Would it perhaps get her off my case for a few more hours? But something keeps holding me back from telling her my past. If I tell her one detail, she'll just want another—one about Jeffrey, or our college, or my mother. I still have not even told Tina my real name. A part of me wants to trust her, but I haven't trusted anyone with these things in nearly a decade. I barely trust myself with that information anymore.

She goes on. "Isn't Yugoslavia not even a country anymore? How can you be the prince of a country that no longer exists? I expect it must take a good deal of effort, lording over an imaginary country."

Tina stares at me with those bewitching green eyes. "She could have done better," she tells me, placing a desert-roughened hand on mine. She thinks she means me, but she doesn't know me. She weaves her fingers in between mine and grips like a vise.

"No doubt," I say, pulling my hand away. "There must be all kinds of real countries with princes still out there."

She laughs. "So. Tell me about wanting to be a tennis pro."

I scrunch up my face for a minute, for I feel that the memories are deeply buried somewhere and it will take time to unearth them. To my surprise, they're not—they're still right there at the forefront of my mind.

"There was this kid, in my hometown, named Henry Waterford. Everybody loved him. He was funny, and his family was rich. I guess you could say he was sort of the de facto king of our school. But he was nice about it. He'd charm all the teachers, beat up the bullies, and tell you if your underwear was showing or something, but quietly. Nicely, you know? And his sister was this beautiful . . . "

Tina's eyes glow like jade, and I have to swallow a lot of beer in order to change directions. She's already read the story I wrote about this, a long time ago. She found the whole damned novella in my luggage one night. I woke to find her there, half dressed in the African moonlight, poring over the pages, chewing on her hair. Now she always tries to get me to tell her how true those stories really are. She likes to see if she can trick me into forgetting the little details I changed.

"Anyway, he was the big man around town. Around all of West Charlotte, really. And I wanted to be just like him. I took a job stringing rackets so I could buy clothes as nice as Henry's. Then I joined the school team. I wanted to do everything he did."

"That's adorable," Tina laughs, as if she thinks it's silly. But she feels she is making progress. She thinks she is coming closer to figuring me out. "Whatever happened to Henry Waterford, then? I bet he's not a globe-trotting writer like you."

"He got slammed in the head with a tennis racket. Some brain damage. Never was the same after that," I say.

"Just like in your novella?" she asks softly. "You said you made that up?"

I don't remember what I said. She doesn't understand that the things I've made up are more real to me now than whatever used to be true.

We drink in silence. Time passes strangely in Africa. When we arrived, in our safari gear, we thought we'd be like Bogey and Hepburn; she'd be irascible and I'd be thick-skinned, and we'd play games with each other for a while before falling madly in love during a vulnerable moment on a steamboat ride down the Nile. Instead, we're here talking about what I keep trying to forget.

"So a doppelgänger?" she asks, finally changing the subject. "Or a *vardøger* . . . "

"Excuse me?"

"Well, if you were Norwegian, you'd believe in *vardøgers*—a sort of glimpse of yourself in the future, doing everything you're going to do in advance. Are you Norwegian?"

Oh, how she *pries*! Like a little insect, trying to find some purchase—some hole that she can nestle into.

"If you were German then it'd be a sign of bad luck."

"Not Norwegian *or* German," I snap. "And we can hardly have *more* bad luck."

"You *could*," she says drily. "It's supposed to be a portent of your own death. Elizabeth I saw herself lying on her own bed. Later that night she died in her sleep. And then Donne? John Donne? He saw his wife's right before she had a miscarriage."

"'Mark but this flea, and mark in this . . .'" I proclaim, the words coming back to me from a freshman seminar, long ago. Rising up from our booth with beer mug in hand, I wave it out to the room. "'How little that which thou deny'st me is; Me it suck'd first, and now sucks thee. And in this flea our two bloods mingled be . . .'"

The bartender shouts something like "Oi!" at me and tells me to sit. The yellowed eyes of four dusty Ghanaian guys all level at me. They are trying to watch a soccer match, can't I see that? Tina gives me a small sarcastic clap as I sit back down.

"Did you and Jeffrey used to recite poetry together?" she asks, relentless. "Was that how you used to get the princess into bed?"

I ding an imaginary bell on the bar table. "Check, please."

"Oh, quit it. Just a joke. I'd have held out longer, is all I'm saying, if I knew you recited poetry."

I give her a skeptical look. Tina and I had leaped into bed together the first night we'd known each other, after a train ride that had left us both on edge. Maybe that was the problem. Maybe it had just been too easy. Maybe she was still simply *too* available.

"Oh! I almost forgot! Wilkie Collins!"

"Everyone always forgets Wilkie Collins," I quip.

"No, I mean for *doppelgängers*. Supposedly he kept seeing a 'Ghost Wilkie' running around London for ten years, on and off."

"Well, that was probably on account of all of the laudanum."

"And wasn't there a story about Shelley . . . "

"Stop it," I groan. "I don't want to hear about Shelley. I'm *dying*."

She pats my hand again. "You're not going to die. Not unless I kill you for making me stay here another week. Now let's find the old man some yams."

And with an apologetic clink of our glasses, we exit O'Bryan's and venture back to the dreaded marketplace. All the while I am scanning the strangers around me for some sign of myself.

Jeffrey Oakes, author of the luminous *Nothing Sacred*, has made no media appearances, given not a single interview—even to Oprah—and has accepted not a single prize or honor in nine years, though he's won several. For those somehow unfamiliar, *Nothing Sacred* had the rare quality of seeming like a classic on the day it was first printed, with a clever consortium of low-lying postmodern puzzles to occupy the highbrow and heartfelt hijinks to captivate the lowbrow. It is the rare sort of book that resembles nothing else and yet somehow seems intensely familiar. From the first line you feel your own heart begin to beat differently. Once it's over you want to begin it again. It is a love letter; it is an atom bomb; it is literature we'd forgotten could be written.

Only now, after eight years with no follow-up, eager critics have begun to claim that Jeffrey's relentless dedication to his art must have pushed him over the brink—that the pressure to measure up to *Nothing Sacred* has undone its creator. Certain loyal factions speculate that he is, actually, hiding away only to create more of a frenzy about his next novel. If he is, it certainly appears to be working: the latté-shop gossip rages on. Some believe Oakes is merely doing research and that he is furiously crafting his next masterpiece in a padded room somewhere. Others believe that it is all a stunt. Some believe that he's gone full-Salinger; that he will never resurface, not even if they give him the Booker Prize for the next book—which most everyone agrees it was a *crime* that he did not win last time, despite the fact that he has not lived in England for nearly twenty-five years, and though he was born there, even his parents have now officially relocated to France. I wonder if I'll dash his chances when I verify, in the tenth chapter of his biography, that he once flung his EU passport into the Hudson, to protest the cancellation of his favorite BBC children's television program. Still, each month *Nothing Sacred* remains on the bestseller lists and the flames are fueled further.

This is why my editor has brought me here to the Gold Coast—to the "White Man's Grave"—to the "least-failed state" in Africa: the Republic of Ghana, where the oldest of the Oakes still resides. Jeremiah Oakes, Jeffrey's beloved grandfather, lives thirty miles outside of Kumasi, near the sacred Lake Bosumtwi, where Jeffrey spent his childhood summers playing around in the catacomb of Ghanaian gold mines, which had been in his family's possession since colonial days.

Now the mines are run by the KMS Mining Corporation, and Jeremiah Oakes remains only because he refuses to go. He has lived in Africa nearly all his life, and I imagine he'd prefer to die there than leave. As Jeffrey's first exposure to the literary dimensions, the old man is all I need to fill in the last remaining sections of my illuminating biography— for which the world waits impatiently. This has unfortunately proved more difficult than I anticipated.

As I come up the long driveway to the Oakes Mines & Estate, my driver, Kojo, swerves his rusty Hyundai to avoid an incoming rifle shot. A hundred yards away, on his sagging porch, Jeremiah Oakes wobbles from the blowback of his ancient firearm. Fortunately, he is almost as blind as he is senile. Before he can regain his footing and reload the rifle, I am out of the car rushing at him with the yams raised.

"It's me!" I shout, as the dust from the car settles. From somewhere around the house, his two housekeepers, Efua and Akuba, come running. When they see it is I, they are only slightly less annoyed. They glare at me as they call out to Kojo in singsong Twi. All three speak English quite well; they converse in Twi only when I'm around if they don't want me to know that they think I am a liar and a thief. Which I am.

"Jeffrey!" shouts the old man. "Come on inside! I've been traveling! There's so much I need to show you."

The old man has no more been traveling than I am his grandson, but I do not dissuade him of either delusion. Lowering my yams, I once more trudge up the creaking steps that lead into the crumbling House of Oakes.

Inside, the air is full of flies, and Jeremiah leads the way back to the room he calls his "study." A room where he wrote six or seven novels, back in the late seventies, none of which is still in print. I have tracked them all down and read them all cover to cover. They remind me a bit of my own efforts: not bad, but not Jeffrey.

A gigantic fan revolves lazily above our heads, sending just enough cool air down to bristle the photographs and scraps of newspaper he has pinned on every walled surface: old illustrations from books of World War II submarines, articles in Spanish about boys killed during the running of the bulls, and tattered letters handwritten in Hebrew. On a long, narrow desk sits a typewriter—the same faint-inked thing that Jeffrey typed his first stories on—and beside it, thin bundles of monogrammed paper, stolen from hotels worldwide, some of which haven't existed since the 1950s. There are guns everywhere—some antique showpieces and some roadside finds. Some loaded; some not. The floor is covered with skins: a warthog, a zebra, a lioness, and an antelope—most of which, according to Jeremiah, escaped from the preserve and came waltzing right in through the wide set of French doors, which he leaves open, day or night, to the terrace outside. The jungle is a hundred yards away.

Checking my watch as if I have somewhere else to be, I say, "So, I think we're *nearly* done. I'd love to ask if you have *any* other memories of teaching me to write here, when I was young?"

He settles into a leather reading chair and lifts a glass of something dirty, brown, and surely intoxicating off a stack of books piled to serve as a side table.

"Oh, sure, sure," he says. "You used to sit right here in this chair and write. Every morning. That's how you make progress. Every morning. You write. Even if your leg is being chewed off by a hyena. You keep writing."

"How old was I when I first came to visit?"

"Oh, maybe about twenty-two," he says, staring at the ceiling fan as it drowsily completed a revolution.

"Wasn't I maybe six or seven?"

"Yes, six or seven. And you'd sit right over there banging away on the keys."

"So, I sat there at the desk?"

"Yes, that's right."

"Because a minute ago you said I was in the *chair.*"

The old man frowned. "Well, sometimes we'd do it that way."

Whipping out my nib pen, I add this note to my calfskin book—along with hundreds of other similar, contradictory statements. The truth is, Jeremiah says something different every time we speak. My notebook is a garden of forking paths. Jeffrey came to Ghana because of early childhood asthma, or because his great-aunt became ill. Jeffrey's favorite childhood book was *Moby-Dick,* and the next hour it was *The Iliad.* His first work of fiction was about an ogre named Claude. Unless it was about a Swiss chocolatier named PJ. One day certainly the former, and the next certainly the latter. The man is in his eighties and his brain is worn through, like a shirt loved too well. When his daughter calls to make sure everything is well, and he tells them, "Jeffrey's here talking with me," they don't even question it.

"You mentioned yesterday that I wanted to be a librarian, as a child," I lie, just to see if he'll notice.

He furrows his narrow brow, which is speckled with brown spots that I'm sure must be melanomas. Will he remember? That he actually told me Jeffrey wanted to be a scuba diver? The spots swim in the fleshy wrinkles for a moment and then flatten again.

He laughs. "You liked the idea of climbing all those ladders, I think. You said you'd want to be a librarian only if they had really tall bookshelves, and ladders, with wheels."

The fictions that Jeremiah sparked like furious flints in his neurons for decades have now caught fire and consumed the remainder of the truth. Does he really believe these things? Or does he fill in the blanks with his best guesses and hope that he's right? Most times he'll run with whatever I suggest, like a freshman writing student eagerly jumping into a story after being given an opening line as a prompt.

With a long sigh I stare out into the darkened jungle. Tina is right. If anything, Jeremiah is a plagiarist's wet dream. I can put words into his mouth and he'll never remember they weren't there to begin with. All day I feed him fictions and listen to them echo back as truths. But still, this hollow feeling grows.

"Do you have any of my early stories?" I ask, as I do every day.

"No," he says firmly. "Definitely not."

It is the only answer he gives the same each time, so I am sure it is a lie.

Jeremiah takes out a knife and expertly plunges it deep into one of the yams I have given him. He works the blade through the flesh and divides it neatly in two. He stares inside of it with a childlike curiosity. I wonder if he knows that you cannot eat them raw. I wonder if I would stop him. I think that I would.

Looking back at the gentle undulations of the palm fronds, I exhale and try to think of how I could get a look around without his stopping me. Occasionally he naps or uses the restroom, and I sneak in and dig around—but I've yet to find anything of use. There is only one drawer in the desk that he keeps locked. If I am ever going to get it open, I'll need to buy myself more time. Then, out on the edge of the jungle I see something moving. Jeremiah sees it, too, and he points, the knife outstretched.

"What is that?" I ask, straining my young eyes in the glare of the light.

"Is that Jeffrey?" he asks with a laugh. "What's he doing out there?"

Blinking twice to be sure it is no mirage, I look again. There I am, creeping through the low-lying brush. My doppelgänger has ditched the tweed jacket, as I have—the heat is simply too intense. His silver wrist-watch glints in the light.

"What's Jeffrey doing out there?" he asks again. Suddenly I wonder if it *is* Jeffrey—the *real* Jeffrey—and my heart leaps into my throat. But it can't be; Jeffrey would sooner roll around in his own feces than crouch in scrub brush.

My double is perhaps a hundred yards away, and he ducks out of sight. When I turn back to Jeremiah, he is standing with his knife point-ing at me.

"If that's Jeffrey, then who the hell are you?"

It takes an hour to talk him back down again. By the time I'm done avoiding being stabbed, I've gotten absolutely nothing factual or firm, and the sun is going down, so once again I return empty-handed to the Hyundai, and Kojo takes me back to Kumasi.

"How much longer will you and whatever the beautiful editor stay?" he asks me. Kojo thinks that he will sound more American if he says "whatever" as often as possible.

"Not much longer," I say.

"The old man whatever, he is crazy, yes?"

"Yes. He is crazy."

"I think maybe that you are crazy, too."

"I think that maybe you are right."

The sun has become enormous and red against the rippling surface of Lake Bosumtwi. The locals are gliding home again, having fished all day off of long wooden planks. Huge dead trees line the distant shores.

The guidebook tells me that it was created by a meteorite that struck the rain forest a million years ago. There are thirty or so tiny villages around it, but no one knows exactly which are where because the lake floods whenever it rains too much and swallows any villages that are too close. Some of them have names like Pipie Number Two, because Pipie Number One was swallowed up the year before and rebuilt later. Others have no names at all.

Kojo told me once that the locals will not allow any metal-bottomed boats to touch the surface of the water, because the lake is considered sacred. The souls of the dead gather there before departing for the spirit world and say their farewells to the gods.

Now Kojo sees me staring out at the lake and purses his lips. "Whatever the fishing has not been at all good this season. Efua tells me that tonight the locals are preparing a sacrifice to whatever appease the gods."

"What do they sacrifice?" I ask.

"A cow," he says, making little horns with his fingers to demonstrate. "They take it out to the rock in the center and chop it all up and throw it in the water, whatever."

"Seems like a fair trade. One cow for a good season of fish?"

Kojo shrugs. "These village peoples still believe in that whatever."

"You don't believe in spirits or ghosts then?"

He clicks his tongue a few times and looks around, as if worried that someone else will overhear him. "My grandmother tells me you have your thought-soul and your life-soul. When you die, the life-soul goes away. But your thought-soul sometimes it stays here for a few years. But sooner or later it goes away, too."

I chew this over. It is growing darker and the city is still some distance away.

"Can the two ever split up while you're still alive?"

"If you are in danger," he says, nodding, "your life-soul may go away and hide. And if then, you are hurt or wounded, you will still not be killed. And then, when you are better, it will come back again."

"That sounds like a good system," I say.

"Well," he laughs again. "It is all just nonsense. Whatever."

The tiny Kumasi hotel room that Tina and I have been inhabiting is home to bugs both crawling and winged, and we pass the evening as usual, under the sanctuary of the heavy gauze mosquito netting that hangs over the bed. We eat; we make love. I drink; she smokes. We watch the black oblong shapes hum across the transparent curtain. It is too hot to sleep, but we pretend for a while that we will.

"So, what happened to Shelley?" I ask. "You were starting to tell me before."

"Percy?" She smiles to think that I've been mulling it over all day.

"I didn't realize you two were on a first-name basis."

"Well, he wrote in his diaries that he kept seeing himself through the windows, walking around on this high terrace garden outside his house in Italy. Once or twice he chased his double through the garden, but always lost him at a low wall, which dropped hundreds of yards on the other side, down into the town. He decided never to tell Mary about it, but then one day, when she was sure Percy had gone into town, Mary thought she saw him out in the garden. She went after him—wondering what he was doing back—and chased him all the way to the wall, where he vanished."

"*Poof,*" I say.

"She screams out," Tina says, gesturing with her hands as if it is she who is doing this screaming. "And the gardener or somebody comes rushing over and says, 'Mrs. Shelley, Mrs. Shelley. What is the matter?' "

Tina's gardener sounds like Charlton Heston, which is to say, he sounds like every impression she does.

"And she says she's sure her husband has just leaped over the wall to his death. And the gardener or whoever says, 'But, no, that's not possible. Mr. Shelley has gone into town.' When Percy finally gets home, Mary is a wreck. Relieved to see him all right, but a wreck. And so he finally tells her that he's seen this reflection of himself as well. And a year later, he is dead."

"That's quite a story," I say. "I wonder if it's true."

"Oh, what does *that* matter?" she groans

"It'd just be nicer if it was, I think. They're both writers, you know. Between the two of them, they could have made it all up."

"You're no fun." Tina pouts, then blows a smoke ring at me.

"You like the Shelleys?"

Tina chews on her lip a moment, as if she cannot decide if she should talk to me anymore. "When Percy died," she says at last, "they burned him on a pyre by the sea. Only a disturbed fan came rushing up and into the fire. People thought he was insane—trying to die with him, or something. But then he rolled away, all burned and on fire, with Percy's heart in his hand. He rushed off before anyone could stop him."

"Crazy," I say.

"That's not even the crazy part. Because years later, when Mary died, they found a little parcel in her desk. One of his original drafts of *Adonaïs*, his elegy for Keats, and wrapped up in it, this withered, burned-up lump of Percy's heart."

"I've heard that before. It's just a myth," I laugh.

"I think it's the most tremendously romantic thing I've ever heard."

"Would you have my heart stolen from my funeral pyre?" I ask.

"I would," she says. "Would you have mine?"

"Of course," I say. It is a lie—but oh, it is a great lie—one I'd love to be true. I feel bad, but not too bad, considering she's lying as well. Jeffrey's heart, maybe, she'd steal, but not mine. A great buzzing scarab thing goes by the netting so quickly that it makes me jump.

"Come on," I say. "It's too hot. Let's go out."

We had not known it was Saturday; O'Bryan's has jazz on Saturday nights. We walk in and it is dark but cool, despite the crowds of people that clog the place. Someone else is in our usual booth, but we hover nearby in the hope the interlopers may leave. News of the world flashes on the muted televisions. A few men stare vacantly, waiting for the sports scores to float by at the bottom. Up on the stage, all the way across the room, a little Ghanaian ensemble is playing something all horns and bluesy, while a large dark woman moans like she's never seen things so bad in her life. Tina gets two beers for herself and two beers for me, and we set about drinking them down.

"Get anything straight out of the old man?" she asks hopefully. "True tales of the early oeuvre of Jeffrey Oakes?"

"We only got about ten questions in before he pointed a knife at me."

And as I say this, I see myself again, all the way across the room, leaning up against the wall in another dark corner. He—me—is listening to the singer, who is going from moan to howl now, as the song circles up and up out of the blues.

"That's him," I say before I can stop myself. "That's the guy."

He is standing with another white man, about our same age, not paying attention to me at all. He and this other man are standing very close. In the dim light I see him whispering in the other's ear.

"He *does* look like you," Tina gasps when she sees whom I mean. It takes her a moment to realize what he is doing, exactly. "Oh, dear. Darling. I think your doppelgänger is gay."

She thinks this is *very* funny. I'm mostly just glad that she can see him, too.

"He was by the house today. The old man thought it was Jeffrey."

Tina squints and tries to look through the dark throngs, rippling in time to a saxophone solo. "It's *not* Jeffrey, is it?"

There's an excited squeak in her voice, as if it were Mick Jagger or Leonardo DiCaprio standing across the bar from us. For Tina, maybe Jeffrey is of that same caliber; after all, her copy of *Nothing Sacred* has more dog-ears than the Westminster Kennel Club.

After a long, long pause, I say, "It's not Jeffrey. But I think that I might know who it actually is." As I start to cross the dark floor, Tina moves to follow me and I stop. "I need to do this alone, if that's all right."

"You're joking!" she laughs. "Come on, seriously. I want to find out who he is!" I can see it in her eye—this predatory feline glint—sure that she is about to unearth some big secret.

"I'm not joking," I say firmly. "I need to talk to him alone. Can I meet you back at the apartment?"

"Why don't you want me to meet him?" she says, and she seems upset at my change in tone.

"It's personal," I say. "He's someone I knew a long time ago and . . . "

She stares at me for a while, finishes her drink, and starts in on mine.

"Why are you *like* this?" she asks.

It is the question—the real question—she's been trying to ask me for weeks. Since I met her, I'd been asking myself the same thing. Watching my double at the end of the bar I begin to worry I'll lose him again, as the people in the bar keep swelling with the sad songs coming from the stage and sighing with the sadder songs that they alone know.

"You wouldn't believe me if I told you," I say.

"I'd believe *anything* you told me," she says. There are suddenly tears in her eyes, and I can't look at them. But she turns away, thinking she's robbing me of the satisfaction of seeing them.

"Well, that's just the problem," I snap. "You would believe anything. And I'm a liar! That's just what I am. I lie like I'm breathing. I lie to everyone, myself most of all. But with you it's just too easy. I can't even stop myself, because you'll believe *anything*."

It's a mean thing to say and it stings her, I can tell. And it's difficult to get out straight, because to be honest it's the opposite that's become true. I can hardly *stop* myself from telling her the truth. I feel it seeping out of me faster than my sweat. What's truly too easy is forgetting all the lies that I've been believing for years.

But she buys my lie, and so I follow it with one more, without even realizing that it will be the last one I'll ever get to tell her.

"I'll be back in an hour, I promise."

She gives me a look—a pitiful, pitying look—and then I think she really *would* grab my heart from a funeral pyre. For a second I think I would grab hers, too, but then she moves off into a darker part of the bar and is gone.

The trumpets tremble while the bass guitar aches, and I cross over to the bar and begin to work my way down toward my double through the crowd. My double looks up at me and realizes he's standing in a corner and there's nowhere to go. As I work my way across the room, I see him telling the man he's with to give him a few minutes. The other guy sees me coming and begins talking very fast in French. Then suddenly it is only my double and me, standing face-to-face.

"Henry Waterford," he says with a smile, reaching out a hand to shake. The blue lights above the jazz group gleam off our watches and now they look the same. Then gesturing to my clothing, he says, "They say great minds think alike."

And now I see. My double doesn't look like me; I look like my double. This is the boy I grew up wanting to be. And, twenty years later, I've become him.

"But fools seldom differ," I say. "You followed me out to the lake today."

"I'm sorry for that," he says, reaching for a cigarette—a new affectation for Henry. He offers me one but I decline. "But you'll know what I mean when I say that it's not every day you meet a twin you didn't know you had. My driver followed you out to the lake. I'm afraid my snooping skills leave a lot to be desired."

"You don't remember me, then?" I ask.

"From the accent I'd say you're from around West Charlotte," he says with a shrug. "If you know me from there, then you know there's a lot I can't remember about those days."

He's right—my Southern drawl has crept back in, despite a decade of firm repression.

"Billy," I lie, shaking his hand. "We were on the high school tennis team together."

He laughs and studies me carefully, as if trying to remember me. "Of course!" he lies finally. "Billy. It's so good to see you again."

"What brings you to Ghana of all places?"

"Business," he replies vaguely, finishing his cigarette after three shaky drags. He's looking around to see if his friend is still nearby. "You remember my family was involved in telecom?"

I don't remember ever knowing this, but I nod.

"Well, Africa's the new frontier in the market," he says. "Fiber-optic cables. Cell towers. Wireless hot spots. They've sent me out like some kind of a scout. *Boring.*"

"Didn't you have a sister?" I ask, a little breathless.

"Married. Kids," he says, as if this is all there is to say. I suppose that it is. Still, it makes me wince, just a little, and while Henry can't quite place me, he looks just a tiny bit uncomfortable at my reaction. Perhaps I am not the first man to ask after his sister in a dark bar somewhere. He fidgets a little. "Anyway, what brings *you* to Ghana, Billy?"

"I'm a writer, Henry," I say, gesturing toward the bar. The singer is burning up a rough imitation of Ella. As the bartender sets two whiskeys down in front of us, I feel Tina coming up behind me. I turn to look at her and so does Henry.

"Another American!" he cries. "This really is the spot tonight. Do you two know each other?"

Tina catches my eye, daringly. She lets a moment go by. *This is your last chance,* her eye tells me. *This is it, right here.*

"No," I say. "We've never met."

"Well, I'm Henry! Henry Waterford! Come on and join us for a whiskey! And this is Billy. Billy . . . "

He pauses, not sure what my last name is. I am about to supply it, when Tina does.

"Littleford."

"Oh, so you *do* know each other!" Henry says.

"No," Tina says. "I suppose we don't, really. I'm just a great fan of his work."

I can't even look at her. Henry doesn't let the beat drop, though, bless him.

"He was just telling me all about it! Join us, join us!"

I hazard a glimpse and know immediately that for years after, I'll wish I hadn't. She looks so incredibly sad. Not for herself, but for me.

"Christina Elizabeth Edgars-Boyleston," she says, shaking Henry's hand. "Thank you so much but I'm afraid I'm leaving."

"Tomorrow, then?" Henry says cheerfully.

"No," Tina replies, "I'm taking off tonight. There's a red-eye at six AM. Got to get back home. Got to hurry—there's a lot to pack."

She gives me a defiant look. *I'll do it,* she seems to say. *I'll really do it.*

Henry gives her a pleasant smile. "Next time," he says.

"Yes, next time," I echo.

Tina looks as though she's about to say something, but she just fakes a smile and turns away.

Henry shrugs and sips his whiskey thoughtfully. "What might have been, eh? Makes you wonder, sometimes. You know a friend told me I ought to write a novel someday. About everything that's happened to me."

"But you don't *remember* anything that's happened to you," I say. I wonder what would happen if I showed him that story I wrote twenty years ago. Would he even know it was about him?

Henry laughs and sips his whiskey. "So, then I'll make it up! Who's going to know? Anyway, tell me. Is it exciting, being a writer? I'm so *bored* with my whole *existence,* I can't even tell you."

I smile at Henry. At last I can see my way out of this place.

"Well, I'll tell you all about it. But if you've got some time tonight, you may actually be able to help me out."

I convince Kojo to come back with the Hyundai by promising him all the money I have left. He was off happily cavorting somewhere with one of his many lady friends, and he is not all that pleased when he arrives in the car, nor is he all that sober. When I introduce him to Henry, Kojo blinks two or three times, as if to make sure the drinking has not left him seeing double. When Henry calls me Billy, Kojo blinks again, at least until I pat him on the back and ask him if we shouldn't get going.

Driving out to the lake after dark is "not advisable" according to Kojo, but I insist that it is important. The old man never sleeps; I am sure that he will be up. As Kojo guides us along the dark and winding nighttime roads, I catch up with Henry about our hometown. Everyone we ever knew is married now; half of them have released some tiny versions of themselves out into the world—a world no larger than the city limits. Everyone we used to know is exactly where we left them, only now they have doubles and triples.

"Tell me more about being a writer," Henry says. He is thrilled. This is more fun than he's had in months, clearly. "Truth is, I really like the idea of being a writer."

For years I wanted to be everything he was. Now that it seems he wants to be what I am, I'm not quite sure what to make of it.

"The idea of it's great," I explain. "But then there's the actual *thing* of it."

He nods and looks wistfully off into the blackness. Tina told me once that, in her line, you come to realize that just about everyone is a part-time writer. Even people who never wrote a full page in their lives think that they might, soon, sit down and churn out a masterpiece. The really good ones, I suppose, make it seem like anyone could do it.

"Thing is, I actually wrote, like, a chapter already," Henry laughs. "But I'd never show it to anyone. It's so terrible."

"I'm sure it isn't," I lie. This is how it starts—in an hour or so he'll be asking me to take a look. In another hour, he'll be asking if my editor might be interested. Tina knew what Jeffrey, and Jeremiah, and I know. The real thing—the true thing—takes more time and effort than most people would ever imagine. Whole productive lifetimes for a few hundred pages that most assuredly won't outlive us.

"Hey, now. What's happening out on the lake?" Henry asks.

Clusters of torchlight surround the wide lake, though it is hard to see through the dense rain forest. The wooden plank boats carry more flickering flames.

"The Asantehene arrived," Kojo explains. "He is the king of the Ashanti."

"They still have a *king?*" Henry laughs. "In this day and age?"

"England still has a queen," I counter.

Kojo shrugs. "Whatever. They will bring the cow out to the rock in the middle of the lake. They will leave his intestines and guts and whatever out there for the gods, and there will be a feast made out of the rest."

Kojo won't stop the car, for fear of what may jump out at us, but through bouncing binoculars I am able to see one highly confused cow, tied up on joined planks, surrounded by men with ceremonial swords. At first it seems to me completely absurd: the men shout and try to avoid the scrambling of the cow, which is either unhappy to be profoundly out of its element or somehow aware of what will become of it out on the approaching rock. But then I wonder how many times, in how many hundreds of years, they have done this. The people on the neighboring boats are jubilant. Soon there will be food, and drums, and dancing— and in a few weeks maybe things will begin to get better. The gods will bring them fish, and they can survive another season. Another year of dry heat followed by rains that will wash their village away. Nothing to worry about—they will build another. And another.

As I suspected, the light in the study is on when we approach the long driveway. I duck so that the old man won't see me, and then pull Henry down, too, just in case he has decided to do a little night shooting. Henry grins widely. Probably he thinks I'll mention this in my book, or more probably that I'll know someone who can get him a book of his own so he can mention it himself.

"Just keep asking him questions," I say. "And jot it all down in your notebook. Don't worry if he says things that don't make sense. He might call you Jeffrey. Just go with it."

"Finally, some fun," Henry says with a boyish grin.

I hesitate. "And if he starts playing with his guns, keep an eye on him."

Henry's smile shrinks slightly, but I give him a quick laugh and he thinks that I am joking. Guilt begins to creep into my gut, but the idea of sitting on an airplane bound for America by daybreak squeezes it away again. Kojo says nothing but stays with the car, listening to the distant sounds of the ceremony. Not that I have any money left, but if I did, I'd wager that the moment we leave, he'll head out there to find Efua and Akuba.

I stay in the shadows as Henry enters the lighted kitchen.

"Jeffrey!" the old man's voice booms. "Come in! I was just packing for my trip."

It is not difficult at all, walking through the shadows along the side of the house, to get to the back, where the French doors, as always, are wide open. By the time I slip inside I can hear the old man putting a kettle on in the kitchen, and Henry dragging a chair backward across the uneven wooden floor—taking his seat at the table. We are both so close to, finally, taking our seats at the table.

It is even less difficult to find an ornamental knife to pop the drawer open. I've seen one often, resting on a bookshelf containing an odd assortment of Great Depression–era plays. Careful not to make too much noise, I slip the knife out of a golden sheath and press it between the drawer and its frame. It slides open with barely a sound.

Inside are a dozen little jars—once containing baby food, according to the labels. Each one is filled with used pen nibs. Jeremiah's used pen nibs. There must be hundreds of them. Decades' worth of cracked metal. I lift one up to the moonlight and examine them, like tiny arrowheads. Stained with the inky blood of stories ripped from nothingness and into somethingness.

Reaching behind these, I feel around in the shadows for a sheaf of papers, but my hand closes instead on something hard and smooth. Out comes a bottle, still half filled with liquid, bearing a handmade label— the sort that went out of style thirty years before I was even born. The faded lettering spelled out EPIPHANY BROS. DISTILLERY. GENUINE IRISH WHISKEY. FOUNDED IN 1900. Gently I cradle the bottle in my hand, and I think about the first story of Jeffrey's that I had ever read. In it, a man on his thirty-third birthday drinks a bottle of Epiphany whiskey out on an Irish moor. It seems like two lifetimes ago. Just two and a half pages. Just nine hundred perfectly chosen words. It had all started there.

For a long time I stand there, staring down at the bottle. In the kitchen I can hear the old man laughing. Henry is doing a bang-up job. I wonder what tall tales the old man is conjuring out of his addled brain now. Slowly I draw the tough knot of cork out of the bottle. I've always wondered what it would taste like.

Just as I am about to lift the bottle to my lips, I catch sight of something in the far back of the drawer. It shines in the faint moonlight—a lump of gold about the size of half a human heart. I reach for it, mesmerized.

And then something slams into my leg. And the bottle falls to the floor and I fall to the floor and for a few long minutes I have absolutely no idea what is going on.

Lying on the floor of the old man's study, I can feel the wiry hairs of an antelope rug like little needles against my cheek. The antelope is quite dead. It's been dead for years. Unlike the tense, speculative leopard that crouches in the space between those open French doors, halfway between the jungle outside and the jungle in here. I'm half in and half out, too: not dead yet, but I see no way of living through the next ten minutes. The leopard has gotten a good swipe at the back of my left leg, and I know it must be bleeding all over the floor. And the dead antelope. Though my vision is a little blurry, I seem to be thinking clearly for the first time in weeks, maybe months. Maybe ever.

I don't dare move, let alone scream. The old man is just in the next room having tea, but if I yelled, I'm sure the leopard could chew my throat out before the old guy even took a step in my direction. The leopard growls, low but lightly. The same sort of inquisitive purring that a housecat might make. Though it is massive, and all muscle, something makes me think that it is just a child. Probably an adult would have killed me outright. Children just want to play and learn how this whole "killing" thing works.

I can't feel my left arm but it must be just behind my head. I can hear my wristwatch ticking.

All around me are stacks upon stacks: of oft-reread books, of newspaper cuttings, of typewritten pages. None of them are mine. The old man writes in here every morning; sometimes all night long, too. When I first came all the way out to Africa, I hoped that the old man might teach me whatever he had taught Jeffrey. Whatever it was that he had—that he'd always had—that I had always *not* had. But all the old man ever told me was to write every day. And to read whenever I had the chance. I could have gotten the same advice from a one-hundred-dollar Saturday workshop at the New School. Instead I'll die out here in the middle of nowhere, my thirty-three years amounting to a useless education, a few pages no one will ever read, and a few girls I loved and who left. Mine turns out to be just a brief, supporting role. A few lines, but nothing memorable.

The leopard relaxes slightly from its pouncing position and settles down into a crouch. After a long stare in my direction, the cat leans backward and begins to lick at its fur. Working slowly, in little patches, it preens and nuzzles itself. My head throbs in time with my leg. I wait for this rate to slow, or to deepen. I try to count but I lose track. My eyes keep wandering back to the leopard. I keep thinking about how I would describe all this in a story, if I only lived to write it down.

Thinking is all I ever do. Or is it *did*, now? Wasted weeks and months traveling around. I spent whole days in bars, talking to strange people from strange walks of life. As they told me about their lives, I began to envision them on pages. I began to imagine how I'd capture their voices or describe their noses. In the wee hours, half drowned in the local brew, I'd lie in bed alone, composing magnificent stories whose details would be lost in headaches by morning. When I did sit down to carve them into my blank pages, they inevitably came up flat and lacking. Small people with their small lives, I'd spit; I just haven't met interesting-enough characters yet. They must be in Stockholm or Damascus or Vancouver. I'd better get moving. And in the back of my mind I wonder if it's me that I'm dodging. If it's me who is too small. But it's this wondering that is growing louder and louder, now, as I lie here dying. All these stories I've gathered are going to be lost forever, seeing as how I'm about to be jungle cat food. I've wasted them. I've wasted everything in my path.

The leopard is really getting into it now. Lifting one ferocious-looking paw and licking its soft white underarm with long, rough swipes of its tongue. The reptilian tail flops back and forth, making a heavy thud against the doorframe as it goes. Can the old man hear this? I can hear him . . . humming something in the other room as the kettle begins to whistle. Outside, an orchestra of jungle insects plays an endless concerto. I always meant to learn how to listen to classical music. To find themes and know what melodies are. To know the difference between Bach and Brahms and Beethoven. As a child I suspected that the secrets of the universe were hidden away somewhere in classical music. People told me that it was too late for me to learn—that music was a language you had to learn when you were little, and so it was already too late. But now I think I could have cracked it—if I'd only tried. I think I could have learned; I could have changed. But I never did, and so I never will, because this is it.

What kills me the most—pun most definitely not intended—is that I have already read this story. It is one of Hemingway's better ones, "The Snows of Kilimanjaro." About a man who is slowly dying and regretting all the time he wasted in his life. All the stuff he meant to write. It's all there. The greatest, and last, story of my whole life and it is plagiarized straight out of The Forty-Nine Stories, and written forty years before I was even born. I've always suspected that this is a deeply ironic universe. That if there is some sort of God, that this is just how He likes to gets His yuks. Which doesn't give me much hope about heaven, then—if this is how He likes to play things. To Him, if anyone, there's nothing sacred.

There's sort of a circular method to it. The licking. The little pink tongue is covered in snaking black branches. The leopard's eyes shut, as if it were a monk, deep in a meditative state. It is the distant stare of a lover who is thinking about someone else.

Is it just me, or is the ticking of my watch getting louder? Are my senses coming alive, now that I am nearly dead?

Somewhere, in a bug-infested apartment thirty miles away, a woman is packing her bags. She's the only person who gives a damn about me for a hundred miles. No, for a thousand, or even three thousand. The only person who gives a damn about me on this continent and even in this hemisphere. I've said terrible things to her and I've pushed her away at every possible chance, and, given the current circumstances, probably no one in my entire life will love me as much as she does.

Done with its preening, the leopard keeps its eyes half shut and stays tightly curled in the doorway. My heart begins to pound. Is it going to sleep? The pounding of my heart begins to echo in the dull ache of my head, and the pain in my leg gets sharper. I struggle and strain not to move, but suddenly the more I think about it, the more my leg wants to shift. Just a few more minutes, I tell myself. Just until I'm sure it's really asleep. Just until the old man finishes his tea. Maybe then Henry will come in to see what's taking me so long. Unless I bleed out before it's safe to move. I try to keep my eyes open. I gently rub the wiry needles of antelope hair against my cheek. I list all the things I will do differently, if I make it through. I dream up ways of describing how those claws felt tearing through my pant leg and then my flesh. Was it like butter? Too cliché. Like pâté? Too elite. Like a foot stepping into the first mound of freshly fallen snow. Too poetic. Who thinks like that, anyway? It was like exactly what it was. It was like a set of claws tearing through my flesh.

The jungle cat begins to look peaceful. The whole room feels darker than it was a moment ago. The leopard buries its head under its oversized paws. It looks stuffed, except that its whole body swells and falls in gentle rhythm. My leg stops hurting, and the sound of the old man's humming blends into that immense, insectile orchestra, performing to the metronome of my watch. As I try to move my leg, I wonder what exactly leopards dream about.

And just then there is a thunderclap bang, and the leopard's body goes limp, right as mine tenses up. Looking up I see myself, bending over me.

"It's going to be all right," the other me says.

The old man stands in a haze of gunpowder, a rifle in his hands that is older than I am. Both of them begin yelling for Efua or Akuba to come and help dress my wounds. But they're both down by the lake, watching old rituals become unforgotten again.

"Here," the other me says, picking up the bottle of Epiphany. Much of it seems to have spilled out. I want to live. I want to live and let Tina love me. I want to live and find Jeffrey and drag him out of whatever hole he's crawled down. I want to live and every morning I want to write something that's worth wrapping my heart in when I die.

"Don't worry, we'll get you out of here," I say to myself.

And then the other me holds the worn glass opening up to my lips and pours.

9

In the Writers' Colony

It is entirely conceivable that life's splendor forever lies in wait about
each one of us in all its fullness, but veiled from view, deep down, invisible, far off. It is there, though, not hostile, not reluctant, not deaf. If you
summon it by the right word, by its right name, it will come. This is the
essence of magic, which does not create but summons.

—FRANZ KAFKA, *DIARIES*

When I first wake up I usually think I'm still in the hospital, until my
eyes come to focus on all the umlauts along the book spines on my
nightstand. Someone keeps setting them out there. I might like to read
them, if only I could read Icelandic. I find it strange. I find it stranger that
I notice the books even before I notice there aren't tubes coming out of
me anymore. I find it strangest of all that I find myself absentmindedly
skimming their unreadable pages, wondering what is lost in them. Do
they, in their own language, divine the depths of human souls?

The walls here are the same clean white as the walls in my hospital
room. Familiar, too, is the ever-present chill; and the small square window, beyond which are rows and rows of great blue pines. I stare at them
until I remember that I am in the Laxness-Hallgrímsson Writers' Colony, in Iceland, and that I have been here for one very cold week already,

looking for my old friend, Jeffrey Oakes, who came months ago and has, apparently, disappeared again.

When I kick off the down comforter my leg aches. The last, dull reminder of my accident. I roll across the cold, far side of the bed and think of Tina. The nights we spent hiding out under that zippered African netting. She's gone now, along with my watch, my jacket, and my almost-finished biography of Jeffrey. It's gone, all gone, but I try to remember that I'm lucky not to be all gone myself. I limp over to the door, where a pot of dark coffee and two bilberry muffins have been left for me—by whom I do not really know. Probably by whoever keeps putting the books on my nightstand. According to the few writers here who will speak to me, the caretaker is a man named Franklin W. Zaff, but it's been a week and I've yet to meet him. I'm told he tries to keep out of our way.

I limp over to a desk that is too high and feed some paper that is too thin into a typewriter whose ink is too faint, and I fidget in an Icelandic chair that is too modern, and I begin to write.

This is difficult. The keys on the typewriter are not in the American order; more disturbingly, the letters c, q, w, and z are nowhere to be found. The ropey-haired gentleman in the next room told me that pens are in very short supply, and that the letter z was legally eliminated from the Icelandic language, back in the seventies—for crimes I can only imagine. So I have been making substitutions with the odd new letters: á, þ, æ, and ö. These, I find, give my writing a bold, decidedly old-world flair: "Noæ, hours later, I am alone again, sitting þuietly in front of the dressing-table mirror, áaking æhite poæder onto my faáe."

I type these words, as I have each morning that week—only harder and faster than I had typed them the morning before. With minimal variations, I describe a woman sitting in front of a mirror, applying makeup on her wedding day. Then I hit the same spot as always and I freeze up completely. I cannot seem to get inside her head. Anything I imagine seems completely wrong. I do not know what she is thinking.

So I sit. And I sip my coffee. And I try not to think about my leg. I backspace a few times and then space quickly forward, as if pouncing upon the next sentence, but I pause again. So I wind the paper up and down a little. And I pop open the door on the side where the ribbon goes in. And I wish I had a laptop. And I stare out the window at the pines in the dark. The sun never rises and the sun never sets. It is just dark all the time. When I arrived, I noticed a crooked, stone bell tower, but I have yet to hear any bells to mark the passing of time. Without my wrist-watch, the only indication of a day's passing is that periodically there is an odd piercing column of light visible through the window. It comes up from way beyond the woods, for maybe two or three hours, and van-ishes again. Whenever it appears, I give up on writing and I go about making a few cautious inquiries about my missing friend.

The Laxness-Hallgrímsson Writers' Colony is a labyrinth of ancient hallways and rooms that are mostly empty. It was once a medieval church, built into the foot of the Akrafjall Mountain for the fishermen of Akranes. Because timber is scarce in Iceland, when the writers took over they removed hundreds of stones from the walls and used the hollows to shelve books. There must be thousands in every room—all written by Icelanders, in their native language.

Lazily I make my way down to the "chapel," which has been con-verted into a gathering space for the various writers residing at the col-ony. Its three crucifixes have been draped with black cloth, and the pews were long ago ripped out of the long, narrow transept and replaced with long stone tables, where those of us with writer's block or an urge to stretch our legs can engage in a little social activity—or try to, in our socially stunted, introverted, writerly ways. When I arrive, a small cadre of playwrights is busily painting with watercolors. I sit down with a smile, grab a brush, and dip it into a golden-colored paint, waiting for someone to pass me a sheet of paper. A quick look around the table shows that I am not welcome.

"Private session," a woman with thinning gray hair says, grabbing the brush away from me. "For dramatists only."

I have no clue if she is someone in charge or another of the writers. She does not look like a Franklin, though. Upon arrival, I was greeted by a toothless man who did not correct me when I addressed him as Mr. Zaff, and when I handed him my bags, he began combing through them. I thought perhaps this was just heightened security, until he rushed off with all my pens.

Down at the other end of the table, two old men with leonine manes of shock-white hair are having a discussion in some strange tongue, jabbing at a thick stack of pages between them. Hoping they are fiction writers, like me, I walk toward them, but they quickly lean into a huddle and lower their voices. All week I have been trying to pal up with someone who might have seen Jeffrey around, but writers tend to be the least extroverted people in the universe, even in Iceland.

My teeth begin to chatter and I decide to try to find something warming to eat in the kitchen. On the way down the hallway I hear a woman's voice, yelling fitfully in a nails-on-chalkboard brogue. "Na, na, na," she insists. "That's'nt how is'posed to be! That's'nt it at all!" When I come upon her, I find that she is completely alone.

She is quite pretty, not much younger than myself, and stares bluntly at me, as if she's expecting a reply. So I say, "I know the feeling." She blinks twice and steps closer. "Writing not quite going as you want it to?" I add. She tugs at the neckline of her loose, black sweater-coat, and for a second she seems about to pull it off. Then, without warning, she vomits all over the stone floor. I barely leap back in time to avoid the spew, and when I do, pain sparks like a string of firecrackers up my leg and my spine and all out from there, and I crumble to the ground, just a foot or so away from the puddle. Steam rises up through the chill of the hallway.

"Is there a nurse or a doctor anywhere?" I yell into the empty corridor. In the distance I hear hurried footsteps, but as soon as the girl hears them she goes flying down the hallway, swooping her arms around, batlike. My leg is hurting too much to chase after her, so I wait there for whoever is coming the other way. It turns out to be not a nurse but a gigantic man with spiked black hair and a bull's ring through his septum.

"You all right?" he asks gruffly, reaching to help me up. All the nails on his right hand are polished black. He seems to be wearing mascara. The sound of atonal jazz is coming from a set of bulky headphones around his neck. "You tossed up?"

"No," I insist, a little too firmly. "There was this girl. Talking to herself in here. And then she tossed . . . *er* . . . threw up and ran off that way."

The man stares at me as if I am crazy, and for a moment I'm not so sure he's wrong. Not for the first time I wonder if I have, in fact, arrived at a madhouse by mistake. As if reading my mind, the tall man slowly bends down and takes a long sniff of the acrid puddle on the floor.

"Black death," he says ominously.

"Excuse me?" I ask. I did not spend an entire month alone in a hospital bed only to come to Iceland to catch the *plague*.

"Brennivín. It's our national liquor. *Svarti dauði*—or 'Black Death'—what we call it here," he says. "It ought to have a skull and crossbones on the label. Smells of caraway seeds, yeah?"

Without getting too close, I inhale sharply. I get a whiff of bile and beneath it, the faint anise scent of caraway, indeed.

"Sounds like you ran into Molly Collins. Loves the stuff. Says it's inspiring. Iceland's answer to absinthe, only twice as disgusting." He takes a giant step over the puddle and grips my hand in his icy one. "Einar Thorlac."

Einar leads me to the kitchen, where I wash myself off. Then, in the large clean fridge, he locates some *skyr*—a local dairy product that is somewhere between cheese and yogurt—and hands it to me. He grabs some greenish blood sausage for himself. Einar soon proves to be, by far, the friendliest person I have met in the colony since I arrived.

"Everyone in Iceland wants to be a writer," he explains to me smugly while we eat. "Like in America how you all want to eat slug poops on TV for money."

"Hey," I interrupt, thinking of the daytime sociological atrocities I'd seen on the hospital television. "Some of us actually draw the line at the slugs themselves."

"We here in Iceland have just three hundred thousand people, and each year we publish one thousand new novels."

This number seems astounding for any populace, but I have a harder time believing there can be so much to say about this place—which from my window appears to be just an endless, frozen expanse of cold blue trees and snow.

"One book for every three hundred people, every year? That puts even Brooklyn to shame."

Einar lets out a deep belly laugh and asks me some questions about living in New York City, where I haven't really lived in years—mostly how I can live there, what with the many heroin addicts and muggings. And I tell him that it isn't like that so much anymore, and he seems a bit let down. Eventually, the inevitable question comes.

"So how is your writing coming along?" he asks me.

"Quite well," I lie. How can you confess writer's block to someone whose countrymen crank out a Library of Alexandria each year? "And you?"

"I wrote seventeen words this morning," he says proudly. "But I'm a poet. For me that's very good."

We share a laugh and then stare out the window and wonder if the weather will ever clear up. The strange light is on again, cutting through the darkness.

"What is that?" I ask, gesturing to it.

"The Friðarsúlan," he says. "Meaning 'Imagine Peace Column.' Yoko Ono built it out on the island of Viðey in memory of John."

He pauses while I look confused, then adds, "Lennon?"

"Yes, I'm familiar with his work," I say quickly. "Just didn't know his crazy widow had built a giant spotlight in the middle of a frozen ocean for him."

Einar is shocked that this news has not reached America, particularly in the great city where Lennon was shot by one of the many crazies who no longer overrun the place. We're preoccupied, I explain—what with all the slug poops.

"It runs entirely off of geothermal energy," he says proudly. "On the side is written *'Hugsa Sér Frið'*—that's 'Imagine Peace'—in twenty-four languages."

Both of us stare out at the light, which glows bright and steady. It has been snowing ceaselessly for the whole week that I have been here and, even for Iceland, it is apparently untenable. All the roads are closed—the taxi that took me here from the airport ferry drove a snowplow ahead of it and charged me a small fortune. I'm praying the Oakeses will reimburse me, should I locate their son. My mind drifts back to my hospital stay, weeks ago.

One morning I had opened my eyes to find a beautiful older woman in a dark pantsuit sitting by my side. For a moment I'd thought it was my mother, but soon I realized that it was someone else's mother—Mrs. Pauline Oakes. Not entirely certain that she was not a by-product of my morphine drip, I ventured a hello. Glad to see me awake, she skipped the pleasantries and got straight to the point.

"My father called from Africa, about your . . . accident. At first we thought he was completely out of his mind. He kept saying Jeffrey had been hurt. But then a nice young man from North Carolina whose family is well known in the telecom business was there, and he confirmed that you were actually just a friend of Jeffrey's and, well—. Look, let's just take all that nonsense from the past and leave it there. Close the book, as it were."

I must have nodded groggily. I barely remembered who I was, let alone who Jeffrey was. Let alone why I'd been in Africa.

"Jeffrey has checked himself in to some writers' colony in Iceland, and he hasn't called or written in two months. And, despite the threat of a lawsuit, the caretaker there has refused to respond to me."

Mr. and Mrs. Oakes were the owners of Oakes International, which imported and exported wines and other luxury foods around the globe, and they had more or less raised Jeffrey in the vineyards of the Loire Valley, the caviar farms of the Black Sea, the Merino sheep pastures of Norwich, and in the finest real estate in all of Manhattan.

"How do you know he's still there?" I asked.

"*Someone* just ordered twelve bottles of the Petit Pineau to the colony," she said. "The 1998. That's Jeffrey's favorite."

"What do you want me to do about it?" I asked. Maybe she didn't know that Jeffrey and I hadn't been on speaking terms in more than ten years, though we'd been quite close before his worldwide success had settled in, and unsettled him.

Mrs. Oakes made a face. "You're a writer, too, aren't you?" She said "writer" as if it were approximately one rung beneath sanitation engineer. "I'll pay you to go there and find my son. If you can persuade Jeffrey to come home, I'll be quite grateful."

She said "grateful" in a way that made me feel that there would be even more money involved if I succeeded. When I stared blankly at my swollen, bandaged leg, she coughed and added, "And, seeing as you have no health insurance to speak of, as a sign of good faith, and on the condition you won't sue my father for any involvement in your injury, my husband has already settled your sizeable hospital bill."

She got up and gave me a smile that was almost kind, and then she left. For a long time I lay in bed, jamming the buttons on the TV remote that was built into the side rail, scanning endless airwaves. Feisty judges hollered at civil court plaintiffs about unpaid child support. "Real" housewives who appeared to be 90 percent silicone drank and squabbled over their marital troubles. Parents herded their eight, twelve, possibly thirty-seven children about like goats. I thought about Mrs. Oakes, worrying after her son. I thought about my own mother, to whom I hadn't spoken in years. She did not even know that I had nearly died. She might even be dead herself. How would I know?

Shaking off these sobering thoughts, I half consider asking Einar for a bottle of Brennivín.

When I look back at the table, I notice that both Einar's plate and mine have been cleared. He is flipping through a small book of poems that he has pulled down from a nearby shelf—even the kitchenette has perhaps a hundred books tucked into its walls.

"Did you clear that? Was someone else in here just now?" I ask, thinking that the elusive Franklin W. Zaff must be close by at last.

Einar shrugs, nonplussed. "The caretaker tries not to distract us. Unless of course it was the elves."

He smirks slightly at this last statement, and I cannot tell if he is serious. According to the brochure I found, Icelanders are extremely superstitious about what they call "hidden people"—rumored to live underground and inside of rocks. Superstitious to the point where Reykjavik's new state-of-the-art opera house was carefully constructed so as not to disturb the surrounding bedrock and features a crystalline upper floor resembling the mythical dwellings of the hidden people. Perhaps they hoped to entice a few to come up and check out *Le Nozze di Figaro*.

"Don't tell me you believe in that stuff," I say.

Einar shrugs. "Most Icelanders don't believe, really. We just don't *not* believe. Some of us think of them as a mischievous force, not little things with pointy ears."

I scoff and mutter, "Say what you want about reality TV, but at least in America we don't believe in elves."

"Oh," Einar says wryly. "Well. You win."

Figuring I may as well take my chance, I lean in closely and ask Einar if he knows another American, my age, staying at the colony, named Jeffrey Oakes.

He arches his pieced eyebrows and leans in. "Jeffrey Oakes?" He whispers even though there is no one else in the room—except perhaps the elves. "He's *here?*"

I nod. "At least he was here. I'm sort of looking for him."

Einar shakes his head. "I haven't seen him. But the caretaker's office is over at the carriage house. Zaff'll tell you what room to find your friend in."

I wince, looking out the window. The dark carriage house appears to be a half mile away, up a snowy hill that I'm not sure I can climb, given my leg.

Einar invites me to stop by his room later to try a little Brennivín.

The lining of my throat prickles at the thought of some new, strange nectar of the writing gods. But even as I promise to join him, the smell of Molly's caraway-tainted puke rises in my nostrils again, and I have second thoughts. Einar goes back to round his word count up to an even twenty for the day, and I return to my own room. There are six more books on my nightstand and my sheets have been changed. My typewriter has been reloaded with paper and my morning's stalled draft has been placed on a pile with the dozens of similar drafts from previous mornings. I begin to put on every warm item of clothing I own. I decide I am going to make it out to the carriage house and find the man in charge of this exceedingly strange colony—and perhaps, even, Jeffrey. If I die in the attempt at least I won't have to finish my novel.

Reaching the carriage house seems even more impossible as soon as I am outside in the brutal elements. Even bundled in two coats, I feel the glacial cold freezing the marrow inside my bones. It is still dark out and the air carries the faint smell of a distant icy sea. My injury forces my steps to be deliberate as I traverse the waist-high snowbanks that cover the path. As I tunnel up the hill, I wonder how Franklin W. Zaff could possibly be doing any caretaking without maintaining a better path through these mounds of ice. The edges are so high that I can't see the cabin after a while. But I keep a bearing on that strange light in the sky, as it reflects off snow that is falling steadily, many miles away.

My leg is throbbing and I think I am barely halfway there. I turn around and see that the walls of my path have collapsed in places, and it will be hardly easier to get back down again. There is a new, duller pain in my fingertips and toes that I suspect vaguely as probably frostbite. I wonder what would happen if I lost my fingers. Screw the toes. I could live without toes. But without fingers I couldn't hit the keys on the typewriter or grip a pen. At first I think this may be some sort of sweet relief—a reprieve from writing the same scene over and over. But the writing over and over isn't really a sign of madness. It's the only thing letting the madness out. With grim certainty I decide that if I feel a finger snapping off I'll do the only sensible thing and lie down and die. I wonder if they'd find me—in six months or so—after the thaw. I wonder if they'd understand why I'd given up.

After a few minutes I carve my way into a small rocky outcropping. Just as I'm about to go around it, I see that I can get on top of it. And this gets my head above the drifts. Then I can see it—off to what I think is the southeast—a pillar of white light rising out of the choppy sea, just past the horizon. I forget my pain in moments. There is something absolutely insane yet incredible about it—a memorial built in the middle of nowhere at all, crying "Imagine Peace" to the descendants of last millennium's Vikings. It is the sort of singular, absurd devotional that only great love can inspire. This is what I am trying to build each morning with my steam train of words. Something everlasting for a love that didn't last. When I have my breath back, I press on, carving my way steadily to the door of the old carriage house.

I let myself in and find, to my extreme disappointment, that the lights are out and no one is there. As I enter I stumble roughly over a wooden mailing crate that has been set just beside the door, and nearly fly headlong toward a sleekly modern desk. I catch myself on its edge, and though my leg flares angrily in pain and I knock over quite a few papers, I manage to avoid smashing my head. The room is lit only by the faint glow of Yoko's distant light.

"Is anyone here?" I shout, but there is no answer. "Anyone at all?"

Looking for something—a guest book, maybe, or even a sign-in sheet—I carefully stack up the papers I have knocked over. All of them are written in indecipherable Icelandic, except for the return addresses on two unopened letters, which lie in a pile of unopened mail by the door—all several weeks old from the postmarks. One of them is a crisp, clean envelope from the offices of Emmetz, Moscowitz, and Bing. With only slight trepidation, I open it and find inside a strongly worded threat of pending legal action, on the behalf of one Mrs. Pauline Oakes, that her son be produced immediately. Slowly I begin to suspect that no one has been in this office for some time.

The second letter confirms these fears. Franklin W. Zaff, of 28 Bistle-thwaite Court, Herefordshire, UK, writes the following:

To Whom It May Concern at the Laxness-Hallgrímsson Writers' Colony:

Unfortunately I will be unable to take over the position of winter cura-tor, due to the unexpected moving-up of the publication date of my new novel, THE FINDER'S KEEPER, which as you know was not due out until the coming summer. My editor at Haslett & Grouse requires me suddenly for book signings, readings, guest lectures, etc., and I feel it would be in my best interests, professionally, to make myself available. I do realize, natu-rally, that this is on somewhat short notice, and I hope that a suitable replacement can be found before the current curator departs.

With heavy heart,
Franklin W. Zaff

Crumpling the letter and tossing it aside, I wonder if I might be able somehow to gather every existing copy of *The Finder's Keeper* and burn Franklin W. Zaff on a pyre built out of them. If the postmarks are to be believed, there has been no one in these offices for three weeks at least. The bulk of the writers remaining have been either too self-absorbed to notice that they've been utterly abandoned or too terrified to face this possibility.

Not sure how to proceed, I sit there for a few more minutes, and soon my eye wanders to the packing slip on the large wooden crate that I nearly somersaulted over upon my entry. In the dim light I can just make out the familiar logo of Oakes International. I turn the box and see, to my delight, that the shipment is for "Mr. Anton Prishibeyev. The Suite at the Top of the Bell Tower. Laxness-Hallgrímsson Writers' Colony, Akranes, Iceland."

I stare down at the name for a moment even before I recognize the alias I gave to Jeffrey once, in a piece of fiction written a lifetime ago, but once I do, it brings a very warming smile.

The problem now, however, is that the Bell Tower is all the way back down the hill. And my leg already feels like someone has been sawing it against a pine tree for an hour. My eyes fall onto the thin, wooden desk and suddenly I have an idea. Clearing it off with wild swipes of my arms, I invert the desk and lay it on the snow outside the door. It sinks into the snow only a little; it is of such light, modern construction. Unfortunately, when I throw my emaciated weight onto my makeshift sled, it is not enough to propel us down the path. For a moment I lie there, feeling the falling snow covering me, and I ponder the end. If this is it, I think, then I'm at least breaking into Jeffrey's wine. I reach down to pry off the lid, and then—inspiration.

With my last bit of strength, I lift the box of wine onto the sled and prepare to make a special delivery. This time when I leap into the sled, it inches forward, and I gain a little momentum, and then a little more, and soon I am speeding downhill through a sheet of white spray like an eager child. I can't think of the last time I was so happy.

At the bottom finally, I crane my neck to the top of the old bell tower, peering through the falling snow. Are there faint signs of flickering light in the small dark cutaways? I can't tell if it is a trick of the darkness.

As I climb the stairs slowly, propping the box of wine up against the handrail, I wonder what I will find at the top. I try not to make assumptions based on the empty Brennivín bottles that I keep stumbling upon, which go skipping off down the spiral staircase and shatter fantastically on the flagstone below. But I brace myself for the increasing likelihood that Jeffrey is soaked through like a ladyfinger in a caraway tiramisu. He could be rocking gently in a corner, talking to himself—the result of months without any medication. Or, considering how it gets colder and colder with every foot that I raise, will I find only a Jeffrey Oakes–flavored Popsicle? With each step my leg throbs harder and the sound of typing grows louder.

The staircase seems never ending, and after what feels like a mile, I collapse onto one of the frigid steps. I feel the sweat on my pants' seat freezing to the stone. Not for the first time, I think about what little I'd be leaving behind, if I was to give up and let myself pass out in the cold, cold tower. Hypothermia has me in its grip—all that remains is for me to let it take me. What did anyone really leave behind, I wonder. A family? A home? All I'd ever wanted to remain in my wake was a book. A simple, stupid mass of words. And I'd failed, even at that.

The hammering of typewriter arms against an inky strip echoes down the tower. I seize the box of wine and force myself up against the wall. The typing stops. I feel the fabric rip out of my pants. It remains, iced to the step. A roller is rolled; a sheet extracted and replaced. I command one leg, and then the other, to lift. The typing begins anew.

And for this imperfect immortality, what prices have been paid? How many livers, lungs, and veins? Shredded, polluted, shot? How many children deserted, family secrets betrayed, sordid trysts laid out for strangers to see? How many wives and husbands shoved to the side? How many ovens scorched with our hair? Gun barrels slid between our lips? Bathtubs slowly reddened by our blood and twisting rivers that drowned us? How many flawed pages burned in disgust and reduced to ashes? How many flawless moments observed from just a slight distance so that, later, we might reduce them to words? All with an unspoken prayer that these hard-won truths might outlast the brief years of our lies.

At last I arrive at the top. As I catch what breath I have left, I think back to the last time I saw Jeffrey. I told him he was insane. He called me a fantasist. Neither accusation had been untrue, and yet I wondered if he had injured me half as much as I had injured him. After all, my hopeless cause was only love; his was everything. His entire mind. Over the years, I'd wondered once or twice if he'd seen his breakdown coming. Surely, he must have; Jeffrey was never unobservant, and there was little he was more absorbed by than himself. He must have known the day he signed the contracts that he was signing away his only life preserver—the book that had buoyed him up while all else whirled him down and down in spirals that grew with each passing month. With every milligram of Lotosil that had worked just a little less well than the milligram before. With every substitution he'd tried to make that only came up short. What sort of courage had it taken to let go of the last thing keeping him afloat?

Leaning against the door, I wonder if maybe I've been clinging to a life preserver all my own. I wonder if he can show me how to let it go.

At last I push open the door to find Jeffrey, typing away at a little desk, on the same little Icelandic typewriter I have back in my room. Beside him is a stack of paper, perhaps a foot high—it looks like almost a thousand pages—weighted down with a half-empty Brennivín bottle. As I step in, he catches sight of my reflection in a tarnished mirror on the wall, but still the typing doesn't stop.

"Just leave the box by the door, thank you," he says, without breaking eye contact with his page.

I set the box down and my leg spasms so badly I can't walk another step. The *click-clack* of the keys echoes through the room, bouncing off the stone. I come around behind him so that he will see me clearly, and in the process I pass the mirror and get the first good look at myself that I've had in weeks. No wonder why the others in the colony have been shrinking away from me. Even by the low standards of writers, I look deranged. Beard shaggy in some places and patchy in others. My eyes bloodshot and underlined in inky purple rings. Skin so pale that I swear I can see my skull through it.

"I was *told* that no tips were required," Jeffrey says loudly, the typing slowing but not stopping, his eyes drifting up but not breaking his stare. "But if you insist, there should be some kronor or something in my bag. Front pocket."

Stepping forward so he can see me better, I smile wanly at my old friend, and at last, his eyes lock onto mine. The typing stops suddenly.

"Good God," Jeffrey says, jumping up from the desk. He winces and immediately collapses back into his chair. He looks nearly as terrible as I do.

"I haven't stood up in a while," he admits. From the intensity of his face, I am guessing that "a while" is on the order of a magnitude of days, not hours. From the smell of the place I guess he's been relieving himself in empty bottles and subsisting only on the full ones. He keeps glancing back at his reflection, as if worried it might run away from him while he's looking the other way. I've seen him like this before.

"Your mother asked me to come," I explain. "She wants you to go home."

Jeffrey stares at the typewriter in the mirror for a few minutes. "I haven't quite finished. Just another chapter or two. Should be done by morning. Tomorrow we'll go."

"There's nobody running this place," I say. "And the snow's starting to let up. We should go while we can. Tomorrow might be too late."

"Have a drink," he says, offering the bottle of Brennivín. As he lifts it, the top pages of his stack blow off and I catch one in the air.

"That's not finished yet!" he shouts, struggling to get back to his feet but failing.

I scan a line from the middle of the page:

and here, almost against his deadish look at the man; it is life, as it hasn't been; no promise of redemption visible; in the man others found it that the man had not found; firm lips and eyes open, oh and that self-same expression as in life and it is as it hasn't been and the looking in is nothing and nothing, through the head goes the point

There isn't a period to be found on the page. There aren't any on the page that tops the stack, and I wouldn't have been surprised to learn there weren't any in the whole manuscript. I wonder if he's been typing all of this without looking at it—and yet somehow he's also cleverly avoided any words containing c, q, w, or z. I put the pages back and set the bottle on top of them again.

Poor bastard. He'd leapfrogged his *Ulysses* and gone right to his *Finnegans Wake*. He begins to cough and cough, for a solid minute. While I wait for him to stop, I pry the lid off the box of wine and stack the '98 Petit Pineaus out on the floor. I have no idea how much they cost, but they can't be as priceless as a thousand pages of Oakes. So I scoop up the manuscript pages and set them evenly inside the box. By the time I get the lid back on, Jeffrey has propelled himself halfway across the room on his weakened legs. I see blood on the back of his hand when he finally moves it away.

"Come on," I say, "we've got to get you to a doctor."

Jeffrey doesn't seem particularly enamored of this solution, and he argues loudly even as he lets me get an arm around him and we hoist each other up. When had we become old men?

"You'd better not try to steal any of it," he warns. "Those damned elves keep coming in here, changing things. Well, I told them—Jeffrey Oakes doesn't write by committee. This isn't some Hollywood screenplay here. You don't get producers credits just for bringing me weak coffee and filthy muffins every morning."

I smile a little wider at the familiar, pleasant sound of his babbling. As much as it concerns me, I know that he has been this way before, and that he is not always this way. If he can get better then we both can.

And, now that he mentions it, I wonder who *has* been bringing the muffins and coffee. Not Franklin W. Zaff—that much I am sure of. Maybe Einar wasn't so wrong about that mischievous force.

Soon we'll be lodged in a French château, surrounded by withered grapevines that will be green in good time. And I keep thinking I'd like to go home myself.

"Time to return to the lands of mothers and slug poops," I say.

"I don't mean to alarm you," Jeffrey says, "but you're speaking gibberish."

Jeffrey and I brace against each other, and we head for the doorway, tripping over empty bottles and still more stacks of Icelandic books, which I swear weren't there moments before.

I ask, "Why is it that these people can't stop writing all these books? You'd think they'd run out of things to say about this place."

What I mean to ask is, how it is that they can write so many and I can't seem to manage even one?

"'A book must be the ax for the frozen sea within us,'" Jeffrey says sagely.

"That's lovely," I say. And I mean it.

"Kafka," he says proudly.

"You wouldn't really expect that. From him."

"No," Jeffrey agrees, looking rather blissed all of a sudden.

Through the window, beyond the mirrors, I can still see the warm glow of Yoko's light. It really is a magnificent thing. A pillar that climbs to the clouds, in honor of a great love lost. Now it seems like the only thing that could possibly have been built. And that it could have been built only here, in this void, where nothingness was waiting to be made into something.

As we slowly descend the stairs, words begin ordering themselves in my head. I can see—clearly—that which is not there at all. A woman, sitting in front of an array of mirrors on her wedding day, thinking about waking in darkness that morning and not knowing just yet where she is. And not wanting to know, at first. And then suddenly it is as if I can hear her voice in my own head, and it takes all I have to not run back up to Jeffrey's typewriter and let it out. It's a voice I haven't heard in a long, long time, but I feel sure that it isn't going away now. I hobble a little faster toward the exit. I think that I know how to proceed.

10

King Me

Do not trouble yourself much to get new things, whether clothes or friends. Turn the old; return to them. Things do not change; we change.

—HENRY DAVID THOREAU, *WALDEN*

Jeffrey sits in the window wearing a white waffle-woven bathrobe embroidered with the elegant logo of the Hotel Luxembourg. His left hand moves lazily out in the fifth-story air, as if conducting an invisible orchestra. His right hand pinches a cigarette, which he smokes fiercely while staring down at the statue of Grand Duke Guillaume II in the square below. Then Jeffrey looks back into the kitchenette, where I lean over a newspaper written in Luxembourgish, a language I frankly did not even know existed before we arrived.

"It's just too . . . I mean, *honestly*. You know what I mean? Does it have to be quite so . . . ? Just *look* at them all down there . . . 'Oh . . . I'm blah blah blah. Don't you think blah blah is so blah?' 'Yes, quite blah.' God! You know what I'm saying?"

He tosses the lit cigarette across the hotel room, and it lands in the large empty fireplace, amid the butts of yesterday's pack. His right hand traces a route through his gray hairs, down the freckled ridge of his ear, and then along the shoulder slope of robe to his pocket, where he fishes out his aluminum pack of Chancellor Treasurer cigarettes. He is hardly ever without one for more than a minute. He calls it his "sovereign addiction"—the only one remaining after obliterating pills, booze, and sex from his diet.

"What *is* it about this place? I don't even know what we're doing here."

"You wanted to come," I remind him. "You could have stayed with Pauline."

An electric shudder runs through Jeffrey, and I know he is thinking back on the recuperative months we spent at the Oakes Reserve Vineyard in the Loire Valley—being ruthlessly picked over by his mother while doctors from all over Europe hemmed and hawed in the hallway.

"I keep having this nightmare," he'd confessed as we'd strolled aimlessly down the still-frosted rows of vines. "They cut me up in my sleep and build a new Jeffrey out of aggregate parts. I come out half my size, with one lung, no liver, and a bird heart."

In truth, they'd stuck him with acupuncture needles and fed him kale. They'd injected him with vitamin C and had him drink a gallon of raw milk daily. With each week that passed, Jeffrey did, indeed, appear a bit smaller and shorter of breath, but his antic scratching and midnight outbursts slowly diminished as well. His eyes no longer danced after things that no one else could see. This is when the gray came into his hair. This is when he began staring at his typewriter, never pressing a key.

I wasn't surprised that, when my leg was finally fully healed and I told Jeffrey I was going to head into Luxembourg, he had his bags in the back of his father's Renault before I'd even downloaded the maps. But that was days ago, and by now Jeffrey's mood has swung right around again.

"I'm just *saying*," he gripes, lighting the new cigarette. "Who goes to Luxembourg? Everything about this place . . . is so . . . so perfectly . . . *uhm . . . humph.*"

That Jeffrey can't quite put a finger on his issue with Luxembourg cannot, entirely, be blamed on writer's block. I feel it, too. The trouble with Luxembourg is that you can't quite figure out what it is trying to be exactly. Everywhere I look there are soaring parapets and medieval coats of arms. There are old men playing checkers on a folding table in the park below us and stone gargoyles on the ramparts above us. But even they seem a bit *bored* by it all. In Paris you could complain the Eiffel Tower was not as striking as you'd hoped. In Berlin the beer wouldn't be worth the crowds. In London the fog could be thick but not hiding-Jack-the-Ripper thick. In all these places there were expectations, but in Luxembourg there were none. One might ask how, without any expectations, could anything be a letdown? But that was the thing—there was a delight in *being* let down that Jeffrey thrived on. Here it all just *was*, no better or worse than what we'd never imagined. And Jeffrey was floundering like a saltwater fish dropped into a pond. Everything looked right and yet he was steadily suffocating; all the poisons he'd long ago adapted to withstand were suddenly nowhere to be found.

"This is hopeless," I announce, folding up the newspaper, having scanned each of its pages for any mention of the royal family. Though Luxembourg is smaller than Rhode Island and with half the population, it has been surprisingly difficult to locate one of the duchy's best-known residents. And then again, she's everywhere. It was big news when the duke's fifth son married an American actress—the biggest news in Luxembourg in a decade. After nine years, they still sell DVDs of the ceremony at every newsstand; her face remains printed onto coffee mugs at the tourist gift shops. Down in the lobby of our hotel there is a display filled with plates commemorating the royal wedding. Yet the princess herself has thus far eluded us.

Immediately upon checking in to the hotel, we'd walked down through the sunny Old City to the flamboyantly spired Grand Ducal Palace and introduced ourselves to the guards. They wore olive green coats with red-and-blue braided regalia and snug black berets. With the machine guns strapped across their chests, they vaguely resembled a pair of militant parking attendants.

"*Jo!*" Jeffrey had said. "*Gudde Moien! Ech hu grad een immensen Huttkar!*"

The guards had stared at Jeffrey's head curiously until I discovered in the phrase book that he'd just informed them he'd bought an incredible hat.

"You are tourists?" one had asked.

"Tourists!" Jeffrey had laughed. "Good God, no! We're actually very old friends of Her Highness, the Princess. If you would just buzz on up and see if she's available . . . "

One of the guards had lifted his bulky black walkie-talkie and spoken in clipped Luxembourgish. Jeffrey had appeared satisfied, until seven more parking attendants arrived to remove us.

"You don't understand! I've known her since she was thirteen years old! We went to school together! In America? *Ah-MER-Ik-KAH*. For chrissakes, *this* one's slept with her more times than *you* all have been invaded by Germany."

I thanked any and all available gods—including the one who had toppled the Tower of Babel—that this last bit seemed to get lost in translation.

"We demand an audience with the princess!" Jeffrey had insisted angrily.

"You are . . . "—the guard had begun, communing quickly with his brethren to be sure he had the English correct—". . . not expected."

"I'm Jeffrey Oakes!" he had cried as we were escorted away. "I've never been expected in my entire life!"

Our attempt to storm the palace had not exactly gone swimmingly.

Finally, Jeffrey slides off the windowsill and announces, "I'm going to shower."

"You've showered twice today," I say as I move to the corner desk, where I have a stack of hotel stationery and a bundle of pens. "Why don't you try writing something?"

He laughs until it turns into coughing—fainter, but still with an echo of Iceland. I listen to him bang about inside, under the crackle of the news on Radio Télévision Luxembourg. I sit down to write. Each day I write out all that I've already written and try to gain enough momentum to push through.

Her Imperial Majesty Mrs. J---- and the other ladies leave the room and I am alone for the first time since early this morning. It was still dark out, when I first opened my eyes. Those first few seconds, I did not even remember my own name. My whole universe was simply snowflakes falling lightly onto the evergreens, the yellow rock of moon, high above the encroaching clouds. When I was eight, it snowed on Christmas morning while we were in Atlanta with Grandmother. It was the only time I ever heard my mother call anything a miracle.

Seconds passed and I remembered that I was in Chiyoda, in Tokyo, at the Fukiage Ōmiya Palace. That today would be my wedding day. That I was about to marry Haru, my prince. Literally. That my grandmother is dead and that Christmases are over and there are no miracles and that Atlanta is on the other side of this great sphere of rock.

Now, hours later, I am alone, sitting in front of the dressing-table mirror, caking white powder onto my face. The ladies have shown me how to cover my face with the *bintsuke-abura*, an oily wax mask that holds the powder—used by geishas and Imperial Princesses of the Yamato Dynasty alike for centuries upon centuries. With each dab the excess powder explodes and drifts off slowly through the dead air.

I stop where I've been stopping for weeks. I can't manage another word. I flip through the book on Japan and the copy of *An Actor Prepares* that I borrowed from the Oakes family library; I push down on the French press that room service has brought me. I pick at the flaking spirals of a croissant; I chew on the only white sliver of fingernail I have left. But I am still stuck. No amount of caffeine seems able to push me past that powder, drifting slowly in the dead air.

What goes on inside her head?

For a while I listen to the quiet of the sleepy medieval city outside. Then, finally hearing the sound of shower water running, I push my chair back and cross to the front hall. There, in the bottom of the hall closet, in the bottom of my heaviest suitcase, I withdraw a wooden box, filled with manuscript pages that do not belong to me.

After his third shower of the day, I manage to coax Jeffrey down into the neighboring Place d'Armes for a stroll. He's run low on cigarettes, anyway. Charming blue umbrellas extend out from a few cafés and beer halls, frequented by Luxembourgers at all hours. Rippling in an ever-present breeze, pleasant flags hang along the medieval archways. Men in puffy shirts sell flowers and used books out of wheeled carts, which they push over wobbly cobblestones. One imagines there must be a dedicated Office of Quaintness, dispatching pudgy burghers in velvet tunics all around town to keep covering the bricks with moss.

The travel sites all describe Luxembourg as a fairy tale come to life, but it feels less like a Grimm land of trolls and big bad wolves, and more like Disneyland Paris. Luxembourg is the wealthiest country in all of Europe, and the Old City is overrun by the tax-sheltered children of eBay and Skype executives, moving in Pied Piper phalanxes with their phones out and thumbs flying—casting spells out into the ethernet. Jeffrey and I dodge them as they trample by in their hiply untied sneakers, their ironic and yet inaccurate THIS IS NOT A T-SHIRT T-shirts. They buzz like flies around the McDonald's and the Pizza Hut, although we have learned in time that they favor the Chi-Chi's Mexican restaurant. Meanwhile, their fathers bark madly on Bluetooths at Brasserie Plëss and stuff themselves full of Grillwurscht sausages and plum *quetschentaarts* at La Cristallerie. Which fairy tale these characters feature in I cannot recall.

Jeffrey lingers a moment by some men playing checkers. He pretends to be fiddling with his watch and *not* examining the boards, but I can see his eyes jumping along with a red checker in zigzags, all the way across the board to the edge.

"*Schachmatt!*" one old man says smugly. Jeffrey smiles as the other spits on the ground and neatly places a second piece atop the first, transforming it into a king.

"You used to have a board but no pieces," I remind Jeffrey.

"I played when I was a kid," he answers. I wait for him to go on. "Of course, chess is supposed to be the better game, but I always found it too . . ."

He trails off, searching for the right finish.

"Want to play a round?" I ask, taking a seat at an empty table. Jeffrey tries to pretend he's not interested.

"There aren't any pieces," he complains.

"Here," I say, reaching over to a neighboring café table and grabbing a little bowl full of sugar packets. "You can be the white packets and I'll be the pink."

Jeffrey snorts, even as he sits down and begins to fluidly set up the board. "Supposed to be red and black pieces. That's why I liked it as a kid. Chess was all black and white. I always got stuck being the bad guys. I'm going to cream you, by the way."

I smile and, as promised, he proceeds to cream me. He guides his packets in effortless slanted motions, crossing the board with ease and then, once his packets had been kinged, bringing them zigzagging back across the board again.

"It's oddly democratic," Jeffrey continues. "No bishops and pawns and knights, with elite abilities to move this way or that. In checkers it's only by cunningly avoiding capture—by hopping all the way across the board into enemy territory—that you can gain any real advantage. And all it is—here's the brilliant bit—all being kinged is, really, is gaining the ability to reverse course. To go against the tide, as it were, back to where you've begun. See?"

I nod, just happy to see him finishing his thoughts. We play one game and then another, and as we begin the third we both become aware of a cinnamon-skinned man watching us from a nearby park bench. He wears dark shades and a black suit and sips from a soup bowl of green *bouneschlupp*. He is the only gentleman of color in the Place d'Armes, but what truly makes him conspicuous is his hair, which puffs out in a seventies-style Afro.

"Check out Mr. Black Panther," I say.

"Think he's an assassin?" Jeffrey teases.

"If he is, which one of us is he after?" I muse.

"Depends. Just what have you been up to these past ten years?"

Jeffrey eyes me evenly as he captures my final packet and effectively ends the third game.

"Let's go," he says. "This guy weirds me *out*."

We move off toward the nearby flea market and Jeffrey seems a half ounce lighter. We peruse old coffeepots and empty picture frames. He dawdles for a bit by a used-book cart while I buy a collectible royal wedding stamp bearing a good likeness of the princess. She has her cascade of hair pinned up, which sets off her high cheekbones even more. But what, I wonder, is going on between them? I gaze into her stipple-inked eyes and try to hear the voices inside her head.

Jeffrey and I sit down on the edge of a large marble fountain, and I try to remember sitting beside her on a fountain years ago, running lines. *'Love. What an idea!' Now you say, 'You don't love him, then?' and I'll say, 'But I won't hear of any sort of unfaithfulness!' Remember that.*

" 'This fountain commemorates Luxembourg's two national poets— Lentz and Dicks,' " Jeffrey reads. "That had to be a tough name to get through school with."

I scowl slightly as Jeffrey reads on. "Mr. Lentz wrote the national motto. *'Mir wëlle bleiwe wat mir sin'* . . . 'We wish to remain what we are.' "

It really explains this strange place, I think, as Jeffrey considers the fountain. The gargoyles, the old men, the cobblestones. Maybe it's trying with all its might not to change in any way. Maybe Luxembourg is stuck, just like us.

"You really think you've changed that much?" I ask.

Jeffrey stares down at the rippling fountain water and runs his hand through the gray streaks above his ear again. "Most days I hardly recognize myself."

He watches the flecks of ash from his cigarette fall off and drift down to the water. I am about to accuse him of being melodramatic when a sudden slant of light catches my attention. I look up and see, not far away, that the young woman working at the used-book cart is standing with her sleek cellular phone aimed right at us. She grins and lifts a book off the stack in front of her. *Näischt Helleges* the title reads, and beneath it is a familiar black-and-white photograph.

"Well," I say to Jeffrey, *"somebody* recognizes you."

Jeffrey refuses to go back to the hotel even after I remind him that we've checked in as Timothy Wallace and Anton Prishibeyev. "They'll know we're staying there!" he shouts, and when I try to ask him who "they" are exactly, he rushes off in the other direction, fleeing the park and leading us southward through town, dodging up and down alleys and over bridges, all the way to the Place de la Constitution at the edge of the Old City. But the area around the monument is packed with sightseeing buses and camera-clutching tourists. Panicking, Jeffrey bolts down a set of stairs and descends into the deep and verdant Petrusse Valley.

These stairs take us all the way to the bottom of the chasm, which circles the ancient fortress walls of the Old City, which had kept Luxembourg snug and secure for nearly ten centuries before tanks and planes had come along and ruined all the fun. Down here, Jeffrey rushes along a jogging path until he reaches a little raised outpost—a forward fortification of some kind, now topped with empty park benches.

Wheezing, Jeffrey slumps against the balustrade and looks hatefully out at the wide Petrusse Valley beyond. It's only then that he notices that there are hundreds of pigeons, fat and gray, swarming beneath the benches, feasting on gingerbread crumbs. Jeffrey covers his mouth as he staggers upwind, nervous about the molted feathers that hang in the air. I want to rush over and pull him back, but I stay by the edge, looking up at the Place de la Constitution above us. In its center is a great obelisk that commemorates the Luxembourgers who died in the Great War. At the very top of the monument is a gilded statue of a woman, hovering angelically with a wreath in her hands. From down in the valley, it looks as though she's floating in thin air.

"Come on," I say. "Let's just go back to the hotel. So you have a fan! It's not exactly the end of the world."

Jeffrey just shakes his head. "You don't know what it was like. You weren't there when things got really bad. That Haslett asshole kept on calling, and then Iowa, and whenever I went out, there'd be someone just *staring* at me. It was like I could *see* my words there in their heads. *Crawling* there on the undersides of their foreheads. It was like they thought I *knew* something. And they always ask me, *Is it true? Is it true? Did it really happen?* And then . . . *What's next? What are you working on now?* All of these . . . these . . . these—"

"Expectations?" I finish for him.

He nods and I can hear the crinkle of the aluminum beneath his seeking fingers. When he finally gets a cigarette out, it shakes in his hand so badly that he drops it. I pick it up for him, blowing on it to get the Luxembourg off. He throws it back to the ground again.

"Where the hell did you go?" he demands.

I chew my lip and finally say, "I wish I hadn't."

Jeffrey takes another cigarette out and this time hands me the lighter. Then he leans in and I shield the flame.

So then I tell him where I went. I tell him about New York and Timothy Wallace and Dubai. Jeffrey laughs, hardly able to believe me—except that he saw the passport I used to check in to the hotel. I tell him about meeting Tina, his old junior editor, on the train in Sri Lanka, and I'm surprised at myself—how sad it still makes me to talk about her. I tell him about the way the Tamil boy read *Nothing Sacred* until they tore him from it. He stops fidgeting at this—to hear that his life preserver buoyed someone else, some total stranger, a world away and mixed up in a war started by this boy's grandparents before he or I or Jeffrey was ever born. Last, I tell him about Jeremiah and the biography I never finished, and here he becomes furious, as I knew he would, but he can't walk away without knowing the end. As I take him through it—my double, the leopard, the writers' colony—his fury fades to anger, and then to mere annoyance. When I finish, he peers up at the golden lady and then out at the flock of pigeons, which continues to cruise, like one creature with a thousand legs, all around the park benches. I play awkwardly with the lighter. Jeffrey does not seem agitated anymore but it is hard to tell. His is still a mind I cannot see into.

Then, finally, he says, "I'll flip you for it."

"Not a chance," I reply.

High above, on the wall, a little train chuffs over to the park, carrying three cars filled with bored tourists. Jeffrey angles his face away from them but stays put, even as several of them snap photos of the little outpost and the two of us amid the pigeons.

Then out of nowhere, he says, "She's going to be at the Philharmonie Luxembourg tonight for their opening."

My hand spasms and drops the lighter. It hits the rocky path under our feet and makes a noise that reverberates loudly out into the whole valley. With one tremendous flapping, the pigeons launch from the benches and take to the sky, up alongside the golden lady.

"How do you know that?"

"It was on the television while you were writing."

"It said she was going to be at the opening?"

"No, but she'll be there."

"How do you know?"

"Because," he grins, "they're doing *Hedda*."

And with that he starts to walk back toward the stairs that lead up the fortification and out of the valley. It takes me a minute to catch up. I have to remember how walking works. I think I might throw up. It's been nearly ten years, during which I've tried being someone else, and traveled the world, and lost the love of a good woman, and nearly died, and—for all of this—I would have expected to have gotten somewhere. But here I am, half sick again, and getting nowhere.

The Philharmonie Luxembourg is shaped like an enormous white teardrop. In this quaint fairy-tale land, it is menacingly modern—like an alien craft that has landed on the mountainside, overlooking all the castles and cathedrals. The opening night is sold out, and Jeffrey and I are only barely able to beg our way into two standing-room tickets, at the back of the Grand Auditorium. For once I am grateful that Jeffrey never journeys anywhere without two sets of black-tie apparel—the second not for me, technically, but a backup, in case there should be stains. We stand among the decked-out citizens of Luxembourg, and I feel as if I've returned to Dubai. Gone are the lederhosen and funny hats; here we swim through a sea of tuxedos and top hats, with more cummerbunds than a junior prom, and the women drag silken fishtails behind them and wear roses in their hair. As I scan the crowd for the princess, I feel like a waiter in borrowed clothes, crashing someone else's party. Again.

"*Dier dierft hei nët fëmmen!*" snaps a woman waving an enormous Chinese fan at Jeffrey. He is attempting, once again, to light a cigarette.

"You can't *smoke* in here," I hiss.

Jeffrey is about to protest when suddenly the crowd turns and their heads sweep up toward the box seats where two of the military parking valets have just stepped out from behind the curtained entrance. They mechanically scour the perimeter and one speaks into his sleeve, and the princess steps into view. She wears a golden gown that radiates as she waves perfunctorily at the crowd below. And there it is—unchanged from years ago—that bored look in her eyes. She smiles, and for a moment I feel a shock of static electricity as her eyes pass over the spot where I am standing. There's no way that she can make me out in the crowd, and yet, for an instant I see her eyes flicker in surprise. I think it is impossible that she can have spotted us, until I turn to Jeffrey and see him waving madly up at the box, lit cigarette in his mouth.

"What?" he grins, enjoying a puff, as ladies in fox stoles push away angrily.

But before I can say or do anything, the space between us is suddenly invaded by a smooth, dark hand, which clips Jeffrey's cigarette between its thumb and forefinger and—with frightening precision—crushes it, lit, in the palm. When I turn, we are both looking straight into the face of the Black Panther.

"I'm going to have to ask you to respect the rules of this establishment," he says in perfect English. "Or you are more than welcome to leave it."

Everything, from his gleaming patent leather shoes to the glint in his eyes, is no-nonsense. The stage lights begin to rise behind the neat circumference of his Afro.

Jeffrey gives the briefest pout before saying, "That's understood," and I want to ask him what he's even *doing* here, but the Black Panther steps back into the crowd. I look up, one last time, desperately, toward the box where the princess is sitting, but now her eyes are fixed on the stage. If she did see us, there is no sign of it now. There is a brief flutter of applause as the curtain rises and the set is revealed.

Two actors step out onto a wide stage. It is all done up like a respectable drawing room, with a huge fireplace and a gleaming piano and a portrait of a frightening old general on the wall. One of the women bends before a closed door, to listen.

"Menger Meenung no hunn si sech nach net geréiert," she stage whispers.

Jeffrey and I exchange a brief look. It had not occurred to either of us that the play, like the newspapers and the books and the television, would be in Luxembourgish.

"Madam, ech hunn lech et jo gesot," the other replies. *"Denkt drunn wéi spéit d'Dampschëff zerekkoum gëschter owend . . ."*

Jeffrey makes a jerking motion with his head in the direction of the exit, but as we begin to shuffle toward it, we notice that the Black Panther is positioned squarely by the doors. He gives us another cool stare and, to my surprise, Jeffrey shrinks back again. I've never seen him this submissive before, not even in the presence of his mother. He seems downright shy.

"We've already paid for it," he murmurs. "I think I've read this one before, anyways. This is the one where the lady winds up miserable at the end, right?"

I stifle a snicker.

A minute or two later there is polite applause from the crowd as the actress playing Hedda finally steps from the wings. She is a tall, fierce-looking blonde, and from way in the back I can make out her bored expression as she gazes out over the fine drawing room—its many luxuries no comfort to her. She's not bad, but she's a faker. I can tell she's only *acting* bored. Really, she's thrilled. It's opening night! Why shouldn't she be? Because my Hedda isn't. I look up at the box seats, and wonder, what must it be like for her? To sit there and watch someone *playing* a role that she has *been* before. Is she thinking about that other stage, half a world away, where she spoke these same lines but in English, and made these same gestures, and paced these same steps? She sits up stiffly, as if she's staring at a mirror, not recognizing her own reflection.

After the show I stay up all night. On my stack of hotel stationery I write out everything I've written before, and this time, when I get to the line about the powder falling in the dead air, I keep going. My pen scratches long trenches into the heavy white pages. It digs through so firmly that on the next page I am crisscrossing the ghostly grooves made by its predecessor. My pen spikes and falls like staccato bursts of gunfire. On a grand stage inside my own head, I can see everything. The princess at her dressing table. The mother-in-law hovering nearby. The cherry blossoms falling outside the window. The cool, gray steel of the morning air, ominous, and testing. It comes so quickly that my greatest challenge is to keep up. Her thoughts become my thoughts. The only interruptions come from the next room, where, from time to time, Jeffrey bangs on the wall and shouts that I'd "better stop all my incessant scratching," but this only makes me increase the tempo. May it drive him mad. May it drive him back to the page again.

There is a photograph on the table in front of me to show me how my face is supposed to look. Mrs. J---- wants the servants to do it for me. "That's tradition," she'd said. I told her I put my own makeup on. For a thousand nights, under a thousand lights, on dozens of stages. For Beckett and for Shakespeare and for Miller and for Simon and for Stoppard and for Mamet and for Ives: I do it myself.

"It's part of my process," I explained to Mrs. J——. She's not an unintelligent woman by any means—being an Imperial Princess and all—but she knows nothing about Stanislavsky. "Bring yourself to the part of taking hold of a role, as if it were your own life. Speak for your character in your own person. When you sense this real kinship to your part, your newly created being will become soul of your soul, flesh of your flesh." I've thought of these words many times before, in many dressing rooms, but never have they felt truer to me than on this day. Today I take the role that I will play for the rest of my life. Today I step out in front of the last audience I will ever entertain. I will quicken their breaths. I will make their hearts swell, and break.

Painted on the walls of the dressing room are pink vistas of koi ponds and cherry blossoms and the barren face of Mount Fuji. Next to the table there's an enormous window, from waist to twenty-foot ceiling, and outside of it the snow is falling much harder than it had this morning. The protesters don't seem to mind. The Japanese are stoic that way. There are maybe two hundred of them out there, just beyond the walls to the palace grounds, waving signs I cannot read. One or two have my face on them, though. The ministers all said there wouldn't be a strong showing—a dozen at most. "We Japanese are not like you Americans, in this way," one said. "We do not get so . . . 'rile up' like you." But when an American stage actress marries into the Imperial Family tree—even a limb as puny and removed from the Chrysanthemum Throne as Haru's—it seems to rile them plenty.

I did the math. I'll be fourteenth in line for the throne. If my husband were killed, and all his brothers and sisters were killed, and all their children and all their children's children all suddenly met some horrible end, then I'd be the Empress of Japan. Perhaps the protestors think I'm going to pick them all off, one by one, like Richard III, but somehow I don't think that's the play that I'm in.

The ladies were whispering about the protestors when they left. *"Watashi haso-rerani bomu ganaikotowo nozomu!"* one of them quietly spoke, releasing a flighty, nervous giggle. I don't know much Japanese yet—but I know *"bomu"* means "bomb."

After the months of classes I've taken, I remember mostly the words that they've taken from English. As I apply my lipstick, I rehearse the handful I know.

"*Konpyuu-ta* . . . computer. *Terebijyon* . . . television. *Atommikku* . . . atomic. *Bomu* . . . bomb."

I'm not exactly a hit at parties, yet. But, I'm still learning my lines.

The lips are the most important. The lipstick goes on like oil paint, with a tiny brush of horse's hair—plucked one at a time from the tail of a steed descended from the horses of Samurai warriors, I'm told. Another brush applies red, and then a black one to outline my eyes, and soon, looking into the mirror, I no longer see myself.

Mrs. Haru J---- looks back at me. An Imperial Princess. Actual royalty. A woman worth a considerable sum. A woman with servants, and a horse-drawn carriage, and a private chef, and a private jet with its own private chef. A woman reviled, and not just by two hundred freezing protestors, but by an entire archipelago of citizens.

Back home they think I am simply marrying for money. Tabloids speculate. Reviewers and critics gurgle in their delight as it drowns them. Who does she think she is? This is not how things are done. How could this woman, whom they've loved so from their front-row seats, whose heart they've watched beating faster as she kisses sweating, rakish men that they've dreamed of being loved by, too—how could she leave and marry some stiff-backed alien? But Haru loves me, just as he loves the roaring passions of the stage precisely because he has never quite experienced them in his Imperial lifetime.

And this, I also understand. I only ever have, once, myself.

Here, though, love has not yet conquered all. Traditions are still important; marriages still arranged. But Haru tells me that the younger generation loves America, and they all want to be Jay-Z and to be in love and drink whiskey and eat bacon cheeseburgers. Atommikku Bomu. Now they sell T-shirts with mushroom clouds on them. I see one out there, in the crowd of protesters now.

Where are the critics when you need them?

I've gotten bad press before. Lifeless. Mechanical. Heartless. You shake it off. You prepare for the next role of a lifetime. Mrs. Haru J----, Imperial Princess of Japan. All my life I have only ever been trying to be anyone other than who I am. But each role ends. I can only be Ranevskaya, or Lady Macbeth, or Miss Julie for a few hours before the mystery and elegance slide away and I am only myself again.

There are twice as many people outside now. Why do I keep scanning their tiny faces—half hidden behind scarves? He is not out there.

Stanislavsky suggests using "affective memories"—meaning that the actress should try to recall times when she felt as the character does—to better re-create that emotion upon the stage. And so I think about him—as I do each night before I take the stage. Each night I try to imagine what it was that he wanted from me. What it was that he felt. Some sort of peace. Something I've never really felt, myself—except on stage. Maybe on a Christmas morning, twenty years ago. Maybe in those moments before the day begins, when I haven't yet remembered who I am.

Outside there is a loud cheer. The Imperial Guards are skirting the perimeter. There are cameras and lights now—the cyborg arms of television crews, coming to record this moment, when the people of an island nation are taking a stand. They are angry because their world keeps on shrinking, bound up in fiber-optic nooses, and the more things change, the more they all become the same. In Tokyo as in Manhattan. In Kumasi as in Dubai. In Colombo as in Williamstown. To them I am a corruption. A toxic invader into a once-sacred bloodline. They see it plainly enough—this is the way the world ends. Not with a bang, but with a cancer.

Careful not to crease the folds of my white *shiromuku* wedding robes, I sit again and reach into my bag. From inside a silk-lined cavity I withdraw

I wake in the morning to find my face plastered to the paper on my desk. I peel this off and bits of words stick to my cheek. I stopped mid-sentence, it appears. And as I stumble to the sink to wash my face I realize that I cannot, for the life of me, remember what I had intended her to withdraw. I sit staring at the half-finished line for hours, until I hear the sound of the shower going in the next room.

Out of habit, I wander past the closet where I've hidden Jeffrey's manuscript, and, as he sings French opera in the shower, I extract a few pages and read on from where I left off the day before. I'm nearly finished. While it remains devoid of all periods, *c*'s, *q*'s, *w*'s, and *z*'s, and it is definitely gibberish, I cannot get past the feeling that it is distinctly Jeffrey's gibberish. Am *I* crazy? Or, mixed into this mountain of verbiage, are there specks of gold?

It has crossed my mind, of course, to sell it—surely some collector would pay handsomely for an unfinished manuscript of Jeffrey Oakes's. It has even crossed my mind to keep it for myself. If I could sift out the gold inside, could I then claim it as my own? But now another idea crosses my mind. I slip the pages back into the wine box where I've kept them and put the box into my suitcase and the suitcase back into the closet. Then I lift another sheet of stationery off the top of the pile and write *"Jeffrey—Be right back. I'll get cigarettes. Don't worry."*

Out the lobby, past the souvenir plates, I head into the Place d'Armes once more. The old men are back at their checkers. One shouts, *"Schach matt!"* at the other. Out of the corner of my eye I see the Black Panther and again it seems as though he is also watching me. But I make my way to the used-book cart, where the girl we saw the other day is reading from the Luxembourgish edition of *Nothing Sacred*.

"Do you speak English?" I ask.

"Englesch?" she replies, shaking her head—no.

"Jeffrey Oakes," I say, pointing to the book.

She nods and grins. *"Frënd?"* she asks, pointing to me.

"Yes, friend," I say. "Old friend." I think about adding "Only friend" but she won't understand me, anyway. She's hyperventilating, and though I've never really seen anyone swoon before, I'm pretty sure this is what she is doing.

"Léift?" she asks, pointing to me. She puts her hands over her heart and then puts one onto the book. But I do not understand. *"Léift! Léift! Léift!"* she keeps crying.

"Love?" I say, pointing at the book. "Yes! *Léift! Multo . . .* grande *léift!"*

Immediately she proceeds to gush in a torrent of Luxembourgish. She shows me her phone, and the photo of Jeffrey that she took. She's posted it to a website called The Oakes Literary Society International, or TOLSI, for short, and there are 3,479 replies. From "hottentot19" and "GurlyGurl" and "WildeOne" and "echolalia" and "MrSmudgyMan."

They demand that she find out where he's staying. What he's doing. If he's crazy. Some squeal in abbreviations. Some, more erudite, quote his passages. The critics are immediately fired upon by the loyalists. Some girl posts a photo of a tattoo she's gotten on the small of her back that's etched with NOTHING SACRED. It's the ninth circle of Jeffrey's Inferno, on a four-inch touch screen with 4G speed.

I clap my hands and turn to the girl. "You can meet him. Sunday night."

"*Sonndes?*" she confirms. "*Owes?*"

"Sunday. Night. Tell everyone. *Sonndes owes*," I say, waving my hands out toward the world and then miming typing onto a phone with my thumbs.

"*Wou?*" she asks, looking about, her fingers already flying over the tiny keys.

"There," I say, pointing toward the palace. "There."

As I enter our suite, the smell of smoke tickles my nostrils and reminds me that I haven't bought Jeffrey cigarettes as I had promised. But it isn't tobacco I smell burning. When I push open the door I see Jeffrey, standing in his bathrobe, in front of the roaring fireplace. It takes a moment to connect the open closet door to the open suitcase on the floor to the open wine box on the counter. To the stack of paper in Jeffrey's arms.

"I thought I'd left a few cigarettes in your suitcase!" he screams, throwing two or three more pages into the fire. "This is supposed to be buried under an avalanche. Blown out of the fucking tower by the Arctic winds and scattered halfway to Greenland by now! Humpback whales should be picking it out of their . . . their . . . those things with the . . . *Christ!*" He hurls furious fistfuls of pages into the fire, stopping only when the flames surge up so high that they consume the bottom of the mantel.

"Baleens!" I shout, trying to wrench the papers away from him.

"Yes!" he cries, as he kicks me back. "Thank you! Baleens! Fucking Moby Dick should be flossing with this . . . this . . . *travesty!*"

With that he trips on the edge of the rug and the rest of the pages mushroom up into the air before sinking down. Jeffrey sits up in the middle of the paper sea, his pages settling like cresting waves that threaten to drown him. He just sits there, as if to let them. Wading in, I sit down beside him and help him to catch his breath.

"I'm sorry," I say, "I've lost too many books of my own. I just needed to save it."

"It's all just fucking *nonsense*," he sobs.

"It's not," I insist. "Not all of it. There's something in here. Something incredible. For the first hundred pages or so I couldn't see it. But then I started to notice certain things—repeating. There's a boy, right? A boy, and he's very gifted at . . . I don't know, there aren't any *c*'s, but you call it—" I riffle through pages, but to find one in the midst of all this would be like reaching into the ocean and grabbing out a fish. If it isn't ash already. I try to remember it, exactly. "A . . . a . . . 'game of slanted moves' . . . 'the oldest game that journeyed from the East, played in the shade of sphinxes . . . '" Jeffrey listens, breathing heavily. And then—a snow-in-Atlanta miracle—I lay my hand on the page I am searching for. "Here! Here here here! 'A game of red and blak, not blak and not-blak'— you meant *black*, right? And 'not-blak' is *white*, but there were no *c* or *w* keys—you're talking about checkers, and chess, right? . . . 'A game of red and blak, not blak and not-blak, for what in this sphere of land and sea is ever all blak or all not, but all is either the dark, dark death or the bold blushing of blood, blue through the skin but underneath it is red, all red, all of ours red, even the bluest blue blood is red, from George to Ferdinand to Louis to Tutankhamen to Buddha to Genghis and every Emperor from the Land of the Rising Sun have been red, red blooded, and all eventually taken by the blak, yes they all played the game, all made their slanted moves over the board, they hopped their rounds, they took them, they arrived at the farthest edge and said, in a thousand tongues, they said, unendingly,

King Me!

Rey Me!

Roy de Moi!

!الملــــك البيانـــات

Rājā mujhē!

Дамка!

王手!'

"You wrote that last part in by hand—how do you know these things? . . . 'And this, this is the phrase on the lips of the boy as he takes the last round of the man his father has hired to train him . . . ' I mean, it's checkers! Yeah? It's all about this boy who plays checkers and . . . well, help me find the next part, why don't you? It's got to be here somewhere . . . "

Jeffrey's gone quiet. The fire has died down a bit. The pages lie flat now, all around us, a still white pond. I pick up one page, and then another, and try fitting them together. I wait for Jeffrey to tell me that *I've* gone mad—that he never so much as thought of a single checker in all the time he was in Iceland. But then, slowly, Jeffrey lifts one page and holds it up against the light from the fireplace. He turns it this way, and that, as if not sure which end is up. Then he takes up another and, scanning the end of the first, matches it to the top of the second, and holds them together between his fingertips.

"Page numbers, page numbers," he mutters. "My kingdom for fucking page numbers."

It takes nearly every available hour between that one and Sunday, but we're not much for sleeping. At first we take breaks only for room service and so Jeffrey can smoke in the window and watch the men playing checkers. The Black Panther barely ever leaves the Place Guillaume II. At all hours we see him there, looking up at us. Watching. Jeffrey makes faces at him from the safety of the room, but only because he has me to send for more cigarettes. But by the third day, Jeffrey has stopped doing even this. His sovereign addiction is replaced by his very first—the steady rush of pen against paper.

We work in tandem, communicating in inks: mine, red cross-outs, circles, exclamation points, and question marks; his, black insertions, deletions, refusals, and acquiescences. Occasionally there is a great laugh from one end of the room or the other, or else a swift intaking of breath. Not only is it pleasant to work with Jeffrey for a change, but playing editor makes me think of Tina. Late one night I catch my reflection in the window, going line by line over a fresh page, and for a moment I am she, reading something of my own.

Jeffrey's thousand pages are steadily milled down to five hundred, which we sift through further, until we have it at just under three hundred.

The Sunday-morning church bells have long since rung and the sun is coasting down. Jeffrey takes one last shower, and we tie each other's bow ties, and he puts the finalized pages back into the wine box again, and tucks this lighter parcel squarely beneath his arm. Then we head out into the dusk together.

There is a small crowd waiting over in the Place d'Armes. Just a little congregation around the used-book cart, where readers from all over have come to meet the girl who broke the news of Jeffrey's return, and, while they are at it, pick up a paperback or two for the journey home. I spot a pair of aged hippies with white ponytails and circled spectacles discussing a volume of Hemingway with a thin man in a gray suit. A squat, wild-maned lion of a man studies Chekhov through the bottom of his beer mug. Three girls who look as though they might have been classmates of Carsten Chanel's compare translations of *The Metamorphosis* and laugh as if to wake the dead. Jeffrey's whole self tenses as they come into view, but he keeps walking steadily, even as they all look up with one expectant face.

"Am I naked?" Jeffrey asks. "Why are they looking at me like I'm naked?"

"I'd probably have mentioned something earlier if you were," I say.

"*Probably?*" he snaps.

But on we go, past the crowd at the book cart, even when they bring up their phones and hold them out at arm's length like so many Yorick's skulls. Jeffrey flinches a bit when the flashes go off but never breaks stride. We march down one of the cobblestone avenues to the palace, where dozens and dozens of the paramilitary parking squad are keeping their eyes on the assembled mass. I think we've about doubled the population of the Old City. There must be a few hundred of them—Oakes fans from all corners of the European Union. Perhaps there are Chunnel-borne Brits out there; perhaps the sons of sons of Soviets. Perhaps some TOLSI-ites have trekked in from even farther away. And there are so many phones pointed our way, taking pictures and videos—capturing this moment for all time and for all people in all places. I wonder if Einar will watch, or simon/西蒙, or whoever is doing simon/西蒙's homework for him these days. Everywhere there are copies of *Nothing Sacred*, and the air is filled with a tremendous cheering. Still, Jeffrey looks humbler than I have ever seen him. As we move toward the front of the crowd, I find myself searching for a large hat, a burst of gingery hair, a dress fifty years out of fashion—but she will not have come, not all this way. But is she, maybe, at a computer a world away, watching this unfolding in a choppy, pixilated stream?

What I *do* see, as Jeffrey moves into position under a quaint streetlamp, is a window up in the palace, with warm light spilling out. Silhouetted there is a woman in a wide-shouldered gown, guarded on one side by a slim black man with a bulb of dark hair, speaking into his sleeve.

"It's the Black Panther," I say to Jeffrey. "He's with *her.*"

But Jeffrey is not listening to me. He is quite busy extracting pages from the wine box. He places the box on one end and then steps onto it. All the blood in his cheeks has drained elsewhere. But he stares into the crowd, facing the thing he's been afraid of since I've known him. Perhaps longer than that even. Perhaps even longer than the shadow in the window has known him.

"So sorry to keep everyone waiting," he says softly. The words catch the stone walls of the palace and they echo, and in an instant everyone is laughing. Is it my imagination or is he *blushing*? "This is from a work very very much in progress—"

Whatever else he says is lost in a volcanic eruption of applause. His eyes flit over the crowd, from one curious face to the next. There is a glint in his eyes that I recognize. He has them entirely under his spell now, and he's wondering why he ever waited this long. He clears his throat, turns back and winks at me, and then announces,

"This is called 'King Me.'"

He reads for nearly an hour. After he's through, there is a thunderous ovation, and then a somewhat-tidy receiving line that I do my best to help corral. I stand by Jeffrey's side but I don't have to step in even once. He sits on the wooden box as if it were his own tiny throne. He entertains each audience seeker with wit and patience. Two more hours rush by and then, out of nowhere, the Black Panther appears at the head of the line.

"Her Majesty, the Princess, requests the pleasure of your company."

Jeffrey stands and faces the man, appearing to consider the offer.

"It's about time," he says finally.

But the Black Panther holds a hand in my direction.

"Not you."

I feel my throat go dry. I look up at the window but the light is out. She is gone.

"Specifically?" I manage to get out. "I mean, did she say she didn't *want* me to come up or did she just *not* say, because she may have assumed that—"

But Jeffrey cuts me off. "Hold on there, Black Panther–man. He comes, too."

The Black Panther looks Jeffrey squarely in the eye. "You would refuse a request from Her Royal Highness?"

Jeffrey snorts. "I'll refuse it and then I'll say she's got an ice-pop for a heart—it makes no difference to me."

The Black Panther snarls, and then when Jeffrey moves to leave, he gives in.

"Come this way," he says to us both.

And that is that. We are whisked through a side door by the armed guards and shepherded down along a long, dark corridor.

"What is this? Huh? Hello? Mr. Black Panther? Are you taking us to the dungeon?" Jeffrey shouts.

"To say 'Black Panther' is redundant," the man informs us suddenly with the thinnest glimpse of a smile. "All panthers are black. A panther is not its own breed but a name common to all large jungle cats that have a dominant pigment that overrides the natural undercoat of the animal. In America, you've typically got black cougars. In Latin America, we have black jaguars. In Asia or Africa, a panther is a black leopard. From a distance they appear to be all black, and yet—if you've got the nerve to get a close look—you can see that they actually still have their normal markings. Their spots. They're just not visible against a background that is also black."

Jeffrey is speechless, which, from the satisfied look on the man's face, seems to have been the object of the lesson. It doesn't last long.

"Well, thank you, Jack Hanna," he says finally.

At last, we reach a door and the Panther motions for us to go through. He looks sweetly at Jeffrey, much less so at me, as we proceed.

We emerge into a great hall lined with tapestries and suits of armor and flowing banners bearing coats of arms. A dozen servants are lined up to greet us, all dressed impeccably. At the far end stands our old friend, and she looks not a day older than when I saw her last. She smiles and, to the shock of her servants, runs over to us so quickly that she seems to nearly trip on her long golden gown. Before I know quite what to say, her arms are around us both, and there is the most incredible charge in me as her lips press firmly onto first my cheek, and then Jeffrey's.

"That was *fantastic*," she cries, any semblance of royal propriety quite out the window, and then her eyes have locked steady onto mine. "And

it was you, too, wasn't it? Of course, it was. Stay here, until it's completely finished. You must be starved. The chef will whip something up
for you."

Jeffrey strides after her toward the dining room as if he's lived here
his entire life. To an apple-cheeked maid he says, "Yes, I'd like two slices
of wheat toast. *Crusts removed.* Then two poached eggs with smoked
salmon. *No sauce.* And he'll have—"

Jeffrey is gesturing in my direction. "Oh. *Uhm.* Steak, then. Bloody."

The princess adds, "Just have Marcel throw something together
for me."

She takes us into a grand dining room, where a long table is covered
in tomorrow's fine breakfast china. On the walls hang gigantic portraits
of the former dukes and duchesses of Luxembourg, milky skinned and
red nosed, always looking just a bit malnourished, as if they'd left sitting
for the portrait off until they were actually on their deathbeds. At the
head of the table is a massive golden throne, cushioned in red velvet. I
expect that the princess will sit there, but she takes a seat to one side.
The Panther sits behind her, and Jeffrey and I sit across. Wine is poured
and Jeffrey chugs a glass down triumphantly before I can remind him
he's stopped drinking.

"Where's the head honcho?" he asks, thumbing his finger at the
throne.

The Black Panther speaks cordially to Jeffrey, "The duke is with his
three sons in Argentina."

"Argentina!" I say. "What's in Argentina?"

"Don't tell anyone," she replies sweetly. "This country's getting a bit
small for us. We're thinking of invading the Falklands. Do you think
anyone will mind?"

She raises her eyebrows devilishly at me, and while Jeffrey bursts into
laughter, I feel my heart begin to flutter.

"Nothing wrong with Argentina. Some of us might like to be *in*
Argentina," the Panther says, making eyes at Jeffrey, which, surprisingly, Jeffrey makes right back.

"Don't pout now," she says, giving his hand a light smack. "Cyrus was left behind to guard me."

"Seems some rather disreputable foreigners had taken up residence in the Hotel Luxembourg," he said, eyeing me. "Do you believe that?"

"Is that right?" I cough. "Well. Foreigners. Good for trade, I expect."

"Only if you count sales of luxury cigarettes and fire repairs to hotel rooms."

Jeffrey tips back his empty wineglass and taps it with one finger. "We bought some theater tickets! And a lot of room service. And judging from the crowd tonight I'd say there can't be a vacant hotel room for miles!"

Cyrus grins wolfishly, and, if I'm not mistaken, there is, again, the briefest lingering in his looking at Jeffrey.

"So," I say, desperate for any reason to look in the princess's direction. "Is that why *you* didn't go to Argentina? These, *uhm,* 'disreputable foreigners'?"

Her eyes glint like the light on the rim of her wineglass as she drinks from it. "They don't have much need for me when it comes to things like that. Negotiating trade agreements. Four percent this for two percent that. Amortized over six years. Steel for soybeans. Very dull stuff."

Cyrus smiles. "Her Majesty is in charge of the Get Fit Luxembourg! initiative."

She punches the air gently, as if quite gung ho about it, and then she and Jeffrey explode into laughter.

"You know what they're making out of soybeans now? Lemonade! And tuna fish! Out of *beans!* The other day I met three men who use it to make synthetic peanut butter. Isn't it just as easy to grow peanuts? I asked them. Apparently not. That's what it all is now. Everything reinvented! Nothing genuine. Next thing you know they'll be injecting pregnant women with it so the children can breast-feed soy milk! This is how I'll be remembered. 'The Synthetic Princess!'"

"You should have them carve a statue of you out of tofu!" Jeffrey cries.

The idea seems to delight her. "If I put it over on the throne and snuck off, do you think they'd know the difference?"

Their laughter fills the empty dining hall, and in an instant there are tears in the corners of her eyes. Then she reaches both hands across the table. Jeffrey takes one and I take the other—and her fingers slip around mine as if I had held them only yesterday. "You have to stay here a few more weeks. Please. It's *just* like the good old days," she says, smiling as the servers arrive with our food.

And as we drink, and Jeffrey and I entertain Her Majesty with stories about our years apart, it *does* feel as if very little has changed. It's only when I lean back in my chair and into the dead eyes of the portraits on the wall that I remember that we are not having brunch in some ritzy New York hotel. This is her home now. High up on one wall is an empty space. I can't help but think that it is waiting for a portrait of her.

After dinner I am shown to a magnificent guest suite, done up in Far Eastern crimsons and golds. There is a huge canopy bed, a black bear-skin rug on the floor, a huge bookshelf filled with leather-bound classics, a wardrobe the size of a New York apartment, and a spacious writing desk in the corner. A Spanish boy named Roberto brings me silk paja-mas. The moon is high and full in the sky outside the window, and after the meal and the wine and a few hours with my old love, I am desperate to write. But I check all the drawers in the writing desk and there is no paper. I could ask Jeffrey, but he's in the neighboring room, and judging from the way things were looking between him and Cyrus as we left dinner, I think that perhaps I will not disturb him. I hear an occasional faint thumping noise that makes me blush. It's nice having the old Jeffrey back, I think to myself, but I'm worried for him at the same time. Will one bottle of wine lead to twelve? Will the good reviews, already streaming onto the blogosphere, go to his head even more quickly than the wine? And how long until Russell Haslett comes calling?

Just as I'm considering tearing some pages from the back of one of the ancient books on the shelf, I am interrupted by the sound of the door opening.

"Roberto, do you think you could find me something to write on?" I ask.

But it is not the Spanish boy.

The Princess of Luxembourg studies me a moment, her eyes curious, as if surprised to find me where she'd left me. Should I bow? I'm half tempted to curtsy.

"Good evening, Your Majest—" I begin, but before I can get it out she's rushing toward me. Her hands grip my cheeks firmly, her lips devour mine, and though her golden hair keeps falling in our faces, she does not close her eyes, as if she needs to be sure it's really me.

"Don't you *dare* call me that," she says, holding me tighter.

It's what I'd dreamed of for nearly a decade, and yet something about her suddenly makes me nervous. I'd imagined myself all this time as some sort of world-weary knight, a lovelorn Lancelot come to free her from this prison. Instead I feel more like a confused Quixote, lost in lovely La Mancha, tilting at the same old windmills. Would that make Jeffrey my Sancho Panza? If anything, I must admit, it's all the other way around.

"I thought you didn't even want me to come up to the palace," I manage.

Her eyes burn at a thousand watts. More. "I've told you," she says. "You always make me forget my lines."

She kisses me again and the nine interceding years begin to fly away. Yet as they do I find myself grasping at them with both hands. My heart is hummingbird-pounding, and I feel a faint throb in my leg as she pushes me toward the canopy bed—but we don't even get there—we end up on the floor, and I feel the pricking of the bearskin against my cheek. She's heavy on top of me and behind those carefully painted lips I feel the faint tensing of her teeth against my tongue. Her hands are on my shoulders, in my shirt, and all I can see is a frenzy of golden hair.

"What's wrong?" she says, pulling back. The red of her lipstick is all smudged around the edges.

"Nothing," I say, squirming beneath her.

"Tell me you're not thinking of someone else?" she teases.

"No! No one! No one!" I insist, but in my head I am thinking, *Outis! Outis!*

Her smile hangs white as a pearl necklace, just out of my reach. "I *knew* you wouldn't forget me."

We kiss again and I am just about to give up my reservations: her absent husband; Cyrus—who is likely armed and just in the next room; and even Jeffrey, with whom I've only just repaired things; but then I hear the thumping noise again, and I falter. Is it coming from Jeffrey's room? It sounds closer than that.

"Can't we pretend everything is like it used to be?" she asks, perhaps more to herself than to me.

"We wish to remain what we are," I joke.

She grins. "That sounds vaguely familiar."

She is about to come at me again, but then there is another thump, and this time she hears it, too. She pauses, hands in my hair, nose a millimeter from mine.

"Is that Jeffrey and Cyrus?" she giggles, pretending to be shocked.

"That's what I *thought* it was," I say, as I sit up against the bed, pulling slightly away from her so I can hear—brushing her hair from my face. "But doesn't it sound like it's coming from in there?"

I nod toward the gigantic wardrobe. In an instant her face goes very pale. She pushes her thumb roughly over my lips, rubbing away the red of her own. Then straightens herself out and checks herself quickly in the mirror above the desk. She locks eyes with herself, and I know that look—she is getting back into character. She crosses swiftly to the wardrobe door and yanks it open.

Inside is a young boy, perhaps eight years old, dressed in golden silk pajamas. His blond hair is slicked to the side, still a little wet from a bath earlier in the night. He wears rather thick glasses and sits cross-legged with a flashlight in one hand and a tattered book in the other.

"Julian!" she scolds. "I've told you a hundred times, you can't be in here!"

He looks up expectantly at her. At his mother. He folds his arms in annoyance and then, he pouts—it's *her* pout, on *his* face.

"Evie told me I had to go away because she's getting her hair cut!"

She seems quite alarmed by this. "Evelyn's getting a—. Who on earth is giving her a *haircut?*"

Julian shrugs. "Ms. Ruby gave her the scissors for her paper dolls."

Suddenly she's rushing for the door, wailing, "No, no, no, no—" but then she pauses and turns back to me, a devastated look on her face. "Could you just—? I have to—. Before she cuts her ears off!"

I shoot a winning smile at the young boy in the wardrobe, as if he is my very best friend in the world. He ignores me.

"Go on," I say, waving my hands at her.

She looks at me one final time, and her eyes are dim now with gratitude and sorrow and grief and relief all at once, and for perhaps the first time since I've known her, I am sure that I know what is happening behind them. She rubs a thumb under her lower lip one last time. She goes and I am alone with the boy.

The boy who is her son.

"Mothers," I sigh conspiratorially from my spot on the floor. "Honestly."

The boy looks up at me curiously. "Do you have a mother?"

"I do. But she's not here, though. She's at home. I mean, where I grew up."

"Why aren't you where you grew up?" he asks.

"I went away," I said. "I got older so I left."

He seems perplexed by this. "I'm *never* leaving home. I'll stay here forever."

I'm about to argue with him until I realize that, perhaps, he's right.

·

Could a future prince of Luxembourg just pick up and start a new life in Belize or Katmandu?

"Well," I say, looking around, "at least it's quite nice here."

"It's *boring* here," he says. "I want to go to Africa!"

"I've been to Africa," I say. His eyes light up but then I add, "They make you take medicine to go there," and he retches.

"Do you know my mother?"

"She and I are old friends," I say warmly, trying not to arouse his suspicions about the fact that I am still sitting on the floor where she pushed me down, only minutes before. I wonder what, if anything, the boy could see through the crack in the wardrobe doors. You can see a lot from under closet doors—I remember well enough. You can see a lot of things you shouldn't. It seems like yesterday that I *was* this boy. But tonight I am the man on the other side of the closet door, and this simply cannot be.

"What are you reading?" I ask.

He holds up his book—a yellow cartoon crane beams up from the cover, the title in indecipherable Luxembourgish.

He holds the book open in my face. "Read it," he commands.

"I can't," I say. He looks appalled. "I mean, I can *read*. I just only know English."

He snorts, as if he can hardly believe anyone wouldn't know more than that.

"English books are *there*," he points. I get up and browse the shelf of old books for something the boy's speed. After thumbing past the philosophy, some Woolf, and a few books about the Harlem Renaissance, I finally pull one out that I think he'll enjoy. When I hand it to him, he reads the title off slowly.

"*Just So Stories*. By Rudard Kippler."

"Rudyard *Kipling*." I sit down again on the bearskin rug, closer to the wardrobe. He seems embarrassed to have said it wrong, so I add, "Your English is very good."

"My mom's from America," he explains.

"Is that right?"

He nods and holds the book open in my face. "Read it," he commands.

Taking the book from him, I look up at the open door, hoping maybe his mother will return, but I suspect that she is dealing with Julian's freshly bald younger sister and has forgotten all about us for the moment. The boy begins to get comfortable, tucking his trusty flashlight into the pocket of his pajamas and arranging some soft extra blankets out on the bottom of the wardrobe. He knows just how he wants to lie on the blankets. I suspect he's gotten scores of maids and footmen and butlers to read him bedtime stories while his mother has been preoccupied with her royal duties.

I wait for him to settle in. It is important to be comfortable when you're just a small boy, alone in a big place. He'll change, but this fact never truly will. He'll go on, day after day, unsure if he's all that different from the day before. Later he'll look back at the things that are happening now and he'll think they were almost like something he read about. He'll know they happened to him but they may well have happened to another person, with another name, in some other place, where the clocks are on other times. In the story of tonight he'll be himself, but costumed in the gentle lies of memory and the soft fictions of yesterdays. Some stories he'll lose along the way: in truck stops, on old computer drives, in boxes in dank basements. Still, each day he'll wonder, has he changed and everything else is the same? Or is it exactly the other way around?

Someday he'll see that he can't have one without the other. He can't know he is the same unless everything around him has changed. It's like black spots on black fur—you can't see them, but they're there, all the same.

He'll think he's moving in zigzags, getting anywhere but where he meant to go. But there are edges to the board, and someday he will reach one, and it is only then that life will place a true crown onto his head. It's only then that he'll be able to turn around and see for the first time a glorious path back from where he came.

"You're not *reading*," the boy complains.

"Sorry," I say, "I thought you weren't ready."

"I'm ready," he insists.

"Oh, this one's a good one," I say as I flip a few stories in. I pause, remembering that I read it once, when I was little, at a tiny bookstore in a big airport terminal. I'm delighted to find it hasn't changed at all—only me. King me.

"You have to say its name," he demands.

"Its name," I say, "its name is, 'How the Leopard Got His Spots.'"

I left Luxembourg and my apologies, scrawled onto the blank end pages of the Kipling book. I'd come looking for someone I'd made up, a long time ago, and that as fun as it might have been to break character for another night, I owed her more than that—much more. For years we'd had a kind of make-believe love, in its way so much better than the genuine article. She'd called me after good auditions, but never bad ones. I'd seen her break men's hearts, but I'd never once seen her heartbroken. Our story had been all romanticism, never realism. We'd had affairs, but we'd never once made plans. Now I saw that, even playing the role of the Princess of Luxembourg, she had no fairy-tale life: she had a country to think of, overweight citizens to inspire to exercise, real duties to carry out! A royal life was still a life: soy products to endorse, a husband to miss when he was away, and children getting up to mischief on opposite ends of the palace. Running away from it all for just one night would have made neither of us any happier, in the end. If Jeffrey had proved anything to me, it was that no one could escape forever. Maybe he'd been right, long ago, when he'd told me that I'd never really loved her. Nothing I'd felt for her then even began to match what I felt when she'd looked that child in the eye and had seen her own eyes looking back.

Of course, I didn't say all that, exactly. Rather, I left my apologies in the form of a story. One that I'd written again and again, about an actress preparing for not merely the role of a lifetime—but a lifetime of a role. A story I'd been unable to finish, until then. When I'd finally finished it, I'd signed my name—my real name—at the bottom, and set the book down beside the sleeping head of her son.

Now, on this airplane, I am writing it all again, while I soar over the great black gap of the ocean, in as straight a line as the curve of the earth will allow. A flight attendant reminds me sweetly to be sure and change the time on my watch. I tell her that I wish I still had a watch. I tell her that I so loved watching its hands winding backward, making time where there was none before, catching seconds from the air and putting them back where they belong.

The sun is rising fast in the east behind us, but we are faster. Everything stays dark, as if the night itself were trying to take longer, so I can finish. I write until the instructions come to put my table in the upright position. Then, as we descend, I keep on going, pressing hard against the back of the seat in front of me. Just before our wheels touch the ground, I, at last, am finished.

Careful not to crease the folds of my white *shiromuku* wedding robes, I sit down again and reach into my bag one last time. From inside a silk-lined cavity I withdraw a small painting, about the size of a page in a book, of a woman rendered entirely in gold. The fluid lines, the precise strokes, can only have been painted by someone imbued with a great and unabating passion. In the glint of the woman's breasts I can trace the serene gaze of its unknown artist. And just to the left of this there is a small smudge—a faint oily spot left behind by the pressing of a single finger.

It took me some time to find the portrait, on loan to a private collection at a North Carolina art museum. When the owners noticed the finger smudge, they were aghast, and offered to lower the price or have it professionally restored. But I would not allow it. I want the smudge, I'd said. Get rid of everything else if you want. It's the smudge I want.

I stare at this single, oily spot as I have every night before going on stage. And after a few moments I am prepared. I rise from my seat by the dressing mirrors and adjust my wedding robes one last time. I pass through the doors of the dressing room and I am on a stage. The curtain has fallen and I can hear the roar of the crowd building, steadily, like a madness. The snow is still drifting down in the dark space before me. Up in the catwalks, some stagehands scurry with last-minute tasks. I am my role. The curtain stirs gently in the draft. And when it goes up, I will feel that one face—those two eyes—that gaze I must avoid all night. But I will feel those eyes watching, every moment, knowing I can never look back into them, because they would undo me.

The wait is over now. The curtain begins to rise.

Terminus

"Lowly faithful, banish fear, / Right onward drive unharmed; / The
port, well worth the cruise, is near / And every wave is charmed."

—RALPH WALDO EMERSON, "TERMINUS"

Here again, she tells herself. She reaches the top of the escalator, yanking
her suitcase by its taped handle to keep it from catching in the mecha-
nism. The sides of her case are freshly smudged with red sub-Saharan
dust. This same dust is caught in the lengths of her auburn hair and
pressed into the pale swirls of her fingertips. Just as it had been the last
time she'd passed through this very same airport terminal. *Here again,*
she tells herself, *and again empty-handed.*

Through a barrage of static, the speakers above her head announce,
"Boarding will . . . in just a moment for . . . two thirty-seven to New
York City."

She peers quickly around Terminal B for a clock but cannot locate one
anywhere. She certainly does not notice him, over at the farthest table—
the man fussing about with stacks of pages: dividing them into parts,
ordering, reordering, deleting, stetting. Hesitatingly he scribbles question
marks onto the wide, clean margins, branding them with each of his infi-
nite doubts. She doesn't see how aggravated and nervous he is, or how
completely exhausted. Everything that was inside of him has been emptied except the overwhelming fear that what's been emptied is nothing
special. He thought that he would be much surer by this point. He knows
that there is so much missing—so much that he's lost and will never be
able to find. He worries that perhaps they are all the wrong words. He

thinks that perhaps they are all in the wrong order. He wonders if perhaps those who read them won't be able to see all that they should.

But really he is lying only to himself, again. Really, his fear is just the opposite. Really, he's worried that maybe they *will* see—all the terrible things that he has done and has been. He's thinks that he has changed his spots—he's sure he has—but now everything is in there: the lies he's told and the truths he's invented.

But she doesn't notice him. She's still pacing up and down the terminal, looking for a clock, but there are none to be found. Not near the Emerson Books. Not across the corridor by Phil's Coffee Hub, or W. W. Gould's Good Eats, or the Jewels, Jewels, Jewels! kiosk. She knows only that it is far too early in the morning, but that to her it feels like the depth of night. She hates taking the red-eye back to the city. She hates arriving into its jubilant, awakening arms feeling so deeply burned out. She continues, legs cramped and stiff, the little wheel on her bag squealing incessantly.

The bag's wheel had a bad encounter with a busted step at the old man's house—the axis knocked a few degrees off balance when she was racing inside to try to catch the end of his estate auction. She'd been so sad to hear he'd passed. She'd never even gotten to meet the great Jeremiah; she'd never been allowed. And after so much anticipation, she'd shown up very, very late. Kojo's rusted Hyundai had blown a tire, hours earlier, and she had been forced to wait out there in the miserable heat while he walked to the nearest village to scrounge up a replacement. By the time she'd gotten inside the old man's house, nearly everything had already been sold. She'd soon spotted an editor from Sandford Books, locking up a briefcase filled with yellowed pages. Early stories? Diaries? Letters? She still doesn't know. Like the rest of the world, she will have to wait and wonder and see.

She continues to scour the walls of Terminal B—she thinks, *What sort of backwoods airport has no goddamn clocks?* There had been ten of them, all in a shiny row, back in the far-nicer Terminal A. *You'll be back in true civilization soon,* she reminds herself. But then a second thought hits her. *By lunchtime you'll be sitting in Haslett's office, trying to explain how you—the only one who had been out to the damned Oakes Mines & Estate before—got scooped for the literary find of the decade.* She dreams about rolling herself a perfect little cigarette, but she does not want to go back outside and risk missing her flight. People are already piling up at the gate, though the attendants are not letting anyone board yet. She thinks she might have a tall glass of gin instead, with parasite-free ice cubes in it. It's early, sure, but she is still on Africa time.

She stops in her tracks and reaches for the side pocket of her purse. From inside it she removes a watch. It is bright gold and quite elegant—but far too big for her wrist. It belonged to the man who broke her heart. She'd found it deep in the pocket of his jacket, which had been auctioned at the estate sale; she'd gotten it for practically nothing. She checks the watch and sees that she has at least twenty minutes before her flight should leave. Just then, a modest sign halfway across the terminal catches her eye. TEN-MINUTE TIMEPIECE REPAIR. *Ten minutes to get the watch taken in,* she thinks, *ten minutes to get my drink.* Wristwatch in hand, she moves swiftly toward the kiosk—closer and closer. She startles a slim man behind the counter. He sits on a high chair, reading a newspaper.

"I'll need some links removed from this, please," she says.

The static comes on again. ". . . flight two thirty-seven to New York . . . now begin boarding."

The slim man sets the newspaper down and, with a genial smile, turns the watch twice in his hands. "They sure don't make them like this anymore."

She does not particularly care. She is staring across the way, at the disorganized line of passengers beginning to move, then over at a turquoise blue gin bottle, which glints behind the bar at W. W. Gould's. If she would just look *ten* degrees further to her left she would see him, lifting the pages up by their edges and hefting them lightly in his fingertips as if, by weight alone, he can estimate their value. Like so many a long-gone prospector he is worried that what remains after his patient sifting may not be enough. But its millesimal fineness cannot be weighed, only determined beneath a careful squint through an eyepiece. He thumbs through the pages. What percentage of its parts is pure?

She looks back at the watch man, holding the timepiece up close to his work lamp and studying it under his extendable magnifying glass for a moment.

"You from around here?" he asks.

"No," she says. "I'm an editor in New York City."

He gives the requisite impressed look. "Where'd you get this, anyway?"

She certainly does not feel like explaining the whole sordid story to an oddball watch repairman in the middle of a tiny, time-forgotten airport.

"Could we just hurry this along? I have a plane to catch."

The man smiles and swiftly begins his work. She watches out of the corner of her eye as, to his credit, his delicate fingers wield the tools of his trade with precision. As the watch man works away she wonders that there are still people in this world who learn a skill from their fathers and then apply it, day in and day out. If Mr. Haslett fires her, she decides, she'll go back to Chicago and make her father teach her how to be an electrician. Wouldn't there be something satisfying in that? Tearing open walls and tracing lines of copper and plastic from switch to bulb? People need lights. People always need light. She could bring light to the world. Plus she thought it might be nice to be in a union. Gripe about taxes, worry over pensions—that sort of thing.

Then, suddenly—finally—the thumbing of pages stops. The uncapped pen falls from his paralyzed fingers and leaves a jagged squiggle on the title page. He has noticed her, *at last*. There, fifty yards away from him, is the woman he left in Africa many months ago. With the same luggage. Talking to the man at Ten-Minute Timepiece Repair—of all places to have stopped!—and they are examining *his* watch.

The sheer coincidental madness of it all sends a primeval panic up his spine and he lurches back, looking for some way to escape. *But wait!* he tells himself. *No more running away. We've put that all behind us now. We've changed our spots, haven't we?* He doesn't even know why he's referring to himself in the plural—the "royal" we—he doesn't know it is because he's speaking to the pages now, too.

Just as the woman is about to apologize for having been so short with the watch man, she hears the rough vibrations of his chair being pushed backward against the linoleum. She squints toward the origin of the noise—the small round table beside W. W. Gould's. Early morning sunlight blinds her, but through its golden shining she can *just* make out the man whom she has hated, and loved. A man whose real name she doesn't even know. He looks once into her green eyes and then, with a smile so faint she nearly misses it, he glances down at the table. At the pages. Then, before she can even react, he rushes away. He has a slight limp, but he is quick as a jungle cat. As the man steps onto the escalators, he looks back over his shoulder—just for a moment, directly at her, and again at the pages—and then he is gone.

She twists and takes a quick step, as if she might rush after him, but then she remembers the watch. She remembers the gin. And her flight.

She tells herself that it is obviously just the jet lag, playing tricks. *Must be his doppelgänger,* she jokes to herself. *Why would he leave all his papers behind like that?*

". . . all rows, all rows . . . flight two thirty-seven . . . "

The slim repairman slips the watch onto her narrow, pale wrist. It fits perfectly and she smiles appreciatively. Then he hands her a small plastic bag containing the links that he's removed. She fumbles in her purse to find dollars amid all the cedis she'd forgotten to exchange back in Terminal A. *What on earth can I do with those now?* she thinks. Then, as she turns to leave—as she begins to move toward the abandoned pages— the young man jabs his thin, pink fingertip at a small mark on the golden edge of the watch. "That's our stamp right there."

"You stamped it?" she asks, studying the near-microscopic insignia.

He shakes his head. "Was stamped already. You must have had work done on it here once before."

"I sincerely doubt it," she says, thinking, *I have just ten minutes.*

The man shrugs. "Bring it back anytime. If your wrist ever gets any bigger."

"I'll be sure to do that," she says. Then, at last, she tugs her broken suitcase behind her over to the bar at W. W. Gould's. She is so close now.

It takes only a minute to get the bartender's attention, and another two for him to pour the drink. As she pays, she watches the line of passengers moving slowly through her gate. The watch feels heavy and good on her wrist. It says she has eight minutes left, so she sits down at the closest table and drains the glass in four long, slow gulps. She shuts her eyes and breathes out deeply. She thinks that now she will be able to sleep on the way back to the city, and that her impending execution in the Haslett & Grouse offices will not sting quite so badly. She thinks maybe she can run over to Emerson Books and find some sort of *For Dummies Guide to Electrical Wiring*. She'd at least like to have *something* to read—

And then her eyes fall onto an untidy stack of papers at the next table. Now that she has a better view, she knows exactly what it is. She knows a manuscript when she sees one. Manuscripts are her roommates and best friends. They live on the floors of her apartment and the spare chairs of her office. Stacks and stacks of stories and words.

She looks around but there is no one else sitting anywhere nearby.

It sits patiently on the table. It is all it can do. She checks her watch again. Slowly she stands up and, still starting, checks the watch—*her* watch—again.

This is where that man was sitting, she thinks. *The one who just bolted out of here. The one who looked just like*—

Reaching over, she picks it up by one corner and looks around her. No one takes any notice of her at all. Tentatively she studies the title page. "The Unchangeable Spots of Leopards." There is no author's name—no address or phone number—no e-mail. But she knows that title. She's seen it before.

". . . two thirty-seven to New York is now . . ."

She reaches into her bag and pulls out another stack of pages. These, she stole them from the luggage of the man who owned the watch. Before she left Africa the first time. She's carried them around ever since, and has read them so often that she could recite them by heart. She sets the stolen pages down beside the ones she's just found. They seem to be about the same height. The same consistency. She lifts away the title page and places it gently on the table beside her glass of ice. She begins to read the Author's Note and as she does the world of Terminal B falls silently away around her: her flight, her gin glass, the watch repairman. The only noise she can hear is the faint ticking of the watch. She lifts each page up to the shortening light; her hand leaves faint red smudges on their margins. Steadily, she runs her finger beneath the opening line and begins reading: *I've lost every book I've ever written. I lost the first one here in Terminal B, where I . . .*

Acknowledgments

This book would not exist today if not for the generosity, time, and faith of practically everyone I know. Most especially I'd like to thank my wife, Leah Miller, who has been my secret weapon for twelve years and counting. Immense thanks to Chelsea Lindman, Maggie Riggs, Clare Ferraro, Timothy Lane, Hal Fessenden, Paul Buckley, Alison Forner, Alissa Amell, Elaine Broeder, Lindsay Prevette, Carolyn Coleburn, Nancy Sheppard, and everyone else at Viking/Penguin and the Nicholas Ellison Agency who believed that this novel could be turned into a book.

Many thanks to my parents, Deborah and Dennis Jansma, who sent me to summer writing camps and at least two universities so I could learn how to do this. Thanks as well to Oma, Jonathan, Jennifer, Dennis Miller, Susan Braunhut, Theodore Fetter, and all the rest of my family.

I'm lucky to have had many great readers along the way, including Elizabeth Perrella, Andy Dodds, Neil Bardhan, Robin Ganek, Rachel Panny, Kara Levy, John Proctor, and David Hellman. Thanks to Jordan Dollak for composing all the music in my podcasts out of the goodness of his heart, and to the brilliant photographer Michael Levy, who makes me look good. Thanks also to the many people who checked my facts and translations: Hanna Miller, Emily Ethridge, Natalya Minkovsky, Sadena Thevarajah, Kelly Johnston, Jennifer Breithoff, and Chantal Flammang at the Luxembourg City Tourist Office, and of course the tireless and thorough John Jusino. I'm grateful to Martin Marks and

Ariel S. Winter for inspiring me since day one of freshman year and to The Doug for keeping me honest for just as long.

This book is what it is today because of the generous people at Johns Hopkins University, Columbia University, the New York Public Library, and, especially, B Cup Café. Great thanks to my colleagues at Manhattanville College and SUNY Purchase, including Andrew Bodenrader, Jeff Bens, Catherine Lewis, and Monica Ferrell.

Absolutely none of this would have happened if not for Mrs. Inglis, my seventh grade writing teacher at Oak Hill Academy, who gave me my first C on a paper, because she knew I could do better if I tried.